Starlight Bender

Sofia Nedic

NOTE: This is a work of fiction. Names, characters, places, and incidents are either the product of the author's imagination or used fictitiously, and any resemblance to actual persons, living or dead, business establishments, events, or locales in entirely coincidental.

Names: Nedic, Sofia, author.
Title: Starlight Bender / Sofia Nedic
Description: First edition. | Self-published through Amazon KDP. | Audience: young adult.
Summary: Imani has to hide her magical power to bend starlight in the time of civil war in her city. However, the news of the incoming invading army draws her out of hiding, and she has a choice to make whether to join the queen's legions and fight in the battle.
Identifiers: Paperback ISBN: 9798399377247| E-book ISBN: 9798891214545
Subjects: Starlight Magic—Fiction. | Courts and courtiers—Fiction. | Mothers and Daughters—Fiction. | War—Fiction. | Celestial—Fiction. | Mythology—Fiction.

Text © 2023 Sofia Nedic
Cover design by Katarina Naskovski
Map illustration by Centaur Maps
Book Design by Rohit Solanki

Copyright © 2023 by Sofia Nedic
All rights reserved. No portion of this book may be reproduced, stored in retrieval system, or transmitted in any form or by any means, mechanical, electronic, photocopying, recording, or otherwise, without written permission from the author.

For my dearest grandma Nedic, a true woman of the hills who is watching over her daughters and granddaughters from the star lands. Until we meet again, I love you.

ACKNOWLEDGEMENTS

This story, like many others, took almost two years and an endless number of revisions to complete. And I would have never been able to finish it without the incredible tribe of women in my corner.

A special thank you to Stephanie Francis, who read and reviewed the early, hectic versions of this book, as well as many revisions since. Her thoughtful feedback, love for spirituality, and an incredible knack for storytelling helped me flesh out Imani and the rest of my characters and their world. If it weren't for her, this book would have never been molded into its final form.

Thank you to Vanessa Dremè for her witty and concise comments that always made me smile, and to Dior Bingley whose feedback alone reads like poetry. To Janelle Brown, for her attention to detail and honesty. And to Samiat Bakare, for her thoughtful and thorough assessments of my work. I am truly grateful to have found such an amazing group of women who improved my writing tremendously over the course of last year.

My biggest thank you goes to Katie Randolph, my incredibly talented editor and a wonderful, creative soul. From the ever-shifting tight deadlines, to having to correct my grammar and word choices at every turn due to my second-language writing skills, she is absolutely essential to my work. She is a teacher and an artist, and I don't know what I would do without her help.

Lastly, thank you to my dear husband who is my rock. From the numerous nights I spent behind my laptop writing, to figuring out every logistic related to indie publishing—he never fails to encourage me or offer a helping hand. And to my family who has always been my cornerstone and a safe harbor. Thank you for giving me the confidence and the strength to always pursue my dreams, no matter the odds.

Starlight Bender

LUMENOR

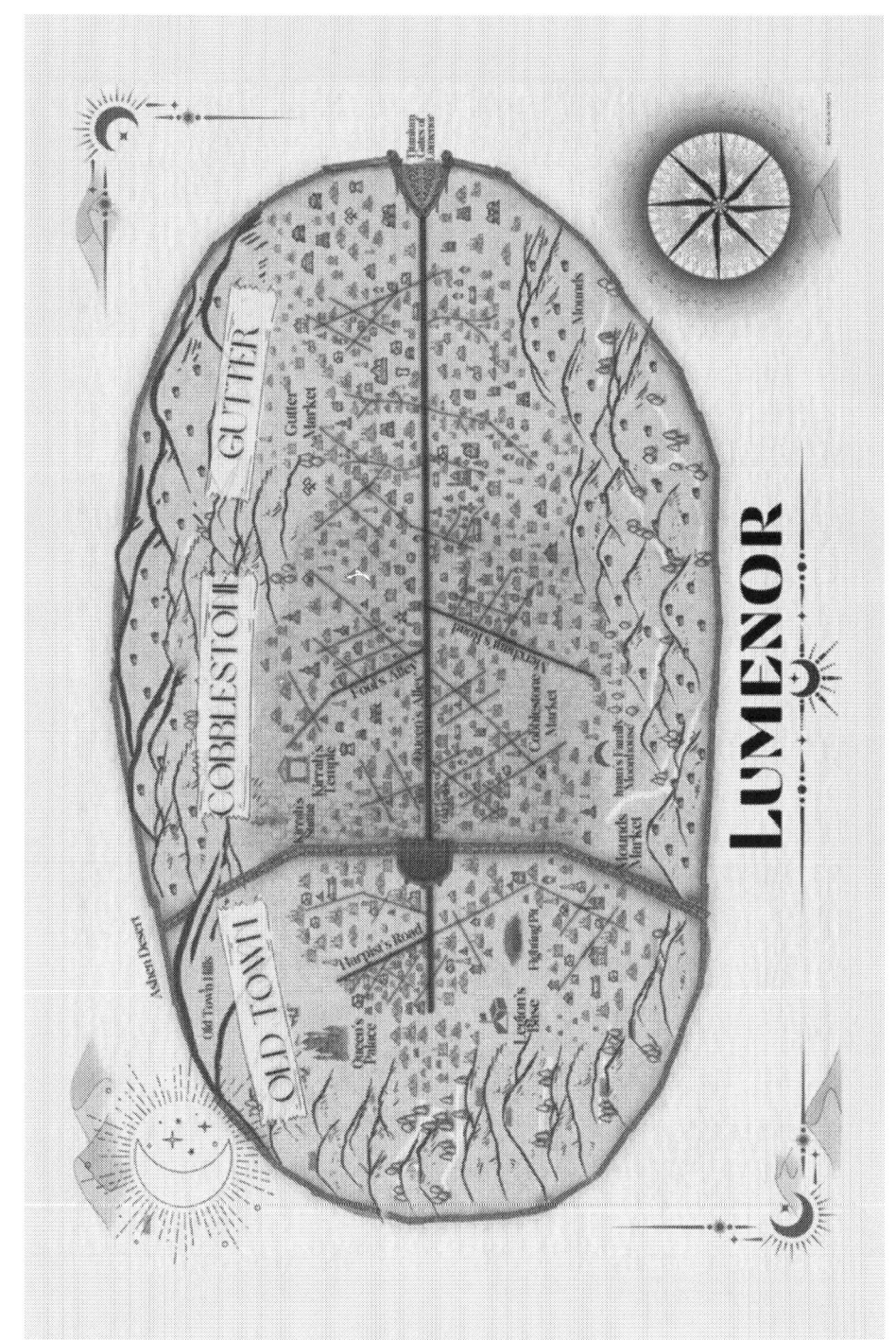

CHAPTER I
Three Draws

Three crescent moons shimmered over the Mounds, the jagged hills that cradled the ancient city of Lumenor where I was born. The moons' names—Tora, Assan, and Shei—were taught to every Lumenor-born as soon as they were old enough to learn anything.

Having just finished planting the last batch of echinacea roots, with my fingertips dug deep into the soil, I glanced at Tora's crescent tip from our garden. A murky gray fog soon washed over its gleam, but even the shade could do little to hinder the moon's beauty.

"Imani—wash that mud off your hands and place seeds on the table!" Mother's voice trailed from the round doorframe of our moonhouse. "You know it's a bad omen to be late to one's foretelling!"

"In a minute!" I shouted.

Echoing steps of wooden clogs plodded against the pebble-paved walkway, treading towards the shoulder-high evergreen fence that encircled the yard. Mother stumbled down the path hastily, balancing a heavy load of freshly brewed soil-feeder potion before she dropped the cauldron on an empty garden bed. A tiny drop of green liquid trickled along the edge before spilling over, and she wiped it off with her sleeve.

"I told you to get ready! Zana will be waiting!"

Zana was Mother's childhood friend and a *teller*. Telling, a long-forgotten ancient practice, was considered nothing but a laughable matter, earning Zana quite the reputation. The last time I saw her at the market, people gossiped as she passed, giggling about the colorful gems and tarot-inspired embroidery on her dress. Still, the Lumenoran elites visited Zana every so often, cloaked head to toe to avoid the watchful eyes of surrounding Mounds.

I bit off a chipped end of my nail, tasting the dry, sweet flavor of soil in my mouth. "Must we get a reading every moon cycle?"

The night was growing old and I was growing tired. I spent the entire day at the market, selling the ointments and potions Mother and I had brewed. The wind at the market had broken at my back, and the customers grumpy with chill hadn't made it any better. I was ready to sink into my sheets and call it a night.

Mother, however, had other plans.

"Yes, we must. I'll be waiting by the gates. *Hurry.*" She rolled up her sleeves, and a silver thread beaded with citrine gemstones slid down the umber skin of her wrist. Her hand fell on it out of habit, as if making sure the healing crystals were still there. "And make sure you bring your quartz ring this time, I will not have us worsening Zuri's fever! We must be careful."

I suppressed the desire to roll my eyes, and went to fetch the ring before departure.

My mother was a superstitious woman, especially since my little sister had grown sickly. She arranged crystals in a particular order around Zuri's bed, and spent the coin that was already hard to come by on magic healers, fortune-reversers, and just about any other pocket-turner she could find. It was her way of coping with Zuri's worsening condition, so we all played along—even Zuri herself.

It feels good knowing people care about you, my sister told me once.

Mother tugged my sleeve, urging me to quicken my steps. "Remember—the poor glassmaker lost her son to the rebels only two months ago, so best not mention the neighbor's girl who just joined their cause. And make sure you drink Zana's wild nettle tea, but not too much. It gave me the worst headache last time around, I suspect she spikes it with rum."

Isn't that the point?

The dwindling luster of three moons had broken through the fog, enkindling the hills, until black clouds coasting from the north began to cast their shadow over the Mounds.

"Another bad omen," Mother whispered, gazing up and shaking her head. Her midnight-colored eyes reflected the fading flecks of gold in the skies, the silver braid that fell over her shoulder glinting with sapphire cuffs.

I rolled my eyes. "Come on Mother, it's only the sky!"

The growing absence of light didn't matter anyway—I could make the trip to Zana's house with my eyes closed. I built a deep bond with the hills of Lumenor at a young age, playing hide-and-seek and chase-a-thief with Zuri over the years. I knew their cold river streams and blue rock bones more intimately than my own body in some ways.

Mother paused at the base of the next hill. "I don't need to remind you to watch your tongue regarding..." She peeked over her shoulder to make sure we were alone. "Regarding you know what."

I sighed. "You don't need to say it every time. *I know*."

Zana lived one hill over, in the same house as her mother, her mother's mother, and so on. Her moonhouse was so old that the rugged surface of granite had assumed the shape of a half-moon. In contrast, the more recently built moonhouses were shaped like full moons, resembling round pebbles perched atop the Mounds from a distance. They had underground levels to store winter supplies, or draw a warm bath from the hot springs underneath.

Mother knocked thrice, pressing her ear against the circular mahogany door.

Zana swung it open within seconds, greeting us with a deep exhale. "Ah, my dears, I am so glad you could make it—I am already running behind!" She pushed a plate of freshly-baked pie into my hands at the doorstep. "Imani, my sweet girl, please find a place for it in the living room, and see that it is as far from my seat as possible."

I wrapped my fingers around the plate, inhaling the sweet scent of the pastry. "But cherry pie is your favorite?"

"Unless my cousin Tena makes it," Zana whispered, leaning in. Glittering golden powder on the teller's eyelids shone against her bone-colored skin, and she arranged tiny gems around her temples to form a star pattern. The stones were the color of her eyes—vibrant emerald-green. She winked, spinning about her heels, and we followed her inside.

Zana's home was decorated according to the fashion of our ancestors. Second-hand velvet curtains hung from round windows, blue-flamed candles dispersed all about. Mimi, Zana's firebird, whistled a high-pitched tune from a swinging iron cage, her red and orange feathers bathing in the candlelight. Incense smoke carried the scent of myrrh, and the curving ceiling was painted with scenes from Lumenor's mythology. My eyes were drawn to the swirl of golden brush strokes that told the tale of Tsehai, the sun goddess, as she stormed the skies in search of her fallen lover. In the center of Zana's living room squatted a sculpture of Kirrah, the starlight goddess, locks of her silver hair that graced the heads of all Lumenor-born folk carved to appear almost life-like.

The teller's tea parties were attended by the women from all ranks and parts of Lumenor, which was rarely witnessed on any other occasion. The wealthy ladies from the Old Town sat next to the beggars from the Gutter, sighing when their misfortunes were being told. They put their soft hands over the beggar women's shoulders when they cried, yet they tightly clutched their purses when the time came to go home.

All of Zana's guests settled in the cushions surrounding a tea table, and Mother pulled me down by her side after I left the pie as far from the teller as was possible without her cousin noticing.

"What are we feeling tonight, ladies?" Zana asked. The sleeves of her robe were embroidered with dozens of purple jewels, woven into the cloth with a single string of red silk. Even her paling braid clattered with crystals, the gems flickering in dim light like thousands of distant stars every time the teller shook her head.

"I was hoping for a card reading," the glassmaker replied. Her eyes were red and swollen, unlike the rest of her face that lost all color and vigor, drifting into a hollow grayness. She had only recently lost her son to the rebels. He had only been sixteen.

I shifted in my seat uneasily.

"Cards it is." Zana reached under the table, fetching a sparkling, night-hued deck. "I say we read directly from Kirrah's hand tonight."

All women nodded, including Mother, passing the nettle tea around. I poured a cupful down my throat before reaching for a refill, but Mother saw me and stopped my hand with the tight-lipped *I-told-you-not-to-do-that* look.

Zana rolled her sleeves up. "Now, who would like to go first?"

"The young shall go while the night is still young," the glassmaker whispered, staring at the floor without blinking.

All gazes drifted my way since every woman in the room was old enough to be my mother, if not grandmother.

Just what I wished for.

An elderly woman to my left cracked her knuckles. The woman's flame-kissed face was textured with deep creases, paved by the long decades of the past, complimenting her narrow cheekbones and dark brown eyes.

"Aye, my turn shall never come in that case. I doubt that even night grows this old," she murmured mostly to herself, chortling.

"And yet you are here," another hill woman said, glancing my way and clicking her tongue. "My daughter wouldn't come along even if I tried dragging her by her hair! All she cares about are her friends, eye powders, and taverns! The youth nowadays have no respect for ancestral customs."

Many women in the room shook their heads with her, Mother being one of them.

I am here, am I not?

Zana went on to shuffle her deck so masterfully that the glittering cards spilled down her fingers like the waves of starlight. One by one, the cards fell into the pool of sparks inside Zana's hand. A familiar itch tickled the centers of my palms, and I tucked them into my lap hastily. I knew better than to give off even a subtle sign.

How long before their motherly stares turned into the looks of disdain and fright if they found out? How many hours before I am reported, dragged away from my family by the legionnaires, or worse—killed by the rebels?

I wondered which one of the women would betray me first, settling on the merchant's wife from the Cobblestone I've met once before, who looked away quickly any time our gazes locked. She had grown up in the Mounds, judging from the long silver braid that fell down her back, woven from hundreds of small braids. The hairstyle dated all the way back to the Ancestors' Era, and many Mounds-born women still donned it to honor the hills' tradition. I often wore the braid myself, its weight leaning against my shoulder and smelling of jasmine flower.

Zana grinned politely, but the smile didn't touch her eyes. "Then it is decided. Imani shall start us off." She scattered the cards all over the tabletop with one wave of her hand. "You know the rules. Pick one card at a time and let your intuition guide your finger, not the other way around. You get three draws."

Alright. I closed my eyes, hovering my hand over the pile longer than it was necessary to tickle the crowd's anticipation.

"That one," I pointed at last.

Zana flipped the card. A woman with a torso that twisted into a snake's tail at the bottom was painted on the front, her unnatural golden eyes staring right at me. Even when I looked away, I could feel her piercing gaze like a broken thorn in my foot.

A few of the women gasped, my mother amongst them.

"This is Teysha, a deity of old," Zana laid out. "Some know her as the Back Stabber. Her poisonous tongue sent kings and queens down a treacherous path, ultimately leading to their demise. Be careful of the women in your life who pose as friends."

Mother's deep umber face grew still.

Oh great, as if she needed another reason to nag about me going to the taverns with Summer and Ayla!

I tapped the back of the second card, followed by another synchronized gasp from the crowd, again including my own mother.

"The Midnight Rider," Zana said. "He destroyed all life on earth once before—may his like never be seen in our lands again. He brings bad luck."

I was not sure if any man, dead or alive, had the capacity to destroy all life on the planet. I only saw a handsome, black-eyed rider smirking confidently from his horse. *I could use one of those,* I thought counting how long it had been since I last felt the tickle of butterflies in my stomach. *Maybe I'll stop by the taverns on my way back from the market tomorrow.*

The impatient glances from Zana and Mother forced my hand back to the tabletop, clearing the growing tension. "Let's go with this card last."

Zana didn't even need to turn the card—we both knew what I drew. Mother knew, too, holding her breath, and surveying the room carefully. No matter how many times the teller read my fortune, Kirrah's ethereal face embellished the card I picked out last. Cloaked in the starlight itself, with a crescent silver moon tattoo on her forehead much like my own, the goddesses' midnight skin contrasted the moonlight-kissed curls that fell down her back. The rarest draw of all.

Another gasp.

"What does it mean?" the glassmaker asked.

"It means that I was right," Zana lied, "this must be a very special night indeed. The goddess is with us."

We both know that is not what it means.

The elderly woman to my side uttered a prayer to Kirrah in the ancient tongue, her lips parting gently to draw a deep breath before mouthing the words in a half-whisper.

Zana cleared her throat, pouring another mouthful of nettle tea into her cup. "Now—who would like to go next?"

Many flipped cards, Zana's interpretations, and cups of nettle tea later, Mother and I headed back home. The night was rather cool for an early spring, breaths slipping between our lips like the wisps of smoke.

"I am worried about that snake woman you drew," Mother said as soon as we left Zana's, just as I thought she would. "You better be vigilant with the girls you hang around these days. I don't want them leading you astray."

I did my best not to make a face. "Come on Mother, those are only hand-painted cards! I have known Summer my entire life. Besides, you were worried about me being stolen away after I drew the Spell Binder last year. I am still here, am I not?"

The quiet in the Mounds past dusk was comforting, like a soft blanket one wraps around themselves to feel safe. The Mounds-folk labored all day, working the fields, the mines, or the markets, and had no strength left to dwell deep into the night like the Old Towners and Cobblestoners. The residents of the Gutter were only truly awake under the shadows of Kirrah's cloak, smuggling and exchanging goods that the queen didn't allow within the walls.

A distant tumble of rocks drew my attention to the edge of the tree line where two silhouettes emerged from the dark. Blending with swaying oaks in the background, their feet crunched over the bare, rocky hill.

The rebels.

"Who comes our way?" Mother cried out. The trembling in her voice was all that it took to raise the rebels' suspicion. I reached for her hand, squeezing my knuckles between hers.

It will be alright.

A man and a woman approached, never breaking eye contact, half of their faces hidden behind their grey-hooded cloaks. Short blades were fastened on their belts, black leather boots soaked by the shallow river streams they passed through. The city folk didn't know the secret ways of unpaved roads and rolling hills, making it much harder to navigate around, especially at night when fog blurred the view.

The man was missing an ear, and thinning, unruly hair fell down his shoulders. His eyes jumped from Mother's face, to mine, and back, examining us thoughtfully. The woman to his side was free of injuries but seemed wary of either cold or fighting. The tip of the blade in her hand was stained, fresh blood dripping to the ground. I made an effort to pretend I didn't notice the knife. Still, my eyes fell to the dripping edge on their own.

"Names?" the male rebel asked.

"I am Kamari Stone," Mother replied, "and this is my daughter Imani. We live up the next hill."

The man's trained eye was not easy to fool. No one could smell starlight, but the rebels sniffed the fear out of folk fast enough. "Whose side are you on?"

Mother squeezed my hand tighter, stopping my blood flow. "We don't pick sides—Old Town or Gutter, it's all the same to us.

Legionnaires or rebels—what difference does it make to the common folk? We worry our own worries, and sell the potions at the market is all."

The rebel woman flinched at Mother's words, tightening her fingers around the blade pommel. Her companion flashed an arm across her belly to prevent her from leaping at us. She hissed, begrudgingly biting her lip, but she stayed in place.

A tear of cold sweat ran down the back of my neck.

"You don't pick no sides, you claim, yet you sell your soul for copper, taking their blood money," she uttered.

Ironic for a woman who earns coin by slicing other's throats. The words almost rolled off my tongue, but if the rebel woman didn't murder me upon saying them, Mother surely would.

"We *all* get by whatever way we can," Mother retorted in a sharp tone she often used when reprimanding Zuri and me for leaving the herbs out for too long. "Now if you'll excuse us, it's cold and it's late. Play your little games with some other folk."

We started for our moonhouse, but they had none of it. The rebels did whatever they desired, and they always got their way.

"Girl." The man's cold fingers wrapped around my wrist, sending shivers up my spine. "Palm out."

I stood still for a moment, blinking up slowly to tease his impatience.

I knew I could bend starlight for eight years, ever since I was ten. The ancient magic of Lumenor often skipped generations, and I was the only person in my long family tree born with power to wield the force that breathed life into the world. My options were to report for duty and join the legions patrolling the city and the Ashen Desert beyond, or stay in hiding like many of the others. Mother chose the latter for me, never asking my opinion.

I am not having you die fighting for their cause, wasting away in the Ashen Desert with the rest of the Mounds-born starlight benders, she said whenever I begged to join the legions. That also meant I never received any proper training, never learned how to bend with precision...

And we could really use it on nights like this.

Mother clenched her jaw, holding her breath despite knowing I had passed their tests before. She stepped forward, maintaining a firm grip on my hand.

"Is that truly necessary?"

I shook my head. "Don't waste your breath Mother, I don't mind."

Pulling my free hand out of the long sleeve of my fur-lined azure coat, I extended it towards the rebel. He twisted his mouth as though attempting to savor the vanishing flavor of ale beneath his tongue, and dropped a coin-sized moonstone charm into my palm, hoping it would draw the starlight out.

Nothing happened.

The rebel woman snarled, cursing under her breath before loosening her grip on the knife. The rebels were always on the lookout for young starlight benders, hopeful to catch them before they joined Queen Astra's legions. Doing the noble work of cleansing the city, they claimed. They didn't worry about the folk of mature age, since bending power faded over the years of one's life.

The man was equally disappointed, sneering as he retrieved the charm.

Fools. Had they held their blades against my throat, they would have learned what they wanted. Starlight was designed to protect itself, attacking by instinct if it felt endangered. But the rebels didn't know that since they probably never stopped to have a word with a starlight bender in their lives.

They only kill us for the thrill of it.

"You are free to go," the man said after a long pause, his lips forming a thin line glazed with suspicion. He studied my face as if making sure to remember it should we cross paths again.

Mother's chest slowly collapsed as we climbed uphill, the unspoken tension we long-held against each other painted all over our silent frowns. There was no point in arguing over it for the hundredth time, so I kept her pace with my tongue tied in a knot, digging my teeth into the inside flesh of my cheek.

I wish you would let me make my own choices in life for once. I wish you didn't hold Zuri's sickness over me to prevent me from joining the legions.

I knew what Mother's response would be, I'd heard it dozens of times before.

Don't be reckless—I do it for your own good.

I cast a biting glance her way. She returned an even sharper one before spinning her head in other direction with her lips pursed.

Well, my own good almost had us killed tonight.

We arrived at the front yard of our moonhouse at last. The muffled whispers of the pines tickled my ears, the scent of rain still lingering about, soothing my mind. The front door opened before I reached for the knob, and Father's smile peered out from behind it. His fading silver coils were cut short, drinking the moonlight, his broad shoulders slightly hunched underneath the gray spring jacket Mother had sewn for him.

"I was wondering if Zana's infamous tea held you two back," he said, and winked at me playfully. "It's getting late."

I reached for his hand, callused from the years of working in the crystal mines deep beneath the hills. "Not this time. We ran into rebels on our way back."

Father's ebony eyes diverted to Mother in an instant.

"Do not worry, dear," she whispered, waving a hand away. "The danger has passed, we are safe now." Her glare narrowed on the cloth pouch swinging from Father's shoulder. "Did you remember to pack your food? I made a spiced meat porridge before we left."

He nodded, the sharp edges of his narrow face softening. "I packed it—the porridge smelled delicious! Thank you for making it, dear, it is quickly becoming my favorite. I will be leaving now, I am already running behind," Father said, and gave us each a hug.

"Be safe, the rebels are lurking about," Mother pointed out before disappearing inside the house.

Father caught my hand before I followed her footsteps. "Zuri and I made a bit of a mess in the kitchen, it will be best if you head upstairs right away. Your sister is looking after your slice of blueberry pie, so better hurry," he mumbled into my ear, then proceeded to head out. Not even working in the darkness of the mines could cast a shadow on Father's cheerful spirit, yet it broke my heart to know that he had to do hard labor while we rested. And he was doing it for us.

I listened to his advice and went straight to Zuri's and my room in the attic. Zuri jumped to her feet as soon as she saw me and ran into my arms. Her silver curls smelled like rosemary, small hands holding a wrapped slice.

"Father made a pie earlier, I saved you some!"

I held my little sister's soft, night-kissed cheek. Her skin was warmer than usual. "Thank you, that's very thoughtful of you," I said, settling on her bed. I always read fairy tales to Zuri at night before we went to sleep. "Mother and I ran into the rebels on our way back from Zana's reading tonight."

Zuri's oval face lit up. "You did? How many were there? Were you scared? Did you bend starlight to get rid of them? Oh, I wish I'd been there! How exciting! Tell me everything, please!"

I chuckled. "I didn't bend at them, there was no need. They never found out I could."

My sister pouted her mouth in disappointment. "Alright. Were they scary?"

I swallowed, thinking back to the rebel man's missing ear. "No, not really. They didn't know their way around the Mounds either."

She smirked. "The city folk never does. Will you read to me?"

"Of course," I replied, and tucked her into the star-covered sheets. The window in the round ceiling offered a view of Kirrah's cloak in the night skies, a smear of gold and silver glittering on black canvas. "Which story is your pick for tonight?"

Zuri's long lashes fluttered twice. "Any of Uche's adventures, please!"

"We read about her last night, and the night before."

Her small hand fell on my forearm. "But I love Uche! She was a fierce warrior, and a starlight bender at that, just like you!"

I am nothing like her.

I can't even bend properly, let alone call myself a warrior.

I bit into my bottom lip, but read myths about Uche anyway until sleep came to Zuri's ever-curious eyes. My sister's slow breathing followed the rhythm of my voice, telling tales of an ancient warrior woman who protected Lumenor over the span of four decades. Uche was brave, powerful, and just. She stood up to protect those she loved.

I may not be like her just yet, but I will be someday.
Even if it is the last thing I ever do.

Chapter II
Whispers of War

I tried my best to forget the events of the night before as I walked along the cobbled streets.

The day was gray and gloomy with the threat of a storm. The pale glint of our silver sun hid behind the clouds, casting a shadow over the market. The folk roamed about in search of supper ingredients, tea brews, or crystals for temple offerings. Their cloaks, in many shades of blue, swirled about in the breeze, everyone's bright silver hair contrasting with the dark skies above.

"Two fenrir livers for the price of one! Two fenrir livers for the price of one!" a boy yelled in front of the butcher shop.

A tall hill woman pushed her cart down a narrow passing between the tightly packed stands, handing out free samples of moldy cheese. Several beggars saw her and lined up for a taste.

"Hush now, all of you! No wallet—no samples!"

I arrived at my stand at last. The tomato farmer waved at me from his station as I began placing the ointments in their usual place—the headache potion in the front, right next to the wound binder, our most popular brew.

The butcher's son, who liked to flirt with market visitors on his father's dime, stopped in his tracks when he spotted me. He had the thick arms of a butcher and the confidence of a giant, always walking with his nose in the clouds. Some jokingly referred to him as the Market King behind his back as a result.

"Aye, Imani, what are you up to these days?" he asked, wiping the fenrir blood against the stained white apron tied behind his back.

"Not much." I shrugged. "Same as always."

In truth, I was still shaken from my encounter with the rebels.

The butcher's son picked up one of the stomach relievers from my stand, tossing it from hand to hand. The black liquid inside the flask splashed all over the glass. "Is this one of them nighttime potions that everyone in the Mounds raves about?"

"Why, are you in need of one?" I winked, and he put the potion back down in an instant.

"A tease, aren't ya?" He glanced about to check if anyone had heard me. "Either way, I stopped to invite you to the Moonscar Inn tonight if you are free. It's my brother's name day. And if you can come, bring that friend of yours—Summer, was her name? Say what you will, but I always had a fancy for the pretty girls from foreign lands."

Summer was about as foreign as the herbs in my mother's garden. Despite being born and raised in the Mounds, she'd inherited burgundy curls from her ancestors in the east that remained resistant to the moonstone, making her appear foreign-born to the silver-haired Lumenorans.

"I will have to check with her first," I said, noting to tell Summer about his invitation at lunch. I had no intention of putting my friend through the inevitable disaster of being on the receiving end of his flirtation, but I still wanted to go to the taverns.

We'll need to remember to steer away from the Moonscar Inn.

The day was drifting away slowly, every minute feeling like an hour. I was ready to begin packing my things when ten legionnaires of mature age entered the market. A stir rippled down the stands faster than an earthquake. The legion of starlight benders split up, moving silently between the stands, eyeing us all sharply. Hundreds of nosy glances followed them from behind, yet not one pair of lips moved.

My stomach churned.

Kirrah's cloak, what are they doing here?

One of the legionnaires approached my station, and my heart skipped a beat. She was a short, square-shouldered woman with a rigid stance that commanded respect. The woman's skin was the color of ivory, the split ends of her braid dipped in an indigo paint, revealing her Mounds' heritage. The paint was an old hills' custom, even older than the braid itself, and only a few hill women still kept it.

The legionnaire glanced at the flasks atop of my stand and proceeded to inquire about every single ingredient of the potions she pretended to be interested in.

"This is for the woman's ache, I presume?" she asked in a gentle tone, running her hand over the flasks I polished earlier. My mouth tightened at the sight of her fingerprints smudging all across the crystal-clear glass. If Mother was there, she would have surely slapped the woman's hand away, legionnaire or not.

Then again, Mother didn't shoot starlight out of her palms.

I nodded. "Yes, the woman's ache. A drop of aries' blood, a spoonful of chopped eagle feathers, one root of ginger, and two sprinkles of cinnamon powder brewed in chamomile tea."

"Hm." She tilted her head, leaning closer to the potions, yet her light blue eyes traced the lines of my face. "What about this one?"

I kept my palms behind my back, acting like I couldn't tell what she was trying to accomplish. The key was to always remain calm when being suspected. Still, it was one thing to fool the rebels. It was another to go undetected amongst the other starlight benders who knew all the tricks up my sleeve. A sudden move could set me off and send specks blazing from my hands.

I would never admit it out loud, but a small part of me grew excited at the thought. I'd dreamed of being a legionnaire my entire life—dreamed of wearing the uniform and of having the freedom to bend magic without fear.

"That potion is meant to help with bone pains," I replied, raising my chin. "Turnip greens, horsetail, arnica and crushed jade rabbit's teeth."

"In which manner is it made?" she asked, like she would know any difference. All of her peers were doing the same—questioning the youthful market workers and their customers alike.

"It is boiled in water for three turns of the clock. Then, the ingredients are left to dry in sunlight for two days before being soaked in the same water again."

The legionnaire twirled her indigo-dipped braid around her thumb, observing me in silence. "Very well. You are quite knowledgeable about herbs for a young girl."

"I have my mother to thank for that," I said.

Sparks ignited in the legionnaire's eyes, her tongue wetting the corners of her mouth. "And where is she? Your mother? Curious, she lets you work here all alone."

"My Mother is taking care of my little sister," I replied, and her stare widened. "She worked at the market while she could, but Zuri…". My heart lurched and I shook my head. "Mother can't come here any longer."

The legionnaire arched an eyebrow, clasping the invisible clutches of her stare around my cheekbones. "Your sibling is ill?"

"Yes. She has been ill for some time. My father helps whenever he gets back from the mines. I do, too."

"Hm." Her gaze drifted off, and if I didn't know any better, I would think I saw a tear in the corner of her eye. "I know what it's like to carry the burden of being…*the other sibling*. Be sure to omit that story in the future, should my peers ever ask you questions. Otherwise, we'll be seeing each other again much sooner than you expect," she said and walked away.

I exhaled deeply as the legionnaire's silver-wolf coat disappeared amongst the crowd. *Was I just…let go?* I asked myself in disbelief. *And why should I not tell the others about Zuri?*

The smell of fresh vegetables and fruits saturated the air, spiced with the fragrances of resin glue and cheap moonshine. The squirrels chased each other over the damp tar of the earth, collecting crumbs and spoiled chunks of food that the merchants had tossed away. Still in shock, I locked the ointments inside the stand. I wanted to head straight to Summer's home; I knew Mother would never let me out if I went home first. The promise of rain was fulfilled at last, and I tossed the hood over my head to keep dry, before the drops soaked in my braid. The hour was late, and most merchants had already left. I paused to relish the last flavor of the market before departure.

I better hurry.

Summer's family lived atop one of the outer hills of the Mounds, one that led towards the guard watchtowers that lay nestled along the wall. Lumenor was built in a valley surrounded by the natural ridges we called the Mounds. Our ancestors had wrapped the Mounds within the high granite walls, ages before my time, to protect us from invasions. The wall needed to be repaired every now and then, but it still stood tall.

Forests of pine and oak covered the rolling hills, contrasted only by the clusters of weathered moonhouses built from hard granite. Wind chimes whistled outside the homes' circular windows, and azure firelight glimmered from swinging lanterns.

"There she is," Summer said, giving me a hug at her doorstep. "Sorry I couldn't come see you at lunch. Father's shop was unusually busy."

"No worries." I took my coat off and placed it on the chair. "You wouldn't believe the day I had."

Summer's dark brown eyes narrowed. "Anything worth mentioning?"

"Mmm, maybe another time. Ah, I almost forgot. We need to stay away from the Moonscar Inn. Market King asked about you again."

Summer shook her head, laughing. "Kirrah help me. Let's get you a drink."

The ruby-embellished dress matched the color of Summer's hair, layered sleeves flowing against her bronze skin. The legends had claimed that Lumenoran sunsets were once crimson like blood, the flames red like the gems on Summer's dress. All we were left with nowadays were gloomy, gray skies and a faint silver sun with its river-blue flames.

Summer pointed at a tangle of dresses on her bed. "One of these will fit you nicely, take your pick. Ayla is powdering her face, and then we'll be ready to head to the Three Singers."

―✿―

The tavern was filled with young and old alike and already packed to the last chair. I picked my favorite of all Summer's dresses to wear tonight—a dark blue, long-sleeved velvet that complimented the warm undertone of my umber skin.

The scent of rain intermingled with the whiff of cheap ale, yet I craved it just the same, as if it were the finest northern wine. The floor was sticky with spill, and we had to watch our steps over the chunks of broken glass. I used my change from the market to buy the first round of drinks. A young bartender uttered a cheeky comment as he poured, blowing bitter smoke into my face.

I wonder if he would be so daring if he knew I can puncture a hole the size of my fist in his chest? All it would take is one wave of my hand. I hushed the thought away and pushed the cups into my friends' hands.

Senar, Summer's brother, waved at us from the corner, where five of his friends accompanied him at the table. They crammed closer in their seats, and I ended up sitting between two strangers after Ayla pushed past me to squeeze next to the guy she fancied.

"I am Aubren." Senar's friend to my left shook my hand with a firm grip. His moonlit hair was cut short, and his handsome, mahogany face had a freshly trimmed beard. He had a pearly smile to match.

"Imani," I said. "Aubren is a foreign name… where are you from?"

"Five hills down from here." Aubren laughed. "My mother deems herself a worldly woman, you see. Luckily, I didn't get the worst of it—she named my brother Blue!"

I giggled. "Blue like the color?"

"It is fashionable in the east, she claims! The farthest east that woman had stepped her foot to are the second-hand shops in the Gutter."

"I guess Blue is rather fashionable in the Gutter then!"

We chattered the night away, flirting with our eyes and pouring one cup after another. Aubren smelled of eucalyptus and ale. I relaxed into his arm that loosely hung around my shoulder. I learned that his father worked at a nearby farm, and that he was studying to become a smith's apprentice in the Gutter. His brother was still in school, struggling with numbers and sneaking out to the outer wall with his classmates. I was enjoying myself so much, I almost forgot all about my troubles from the previous evening.

But not for long.

The tavern doors burst open, and three middle-aged starlight benders marched inside, pounding on an empty table until everyone stopped talking. Their legionnaire uniforms were made of a sturdy ashen flax—one of the most expensive materials that Lumenoran coin could buy, second only to the silver-wolf's fur of their coats. That, and the three titanium arrow brooches pinned to their chests on either side of their necks, clipped over the rounded-edges of their shoulders. Throwing blades rested in sheaths down their sleeves.

"Curfew starts immediately, everyone is to head home! I repeat, the curfew starts immediately, head home now! What are you standing around for? Get out!"

Senar leaped from his chair. "We are *not* going anywhere! Your daily brawls with the rebels don't scare us."

The legionnaires exchanged a dim, knowing look.

"Boy—if Queen Astra commanded a lockdown every time those beggars decided to slice some innocent flesh, you would never leave your house."

Aubren's arm tightened around my shoulder. "Then, what? Why is a curfew being put in place?"

The legionnaires hesitated for a moment, and it felt like the whole tavern held its breath waiting for their response.

"The news we bear is much more troublesome, I am afraid. Akani Warriors conquered the ancient city of Vatrion in the north, and all that is left of our sister kingdom is a burning pile of bones."

Summer's palm went over her mouth in an instant. Ayla gasped, and the ale in Senar's cup rippled before spilling to the floor. The sound of breaking glass screeched over the muffled whispers that made their way around the tavern, yet everyone was too afraid to speak up. We were all hoping the truth would go away as long as we pretended we didn't hear it in the first place.

My mouth went dry.

"What about their crystal?" I asked.

The legionnaires exchanged another knowing look. "The ruby crystal is in the Akani's possession now. No one was left alive to defend it."

"Not even, umm, *your* people?" Summer asked, her hand still covering her mouth. In fact, no other part of her body moved except for her lips. "The starlight benders?"

"*No one*," the legionnaire replied. "And the Akani are headed here to seize the Lumenor's moonstone crystal next. The journey from Vatrion will take them three turns of the moons or so, and then... Kirrah help us."

The rain had stopped. Aubren offered to walk me home since the chaos had already erupted in the Mounds. The whispers of war traveled faster than light, or so it seemed, and the hills were set ablaze with candlelight coming from every single moonhouse. Clusters of round, granite homes resembled the stars of Kirrah's realm, forging a ring of burning firelight around the tall, stone rooftops and gold-coated domes of Lumenor. It was well past dinner, and still the entire city was only waking up.

Mother will be furious with me. She must be worried sick!

"What do you think will happen next?" I asked, glancing over my shoulder to check if we were being followed. The legionnaires left the tavern at the same time we did, but there was no trace of them anywhere in the woods. Apart from an occasional shout, the hill we were crossing was otherwise too quiet for my liking.

Aubren shrugged. "Exactly what the school teachers told us happens during invasions, I presume. The queen will bar the city gates, instrumenting the Lumenor-wide lockdown. The guards will begin recruiting all commoners of fighting age, and the legionnaires will be on the hunt for the starlight benders in hiding."

Little does he know they already began.

I took a deep breath, remaining close to Aubren. He gazed at me the same way he did at the tavern, seemingly unaffected by the news of the upcoming battle. The scent of eucalyptus on his skin swirled into my nostrils, when a distant clamor clanged through the woods—the clashing of blades slicing through the night.

The rebels.

"We should hurry," I urged, hoping to avoid another unwanted encounter with them.

Aubren's eyebrows shot up, and the beam on his face faded away. "What are you worried about? The rebels don't harm the non-bending—"

His throat swallowed the rest of the sentence after a chilling rustle creeped in from the darkness, coming from the cluster of evergreen bushes behind us. Every muscle in my body stiffened, my eyes searching through the blackness of the forested hill. But I couldn't see, I couldn't find anything that could have made the sound.

My voice trembled. "Did you hear that?"

Aubren nodded, pressing a finger against his lips.

We stood in complete silence for what felt like an eternity before something jumped out of the bush. I gasped. A wave of light rushed over my palm, illuminating a patch of grass beneath us. A silver squirt ran down the path, and I blew a sigh in relief before I realized what I had done. One look at Aubren's widened eyes told me that he was aware of it, too.

He knows.

I accidentally summoned my power in a moment of fear.

And he did not like that.

I backed away a of couple of steps instinctively, freeing my other hand from my pocket, keeping my gaze on Aubren. His large, brown eyes followed my palms without blinking. Standing motionless, Aubren's fingers slid towards the pocket of his black pants. The blue pommel of a knife appeared from it.

I took a deep breath.

A goddamn rebel!

"I wouldn't try that," I said. My palms were now in the air, facing him directly. I tightened my fingers to prevent them from shaking and drew a silent gasp.

The last thing I need is for him to sniff the fear on me.

Aubren's smile returned, but it was not the kind, comely smile that'd greeted me back at the tavern. Instead, a cold, ruthless rebel who was ready to duel his enemy to the death watched me from the darkness.

One wrong move, and I am dead.

"You are not trained," he said. "You will only hurt yourself if you bend."

Aubren took a confident step forward, only to halt as two tiny balls of translucent, sparkling light emerged from my palms, leaving my skin intact. His mouth gaped as the reflection of beaming magic that glittered in his eyes.

A wave of warmth washed over my chest, the release of my power smearing a sweet flavor over my lips. My heart was still pounding, but I was no longer afraid.

I raised my chin, pointing the tip of my nose at his forehead. "You are right, I am untrained. And if I fight you, I may injure myself, that much is true. But I will most certainly *kill you* in the process."

My threat didn't sit well with him, judging from the way his fingers curled into a balled fist, and yet he was still hesitating to reach for the dagger. He leaned forward, contemplating his next move. I didn't have much time, and I couldn't spend the entire night staring him down. Besides, one could only bend for as long as they had stamina left. Even though I could forge a lot more starlight than two tiny balls before draining myself, my knees would eventually weaken, and my vision would blur.

Retreating a few paces further, my eyes bounced around hastily. All I could see were numerous swinging trees, some moonhouses in the distance; all I could feel was magic at my fingertips. I split each ball into five with my mind—a trick that took me four years to master—and came up with the plan. Directing all my attention at the oak halfway between us, I waved my arms in a throwing motion. The specks left my fingertips hurriedly. I aimed for the tree in hopes of knocking it over, and buying myself enough time to escape.

I missed.

Everything that followed happened so quickly. One moment I was bending, the next running for my life.

My feet raced over the thickening mud, all while Summer's velvet dress loosely billowed around my legs, allowing me to run free. The tree line grew denser as I darted deeper into the woods, hoping Aubren would eventually lose my tracks. But whenever I peered over my shoulder, he was right behind me, and his long strides would have caught up with me already if he was not afraid.

At least I didn't have to worry about him throwing daggers at me. It was way too dark, and he seemed to only have one knife on him.

With only one breath to spare, I stopped running and turned back. My thighs were throbbing. The cool evening air chilled my chest. The warmth of starlight within me had vanished. Aubren's quick feet pounded against the hill before he reappeared within arm's reach.

"I've never harmed another person in my entire life! I am not your enemy," I shouted.

He scoffed, piercing me with a pointed stare. "And I am not a fool, *starlight bender*."

I rolled my eyes. "What are you going to fight the Akani with? Sticks, stones and blades? They have an ancient crystal in their possession for Kirrah's sake!"

Moons help me if anyone has ever managed to reason with a rebel!

"Won't make much difference to you." Aubren's cold smile spread his lips wide again. "You won't be there to see it."

I swallowed, attempting to reason with him one last time. "I thought that you liked me, I thought that we could be friends!"

A one-sided smirk flashed across his lips, fueled with contempt. "I don't make friends with *your* kind."

Can't say I didn't try.

My fingers split apart like the petals of a blooming flower. Feeling my connection to the black skies above that shimmered with flecks of gold and silver, I opened my chest wide and drew on my power. All matter was created from stardust, but it was starlight that breathed life into our world.

And I had the power to summon it at my fingertips.

Aubren shifted his weight forward, watching my palms light up, breathless. I doubted he ever faced a starlight bender in his nineteen years. Even untrained, I was more powerful than any boy or girl he had aimed his daggers at before. My own dagger was leagues beyond his reach, ready to turn him to dust.

"This way! A starlight bender!" The wind carried his shouts.

Coward.

One thing I discovered about my power early on—once I unleashed it, it was almost impossible to let go. Feeling every muscle in my body, every bone and every vein fill with magic, was like taking the first sip of mulled wine on a frosty winter night. It reminded me of my first kiss and of the fireplace in the living room of our moonhouse. It reminded me of my sweet sister's soft hand wrapped around mine before we went to sleep.

Not allowing myself to think, I released all the air from my lungs, and starlight left my hands again. Only this time, instead of two faint, marble-sized balls, streams as thick as tree trunks rushed out of my palms. They intertwined, slipping out of my control like a glass cup out from a wet grip. The magic kept flowing out of me, the waves thickening with every drop. I couldn't stop bending, couldn't resist the sweet tickle of power on my lips. My head hurt from trying to focus, and not much time had passed before I couldn't bind the streams to my will any longer.

Only Aubren didn't know that, and he disappeared back into the woods a moment before starlight crashed into the pine next to him. The entire tree was set ablaze from the root up, its branches and needles glistening, illuminating the entire hill. Starlight spread like wildfire. The shine of it all was as bright as though all three moons landed on earth for the second time, bathing it in their glimmer. Every pore and every crease in the tree-bark filled with blinding magic, drinking the streams of light that crashed into them.

Then the pine and surrounding trees burst to ashes, and I fell to my knees.

Aubren had fled out of sight, but screams echoed from a distance, growing louder with every blink of an eye. My little showdown caught the attention of every single rebel in Lumenor, and they were undoubtedly making their way to me. The legionnaires, too.

I will either be killed or arrested if I don't leave.

I was exhausted, kneeling in the dirt, fighting for breath. My world was spinning about me, cold sweat beading my cheeks. All I wanted was to curl up and drift into sleep, and I wanted a rest from the overwhelming pain that felt like a thousand blades slicing through my skin. The weight of it pinned me to the ground.

No help was coming—only more danger. So, I mustered whatever strength I had left in me and ran into the night.

Chapter III
Gutter-born

Shouts raced through the darkness behind me like the nearing steps of a wild beast, chasing and hunting me down. "Who attacked you, boy?"

Not allowing myself to think, I pushed forward one cautious step at a time. Synchronizing my exhales with the passing gusts of wind, I was as silent as a hill ghost.

"A girl of eighteen! I met her at the tavern tonight!" Aubren's response whistled by my ear, carried along by the chilling breeze. Every little hesitation in his voice bought me an additional crumb of time to get away.

He is worried they'll think he was helping me.

Aubren's questionnaires were not satisfied. "Who is she? What does she look like?"

He finally gave me up. "She is as tall as my shoulders, uhm, black-eyed and deep brown-skinned, with long silver hair tied in the Mounds' braid. Her coat and dress are blue. She ran that way!"

Kirrah damn him!

My knees throbbed with every step I made despite the soft mud that gently padded the soles of my boots. Shifting shadows from the branches cuddled my face, and the whisper of cold brushed against my neck. I was shivering.

"Boot marks! This way!"

I had to run despite the exhaustion. It would have taken a few hours of good sleep to recover, and I only had minutes to spare, if that.

Think. You know the Mounds better than Zana knows the lines on Mother's palm, and that is saying something.

I glanced around, my eyes narrowing at the impenetrable darkness. The stench of smoke and liquor billowed from the Three Singers, two hills over towards the north, if my nose did not betray me. I was not exactly counting hills during my chase with Aubren. The tavern was built halfway between the two forks of the Mounds' river, rushing northbound towards my home. If I located one of the streams and followed them, I would be at my door in half an hour or so, at my pace. Granted I didn't get caught.

But I couldn't go home.

Mother had always instructed me to run to her if I was ever found out, but everyone knew the punishment for not reporting a bending child to the legionnaires. My parents would be imprisoned, and I would be carried away, leaving Zuri to fend for herself.

The rebels, on the other hand, surprisingly left the families alone—it was against their code to harm the non-bending folk unprovoked. Still, I couldn't place the safety of my family into the hands of the people who hunted me down at this very moment to murder me.

Zana's home? No. That's the second place they'll search for me. Mother and her had been inseparable since childhood.

I considered running to Summer's house, wondering if she would accept me if I did. Her family didn't support the rebels, but they were not exactly fond of the legionnaires either. Besides, she was the one who brought me to the tavern and introduced me to Aubren. I had caused enough trouble for her already.

There was only one choice left.

The choice Mother never allowed me to make or even consider. One thing I had always wanted. I had spent countless nights under the blankets with Zuri, imagining I was a legionnaire. My little sister loved watching me perform fun bending tricks that I'd invented for her amusement. Splitting the starlight balls into five was always her favorite. Her sweet giggles echoed in my mind whenever I thought about those tender moments of our sisterhood.

I should have practiced aiming with precision more while I was at it.

But I always had to hide: from Mother, from Summer, from the rest of the Mounds. I only had trinkets of time in the woods during the day, when starlight was harder to detect. And even then, I had to be careful.

The bushes rustled in the dark. My pondering had caused me to slow down my pace without noticing, and I only had seconds before my pursuers caught up with me. The rebels expected me to head home, and Aubren knew exactly where I lived thanks to my big mouth at the tavern.

Moving as quietly as I could manage over the sparse patches of grass, I crawled into a narrow opening in the nearby evergreen web of bushes. I only pushed my way through the branches as much as I needed to blend in, careful to minimize their cracking under the pressure of my movements. Making noise kind of defeated the purpose of hiding.

"The tracks stop here," one of my chasers noted. Steel whispered against leather as a woman walked into view and pulled her dagger out. I clenched every muscle in my body, afraid to breathe.

"Probably climbed a tree or something," her peer said. He sounded young, like a boy whose voice had yet to thicken into a man's rasp.

"Don't be stupid. If it was truly just one, untrained girl like the boy claims, she should be half a corpse. They can only learn how to bend the power within themselves on their own, so untrained folk drain quickly."

So the rebels know a thing or two about starlight benders.

"Then what?" the boy-rebel asked. "Where is she?"

The woman paused for a moment before responding. I dug my nails into the skin of my palm, biting the flesh inside my mouth. "Let's head downhill, she can't be far," she decided. "We need to find her before the legions take her in."

Thank Kirrah.

I crawled deeper into the bushes once the footsteps faded farther down the hill. My body was at the point of fierce exhaustion. The moonlight couldn't penetrate the thicket, providing a sanctuary for the night. There was no point in trying to escape amidst the active search for me—I would only be a sheep walking straight into the wolves' den.

And I am no sheep.

I tucked my legs underneath the velvet of Summer's dress and rubbed my hands against each other to warm up. Lingering raindrops from the storm earlier still slipped down the branches, plopping onto my azure coat. I was caked with crusting mud. Cold, discomfort, and angst rocked me to sleep, until my heavy-lidded eyes sank my mind into darkness.

I woke up with the first blink of dawn.

Only a vestige of light hung in the east, making the sky a gradient of dimming shades of gray. A trickle of pale sunlight spilled over the city, waking Lumenor from its dreaming.

I wished my last night had been a dream, too.

My boots were drowned in caked mud, the dress around my legs dirty and dyed brownish-gray. My braid rested heavily on my shoulder, its bottom half soaked with dripping rainwater. My fingers and toes were numb, and my bones felt like they were breaking every time I moved.

Yet the resemblance of a grin escaped my lips.

I am going to Old Town! Mother and Father will be spared if I join the legions on my own accord like I always wanted. The legionnaires are brave and powerful. I hope they accept me.

Listening for the commotion, I left the safety of the thicket. Only the copper-eyed owls and domestic animals from surrounding farms made any noise, not counting the miners on their way back from their night shift. Father was likely amongst them, unaware of the news that awaited him at home. I was tempted to take a peek at the road beneath the hill, and look for his warm, fatherly gaze.

This is no time to get sentimental. I will see Father again.

The safest route to the Old Town led through the busy streets of the Cobblestone. One could easily pass by its markets, merchant shops, and townhomes unnoticed if they kept their head down and their lips sealed. To get to the Cobblestone, I decided to pass through the spice farm that crouched at the very tip of the southern Mounds. Even the rebels avoided the perimeter of old Vasin's lands since the farmer was known for being an avid knife-thrower. Zana had claimed a legionnaire once threatened Vasin in his youth, so he learned the skill for self-defense before taking a liking to it.

Sneaking my way through the quiet of the morning, I felt my strength return in waves. My head wasn't aching any longer, and my muscles pulsed with energy. Tiptoeing around Vasin's piled stores of dried spice, careful not to alert him, I tasted the flavor of turmeric and basil in the air.

My stomach growled.

I came upon the edge of the Mounds at last, to the vantage point that overlooked Lumenor before a steep drop into the city. The Gutter—the poverty-stricken home of the rebels—squatted to the east, its decaying roads and homes sinking back into the soil. The wide alleys of the Cobblestone lay west, its roads still empty despite my expectations. The streets crossed at dramatic angles like blades clashing mid-fight. Kirrah's Temple was erected at the Cobblestone's neck, with the goddess' gem-studded stone statue watching over the city. Old Town stretched behind Kirrah's back, vast and gated and richly ornamented with gilded domes and theatrically twisted columns.

I didn't dare think or look back.

You don't have a choice, I told myself, *yet the choices we are forced to make shouldn't feel this good. Besides, if the rumors are true, the legionnaires are paid rather handsomely, and Kirrah knows my family could use the coin.*

Stepping over the edge, I descended down the steep-sloping hillside and entered the Cobblestone at its base.

The sound of awakening life in the Mounds died with distance, and an eerie silence numbed my ears once I reached the bottom. Despite my expectations, the town was filled with nothing but void. Not a single person lingered in the streets, and both the legions of starlight benders and the city guards were out of sight, surely busy fighting the rebels. Every so often, a scream erupted from the depths of the Cobblestone's belly, startling my already hesitant steps.

I abandoned my original route and chose the way of back alleys instead. In the light of the day, without the crowds to blend into, I felt too exposed going through the Cobblestone's market or the Queen's Alley. What if Aubren was out there, leading others to me? What if they were waiting at the next corner? I slipped inside a narrow lane, crawling behind a long array of closed merchant stores. I was wrapped in the cold shadow of their stone walls and backdoors.

I only need to make it to the gates of Old Town, how hard can it be?

It turned out that it was pretty hard.

I spent very little time in the Cobblestone before, save for the occasional trip to the outermost cluster of taverns. Unlike the rolling hills overgrown with bushes and pine trees, the city was a maze of granite towers and painted glass windows that all looked the same to me. I lost my way more than once, turning into dead-end alleys or dark passageways between the stores. The city smelled stale and of a nearby forge; of rosemary-scented vinegar cleaner, and morning tea. Clinging to the direction of the Queen's Alley, I aimed towards the statue of Kirrah, whose head could be seen from any point in the city. The goddess' hair was carved to a curly texture and dipped in white gold to mimic the color of starlight.

Turning from one street and into another, I jumped at every little sound—distant screams, rats digging through the rotting food, the wisps of wind overturning litter. Still, I couldn't resist peering inside a couple of townhomes, entering the world of town folk, if only through the glass. To my surprise, they looked much like the moonhouses in the hills—filled with crystal bowls, swaying moon phase garlands, star constellation paintings, and sun calendars. Only, it was grander.

Nearing Kirrah's Temple, I watched as the statue's head kept growing bigger with each yard I crossed. The stone goddess was a hundred times the size of a person, if not more. I stared at her without blinking when a shred of burbling laughter sent me leaping behind the piles of trash in the corner of yet another back alley.

"How many so far?"

I didn't know who was speaking, or where they came from. I only hoped they didn't see me.

"Well, let's see. Three dead in the Mounds, seven in the Gutter, and two so far in the Cobblestone," someone else replied. Both voices were deep yet of ambiguous maturity. "Not bad for one morning, I'd say. The news of the Akani really scared the starlight folk up, drew them out of hiding."

The laughter erupted once again. "That's what they get for poisoning the city!"

A nearby crash interrupted the rebels' conversation. Judging from the sharp sound, starlight had crumbled the wall of one of the surrounding buildings. Then someone stalked by, their boots pounding against the pavement in a rush.

"There, look! A starlight bender! She's getting away!"

The rebels broke into a run, chasing another person with my abilities. I tapped my foot against the cobblestones, tasting trouble at the tip of my tongue. I swirled my hand and a sparkling mist of starlight rose from my palm.

My magic had returned in full force.

If anything, they'll lead me straight to Old Town. I'll stay in hiding and trace their steps.

The ones doing the chasing were rather easy to follow without being spotted. The rebels dashed towards the statue, never looking back. I trailed behind them, fighting the urge to attack. Pausing at the corner of the Queen's Alley, I looked to all sides to make sure it was safe to step out.

It wasn't, not entirely, but I did it anyway.

Mother would have me polishing flasks until my fingers fell off if she saw me acting this way! Good thing she is not here.

The starlight bender that the rebels were chasing turned out to be a girl of my age. She danced around the fountains in front of Kirrah's Temple, avoiding the rebels' daggers with skill. Appearing to be somewhat of a master knife-thrower herself, she returned their attacks with as much, if not more, zest, pulling one blade after another from her pockets and sleeves. Her Lumenoran hair was cut short by an untrained hand, the upper-half tied up; her skin was pale like daylight, eyes blue like candle flames. The crescent moon tattoo on her forehead faded at the tips and her rags were ripped in more places than I could count. A gray leather bundle hung from her back.

A Gutter-born starlight bender.

The girl continued her dance while I watched, hunched over my knees, hiding behind the nearest merchant shop's wooden posting. It was an unfair fight, five against one, and while she must have been one of my kind to be chased so viciously, I had yet to witness any of her bending.

The rebels closed in, backing her into a large fountain at the center. They were hesitant to approach within the reach of starlight's precision, but their flung daggers became increasingly more difficult for her to avoid.

I have to help her.

Straightening my back, I stepped out from hiding. The girl's fire-blue eyes widened at the sight of me. I forgot what I had been through, what I must have looked like in my once-beautiful dress covered in mud and dust.

Not that any of that mattered.

Breathing in, I summoned magic to my palms. A bright flash of starlight broke through the dullness of the day, drawing the rebels' attention. All gazes steered towards me.

"One behind you—duck!" the girl warned me.

I listened, and a sharp-edged dagger flew above my head with a *swoosh* a second later. I waved my hand behind my back without looking, and the stones crumbled, forming a barrier between me and my attacker.

The rebels flung another knife in my direction. I shattered it with starlight only inches away from my face, barely in time before it got close enough to split my skull in two.

I really should have practiced aiming more.

The girl positioned herself directly across from me, forcing the remaining rebels into a tighter squeeze between us. Smart. They couldn't pause and focus on their knife-throwing if they were attacked from both sides. I attempted to release my power scarcely and only as much as it was necessary to keep them at bay, afraid of draining myself. Unfortunately, I had very little control over my bending. The weakness of my lungs and muscles slowly crept in, tiring me out.

The girl ran out of her blades, though that made very little difference in the end. Her starlight attacks were not much different than her dagger ones, save for their composition—they were precise, short, and pointed, shattering the rebels' knives. When I thought about it, everything about her seemed sharp and pointed. Her nose, the edges of her face, her arms, elbows, even her movements.

We were on the verge of winning, the rebels' backs pressed against one another, eyeing the knives laying out of reach on the cobblestones. The girl's fire-blue gaze met mine through the gap in their formation, and a look of recognition molded both our features in a similar fashion. It was not each other that we recognized—I was certain I had never seen her face before. Rather, it was a decision that every starlight bender had to make once or twice in their life that we were both familiar with.

To kill or not to kill.

I knew which one I would choose, if I could help it. She appeared to agree based on her relaxing stance. But before we had time to discuss the best course of action, one of the rebels pulled a hidden dagger from his sleeve and turned towards me.

As if time had slowed down, every inch of his movements took longer than they should have. The girl's mouth half-opened, her hands shaking. Just as I angled my palms to face the rebel, two violent waves of starlight rushed from behind me, curving around my body before plunging into the rebels. The radiance of the clash blinded me, and I covered my eyes in pain.

The fountain sounds soon washed over the horrified screams, the peaceful song of water flow soothing my ears. I opened my eyes to find a thin pile of stardust caking the top of the pavement where the rebels had been, the girl's face staring at it in terror.

"You are welcome," a voice behind me said. I turned towards it and found myself looking at a regal-looking legionnaire. "I'm Raina."

Despite the authority in her voice, Raina looked about our age. She strode past me with more confidence than I had the previous night wearing Summer's velvet dress. Her glossy curls were tied up high, the moon tattoo gleaming brighter than Tora on a cloudless eve against her forehead. A bronze undertone glowed beneath her spotless brown skin, like the harvest moons in twilight. Golden jewels shined from the creases of her chestnut eyes, glued symmetrically with needle-thin precision. Lean, hard muscles curved beneath the thin flax of her uniform.

The waves that killed the rebels were hers, too.

They had to be.

Raina was joined by two other legionnaires, boys of her age and tall as statues. Both of them were Lumenor-born, judging from the pale, starlight-colored hair on their heads.

The legionnaire to Raina's left stepped out of the shadows without hesitation. Midday sun rays spilled over his deep, brown skin like liquid silver, shining onto the shortly-cut coils of his hair. A sneer curved his lips—an expression of disdain for the rebels mixed with the delight of their untimely deaths.

I shuddered, averting my pointed stare.

They are different from what I expected.

The only remaining legionnaire caught my eye. He observed us quietly from the shade before joining his companions. Short silver hair fell down his face in an orderly fashion, accentuating the fine lines of his jaw. The flax material of the legion's summer uniform clung to his arms like a second skin, outlining his squared shoulders. His large, gray eyes were piercing, and our gazes locked briefly before we both looked away.

"Welcome for what?" The girl from the Gutter asked through her teeth. Despite her threatening demeanor, she had a high-pitched, tender voice.

"The rebel was hesitating," I added timidly. "We didn't need you to swoop in, and—"

Raina pursed her lips. "And save your life?"

The boys behind her looked to each other intensely, as if they were having a conversation of their own in silence.

"You can thank me later," she continued. "It is time we drop you off at the incomers' base to be processed and continue with our patrol. We'll chit-chat another time."

The Gutter-born girl stepped back, leaning into a fighting position. "You don't get to order us around! If we come with you, it'll be on our own accord."

"That's not how it works," Raina sneered, peering over at her companions. "We don't have time for this."

The Gutter girl's daylight-colored face went purple, and she abruptly raised her palms above the hip level. I froze in place, listening to the pounding of my rising heartbeat.

Does she mean to get us killed after all?

I glanced at Raina, whose palms shot up a second later, aiming back at her. Having been so thrilled to join the legions, I never stopped to think if they would be thrilled to have me. Raina certainly didn't showcase an ounce of excitement about us coming on board, yet she wasn't willing to let us go.

"Seriously? You are going to aim at your own kind?" The legionnaire boy who stepped out of the shade first asked, sounding as if the Gutter-born girl offended him by raising her hands in protest.

Another legionnaire rule, maybe?

I stood motionless, waiting for the fire-eyed girl to give up and put her palms down.

She never did.

Raina sighed. "You are forgetting yourself, I'm afraid. You might've been the most powerful fighter in whatever hole you crawled out of, but you are only an untrained girl at the end of the day. Even your friend here has some sense to step away from the fight. Retract your claws before you get bitten."

"I think not," the girl replied.

"Kirrah's cloak, put your hands down!" I urged. "You don't have a choice but to join the legions. You know this."

She shot a sharp look my way after my fingers intertwined behind my back.

The legionnaires ignored and began encircling us, waving their arms apart, forging an inescapable whirlpool of starlight around. The specks thickened, merging and making the fountains, the temple, and even the statue seem like an illusion—a dream made of light. My Gutter-born companion and I gasped. I had never witnessed starlight link before. I didn't even know it was possible! Mesmerized, I stared at the twirling waves of magic that encompassed us, nudging us closer together.

I looked to all sides, but there was no room to escape.

"What are you doing? I wasn't even trying to run away!" My voice echoed through the whirlpool.

Raina shrugged off. "As I said, we don't have time for chatter."

The whirlpool finally forced me within her reach, and the last thing I saw was her fist whistling towards my temple before the world turned pitch black.

Chapter IV

Trials

Teardrops of muck dripped from the ceiling. My neck was stiff, head pressed against the hard stone floor. The air reeked of rusting metal, and the only light came from a dying torch on the wall, illuminating the long bars that guarded the prison cell.

"You should've joined the fight instead of keeping your palms down. That was stupid," a quiet voice said.

I propped my head up with my elbow just enough to see the blue eyes of the Gutter-born girl stare me down from the opposite corner.

"You're one to talk," I snapped. "Who in their right mind fights five rebels on their own, let alone raises a palm against trained soldiers? I, unlike you, want to become a legionnaire. I only ran to your aid in the first place because you looked like you needed my help."

She snorted. "Thank the moons I had it, then! I'd probably be locked away in a prison cell somewhere otherwise." She winked, cracking a sliver of a smile. "My name is Shei."

"I am Imani. Shei like the moon?"

"Mhm."

I rose to my feet clumsily and stumbled towards the wide bars of our cell. The gaps between them were needle-thin but for a shut square window at my eye level. The bars were cool to touch, the kiss of magic-forged titanium sending shivers up my fingers. Naturally, the Old Towners built this prison for starlight benders out of the only material our magic couldn't penetrate. The rebels would have surely built every knife and shield from it, if the price of a single gram of titanium didn't amount to a small fortune.

"Don't bother, I already tried," Shei said. She pulled a dried mint branch out of her pocket and started chewing on one of the leaves.

I slid back to the ground and rested my chin on my clammy palms. My head was throbbing where Raina's fist crashed into my temple.

"So, what now?" I asked.

"Now we wait. They won't let us rot in here, they need more starlight benders of young age."

Shei clenched a mint leaf she previously plucked from the branch between her teeth. Her jaws made tiny, bite-sized chops until there was nothing left but the ground mint she swirled in her mouth.

My curiosity got the best of me. "What are you doing with that leaf?"

"You've never seen someone chew mint before?"

"No?"

"They don't chew on herbs in the Mounds?" she asked, glancing at my braid—the mark of my people's tradition.

"No, I'm afraid not. I mean, we use herbs for tea, stews, and potions, but we don't chew on them. Can I have one?"

Shei plucked a heart-shaped mint leaf with her front teeth, took it between two roughened fingers, and passed it to me. I thought about all the things Mother would scream into my ear if she saw me put an unwashed herb into my mouth, let alone the one a complete stranger bit off for me. I thought about her and the rest of my family. The rebels never harmed the relatives of starlight benders caught in hiding, but I wished to know if my parents and sister were safe.

They must be so worried.

"Not bad," I said after grinding the leaf to shreds. The mint tasted a little off, probably from sitting in Shei's pocket for Kirrah knows how long. Its pieces got stuck between my teeth, but it was something to do.

She winked. "So, what were you doing sneaking through the Cobblestone in that filthy dress?"

Where do I begin? The market, the tavern, Aubren?

I yawned. "I revealed I was a starlight bender to a rebel by accident, so I had to run."

"You revealed you're one by *accident?* How?" Judgement leaked from her voice.

"He was handsome, and I'd had a couple of drinks, alright? I'd heard something in the dark and my palms flashed with starlight. The next thing I know, he's chasing me over the hills, and then I burned that pine tree down..."

Shei's stare widened. "That was you?"

Nodding, I felt a small part inside me plume in pride at my deeds. I'd never had an open conversation with another starlight bender before. It meant something to me, to be able to speak freely, to *feel free* for the first time despite being locked in a prison cell.

"Imani—that's amazing! *You* did that! I change my mind, I'm glad I'm stuck in here with you."

A tingling heat flushed up my cheeks. "What about you? Why were you chased down by the group of rebels?"

"They caught me eavesdropping." Shei waved nonchalantly, as though it was a meaningless matter, an everyday occurrence. "If one gets into technicalities, a loose roof tile gave me away."

She climbs roofs? I can't even run up a hill without panting!

"What were they saying?" I asked.

"The rebels? Oh, they were thrilled about the news of war. They hope Akani Warriors take the moonstone away once and for all."

A shudder wormed up my back. I forgot all about the upcoming invasion while trying to escape the rebels. "Kirrah's cloak, why? The moonstone is the only reason why we are able to survive, Lumenor's only protection against the wrath of the Ashen Desert! Everyone knows that, even the rebels!"

"I'm only telling you what I heard." She shrugged.

The thunder of marching steps came from the hallway, growing louder with each heartbeat. Shei and I both leapt to our feet, and her hand fell on her pocket, reaching for a knife that wasn't there.

A man as tall as statue opened the large square window built into the door of our cell. He was followed by a scrawny guard who peeked over his shoulder. The man's legionnaire uniform outlined his hard muscles without one fold or crease in the flax. His silver beard and hair were fading to pale white—a sign of mature age by which most starlight benders lost the ability to summon their power. However, I found it hard to believe that he couldn't crush us both with one pound of his fist.

Not that I was in any rush to find out.

"These are the two my daughter caught dueling rebels by the temple?" The man's voice fitted his stature—it was stern and deep.

He's Raina's father?

Shei must've figured as much. She clicked her tongue. "Your daughter wouldn't have stood a chance if she didn't have help!"

The smaller guard's glare narrowed as he sent a reprimanding look our way. "My apologies, Commander Izaak, the girls are not from here, they don't know—"

Commander waved the guard away as though he was a mosquito buzzing around his head. "Obviously," he let out an exhausted exhale. Commander Izaak took a moment to measure each one of us up and down, expressionless. I shifted on my feet, struggling to find comfort.

"What do two girls from the opposite sides of town have in common?" he asked. It was easy to guess where we were from based on our appearances, after all.

Shei and I traded a quick, eyebrow-dancing *you-answer-it-no-you-answer-it* look.

"Nothing apart from being starlight benders in trouble," I replied at last.

Shei's finger shot up. "Also, we both like chewing mint. Does that count?"

I giggled, but Commander Izaak was not amused, watching us while remaining as still as stone from the other side of the bars. "How did you get yourselves in this trouble you speak of?" All his sentences were even-toned, and none sounded like questions—they were demands.

"Let's see. I got caught spying on the rebels, and Imani here set the Mounds on fire last night!"

I gasped. "Shei!"

She will get me expelled before I ever make it into one of the legions!

"What? It's true, you said it yourself!"

The commander's expression changed. His stare narrowed on me, examining my face once again. "Curious," he muttered. "Lazzor and Tain were quite impressed with both your skills, having in mind you haven't been trained. Impressed enough to grant you participation in the trials for their legion tomorrow."

A moan left my throat. "The trials?"

"Yes, the trials." The commander nodded. "My mother used to say that it was more important to be at the right place, at the right time than it was to work hard for something your entire life. You two are proof of that."

Ouch.

He headed out, tossing commands at the guard as he walked away. "Make sure they are well fed and rested. Bring them blankets and a change of clothes. We will test these powers they like to brag about in the morning."

―◊―

Shei was up early the next day, twirling the chewed-out mint branch between her fingers as I awakened.

"Jitters?" I asked, washing my face with lukewarm water that the smaller guard left with us before sleep.

She took a deep breath. "No, not really. I'm not afraid of some stupid trials. I worry about my uncle—it's always been just the two of us, you see."

"Oh." I looked to my feet, thinking of my family. I prayed to Kirrah they were safe all over again and decided I would write Mother a letter after the trials, assuming I was still in one piece. "How did your parents…?"

"The legionnaires killed them," Shei replied grimly. "Ironic, I know. Being rebels didn't prevent them from giving birth to a child who can bend."

Her parents were rebels?

"I'm sorry," I said.

Her smile was a weak, solemn one. "Thank you. They made their choices and a lot of time has passed since. I found my way to live with it."

"And you're fine with joining the legions?" I asked. "You didn't seem so keen on it earlier."

Shei shrugged. "That's because I am *not* keen on becoming a member of the order that murdered my family, valid reasons or not. But I can't go back to the Gutter, can I? Everyone there knows what I am now, and they'll stop at nothing short of killing me. I have no choice but to join the legions. Still, I wanted it to be on my accord." She hitched the edge of her gray shirt irritably, stretching the already thinned linens out. "You have any family?"

"A little sister. A lovely father and a mother who will tear me to pieces once she gets her hands on me."

I made her laugh, and we proceeded to eat the breakfast the guard had brought over. Even the prison food in Old Town would be considered a special treat in the Mounds. We were fed spiced sausages, peppered eggs, ripe cherry tomatoes, cheese, freshly-baked bread and butter, and some blueberries, in addition to chamomile tea to wash it all down.

"This, I could get used to," Shei said with her mouth full. I mumbled in agreement, stuffing a piece of warm bread down my throat before licking the melting butter off my fingers.

A guard opened the cell window. "Time to change. You have ten minutes." He threw two legionnaire uniforms at us and left.

I picked the uniforms off the floor and handed one to Shei. "How do the trials work anyway?"

She shed the worn out linen jacket from her back, throwing it on the floor. "I know almost nothing about these trials. I thought they were just going to ship us to the desert."

"Same here."

I wiped my hands against Summer's blue dress that was now gray-brown. I knew she would never take it back, not after what happened to it. The velvet was damaged beyond the point of repair, much like our friendship. For good reasons or not, I lied to her for eight years.

Shei measured the sleeve of her uniform against her arm length. "These don't seem to be the right size."

They were not.

Her uniform jacket was too loose around the chest and waist and was at least three inches too long. She had to help me wrestle the pants over my thighs, the cloth sticking to my skin awkwardly whenever I stretched my legs out. We both struggled with clipping the arrow brooches over each other's shoulders—they kept falling out of place and dangling around.

"How do I look?" I asked after we finally anchored the arrows the right way.

Shei cackled. "Like you burned a tree and had to sleep in the muck. Me?"

I tilted my chin with a smirk. "Like you got saved from certain death by an occasional tree burner."

We both smiled, and she slammed a fist against the titanium bars. "We are ready!"

A playful whistle trilled in from the far end of the hallway, until two shadows crept underneath the door.

"Nice chamber." Raina opened the window to our cell. "If I knew Tain and Lazzor were such fools to offer the untrained benders a place in our legion, I would've dealt with you back when I had the chance! You two should be patrolling the Ashen Desert."

A female legionnaire who came into view at her side her gasped. "Raina! Get a grip for Kirrah's sake!"

The girl's face was the color of an early evening, the palette of moonlight and midnight blending in her skin, black hair falling to her shoulders in loose locks. Lumenor was first formed by two ancestral tribes—one midnight, one moonlight-skinned—and the centuries of living in close proximity to the moonstone crystal dyed all our hair silver. Raina's friend seemed to have roots from both tribes, unlike the rest of us, although many others in Lumenor shared her mixed heritage. She also appeared to be one of the rare Lumenorans who dyed their hair back to their natural color despite the silvering that continued to fade her curls.

"What?" Raina snapped. "I'm just teasing. Relax Cella, will you?"

"We don't care one way or another," Shei said, rolling her eyes. "Can we go now?"

Cella pulled a key out of her pocket and spun the loop around her finger. Her nails were painted black, matching the crystal choker around her neck that twinkled just above the collar of her uniform. The door swung open, the cell torch casting a ray of firelight on her face.

Raina tapped the sole of her leather boot against the floor. "Must we carry you on your way, too?"

"My feet are kind of tired, now that you ask," Shei jested, stretching her leg out.

I nudged her forward, huffing. "Just go."

Say what you will about Raina, but she could wield starlight better than anyone I'd ever met before. Not that my list was very long. Still, I wanted to learn to be that good of a starlight bender, that big of a threat.

"You...you are just okay with us walking out freely?" I asked before stepping out of the cell. "You are not going to bind our hands?"

Cella and Raina swapped a subtle glance between themselves, biting their lips as if they were trying not to burst into laughter.

"Can you summon sei outside of yourself?" Cella asked.

I squinted. "Sei?"

"Kirrah help us," Raina cried out. "Sei is an ancient...a proper name for starlight. And those who were born with the gift to bend are called sei-sans. You will do well to remember that."

"Oh."

Cella tapped her chin. "So, can you summon sei that doesn't come from inside?" She pressed a palm against her chest, gesturing a draw of starlight.

I shook my head.

"Can you deflect the streams we aim at you?"

I glanced at Shei, hoping that at least one of us could do something useful.

"Don't look at me," she replied, to my disappointment.

Raina beckoned us with one swing of her arm. "Then you are not a threat. Come on."

We marched in front of the two of them with Shei occasionally peeking back to ask Cella more questions. Raina promptly ignored us and only spoke when it was time to give directions. It turned out that we were locked away in the dungeons beneath the fighting pit. The trials took place above the ground. The stench of rot followed us down the torchlit hallways. The air was clogged with the choking, burning smell of tar, and distant wailing echoed hauntingly.

My blood ran cold.

I had observed the pit from the edge of the Mounds many times before. A ring of high stone bleachers big enough to sit thousands encircled the vast platform sheeted in dust, resembling a muddy pond from a distance. I used to imagine myself conquering the tournaments the nobles had hosted annually for practice. Now that the time had come to enter the pit, however, all my confidence vanished.

"So, how do the trials work?" Shei asked.

Cella adjusted the obsidian choker around her neck. "The rules are quite simple. You will aim sei at targets. Then, you will engage in combat against one of the sei-sans from the legion you are being tried to join. Our legion, in your case. There are four of us in total—Raina, myself, and the two boys that helped capture you."

Only four of them in total?

Heat rushed to my head. Young legions were often low in numbers when compared to the mature ones whose power was beginning to fade. But only four of them? I never heard of a group so small.

They must be quite powerful.

"What do you mean, we engage in combat against one of you? Like, *real* combat?" Shei asked, her face paling.

The corners of Cella's lips pulled gently, dimpling her cheeks. "Almost real, with the exception that we aren't allowed to bend sei back at you. It would kind of defeat the purpose of the trials, don't you think?"

Shei's nose wrinkled. "What do you mean?"

"Well, you would die."

Neither of us had any questions after that.

We emerged from the underground labyrinth of dimly lit hallways at last, and my head hurt as silver sun rays shone directly into my eyes. Shei covered her face next to me and grabbed my hand instinctively once the entirety of the pit roared ahead of us.

The pit presented itself as a city of its own, all of its grandiose height and vastness eclipsing any of the actual city beyond. If the stone bleachers crumbled in that moment, we would never see the light of a new day. The dusty platform in the center was spacious enough to fit ten, no, twenty moonhouses the size of the one my family owned. And the worst of it—the bleachers were full to the last seat. Folk from all parts of the city but for Gutter came to watch—rich and poor, young and old alike. They were all eager to witness the new classes of youth multiplying the ranks of their protectors. I searched for my parents in the crowd, but I found no familiar face.

"What are all of them doing here?" The pitch in Shei's tender voice sounded unusually high.

"They are here to see our newly found heroes, of course," Raina answered without attempting to conceal the sarcasm in her voice.

She pushed our backs, propelling us forward and towards the lower level of the bleachers where at least two dozen starlight benders of our age trembled in their seats, waiting to be tested. Shei and I had been alone in our cell, so they must had come at least somewhat willingly, or so I assumed. However, their faces told a different tale, the blacks of their pupils growing like frightened game. They were all dressed in ill-fitted uniforms, their jaws quivering above their tight collars.

Raina and Cella settled three sections away, next to the two boys who helped trap us in front of the temple. Their legion was surrounded by soldiers close to us in age, all looking intimidating to my admittedly untrained eye. The ten-year-old Imani inside me beamed with pride to be considered to ascend to their ranks, but the eighteen-year-old Imani, more wary of the world, wished she could go home and hide.

Now that I see what I am up against, maybe I should have stayed in the Mounds and taken my chances with the rebels, the fear in me spoke.

Shei slouched, short of breath. "I lied. My stomach is turning to water."

I clasped her hand and squeezed her fingers between mine. "You heard Cella, they are not allowed to hurt us."

"No—they are not allowed to aim starlight at us! Pardon my language, *sei*, not starlight." She mimicked Raina's manner of speech, making me chuckle. "They can still kick us and punch us and all the rest!"

I forced her to take a deep breath alongside me. "I watched you shoot starlight the same way you throw knives! Don't let them get close to you, and you'll be fine. I, on the other hand, seem to be in far more trouble with my below average bending skills."

Her chest fell back down slowly. "Imani, you shattered a tree into pieces! What do you have to worry about?"

I drained myself for the night, that's what I have to worry about, I didn't dare admit.

Commander Izaak stepped onto the platform and the pit went silent.

"Good day, Lumenor." His deep voice traveled the distance. "A good day indeed. Despite the worrisome news we received from Vatrion, today we admit new sei-sans into the ranks of our best. Let's sort them out, shall we?"

I was not sure what was worse—watching the newcomers bend starlight or watching them participate in combat. Most drained themselves after aiming at two or three targets, which was surprising. I'd always assumed we all contained an equal amount of starlight within ourselves, but I was wrong. I could see why Raina's friends considered adding Shei and me to their legion. Even untrained, we were far more powerful than anyone who was tried before us.

The incomers' combat skills were dreadful at best, and most gave up before the fight even started. Having never fought another person before, I knew a similar fate was waiting for me. In fact, Raina's punch was the first time I had ever been hit.

Commander Izaak called Shei's name, and both of us froze in our seats.

"You got this," I whispered. "Go, go!"

Shei marched towards the bleachers at a stalling pace, but she composed herself once she reached the platform. Round titanium shields glistened, dispersed around at varying distances and heights, each as blinding as the sun itself. They were the only shield from starlight, the gift from earth infused with magic.

But Shei was not to be deterred.

She stomped her foot behind the line drawn in the dust. Her gaze narrowed on the targets and readied her position. The entire pit was quiet, allowing her to focus. Despite my assumption that we would be mocked and looked down on for hiding, everyone was rooting for us. I knew their encouragement came from desperation rather than genuine alliance, but I was willing to take any support I could get.

She opened her mouth, avoiding looking at Commander Izaak directly. "Can I…uhm…can I have just one knife before I begin?"

The hard lines of Commander's face folded in. "A knife?"

"Yes."

"Fine, but don't attempt anything foolish."

As if any of us would dare do something stupid within the reach of his long arms!

Shei embraced the dagger from his hand and spun the pommel without as much as a glance before clutching it firmly. The blade settled in her grip, and her full confidence returned at once. Focusing back on the targets, she released the dagger, striking the farthest titanium shield on her first try.

The bleachers let out a unanimous gasp.

Shei wasn't good—she was great.

After hitting the most challenging target, first with the knife and then with her power, she proceeded to bend starlight at the remaining shields at a rampant speed. She only missed two and only by a hair.

The applause rose like dust from a horse when she was done.

I'm doomed, I thought. *I should have asked her to teach me a couple of tricks while we were locked away!*

The commander nodded in approval. Cella joined the clapping that swarmed through the audience while Raina looked bored with her arms crossed over her chest, peering at the skies.

The commander pointed at their section. "Pick an opponent now."

As if to add salt to our wounds, we were allowed to select a fighter from the legion we were being tried to join. Shei was a tad drained from bending, standing with her back hunched. Her eyes searched the section for an easy pick. The problem was that there weren't any. All four of them pulsed with strength and starlit vibrance, and all but Cella looked thrilled to toss us about for giggles.

Shei pointed at one of the boys—the handsome, gray-eyed one. "Infamous Gutter Prince, would you do me the honors?"

She means to fight him?

People gasped, but Raina licked her lips as if staring down at her favorite meal. The boy Shei picked smirked and got up.

The combat was over before it even started. The legionnaire deflected Shei's streams without breaking sweat, and he even threw her over his shoulder a couple of times. His stature was as frightening as the commander's. I watched him duel with astonishment, envious of his skill. He refused to hit Shei, unlike his peers before him, but he still slammed her down with force more than once before Commander Izaak was satisfied.

"Thank you, Tain. Good work, Shei," Commander said, spinning about his heel to face me. "Imani, your turn."

My insides twisted into a knot. Every single gaze in the pit fell on me, gluing my thighs to the bench. I couldn't blink, couldn't move a muscle. I froze. Shei jogged back to me and pulled me up.

"Come on, tree burner! What are a few targets in comparison to setting the Mounds ablaze?"

It was only a tree. And easy for you to say, Miss I-hit-the-farthest-target!

I regretted that thought immediately. Shei had been nothing but supportive of me, and we had only just met. I mustered the courage to stand up in spite of my wobbling knees. If the others could do it, so could I.

I wanted this my entire life, I am not backing out now. I gave myself a pep-talk of a sort. *Where is Mother when I need her?*

I rubbed my hands against one another as the pale earth rose behind me. Standing shoulder to shoulder with Commander Izaak was almost more intimidating than the infinite distance of the titanium shields. He observed me silently from the vantage point of his height, giving me time to prepare. My eyes fell on the nearest target, and I realized I had never aimed that far, let alone farther.

I am about to make a fool out of myself and get sent to patrol the Ashen Desert with the rest of the untrained folk.

A shout echoed from the bleachers, breaking the silence. "Go, Imani!"

My throat tightened. I could pick out Zuri's honeyed voice amongst thousands if need be. There they were, all three of them. Zuri, Father, and Mother.

My family.

Zuri's features were molded in Mother's image—with her oval face, heart-shaped lips, dimpled cheeks, and thick eyelashes. They both donned their second-hand azure cloaks, but where Mother's hair was silver and braided, Zuri's was flowing free in a crown of silver and black curls.

Father's eyes were heavy-lidded from lack of sleep, though they gazed down lovingly at me. He coughed into an old handkerchief; his lungs had been damaged from the long decades he spent working in the mines. I knew he had just returned from the night shift, and yet he was there.

They were all there.

Even Zana had come along to cheer for me, waving what looked like a ripped piece of purple curtains with golden gem embroidery spelling out my name. I let their faces imprint in my mind, willing away the tears.

How did they know? Don't be naive, of course they knew. Where else would I be?

I looked at Mother, expecting her fury to burn me down from the stands. Instead, her face was stoic. She pressed her pointing finger against her temple, then clenched her fist.

I knew what that meant. *Think Imani, think.* Whenever I was in a tough spot, ridden with pressure or insecurity, Mother's advice was always the same.

Think.

I mouthed my thanks and faced the targets.

Shei's strength was in her precision, mine was in the amount of power I could summon. I had about the same chance of hitting the targets that I had beating Commander Izaak in combat. I decided not to waste my starlight on aiming. I would save it for later—for combat.

I swirled my palms and two marble-sized balls appeared in front of my hands once again. Zuri giggled in the stands. If I accomplished what I had set out to do, at least my family would be taken care of. The legionnaires' wages were thrice the amount we earned from selling ointments at the market, even on our busiest month. Shei had said as much, at least.

The audience was quiet, everyone anticipating my next move. I split each ball into five, causing few gasps, all from the non-bending observers. It would take a lot more to impress the legionnaires who had been training for years. I waved my hands as if I were trying to fling water from them. The balls of starlight left my fingers and scattered around.

Needless to say, I didn't hit any of the targets.

I cleared my throat, turning back to Commander. "I am ready for combat now."

Commander Izaak leaned his ear in, checking if he'd misheard me. "Ready for combat?"

I nodded.

"Are you *certain* you don't want to aim again?" he asked, leaning another inch closer.

I smiled sheepishly. "No need."

Shei shot her arms up in the bleachers, motioning me to go back and bend. I didn't move.

"Pick your opponent, then," the commander demanded.

My gaze swept over the legion's section for performative purposes only. I knew which one of them I was going to pick before I even stepped onto the platform.

I extended my arm as if asking for a dance. "Raina," I called out, causing much commotion in her section. "I believe I am owed a rematch."

Cella's head swiveled between Raina and I at such speed I thought she might faint. The boys pounded their chests in jest. Raina rose from her seat with poise. She seemed excited, even. Posting across from me in a matter of seconds, she waited for her father to retreat before bowing and stepping into a fighting stance.

The corner of her lip curved up. "Let's dance then."

Only ten seconds had passed before she snuck up on me and kicked the left side of my face. Blood ran down my nose, plopping onto dust. My head was already pounding, and we had only begun.

"I'm getting up!" I raised a hand, signaling I wanted to continue, slowly crawling to my feet and attempting to catch my breath.

Raina rolled her eyes, looking bored again. I knew I couldn't beat her, but wiping that smug look off her face just once would make it all worth it.

It will serve her well to have her pride tamed from time to time.

She leapt towards me once more. I opened my chest instantly, and her run came to a halt. Two potent waves of starlight streamed out of my palms, and I circled my arms until they merged. Another trick I learned for Zuri, though I never attempted to bend so much starlight while performing it before.

A trickle of my power would have been enough to fill me with a thrill, and I released more than a trickle. Bending felt better than food, better than wine, better than kissing. I would've given it all up in that moment to hold onto my power forever.

My waves had formed a circle twice my height when I felt starlight starting to slip out of my control. The world was beginning to blur, the shadows began to shift—I was starting to drain.

I drew more than I should have.

I forgot about the thousands in the audience, about the commander, and about all of the legionnaires. I only saw Raina through the glittering wall of lumen, her palms raised, ready to deflect what was coming her way. Pushing all the air I gathered out of my lungs, I blew starlight away with it. It was really my mind that was doing the bending, but performing the physical motion helped.

I expected Raina to defend against my power with ease. However, deflecting a giant sphere of starlight wasn't as effortless as I thought. She managed to contain it at the very last second and redirect it towards the nearest target. Titanium rang like temple bells at midnight as the starlight crashed into it, but it didn't break.

The bleachers sighed, the folk clapping in amazement.

Raina bent over her knees, panting, then lifted her head back up.

I struck again.

A smaller amount of starlight left my palms this time, and my world blurred even further, making it hard to distinguish far objects. Still, my power was potent enough to make it challenging for her to deflect.

Then I did it again, before she had time to recuperate.

My gesture angered her, and she switched to offense. I waved my left hand while holding the right pressed against my hip in an effort to remain on my feet. Raina jumped over my stream. The next one she ducked to avoid. The last one, however, brushed against the edge of the sleeve of her uniform, leaving a needle-thin burn in her skin.

"You show her!" Shei shouted from the now silent stands.

A tiny victory but enough to quench my thirst.

For now.

Raina's big chestnut eyes stared me down in a cold rage, and she twirled her fingers, forging a small, spinning current of light. My elbows and knees were shaking, my sight darkening a shade further, tunneling my vision to the ray of magic in her palm.

"It's…it's against the rules," I murmured as my knees hit the dust. I winced, leaning onto to my hands for support, sweat trickling into my eyes. "You're not supposed to bend back at me."

Raina scoffed. "I don't care."

She might had been able to get away with breaking the rules if her father was not right there. Commander Izaak sprinted faster than most boys half his age, stopping midway between us.

"Enough," he grunted, and Raina vanished the starlight.

I let go of one last breath, releasing the hold on my body. My mouth kissed the platform, and the world blurred to complete blackness.

Not again.

Chapter V
Far Hallways of the Mind

Moving images drifted in front of my eyes. Zuri slept amongst a sea of pillows, her forehead wrinkling from old age. Ash and sawdust covered my family's deserted moonhouse. My own hands shook in front of me, unable to produce any starlight. A soldier whose face I couldn't see wrapped his arms around me, whispering softly into my ear. Commander Izaak's groan rang like a thunder, and the legions of starlight benders rushed past him in full armor. Summer's blood trickled down my hands before Aubren's knife twisted deep inside my belly.

Then I woke up.

Another dream.

My years of potion making with Mother had taught me everything I needed to know about my condition. I guessed what the healers worried about based on the treatment they had administered.

Catnip tea soaked wrappings for headache.
Corydalis flower to stop muscle cramping.
Cayenne to increase my blood flow.

I was going in and out of dream lands, my mind constructing the most vivid tales. I could taste the food I imagined and feel the crisp graze of chill on my skin. I swam in the starlight pools of Kirrah's cloak in the skies and rode across far, barren lands. I was in pain, in shock, in wonder, in love.

The healer's aid.

The only potion strong enough to knock one out of consciousness and make them stay there long enough for the healers to perform their duties. I never had the taste of such a potent brew before. Not knowing how much time had passed or when the dreams would stop eased my mind. I was out of control, and I could do nothing but let go.

Two healers hovered over me day and night. They were there every time I opened my eyes. The older one of the two was lanky-fingered and steady-handed, and the words rolled off his tongue gently like poetry. The healer's pale coils contrasted against his onyx-skinned forehead, which always wrinkled when he was focused. He was a master of knives and needles, the one who stitched my knee up after the trials. A cheerful young girl was his apprentice, and she only performed mundane tasks—changing my wrappings or rubbing the turmeric ointment behind my ears and on my chest.

They are worried about inflammation. We always rubbed turmeric on Zuri's skin when her chest burned.

Mother's voice awakened me from another long sequence of blurred dreams. "Where is my daughter? I demand to see my child!"

I parted my eyelids lightly. Faint rays of sunlight slipped through the mermaid-painted window of the healers' wing. The mermaid's gold and black silhouette spilled on the wall across the room, and both Mother and Commander Izaak passed through the hued light, bathing in her colors. My eyelids grew as heavy as Zana's winter curtains, and I had no choice but to shut them.

"Imani was given the healer's aid to recover, she will not be able to speak for some time," Commander Izaak said.

He was right. I tried moving my lips, but they were fixed in place.

"You administered my daughter the healer's aid *without my permission*?" Mother's hand cupped my cheek before she checked my forehead for fever.

"I don't need anyone's permission to choose what's best for my legionnaires."

His legionnaires? Kirrah's cloak, I passed the test! I passed the trials! I am one of them!

Mother didn't partake in my thrill. "*Your* legionnaire? *My* daughter is going home with me as soon as she awakens."

Commander's voice remained firm, as did his willpower. "The only place you will be going to is prison unless you leave promptly. Be grateful we didn't jail you and your husband for hiding Imani all these years. She is quite powerful, if only she was trained in time—"

"She'd be dead long ago if she was trained, fighting Queen Astra's endless war with the rebels," Mother interrupted. "I think not."

Commander Izaak exhaled through his teeth, running out of patience. "You know you have no say in this matter. If it makes you feel any better, Imani is joining my daughter's legion. I will keep an eye on her."

Mother smacked her lips, and despite not being able to see her, I knew the exact face she made. It almost made me feel bad for the commander. "A fine daughter you raised, she was ready to kill my child! How is that supposed to make me feel any better?"

"Careful now." Commander's tone sharpened. "Leave the bag you brought beside the bed, we will make sure Imani gets it. It is time we leave her to recover. Come on, hurry."

"I will go at my pace." Mother stood her ground. "And shall anything happen to my girl, I will personally hold you responsible."

"As you wish."

Mother planted a soft kiss on my cheek and whispered into my ear. "I love you."

I listened to her receding steps, wishing I could say it back.

Another dream. Blood spilled over cobblestones. The head of Kirrah's statue crumbled onto her temple, crushing its walls. The silver gates of Old Town shattered in a thousand pieces. Skies flashed with stormlight, lightning breaking beneath Assan's full-moon shape. The storm carried frightened screams alongside the smell of decaying flesh on its breath. A gust of glaring starlight pierced my chest, turning it to stardust.

My own scream woke me up.

"Welcome back, Imani." The master healer bobbed his head. He was sitting by my bed, sorting out the contents of the bag Mother had left for me. She fit more ointments inside than I thought possible, three silvers worth of protective crystals, and some clothes. "Don't worry dear, the healer's aid is almost flushed out of your system."

Almost?

"Here, eat this." He reached for a ceramic bowl on my nightstand. The smell of the spiced chicken stew made my mouth water. "I am Mr. Osei, the head healer here in Old Town."

I embraced the bowl eagerly, drinking from it instead of using a spoon. The stew was flavorful and warm, garnished with sage and parsley. I finished it in three gulps.

"Thank you. Nice to meet you, Mr. Osei. How long…?"

"Two days."

I sighed in relief. I'd worried I had been out for much longer. I already missed years of training, I didn't want to miss another day.

The door swung open and Commander Izaak's sharp-edged face appeared behind it. He whispered something into Mr. Osei's ear before turning to me.

"Are you well?"

"Yes, I feel fresh," I said. "Ready to train. I want to learn how to bend properly."

"You will be ready to bend when I say you are."

He spent too much time around Mother, I see.

"But sir—"

His open palm leapt into air. I sucked my breath in.

"Commander Izaak for you, not sir. That is what all legionnaires I lead call me. Commander for short." He paused to draw a long breath without blinking even once. "What you did out there, during the trials and in the Mounds, was a great show of power. Don't smile, I am not finished. It was also careless. Ignorant. And might I add, foolish."

I dropped the corners of my lips back into place. "But what was I supposed to do? Um, Commander."

"Don't interrupt. Do you know what happens if you entirely drain yourself, draw all the sei that resides within you?"

"I faint," I replied.

Commander Izaak shook his head. "No. You die. You would have known that if you didn't hide for eighteen years. So until Miss Yamane, your sei instructor, teaches you how to draw outside of yourself, you are forbidden from bending unless in her or my presence. If I see as much as a speck leave your palms unattended, you will be transferred to the weapon building unit in the Ashen Desert. Clear?"

Do I really have a choice?

"Clear," I muttered.

Commander bobbed his head, then marched towards the door with heavy feet. Mr. Osei and I sat in silence until the doors slammed behind him.

"Just when I was glad to be rid of my mother's firm grip!" I sighed once the commander's footsteps faded into distance.

Mr. Osei chuckled, passing a cup of the steaming catnip tea to me. I blew into it carefully, my breath stirring the hot liquid. "Izaak is strict, but he is not wrong," the healer said with measured gentleness. "You almost drained yourself entirely after all. He is a man of discipline and responsibility, and he will demand the same of you."

I frowned. "I am not the one who put myself into the pit to duel one of *them* before being trained!"

Am I the only one seeing the irony?

Mr. Osei arched a brow, continuing to speak with a calm demeanor. "But you are the one who chose Raina for an opponent. Anyone else would have gone easy on you, and you knew that. Her legion, well, *all* the legions are in need of powerful additions. Now more than ever, and those don't come about often. Not even amongst the youth. Hence you and Shei got the opportunity, despite being untrained."

Shei! Kirrah forgive me—I forgot all about her!

"Shei! Where is she? Is she well?"

Mr. Osei nodded. "Yes, she is fine. She visited you twice every day while you were asleep. Good-spirited girl, the kind you will want to keep around."

I grinned. "Can I go see her?"

The healer rubbed his eyes, his mouth opening to a yawn. "You can. I will leave the room so you can change. Your mother left you some clothes. We are already inside the Old Town's base. Your legion's quarters are two floors up. I will take you there."

"Thank you, Mr. Osei."

His long, crooked finger shot up. "I almost forgot. One thing for you, before you depart." He reached behind the wooden nightstand, and grabbed a bundle of dried nettle leaves tied together with an indigo thread.

"Little piece of home for you. It was my mother's favorite, she used to spike it with rum come dinnertime." The edges of Mr. Osei's face softened, his eyes distant and longing. "I was born in the Mounds, too. I learned half of what I know there. You will find more than one friend around here. If you ever need anything, and I mean *anything*, you come to me first."

Nodding, I thanked Mr. Osei and brought nettle leaves close to my nostrils, inhaling the scent of home.

―――♡―――

The interior of the Old Town base was a work of art. Despite being used to house the legions, the building was more elegant than any room I had ever visited.

Star constellations decorated the ceiling of each chamber and the hallways glittered with minerals in the dark. The hum of a faraway harp vibrated through the stone foundation, traces of frankincense roaming about. The crescent moon-shaped candles emitted indigo firelight, pigmenting the air. We encountered numerous young legionnaires and their commanders along the way, most of them casting nosy glances at me in passing.

The stairwell at the end of the hallway spiraled up towards the unicorn constellation-painted ceiling, even the smallest stars twinkling in the stone. The handrail was made of rich, ebony marble and blue velvet carpeted the stairs. There appeared to be a pattern around the base—all furniture was made of ebony and velvet, and windows and canvases alike were painted with brush strokes of blue, silver, and gold. Sculptures of Kirrah and other deities crouched in every corner, carved into the walls themselves at times. Vivid colors melted into one another, and I couldn't stop gaping at the sheer beauty that surrounded me.

"I am afraid I must leave you here," Mr. Osei said as we reached a wide set of double doors on the third floor. "Shei and the rest of your legion should be here shortly. They will show you to your room."

My hand trembled when I reached for the gilded knob, sweat breaking down my neck. I felt as if I'd sank into another dream, expecting to wake up at any moment.

Am I really here?

The doors opened to a spacious, octagonal salon. Ebony shelves adorned every wall and were stuffed full with color-coded book bindings. The constellation of Gemini stretched across the ceiling, matching my third-moon sign. Blue carpet, softer than a field of flowers, cushioned my boots while a large, seven-pointed table marked the center of the room, seven sturdy chairs tucked into it. Stacks of playing cards laid around the tabletop and were surrounded by the scatter of wine cups, lotus incense sticks, sapphire and sunstone crystals, melting candles, sets of silver keys, and more. I ran my hand across the smooth surface of the sapphire tower placed by the edge when the doors behind me were flung open.

"Is that our dead girl?"

"Kirrah's cloak, Lazzor, get a grip!" Cella elbowed one of the male legionnaires we met by the temple fountains. "She is clearly *not* dead."

"Not yet, at least," I said, chuckling.

Lazzor laughed and shook my hand. Cella hugged me, saying she was glad I was feeling better, and then Shei stormed into the room.

"You had me worried for a second, tree burner!" she exclaimed before pulling me into a tight hug. Her fingers dug into my back as she gave me a squeeze.

I pulled back an inch, making sure it was really Shei. She looked different. Her hair was at least two shades brighter than when I'd first met her, and it was cut evenly. She was dressed in a legionnaire uniform that didn't fit her awkwardly. A clear quartz choker hung around her neck, similar to the obsidian one that Cella wore. Tiny gems the same color of her eyes were glued beside them, shaping a wing in each corner. Even her moon tattoo glimmered from tip to tip.

"You look beautiful."

She blushed, avoiding my gaze. "All thanks to Cella. She showed me around while you were asleep and did all of this." She pointed at her face, and I smiled.

"It suits you," I said.

My warm welcome didn't last long, though.

"Oh, there she is."

Raina entered the room side by side with Tain, the tall legionnaire who fought Shei during the trials. His short hair was now ruffled, and he smiled as he offered his hand to me.

"I'm Tain."

I took his hand in mine and felt the rough callouses of his palm.

"Imani."

Raina's brush against my shoulder broke our eye contact. "Ready for round three whenever you are."

"Let her settle down first, will you?" Shei took my hand, pulling me aside. "Come, I will show you to your room. We have so much to catch up on!"

Chapter VI

Combat

Waking up on time meant getting up before the sun. According to the commander, if we arrived anywhere on time, we were late, and if one of us was late for any reason—be it a mere inconvenience or a life-threatening obstacle—the entire legion had to endure the punishment. Without Mother to wake me, I would have surely overslept on my first day if it wasn't for Shei.

"Imani! Wake up!" She rocked my shoulder at dawn.

I parted my eyelids slowly, seeing her bleary silhouette hovering above me. "What?"

She threw my covers aside, tugging at the leg sleeve of my sleeping garments. "Get up, we only have minutes! We'll be late!"

I protested but had no choice but to oblige. Shei helped me get ready, and I put my uniform on in haste.

At least this one fits properly.

My chamber was a tussle of silk and velvet with shades of deep blue and pale silver. Starlight-colored drapes veiled my bed, disturbing the otherwise dark decor. The constellation of Pisces watched me from the ceiling, matching my sun sign. Chiyoko, its brightest star, gleamed against painted stone. The star got her name from her mother, the sea goddess Chiyo, who awakened the waters just as Kirrah breathed life into the air. My window glass was stained—a mosaic made of a thousand pieces arranged to shape an ancestral warrior woman. Legionnaire uniforms for every kind of weather hung inside the ebony closet—from summer linens to the silver-wolf fur coats, all marked with the queen's five-jeweled crown sigil. A set of knives I could barely throw lay neatly arranged on my desk, each blade sharper than the previous.

"I'm ready," I muttered after Shei clipped the last of my arrow brooches. "Let's head out."

The legion didn't walk to the pit—we ran. Faint rays of the rising sun broke through the clouds, and the air was sticky with humidity. Tears of salt ran down the nape of my neck. I was out of breath before we left the base courtyard, which was rather plain in comparison to the building's lush interior. The edges of the textured stone were weathered by time, the handprints of wind and rain indenting the gray surface.

"The building is plain so that no one assumes the moonstone is hidden here," Shei said.

She'd told me everything she had learned whilst I'd been deep in dreams, including that the moonstone crystal was stored in the heart of the base. Our legion was meant to guard it if things went sideways and the Akani Warriors penetrated the city walls. Shei claimed that our peers were bearable despite her original expectations, but Commander Izaak was not to be messed with.

"He says—you do. It's as simple as that."

I had a hard time keeping up with the others' jogging speed on our way to the pit. I couldn't remember the last time I'd run on my own accord, if ever. I hadn't been much for sporting as a child, and as I'd grown older, I'd replaced my dolls with makeup powders and taverns. We were about five minutes into training and I was already light-headed.

The run to the pit turned out to be only the warmup. We sprinted ten laps around the platform as soon as we got there, Commander Izaak yelling at Shei and me to catch up with the others. Granite bleachers towered above my head like mountains. My feet thumped against the scattered grains of earth. A desert-dry taste soured my tongue, and I craved a cup of cool mint water to wash the flavor down. Tain led the legion, setting the pace, before the commander made him run at the tail, which meant right behind me.

"Everyone needs to run faster than the person that is in the best shape. No exceptions!" Commander Izaak ordered, staring directly at me.

Kirrah help me.

I tripped over my feet several times, too aware of Tain's measured breathing behind me. He nudged my back when I started falling behind, enough to keep me going.

"Make longer strides," he urged, "it takes less effort that way."

I was afraid I might faint when we were finally done running. Smog washed over the platform like a wave, soaking the pit in a pool of gray mist and making it hard to see. Bending over, I brought my face to my knees. The heat that burned my chest after drawing more starlight than I should was nothing in comparison to the pain I felt gasping for air.

"We might've killed her for good this time around," Raina said, and they all laughed except for Shei.

It was not funny at all. Not to me.

How am I to fight the Akani, the great warriors who stole Vatrion's ruby crystal, if I can't run ten laps? How am I going to face my family, telling them I couldn't keep up?

"Come on." Shei dragged me away. "It's only your first day, it'll get easier. Don't listen to her."

"Everyone line up, five feet apart!" Commander Izaak called out, demanding we practice combat moves next. The legion formed a line. "Ready position, hurry, we don't have all day. Now, chin down, right hand up, elbow in, left fist straight out! Pull it back, left fist out!"

The legionnaires moved in a synchronized motion without skipping a beat, like the two wings of a butterfly. Their combat moves were practiced to perfection, without a finger out of place. It made me feel a tiny bit better to see Shei swing a second or two late alongside me. The commander paced around, correcting everyone's technique, demanding more precision or power in their strikes.

Then he got to me.

"Keep your right elbow in, turn your foot, that's better. Use the rotation of your hips before you strain your shoulder. Don't slouch so much! You can't afford to lose height if you are fighting against soldiers who are a foot taller than you. You are still slouching!"

Ugh.

"Pair up!" The commander ordered next. "Imani and Shei, over here. I will guide you through the exercise."

I muttered thanks to all three moons, not quite ready for a rematch against Raina.

"We shall start with the basics, since you are both about ten years late. There is a reason why we start training sei-sans young, as you can imagine. You have much to catch up on, and not nearly enough time."

We listened and watched the commander as he showed us the proper way to take a stand, to kick, to punch. He executed all the moves with such ease, or so it seemed until we tried repeating them.

"You fight like a street bully," he said to Shei, making me burst into laughter.

"Sorry," I whispered upon seeing her face drop.

This isn't easy for her either.

She brushed it off, returning the jab. "At least I *can* fight, dead girl."

Alright, that was kind of funny.

Not to the commander, who made us run a punishment lap just for joking around. "You must take your training seriously and learn to fight. Come, Cella and Lazzor will now demonstrate how the legionnaires actually engage in combat."

I didn't know if I was more thrilled or frightened to watch the two legionnaires duel. There was an undeniable allure to witnessing what kind of fighter I could become, accompanied by the angst that I would never get there, at least not in time for battle.

"Bending or no bending?" Cella asked, trotting towards the center of the pit. The obsidian choker around her neck drank in the meek sunlight and her leather boots drowned in the ascending haze beneath her feet. Lazzor trailed behind her, cracking his knuckles and humming to himself in preparation.

"No bending," Commander responded, to my disappointment. I was impatient to see starlight—*sei*—used in combat.

Cella and Lazzor posted across from each other in a fighting stance I was yet to master, and the rest of the legion and Commander Izaak encircled them, watching attentively. Tain stood behind me, breaking down every move to Shei and myself per Commander's request. Shei pretended she couldn't hear him, but I listened to every word.

"Pay attention to Cella's balance," Tain said, pointing at her feet, "the direction of her toes. She is stable but not bound to the ground so that she can move quickly."

"I see."

Cella swung first, leveraging the power of her torso to gather force. Lazzor caught her wrist midair, but she was too quick and slipped between his fingers almost immediately. She spun on her heel, attempting to kick the right side of his face. He blocked her foot and swung back. Their bodies tangled and untangled—fists, elbows, palms, knees, and feet storming towards each other's weak spots. They seemed to move at the speed of light, disturbing the rising smog and cloaking their uniforms in a gray shimmer.

"I almost had you!" Cella jeered after Lazzor escaped her kick by a hair.

"Oh! I'm almost scared now!" he called back.

Their combat, despite my expectations, was not a playful dance of limbs. Both legionnaires grunted and panted, focused on each other's moves. It appeared as though they saw no one else, heard no one else, but each other. Lazzor and Cella gazed upon one another with the unsettling expression of a killer cornering its prey. My blood curdled just imagining the Akani rushing towards me with the same determination on their faces.

"Showoff!" Lazzor grunted after Cella's elbow plunged into his chest. He took advantage of her proximity and flipped her over his shoulder, slamming her to the ground.

A gasp died down at the back of my throat.

Shei squinted, looking for Cella's body in the mist.

"Is she alright?" I asked.

Tain's breath rolled down the side of my neck, prickling my skin. "Of course she's alright, this isn't Cella's first time being knocked off her feet," he murmured. "Focus on the way she shifts her weight, how she keeps her distance until Lazzor's attention scatters."

Cella was indeed fine, lifting herself from the ground and sliding straight into another fighting stance. Her ashen-colored uniform was dotted with fresh drops of blood.

"Is it common for male and female fighters to go against one another?" I asked. Shei glanced over, acknowledging Tain's presence for the first time, curious to hear the answer herself.

Tain's hand gave a light squeeze on my shoulder, and despite being tucked underneath the layers of my uniform, my skin pulsed to the starlit warmth of his palm.

He must be quite powerful to beam with so much heat.

"Commander Izaak demands that we let our opponents choose us," he laid out, "not the other way around. But to answer your question, it's very common and there's nothing to fear. I may have bigger muscles than you, but..."

Shei smacked her lips, cutting in. "...she can burn your bones to stardust before you blink?"

I giggled, but Tain's jaw clenched. "And you? Are you tempted to challenge me?"

The question was for Shei, not me.

Why are they so hostile towards each other?

I didn't know which one of them to look at, feeling the rising heat emitted by their pointed glares at one another. Luckily, Commander heard their scuffle and made Shei stand next to Raina since she was not willing to listen to Tain.

Cella's nose was now bleeding and the skin around Lazzor's left eye had started swelling. They were visibly tired, yet both kept their composure. I rubbed my palms against my thighs, holding my breath. I grimaced as Cella's body slammed against the platform once again. She struggled but still returned to a defensive stance. The tension was fierce, and I could not help but to bounce on the balls of my feet.

You got this.

Naturally, I was rooting for her. I saw myself in the other girl, saw what I could become. She gathered whatever strength she had left and charged at Lazzor. Changing direction at the very last moment, she forced him to open the already beaten side of his body and roped herself around him before crushing him to the platform, pinning her knee to his back.

Commander called the fight over.

Cella leapt up, extending her arm to Lazzor who had yet to rise. "You *almost* beat me, I'll give you that," she teased.

"I must change my strategy—you've learned all my moves," he said half-begrudgingly, before cracking a smile and taking her hand. "Until next time, my friend."

I watched Cella wipe her bleeding nose with a ripped sleeve from her uniform. I felt the sudden tug of jealousy in my stomach. No, I didn't want to feel the force of Lazzor's fists on my ribcage, but I did want to know what it was like to win—to be feared and respected. She had done so much damage without even bending! I could only imagine how exhilarating their fight would have been if they'd used starlight.

And I wanted it. All of it.

The thrill, the reverence, the power.

The legion stretched out in the dirt after the combat lesson was over. Commander pushed my back forward, towards my toes which felt more out of reach than the targets during the trials.

"You will get injured unless you become more flexible. Make sure you go to Mr. Osei after the day is over."

Is there anything here that I can do properly?

I soon learned that a cold plunge was mandatory after each combat session, as if I was not in enough pain already. I changed into my swimming garments and tiptoed towards the pool inside the healers' wing, stopping at the edge. A cloud of steam rose from the water, evaporating in the torch-emitted heat of the chamber—a battle of fire and ice playing out in front of my eyes. I didn't know that ice could burn, however, until I dipped my toe into the water.

"No way, nuh-uh." I withdrew my foot within a second. "I swim in the Mounds river every year come springtime, and its frigid stream is warmer than this pool!"

Cella met me at the edge, hesitant to go in herself.

"I've been doing it for a decade, but I hate this part, too. It's too cold," she complained. "Best to get over it quickly. It will hurt for the first minute or two, then you'll lose all feeling in your limbs."

Great, I feel better now!

Mr. Osei watched us from the side, polishing empty potion flasks with care. His apprentice roamed about, preparing towels for when we got out. "I can't start the time until everyone is in the water up to their chest," he said, wrinkling his forehead.

"Up to their chest?" I grimaced. "You might as well kill me now."

That amused Lazzor and Shei, who went on to pretend to be freezing to death, teasing me to get in.

"I really don't have a choice, do I?"

"You can take it up with Izaak," Mr. Osei replied.

Right, so that he can make me stay in here for an hour as a punishment!

I stepped into the water. It felt like thousands of knives stabbed my legs and stomach, and my skin prickled as if I were breaking out in hives. My muscles grew stiff as rocks, and every splash poked like needles. My jaw was shaking and so were my fingers.

Then I went numb.

"See, not so bad after a while," Cella said. She was sitting next to Tain, who had plunged down all the way to his neck. He had his eyes closed, as if focusing, and his lips were turning blue. I realized I was staring and looked away.

"You two need to put some muscle on," Lazzor judged, looking at me and Shei. Raina bobbed her chin beside him.

"Shut up, Lazzor!" Cella sent a splash of ice water his way, cold droplets raining onto his neck and shoulders, making him gasp and shiver.

"What?" He splashed the water back at her. "I'm not saying that to make them feel bad, I'm saying it because it's true. No great warrior in history—"

Cella rolled her eyes. "Not this foolery again! Stop reading warrior stories all night and get a grip. They are both working hard. Besides, it is only Imani's first day!"

Lazzor shrugged his goosebump-ridden shoulders. "It will soon be her last, unless she learns how to fight."

My body fidgeted and not from the cold. Shei and I glanced at each other, both our lips pressed tightly.

What if Lazzor was right? I jumped at the first opportunity to join the legion, never thinking about what it meant. I wanted to wear the uniform and have the freedom to bend, but I never thought about what being a legionnaire entailed. It was far more than a half-fleshed out fantasy of a naive Mounds girl. One combat lesson was all it took to showcase the disparity in our capabilities against the trained starlight benders, and we had not even gotten to the bending part yet.

"Alright, that's enough," Tain said, his lips completely blue. "Since you are so eager to see them improve, you can help me train them. Commander already asked that I take Imani under my wing, so maybe you can work with Shei."

"I can't believe I am stuck with Lazzor as my overtime instructor!" Shei puffed.

The sun was sinking back into the earth on our walk back from my first knife-throwing lesson. We were finally headed towards our chambers after a long day of training.

Shei was miles ahead of me when it came to aiming, and she was a far better knife-thrower than any of the other legionnaires. I was, naturally, the least precise one in the group, but Shei's pointers helped me hit a couple of the targets. The small improvement was enough to lift some weight off of my chest.

"Do you want to switch?" I asked, twirling my braid around my finger. Sunlight trickled down my forearm, its fading glow flowing down my umber skin. "Lazzor isn't careful with his words but he means well. Besides, I find the warrior stories quite intriguing."

"Really?" Shei twisted her mouth as if she'd bitten into a worm-filled apple. "I would've taken you up on the offer if your instructor was anyone other than the Gutter Prince."

That was the second time she'd addressed Tain by that nickname. "Why do you call him that? And why are you so appalled every time he speaks?"

She stopped in her tracks, patting dirt off her leggings. "You are kidding, right?"

I tilted my head. "Um, no?"

"Tain is Queen Astra's adopted son, the first boy from my part of the city to rise through the ranks of Old Town. The queen must've thought that adopting a child from the Gutter would ease the tensions within the city," she hissed, gritting her teeth. "She was wrong."

My nose wrinkled. "Queens adopt children?" I asked, rubbing a sore spot on my arm. Despite plunging myself into the iced water earlier, every muscle in my body was aching—a mark of survival after my first day of training.

Shei nodded, quickening her steps once again. "All the time! Unless their own child can bend, which rarely happens. Queen Astra's husband died young, and she never remarried or gave birth. The Lumenoran throne is passed down to the next most powerful starlight bender amongst the youth, not the next of kin, anyway."

She grabbed one of her combat knives from her belt and ran a thumb across the edge absentmindedly, almost cutting her skin in the process.

I snatched the blade from her hand and slid it back into the leather sheath clumsily. "I've never heard of an adopted child who became a king or a queen," I said, drawing on my half-forgotten school knowledge. The Mounds folk didn't really care about the rules of succession as it made very little difference to us in the end which noble was sitting on the throne. Unlike the elite families of Old Town, we had no say in choosing our next ruler.

Shei pursed her lips, kicking a pebble in her way with the tip of her boot. The stone rolled along the path before crashing into a nearby building. "Tain might as well be the first. I heard there are only a few who could challenge him, and the queen's bending power fades with each new sunrise."

The passing thought of my own power diminishing one day trembled through my bones. *I have to live long enough first.*

"Still, that does not explain why you're not fond of him," I said.

Her face grew serious, thin silver brows furrowing. "He did nothing for the place he came from during the long decade he spent on this side of the silver gates. In fact, things have only gotten worse as of late. Our people are harassed daily and starved. That is why I have no love for him."

I knew better than to suggest that she should ask him for his side of the story and dropped the matter altogether.

An anchored ship does not change its course, Zana had told me once.

"It's settled then, I guess. You are stuck with Lazzor as your instructor," I said, only a tad thrilled to train with Tain.

Chapter VII
Three Full Moons

*T**hank Kirrah for my mother.*
She'd packed all of my hair and skin potions, as well as my makeup powders. My braid cuffs and my aquamarine necklace and earrings had also been tucked away – birthstone jewelry had always been my favorite. Zuri's star-shaped pillow had also been packed. It smelled like sweets—like my little sister. I pressed it against my cheek, thinking of Zuri's enthralled face as I read her fairytales at night.

I complain and we argue, but no one knows me better than Mother.

Placing the labeled jars inside my bath chamber, I stacked them against the wide wooden shelf carved with ancient markings. The passage of time had dulled the lettering, leaving behind an altered memory of ancient life, a retelling of an old story. Zana had taught me a handful of ancestral symbols from the past, but I only recognized one of them on the shelf—the mark of eternal light.

An almost burnt-out candlewick flickered in front of the jeweled mirror, its azure flame sparkling in the reflection of my ebony eyes. Polished marble floor chilled the soles of my bare feet as I shed the layers of my uniform. I gently detangled my hair and reached for my hair ointments and soap before heading into the bath.

A half-moon shaped tub of stone, filled with hot water, waited for me, the scent of rosemary rising with the steam. Warmth flowed against my skin like silk, soothing my tired muscles. I was fighting the urge to shut my eyelids when Shei's loud punches against the door startled me.

"I asked Cella! We are starting soon! Hurry!"

Please don't let it be another training session. I thought we were done for the day?

I got out of the tub in a rush, and rubbed lavender ointment onto my skin, which was still raw from the bath. I oiled my waist-long curls with grape-seed and jasmine flower extract, braiding them into two thick plaits to dry. Just as I finished my mind began drifting.

Shei pounded on the door once again before the knob rattled and the door was flung open, startling me.

Her eyes roamed over the room and stopped on the belongings my mother had sent. "You weren't joking about the crystals!"

Her hand glided over the gems on my shelves—purple amethyst to encourage inner strength, translucent calcite to cleanse one's energy; red jasper to give courage, green malachite to help with transformation, to name a few.

She picked up a dark blue crystal carved into a pyramid shape, the spills of gold and silver trickling down the edges like free brush strokes. "What's this one for?"

"That is Lapis Lazuli, the stone of truth," I replied, rubbing my eyes. "It encourages good judgment and wisdom—something my mother seems to think I lack."

Shei traced the edge with her finger, studying each side of the pyramid with admiration. "A wise woman, your mother."

"Ha-ha." I exaggerated my laughter. "Take it if you like it. The crystal, I mean."

Fluttering her eyelids, she placed the pyramid back on the shelf with caution and withdrew her hand. "No, I can't."

"Take it. I mean it. I only have what—about three dozen left?"

"Well, when you say it like that…" Shei snatched back the polished gem and put it into her pocket with an almost child-like excitement that reminded me of Zuri.

"Thanks," she said. "Ready?"

I pulled the white, aquamarine-beaded sweater Mother knitted for me last winter over my head. The wool was soft, if a little stretched out at the elbows, and smelled like rosemary.

"You still haven't told me what we are doing. I don't think I can handle another training session. The sun is down and it's getting late."

"Kirrah's cloak, no!" Shei blurted out, twisting the gilded doorknob. "We are going just outside the chambers, to the salon. We play cards and dice there every night."

I let out a sigh of relief.

All four remaining members of our legion were already in their seats. Cella and Raina donned fancy sleeping garments made of shining, black velvet, and while Cella's lining remained black, Raina's flashed with gold. Lazzor's broad shoulders stretched out a skin-tight white jacket, and Tain wore a dark blue shirt embroidered with Queen Astra's crown sigil across the chest.

Shei, unlike the rest of them, wore layered gray linens after the latest Gutter fashion, seemingly unbothered with what the others thought of it. I caught myself staring at everyone. I'd never seen any of the legionnaires without their uniforms and weapons before. I'd fallen asleep at dusk the prior evening, before they had all changed, numb from the leftovers of the healer's aid in my blood.

I took an empty chair between Cella and Shei. Cella turned out to be an experienced card dealer, scooping dispersed pieces of painted papyrus into her lap with natural grace. Shei pretended to yawn as she peered over from her seat in hopes of catching sight of one of the cards.

"Cheater," I mumbled and she cackled, but she kept peeking anyway.

"Imani," Lazzor called my name from the opposite side of the table. "Red or white grape?"

I rubbed my forehead, distractedly stretching out my cramped muscles under the table. "Sorry?"

He gestured at two bottles of wine resting beside the tall stack of warrior tomes on the table. Each book was at least six hundred pages long, wrapped in hard leather binding. A golden thread spelled out its long title.

"Red, please," I said. "Always red."

Raina snorted at my words despite drinking the exact same brew. To her not-so subtle disappointment, it didn't take long before I learned to ignore her not-so-subtle jabs.

"Didn't take you for a red grape kind of a girl," Shei said, cupping her glass of sparkling white.

I glanced over at her drink. "White is too sweet. Besides, red is supposed to be good for your liver."

Shei rolled her eyes. "Oh, is that so?"

Cella shuffled the deck of playing cards as skillfully as Zana did before her readings, the back of the painted papyrus matching her night-themed velvets. "I never asked—how *did* the two of you end up fighting rebels by the temple?" Cella asked without looking up. "I wish I'd been there to see it!"

I took the first sip of my drink, savoring its spice-rich flavor. The label on the bottle claimed the wine was two hundred years old, yet it tasted the same as the one-copper-a-cup brew from the Three Singers to me. "We were both running away from the rebels," I responded. "Shei was caught spying on a roof, and I'd revealed myself by burning down a pine tree to get away from a rebel, but I'd released too much starlight and—"

"Sei, not starlight," Raina emphasized.

I clicked my tongue in annoyance. "...I released too much *sei*, and the tree burst to pieces. Rebels had swarmed the Mounds looking for me after that, so I ran."

"Izaak must have been furious," Tain muttered, closing his fingers around a red-jeweled cup.

I nodded. "He called me ignorant and foolish."

"That's the commander for you," Tain sighed. His throat bobbed as he drank from his cup. "What were your lives like before?"

"My uncle owns a blade shop that I work in," Shei replied, not giving Tain as much as a glance.

Lazzor rested his elbow atop the stack of warrior tomes, leaning over the table with his back hunched. "Explains her skill with knives," he muttered under his breath to Raina, who nodded.

"What about you?" Tain asked, turning to me.

"I sold potions at the Mounds market that my mother and I brewed," I replied, my mind drifting towards the countless days I spent behind my ointment station. In spite of becoming a legionnaire like I'd always wanted, finally making my way into the heart of Old Town, I looked back at my potion brewing days with fondness. I was beginning to miss the smell of fresh market vegetables and honey pies, the comely, polite faces of my neighbors and friends as they strolled through the stand-packed lanes. I was beginning to miss home.

Raina's eyes lit up, and she accidentally took a sip out of Shei's cup instead of her own, grimacing as she tasted the white grape. "What I would give to see you behind the stand, bargaining over the price of a jar of a gentleman's aid!"

"It's honest work," Cella scolded her. "Besides, that means Imani knows a ton about herbs, am I right?"

"Mhm."

Lazzor accidentally kicked one of the ebony legs under the table, shaking the tabletop and Cella's elbows with it. Cards fell from her hands like leaves, fluttering all over the table and floor. "Seriously, Lazzor!"

"My fault," he grunted, helping collect the cards.

"No kidding it's your fault!" Cella snarled, licking a finger before sorting through the deck, counting the number of missing cards. Then she returned to our previous conversation. "By the way, you should see the Old Town breweries. They mix everything from healer's ointments to weapon potions."

Summer would be thrilled to stop by—we had so much fun inventing new potions together, though they seldom worked.

I was beginning to miss my friend, too.

Leaning over to help Shei assemble the remainder of the deck from the floor, I reached for the last card that stuck to the carpet face-down. When I flipped it around, unnaturally golden eyes pierced my skin in a familiar way.

The Back Stabber.

Unbeknownst to many, tarot and playing cards often overlapped, as the makers of the latter drew inspiration from the tellers. I chuckled to myself, thinking of Mother's gasp when I first drew the Back Stabber during Zana's reading, before an unsettling thought passed through my head.

Was Zana right? Did Summer know I could bend? It would explain Aubren's immediate attention to me. Is she the Back Stabber?

Shei whistled a popular Gutter tune into my ear while Cella reshuffled and began dealing cards for the moon phases—Father's favorite game. He enjoyed playing with Zuri and me before heading out for the night shift. I only ever saw Father in the evenings before he left for work. He was mostly asleep during the day, exhausted from long hours at the mines. He felt guilty about his absences, having missed my first day at school, my first dance, Zuri's first step, and many other milestones. I used to feel resentful towards him as a child—I lacked an understanding of our family's predicament. If anything, my legionnaire salary contributed enough coin to my family's safety, allowing Father to take a much deserved rest. It hurt a little that I was not there to see it and make up for the time we'd lost.

We will have time after the battle.

"It is time for the war strategist to show off his skills." Lazzor rubbed his hands together, staring pointedly at Cella over the table.

"Hardly!" Cell scoffed. "If you're such a great strategist then why did I floor you at training today?" Shei giggled while I covered the smile on my own lips.

Lazzor shrugged. "Laugh all you want, but I'm nine wins ahead of the rest of you lot."

"Nine wins?" I asked, emptying the rest of my cup in one sip. A hint from the floating cinnamon stick sweetened my lips. "And how exactly do war stories help one with moon phases?"

Tain put his palm up, the embroidered sleeve of his sapphire-colored shirt wet from the wine Lazzor had spilled earlier. "Don't encourage him, we'll never hear the end of it."

Lazzor twisted his neck, frowning. "Tain only says that because he prefers his books to dwell on the meaning of life instead of people who lived it. Don't listen to him, Imani. I can tell we are all going to be good friends. I'm glad you two joined us. We all are."

"Speak for yourself," Raina snapped.

"Don't be rude." Cella admonished her. "We are *all* glad you are here, though we have an odd way of showing it sometimes."

I bit my bottom lip to suppress a grin.

I might belong here one day after all.

"You too, Miss Knife Thrower," Cella added, and Shei blushed.

Picking my cards up from the table, I kept every face muscle in place to avoid revealing the good hand I'd been dealt. Two moons—Tora and Shei in the waning phase—rested amongst others in my palm. I was only missing Assan for a full crescent hand, worth thirty points. Father had claimed that one had to be patient to win the moon phases, but patience was not my strong suit. I dug my toes into the soft carpet while everyone rearranged their cards, contemplating a winning strategy.

Raina, Lazzor, and Tain guarded their hands as keenly as their lives, keeping them under the table in their laps.

"One would think you are hiding the moonstone over there," Shei teased, leaning over to take a peek at Raina's hand over her shoulder.

"Keep your eyes on your own deck before I give you something bright and hot to look at," Raina hissed, perking her chest up.

Shei stuck her tongue out at her before giving up, settling in her seat without looking at my cards. *She wouldn't cheat against me, just like Summer never did.* Something in Shei's demeanor reminded me of my childhood friend. Her quick wit, her uncompromising attitude, even the way she joked about—it all exuded confidence. It was what drew me to her in the first place.

Let's hope our friendship doesn't end on the same note as my relationship with Summer.

"Are any of you…afraid?" I asked after passing a full moon card to Cella. She took it with a grimace, then placed it in the middle of her deck, acting disappointed. I decided to pay closer attention to her, certain she was close to winning.

Raina's chestnut eyes darted to me. "Afraid of what?"

I swirled a gulp of water in my mouth to wash down the sweetness of the wine, wishing I could take my question back. "Well…the Akani. The war."

The room grew quiet. Cella picked at her lip, and Lazzor ran a fingertip down the threaded title of one of his leather-bound tomes. Ironically, the title of the book was *The Last Battle.*

"One would be a fool not to fear them." Tain broke the lingering silence. "Anyone powerful enough to defeat Vatrion's sei-sans and steal their crystal must be taken seriously."

"No kidding," Shei said.

"Are we... are we powerful enough to defeat them?" I asked.

"We'll find out soon enough," Raina replied briskly. "Now, pass the next card. And no more talk of the war in the evenings. We hear enough of that during the day."

I swallowed and continued to play moon phases.

Lazzor ended up besting us in nine out of fourteen rounds, adding another big win to his count. "And that's how you sit back, observe, and keep your hand until everyone else shows theirs," he boasted.

"I swear he is counting cards!" Cella said, throwing hers back on the table. Being so close to beating him, she'd only lacked Tora's card to complete the full moon hand, worth fifty points. She was also the holder of the waning crescent Assan I was missing.

Lazzor raised his chin confidently. "Of course I am counting—only the important ones, though. Cella is jealous because she used to beat me in moon phases when we were children."

When they were children?

"How long have you two known each other?" I asked.

"Our entire lives," Cella answered. "Our parents are close friends and so are we. That doesn't mean I am going to allow him to cheat!"

Lazzor chortled but still refused to admit any wrongdoing.

"I am off to bed. Good night and don't stay up late," Raina said, getting up from her chair. Cella and Shei followed her shortly, closing the doors to their respective chambers. I helped Tain clear the table while Lazzor put away the drinks.

"Ready for bed?" I asked after Lazzor shut the doors to his quarters, too.

Tain gathered the remaining cards that had fallen under the table, aligning their edges with meticulous precision. "Not even close. You?"

I shook my head.

"Come with me then," he said, putting the deck down.

I remained in place, blinking up at him with suspicion. "Come where?"

Circling around the table, Tain offered me a hand. I took it warily, feeling the warmth of his palm imprint on my skin, starlight colliding with starlight. "I won't get you in trouble, I promise. It's your first official night in Old Town. There is something you need to see."

⁓♡⁓

"This is what you call *not* getting me into trouble?" I cried out, mounting the outer stretch of stairs that led towards the rooftop of the base.

"Trust me."

A cluster of star constellations gleamed in the sky—Tora, Assan and Shei illuminating the night in the full moon phase. A chill snuck in underneath the wool of my sweater, but the three cups of wine I'd drank warmed me up from within.

The rooftop was a plain square of cold, weathered stone with only a short railing around it. I was not very fond of heights, dropping to crawl towards the edge while Tain marched with his spine straight. I laid on my stomach next to him, looking out to the east.

"I come here every night before sleep. The view is quite something, isn't it?" he asked.

"Yes," I admitted, looking down at all of the lights and people. "It's breathtaking."

The ages-old rooftops of Lumenor stretched eastward, crowned by the white-gilded dome of Kirrah's Temple. The goddess' statue struck the skies beside it, her jewels gleaming in the night, rivaling the stars. Waterfalls of blue flower vines rushed down the tall stone fences of Old Town, and guards and folk crowded the streets, heading home after a night of drinking. Music spilled through tavern doors, singers' voices blending with the subtle notes of lute and harp. The moonlight bathed the city in its silver gleam.

"The best thing you've ever seen?" Tain asked softly.

He crouched beside me and our elbows touched. I could almost taste the scent of mint and leather that was on his hair and skin. His demeanor was now gentle like the summer rain, contrasting with the quiet storm he carried when we were training earlier. It made me wonder which one of them represented the real him.

I sighed. "Second best," I said. "Old Town is magnificent, but you should see the view from the very edge of the Mounds, the entirety of

Lumenor stretched out before you. Nothing can best it. I stand by that."

Tain was taken by surprise, staring at me in disbelief. He unrolled the sleeves of his shirt to protect his elbows from scratching against the stone. "In that case, you need to take me there. I would love to see it."

The breath of the evening breeze combed through my silky plaits, my lungs drinking in the fresh night air. "It will have to wait. You may be secure in your position, but I'll be sent straight to the Ashen Desert if I move a palm out of line. Commander said so himself."

"After we win the battle, then," he said with a meek grin. Unease crawled up my spine at the thought of Akani Warriors rushing through the moonlit streets, soaking them in blood.

"What can you tell me about them? The Akani?"

He shrugged. "Not much. Izaak called a meeting in his office tomorrow. Hopefully they have gathered some information we can use. My mother swore we'll be the first to know."

His mother, the queen. I almost forgot that Tain was Queen Astra's adopted son until he reminded me. "Why do you come here, besides to admire the view?" I tried changing the subject from the upcoming gloom threatening to evaporate our city. "And do you take every newcomer up here?"

He paused for a moment before parting his lips. "I come here to think. I like the sound of silence. Well, and to watch people from a distance. But no, I've never brought anyone else up to the roof. Only you."

Only me.

I twisted my head to the side before he could see a smile ripple across my features, pretending to admire the view. "You like watching people from a distance?"

I decided not to ask about the *only you* part of his statement.

Tain's blush reddened a shade under the luster of three full moons. "It helps me to see who people are when they aren't aware that I'm watching. I'll need to know them if I'm to become their king."

The words rolled off his tongue so naturally, as if they were a certainty.

The king.

"You actually have your sights on the throne," I said, intrigued. Shei was not going to be happy about that, I thought, but it was his opportunity to prove her wrong. "You can finally help your people in the Gutter if you win the crown."

Tain's stern expression accentuated the edges of his jawline. His elbows shuffled an inch away from me. "All my people are dead or here."

My stare widened. That was not the answer I expected. "Uhm," I mumbled, struggling to find the right words, "did something happen to your birth family?"

One look from him was enough to answer my question. "I would rather not talk about them, if that's alright. And you can tell Shei that she can voice her frustrations with me directly instead of having you do her bidding in the future."

Kirrah help me and my big mouth!

"I'm sorry, Tain. I didn't mean to pry. And Shei didn't ask me to voice anything for her."

The evening breeze turned into gale, running its cold, invisible fingers through his tousled hair. The wind carried the perfumed puff of Old Town—a mix of fragrant oils and strong liquor thickening the air.

"Either way, you can tell her not to worry just yet," he muttered. "The nobles will vote for the next ruler after the battle. It will come down to Raina or myself, since we are the most powerful sei-sans in all of Old Town, but I mean to secure my place by proving myself in battle." He drew a silent, slow breath. "We will protect the moonstone *no matter what*, Imani."

I bit into my bottom lip. His reassurance meant very little, a well-intentioned promise of a boy who wanted to be a king, but those were only empty words and wishful thinking. I felt the burden to protect the city fall on my shoulders.

I owe that much to my family.

"So Raina might be our next queen should your plans go sideways."

Tain's gaze softened, and the gentle tickle of butterflies fluttered in my stomach. "Raina's not so bad," he said, "once you poke through the layers of armor she's built around herself. She acts hard, but she loves her people. Give her some time."

I appreciated that he didn't try to turn me against her despite the fact that the outcome would benefit him. It made me think that maybe he wasn't all bad like Shei believed him to be.

"We should head back," he said, dusting off his elbows. "You don't need to pile sleep deprivation on top of your miseries during training."

I took his hand, letting him pull me up to my feet. The heat of our palms clashed all over again. "If I manage to get my legs out of bed in the first place," I said, only half-joking.

"You will." Tain winked. "I know you will."

Chapter VIII
Magic Blade

Commander's Izaak's office reeked of his rigidness. No artwork hung from the walls but for a rough sketch of Raina and him, unpainted. Commander didn't seem very fond of color—all the cloth in the room was dull gray without exception. There was barely any furniture to sit on but for a set of shrieking chairs that were at least a decade older than any other piece of wood in the entire building. Stacks of scrolls lay neatly arranged on the surface of a long, rectangular table, their edges overlapping perfectly beside Commander Izaak's hand.

We slipped into seats, Shei and I pulling our chairs close enough to sit in each other's laps, if need be. The reality of the upcoming battle settled in my stomach like a rotten meal, although it helped to see that I wasn't the only one feeling uneasy.

Raina shook her foot viciously, disturbing the tabletop. Tain and Lazzor whispered to each other, covering their mouths with their palms, and Cella sat so still, one would think that time had stopped turning.

"Father," Raina spoke at last. "I mean, Commander. What news do you bring?"

Commander cleared his throat in the head seat, his eyes narrowing on the parchment in front of him. He tapped the quill against papyrus in choppy strokes the same way he punched air during combat lessons.

"It is worse than we imagined, I am afraid."

Tain inhaled loudly, sucking all the air out of the room, or it felt that way to me. My lungs choked, begging me to breathe. I gripped the moon-carved armrests, my fingertips sinking into the chiseled dent in the wood.

"Tell us everything, please," Cella said, gritting her teeth.

"The Akani Warriors are far more powerful than we've previously thought," Commander laid out. "And their numbers grow every day... the folk from passing villages join their ranks."

What do the villagers have to gain from joining forces with the Akani?

"How many?" Shei asked.

Her composure was refreshingly calm, arms folded in her lap, a single mint leaf clenched between her teeth. She leaned against the decaying backrest that screeched every time her spine pushed further against the dry wood. I stared at the sharp edges of her face while I felt the panic settle in.

"Twenty thousand fighters, all in their prime."

"*Twenty thousand!*" Lazzor repeated loudly enough for even the Akani to hear him from leagues away.

"What... uhm, what else?" I asked.

Commander Izaak leaned his quill against an ink jar, ruffling the flame-kissed feathers with calloused fingers. He coughed to clear his throat. A single speck of starlight misted out of his mouth before vanishing into the air, and Raina gasped in spite of herself. Commander's iron stare dashed to his daughter, and he curled up the corner of his mouth.

His power is beginning to fade.

I shivered.

If Commander Izaak can't help save us, who will?

"The Akani tread water and land alike atop kelpies, their magical horse-like creatures, and are led by a young warrior called Kalon," he continued. "He is the son of a sorceress from the winter lands, or so the rumors claim. She forged him a blade interwoven with ancient magic."

Kelpies still exist? I thought they went extinct!

Cella gasped. Swiping the tourmaline-brown curls off her neck, she tied them up with a pearl-beaded ribbon. One curl escaped her clasp, twirling down her shimmering cheek. "But it is forbidden to use the ancient magic!"

"It is forbidden here and in other ancient cities where such laws are followed," Commander stated. "But the Akani have little regard for our laws—they are fighting a war, and they mean to win it any way they can."

Beyond the myths of gods and the legends of great heroes and heroines, such matters were rarely discussed in the Mounds' classrooms. "Can someone explain? What's so bad about the ancient magic?"

Raina's long eyelashes fluttered. "The ancestors' spells aren't to be meddled with. They can cause great destruction if used improperly."

Zana had once told me a story about an acquaintance who experimented with the spells—killing all plants in his garden in the process. A realization dawned on me like a long-forgotten truth. "The Ashen Desert is a product of it, isn't it? The ancient magic?"

Raina nodded with a hint of distaste in her mouth. "There are no records of it, but what else could it be?"

So it was not an inexplicable force of nature like I was taught! I wondered how many things had been omitted from our school lectures or taught inaccurately. And even more, I wondered why.

"The Akani Warriors sound like a treat thus far," I moaned.

Cella and Raina looked to each other nervously. Raina fanned her face with a parchment from Commander's stack before he seized it with a stern *I-told-you-not-to-do-that* frown, reminding me of Mother.

"That's not all," Commander added, his voice lowering a note. "The Akani are immune to sei."

All muscles in my body stiffened, and my throat went dry. Commander's words roared in my mind, followed by a pressure in my temples, as though someone rang a bell into my ear.

Immune to starlight?

"Immune to sei?" Lazzor and Tain cried out simultaneously.

Cella let her hand fall on the tabletop with a thump. Raina was speechless, sulking quietly in a way that made my teeth clatter. Her bottom lip trembled, her brows folding into her eyelids.

"How is that even possible?" she asked.

Commander shrugged, sulking in an identical manner to his daughter. "We don't know. Ancient magic, maybe, though our archives hold no record of such spell or potion."

The walls of Commander's office closed in, the entire room growing with darkness. My insides twisted like a water-soaked rag drained by two fists. Even the air cooled down several degrees, prickling my skin. I was frightened of Akani Warriors when I thought them to be ordinary soldiers, before I knew about the magic blade and an ancient horse breed. But immunity to starlight?

How am I going to protect my family? Of what use can I be with muscles fragile like spring flowers, fighting against the sharp iron of their swords without starlight to protect me?

Shei noticed my angst and put her hand in mine, her skin warm against my ice cold fingers.

"Don't fret, we will survive this storm," Commander said, "The Akani may be immune to sei, but their kelpies aren't. Nor are their swords or shields. Not even Queen Astra has enough coin to supply an entire army with titanium gear."

Thank the moons.
We will need all the help we can get.

Shei scoffed. "And what protection do we have? There are, what, eight or nine hundred starlight benders currently serving the city? Half of them are of mature age and a good number are children. How does that pan against twenty thousand soldiers?"

She posed the question everyone else wanted to ask, judging from their cocked heads and half-open mouths. I wanted to know, too.

So much for having a good time being a legionnaire.

Commander Izaak scratched the back of his earlobe. "You are forgetting about three thousand city guards who are not sei-sans. They will fight for Lumenor, too. We also have the wall to protect us. Besides, the ancient magic isn't only available to the enemy."

"You just said it was forbi..." My throat swallowed the words after everyone directed their glowers at me.

Tain paused to survey the legionnaires' reactions before voicing his take. He seemed to measure every thought before expressing it. "Who cares? We must do whatever it takes to protect ourselves!"

Shei rolled her eyes. "No surprise you would think that," she mumbled in a tone too striking for anyone in the room to miss her remark.

Tain's face changed color, the control he had over his usually firm demeanor drowning in fuming anger. His lips tore apart to retort, but Cella beat him to the punch.

"If anyone is against the violence, it is me," she claimed, "but the Akani made the ancient magic a fair game. We should make battle potions and spice them with sei. We don't have a choice, Shei."

"There is always a choice," Shei shouted, her chin aimed at Tain. "The magic of our ancestors isn't to be meddled with, you said it yourselves! If we caused the once grass-covered lands to turn to ash the last time around, what will happen to the city if we employ such methods again?"

Tain leaned over the table, stopping inches away from her face. He was so close I could smell mint and leather on his skin from my seat. Their stares locked, as if they were playing a game, waiting for the other one to look away. "There will be no city left behind this time if we don't use magic-bound potions. Wake up!"

Not even Kirrah could bring these two together!

I grabbed Shei's forearm, afraid she was ready to punch him if not bend at him. Her fair cheeks were now bright red, and she was breathing at the same quick pace she released her knives at during throwing lessons.

"Fine king you'll make," she uttered, "bending rules when it suits you."

Raina twitched to her words. "Who said anything about him being a king? Where did you hear that?"

I slapped my forehead, tired of their arguing.

"He is the queen's son and a very potent starlight bender at that—of course he'll be voted a king," Shei snapped. "So much so he forgot where he came from." She turned back to face Tain. "Do you even care that it is your own people on the outskirts who will be the first ones to suffer the Akani's wrath? Do you even think about that, prince?"

All five legionnaires around me leapt from their seats at the same time, shouting at once, before Commander's fist slammed the table, pounding louder than the earthquake. "Sit down, and everyone be quiet," he ordered. "Don't make me repeat myself."

One by one, everyone sank back into the chairs.

"This is the time when we need to stand together, not bicker like children. Are you children?" Commander Izaak's deep voice rumbled through the stone, void of color and scent, and everyone bowed their heads in silence. "You think I like our odds? You think I want to send my only child to the battlefield? No, I don't. But I shut my mouth, and I do my duty, because if I don't, who will? It is time you all grow up, and listen. Leave the battle plans to me."

Commander had a point.

There were no other choices but to stay focused and train.

"When will the Akani Warriors arrive? How long do we have?" I asked.

"We don't know for certain, but we have estimates," Commander said in a forcefully cheerful voice that contrasted his grim demeanor. "The journey from Vatrion will take them no less than three months, so I suggest you train like the life of everyone you love depends on it. Because it does."

"I am ready for my extra reps with you," I told Tain on the way out of Commander's office. "In fact, I would like to go right now."

Tain's distant stare observed every fold in my face, every pore that leaked my fear. His gaze softened in the same way he looked at me on the rooftop the previous night.

"Imani…"

"Please," I cried out. "I need to train."

He and Lazzor exchanged a sour look, but they agreed.

"Are you coming, Miss Knife Thrower?" Lazzor fondled the upper-half of Shei's hair, trying to make the light out of the situation.

She clicked her tongue, slapping his hand away, but she bobbed her chin. "I have nothing better to do, do I?" She continued to pay no attention to Tain as though he was not there.

Instead of going to the pit, we descended into one of the base's inner courtyards that the legions used in their spare time. The day was cloudy, the skies the color of Tain's eyes, the smell of rain hanging thick in the air. Hard-packed dirt filled the courtyard floor, bare but for a sporadic wooden bench or tree stump. An occasional legionnaire from another cohort sat around quietly, reading a book or resting between training sessions. They all left after we arrived per Lazzor's plea.

"Clear your heads," Tain ordered. His firm composure mimicked Commander's, the way his shoulders squared stiffly across from me.

I picked up a tiny oval stone from the ground, feeling its cool surface slide down my palm. "Yes, let us quickly forget that we need to fight the starlight-immune soldiers with magic swords," I puffed, letting the stone slip between my fingers. "Or *sei-immune*, in case Raina is peeking behind the corner."

"One magic sword." Lazzor pointed a finger up. "Don't you worry about this Kalon fella. I will be the one to take him." He motioned a fist punch, pretending to hit the mysterious Akani leader, then went on to assume Kalon's role, falling to the ground.

If it only were that easy.

"Oh, Lazzor," Shei sighed. "Do you even take yourself seriously?"

He went on to chase her around the courtyard, pretending to be the magic blade bearer himself. She continued to tease him, ducking his fists and returning jabs.

"You may be equipped with muscles, but you'll never have the advantage of sharp wits!" Shei panted, avoiding another hit by an inch.

Lazzor corrected the low formation of her fists, then he continued to simulate punches. "I am yet to be knocked over by wits alone!"

"First time for everything," she insisted and ran away.

Their chase quickly became a background noise for the ringing in my head. I couldn't shake my angst like the two of them. Three months would never be enough for me to catch up with all the things

I'd missed. I thought I would be furious with Mother, wanting to shout "I told you so" from my lungs. Instead, I was worried.

"Wishing you could go back to selling ointments in the Mounds without a worry in your head?" Tain asked. The muscles of his face were pulled back, lips pinned tightly, and sweat beaded along his brows.

"Never," I replied, forcing my mouth into a smile. "But I wouldn't mind having more time to prepare for what is coming."

Tain's hand jerked towards me, but he held back at the very last second. "You can cry over the spilled potion, or you can work with what you have. Three months isn't nearly enough, but it is all you've got. All we've got."

"Alright then, Commander Tain." I bowed deeply. His face lit up to my words despite trying to remain composed. "Teach me how to fight."

Chapter IX
Starlight Bending

I continued to have nightmares for three weeks straight. They always ended with the Akani Warriors climbing the steps of my house, heading to harm Zuri. Despite training with the legion during that time, I had yet to be allowed to attend bending lessons.

"You must increase your endurance first," Commander Izaak refused my never-ending begging, "before you drain yourself and end up in the healer's wing again."

So that was what I did, or at least what I tried to do. Getting in shape was not easy. I ran to the pit, ran around the platform, ran up the bleachers until I could keep up with the rest of the legion. I kicked, jabbed, ducked, and did sit-ups until it hurt to breathe. I ached so much I had begun looking forward to the cold plunges—and I *hated* cold plunges. Shei and I continued to train with Lazzor and Tain in our spare time. While Lazzor taught her how to slice swords with starlight more efficiently, I was stuck getting tossed over Tain's shoulders until I couldn't get up.

Then the day finally came.

I skipped on my feet, hurrying towards one of the inner courtyards dedicated to bending training. We were forbidden from attending each other's sei lessons, but I spied on Shei and her instructor once or twice before.

It was my turn now.

Each starlight bender was paired with a teacher that best suited their needs, one of the Old Town's retired legionnaires who practiced the craft for years. Shei complained that her instructor was a grumpy old man with little to no interest in honing a Gutter girl's skills, so I had no expectations going into my first lesson. Despite needing young sei-sans more than ever, some Old Town folk seemed stuck in their ways. The Mounds were regarded with only slightly more respect than the Gutter, mostly due to the farming and mining that supported the city. Still, learning to bend had been my dream ever since the first trickle of magic left my palms, and I was so thrilled I could jump out of my skin.

The round, titanium shields were erected all over the courtyard at various heights, reflecting noontime rays. Sunlight melted across their polished surfaces, shining brightly enough to blind me. The day was warm and without as much as a cloud in the sky—perfect for bending, although any day was perfect for bending for me.

A woman of Mother's age stood in the center of the yard with the grace of a queen. Her arms were loosely crossed beneath her chest, strands of voluminous indigo-tinted black hair tied behind her head with a jeweled pin. The sapphire-colored moon tattoo that glistened on her forehead matched the crystal charm of her necklace.

Starlight bender from the shores of Sapphire Sea!

My instructor's eyes were two black tourmalines that drank the shade, her cheekbones high and accentuated with the smear of a peach-colored blush. She had the kind of regal beauty a woman was not born with but honed into over the course of many years.

I instinctively bowed to her, then straightened up, realizing I overdid it.

"Welcome to your first bending lesson, Imani," she said. I could cry just hearing those words. "You can call me Miss Yamane."

"I am so thrilled to be here," I squealed.

Despite my expectation to start blazing starlight all over the courtyard right away, Miss Yamane suggested we sit atop the rocks that surrounded a chiseled tree stump in the corner.

"We must review your learnings first," she explained, taking note of my confusion. "You need to be in tune with your power before you begin to train. So tell me, what do you know about sei?"

I thought back to the time when Aubren chased after me, before I made the pine tree light up; to the rush that came with fighting for survival, and to the thrill of my own life force boiling within me. Goosebumps thorned my forearm like a rose stem.

"Well, it shoots out of my palms without harming my skin, yet it would wound me if someone else bent at me? It is more precise when I am focused, but far more potent when my emotions are in disarray."

Miss Yamane nodded. "That is a valuable observation, what else can you tell me?"

What indeed?

"Umm, that's as far as my knowledge goes," I replied, wrestling with intrusive thoughts. I worried Miss Yamane would tell the commander I was a lost cause, better leveraged building weapons than being one.

"Do not worry, dear. That is why I am here," she said, smiling in a way that reminded me of Zana. "I watched you during the trials. Did your chest burn when you forged that sphere of sei fighting Izaak's daughter?"

I nodded.

"That is because you are only drawing from within. Sei uses the air in our lungs and the blood flowing through our veins, and it travels straight from our hearts to our palms." She gestured the flow gracefully. "We do not know if that is where sei originates, but it is the first place where we can feel it. Some go as far as to suggest our minds themselves create the magic."

Our minds create starlight?

That sounded quite strange.

"I can think of one more thing," I said, pointing a finger up. "I suspect that starlight, I mean sei, has a mind of its own. It is always on guard, ready to protect itself. I feel the urge to release it the most when I'm in trouble."

I also had a hard time letting go, but I figured I best not mention it.

Miss Yamane's cheeks lifted into a prideful grin, and I beamed with delight at the slightest nod of her approval.

"Another valuable observation, Imani. Many others feel the same. We can only guess, but I believe Kirrah designed our entire world with the same symmetry, the same mold, in mind, and that all things we ourselves create follow a version of this pattern. All living things feel pain and joy, all strive to survive—why not sei?"

I was enchanted for what felt like a moment stopped in time. I heard nothing but Miss Yamane's melodic voice that painted over the calm silence of the empty yard. I was so deeply immersed in her storytelling that the words echoed inside the chambers of my mind as if they were my own creation.

She taught me many new things about bending, adding layers to my understanding of how mind and body work in sync to invoke my power. Things were not nearly so simple as I thought.

"Sei-sans cannot plainly point their mind at something and expect sei to bend to a weak thought," she said. "Sei requires true intent, for one to be in tune with their body both inside and out. Feel your emotions but don't let them control your thoughts."

If only that was so simple.

"What about bending sei outside of myself?" I asked. "I've never figured out how to do it."

Miss Yamane's hand lightly brushed my shoulder. "I am afraid you will have to wait until our future lessons to find out. You must gain control over how much you draw from within, first."

My nose wrinkled. "But I thought I wasn't supposed to draw from within?"

According to Commander Izaak and Mr. Osei, draining caused death. Yet, despite feeling the exhaustion and pain of bending almost all the starlight inside of me, I have never felt close to dying. I could hear Mother's reprimand in my ears. *Don't be reckless.* But Mother never knew what it was like to taste the exhilaration of bending, its cherry-sweet flavor as the flecks of light left my sei-san palms.

"That is correct. You are not supposed to bend from within. Well, not exclusively," Miss Yamane said after careful consideration. "But in order to control sei outside of yourself, you must link it with sei that resides within. That is how deflecting works, too. You can still drain yourself, but it would take longer. In your case, based on what I have seen, *much* longer."

I couldn't help but grin.

I was almost disappointed when Miss Yamane said it was time to begin aiming, something I didn't think possible.

Even with all my newly gathered knowledge, I struggled with precision. Miss Yamane wanted me to work on controlling my streams, aiming to reduce the amount of power I released with each shot.

"You cannot exhaust yourself with the first sprinkle of magic that leaves your palms," she said after I hit one of the shields with a significantly more potent stream than necessary. "That is a great way to get yourself killed."

I know, I know!

"But I can't contain it! I tried calming my mind—sei still bends the way it intends to! I tense my muscles and focus—it's still potent! I hold my breath—nothing works!"

I puffed out loudly, picking at the arrow brooch chained across my shoulder. The cold kiss of iron soothed me, despite the urge I had to rip the arrow out and throw it across the yard.

I only have three months to master bending, and that's if we're lucky.

Miss Yamane asked me to take a deep breath. "Holding back will not work. True power lies in letting go of fear, in learning to trust yourself. There is no one you can harm here, child. Now, try again."

I calmed my body, sharpening my intent like Miss Yamane taught me. The shining shield I was tasked to aim at was far out of my ordinary bending reach. I needed to focus all my energy, all my thoughts, into hitting it in the center. I needed to hit it as if my life depended on it.

Miss Yamane was fond of my use of fingers to direct sei and wanted to put the years of practice I dedicated to entertaining Zuri to good use. She asked me to forge two balls of starlight and bend them at the shield without splitting them further.

Left hand first. Good, there you are!

I managed to form a ball with my right hand a second or two later, my forearm muscles pinching under the pressure to release.

Be patient. Take a breath. Aim!

I still missed.

"Focus your eyes first." Miss Yamane guided me through the exercise one more time. "Now, your mind. Keep a firm grip on the sei with your will. Take a step forward with your right foot, a little farther, that is good. Now, release."

I jumped and screamed ecstatically after both balls of sei clashed into the shield. Finally, my first proper aim.

Zuri would be so proud!

I sighed in relief, hanging on the verge of crying happy tears.

There is still hope.

"Good job, Imani," my teacher said with pride. "Do it again, this time without my guidance."

My progress at the end of the lesson was the same as with everything else—marginal at best. Learning how to bend was a cumbersome task, but it was the one I utterly enjoyed. I said my farewell and my thanks to Miss Yamane, but I was already impatient to get back to the courtyard for our next lesson.

"It was so good! Not good, outstanding!" I told Shei all about my time with Miss Yamane.

She held onto a mint branch with her teeth. "If only the rest of us were so fortunate! I am happy for you, and, needless to say, for all the pines in the Mounds."

"Oh, shut it!" I slapped her hand, laughing.

We were alone in the salon. The rest of our legion had gone on their weekly patrol of the city that the commander deemed Shei and myself unprepared to join. They used to patrol Lumenor every night before we learned of Vatrion's fate, and of the enemy headed for our doorstep..

"It's strange, isn't it?" I asked. "Being here, in the heart of Old Town. Eating their food, drinking their wine, and earning coin on top of it."

Shei plucked another leaf with her teeth. "Missing your family?"

I nodded. "You?"

Her mouth hardened, and she screeched one of her knives against the ebony table. The noise made me shudder. It was loud and shrill, resembling the howl of a faraway beast.

"My uncle is not used to being alone," she laid out. "They wouldn't let him through the silver gates for the trials, being from the Gutter and all, but they allowed us to exchange a single letter each, how generous!"

Commander didn't want us writing to our families until we adapted to our new lives and duties. It would only create a distraction, he claimed, going on about how we needed to learn to be our own people first. I spent my entire life yearning to leave home, but I found myself wishing I could tell Mother about the doubts in my head and about the fears that turned my dreams into nightmares.

"Is your uncle well? Fine with you being a legionnaire?" I asked.

Shei bit back a solemn frown. "He knows I had no other choice. I would have been killed if I went back to Gutter. Besides, the coin *is* good."

I imagined that Shei's life as a knife sharpener suited her. I could see her enjoying working with blades just as much as she loved throwing them. Her mouth half-opened, as if there was something else she wanted to say, but she closed it once more and looked away.

"How did you learn to bend so well?" I asked, thinking about all the times I witnessed her skills. "By the temple when we met and during your lessons that I've been spying on—even training with Lazzor. You practically never miss."

She winked. "Some of us are just naturals. That, and I practiced a little when no one was watching, mostly in abandoned buildings hidden in the heart of the Gutter."

I felt envious. I'd never enjoyed the same freedoms and had only been able to practice in the sunlit summertime woods to avoid drawing attention. Additionally, I could only sneak out unnoticed when Mother was away, which didn't occur very often.

I arched my brow. "And you didn't have a mother to haunt your every step." I regretted my words as soon as they left my throat. "Sorry, that was… I shouldn't have said it."

Think before you speak, Imani. Think.

She swallowed, her gaze falling into the abyss of deep thoughts. "You should consider yourself lucky, you know. Having parents who love you so much."

Shei was right. Mother may not have allowed me to bend, but she was always there for me. She stitched me up and gave me spiced milk when I scraped my knees climbing walls with Summer as a child. She woke up at dawn every day to prepare my lunch before I left for the market and threaded the garments I ripped apart while playing outside. She'd helped me with my studies, taught me how to brew potions and how to put powders on. She'd even bought me what she thought was my first drink on my eighteenth birthday four months ago. And here I was, complaining.

"I know. I'm sorry," I whispered.

I poured us each a cup of Shei's favorite mint tea, looking for the missing cards amongst loose items on the table. Shei wanted to practice her cheats against me so that she could beat Lazzor in moon phases.

"Found one!" I announced, lifting the sparkling black papyrus from the tabletop.

Shei shook her head. "That's one of Cella's tarot cards."

Zana's face flashed in front of me. She was like an aunt, my second mother in many ways. "I didn't know Cella believed in telling."

The front of the card in my hand was painted with shades of gray, a whirlpool of magic surrounding a single warrior in its midst. The warrior's rags were stained, a broken bone poking out of his shin.

I wonder about the meaning of this card. Where is Zana when you need her?

Shei licked her tea-stained bottom lip. "You should ask Cella about it. Her mother is not fond of her proclivities, but she swears by it. She's been trying to get me to sit with her so she can do a reading."

My brows knitted. "You don't believe in telling?"

"I do," she replied. "I'd just rather not know."

"Scared she'll see a tall, muscled legionnaire in your future?" I teased.

Shei took an oversized gulp of her tea and fluttered her eyelashes. "Where are you going with this?"

I relaxed my shoulders and set my own cup down. "I mean, Lazzor and you have been quite friendly…"

She gasped. "Eww, Imani! I mean, Lazzor is as silly as they come, and I mean that in the best possible way, but I have no interest in him."

"Who, then?" I asked.

She looked down, poorly managing to hide her shyness, an emotion I'd never witnessed from her before. "Alright. Between us, I think Cella is charming. She is quite scary when she fights but is otherwise kind and bright. And very pretty, if I might add." Her entire face turned red like a rosebud. "Don't you dare tell a single soul, or I will settle the Akani's matters with you long before they come!"

I giggled, motioning the stitching of my mouth. "My lips are sealed. I should have known with the way you two ogle each other."

Shei rubbed her cheeks, as if *that* was going to help mop the blemish off her face. "It doesn't matter much anyway. We have a battle to fight, and I can't risk becoming attached."

My palm fell on the rough-textured linens of her sleeve. "What better time to form a bond with someone? As you said, we have a battle to fight."

The doors to the salon burst open, the knob crashing into the side wall violently. Tain stumbled inside. He was covered in blood. His skin was coated in tar, debris sticking to his clothes and skin and dusting his hair.

Shei and I leapt to our feet.

"Are you hurt?" I ran towards him, inspecting the red patches on his uniform. "What happened?"

"Blood's not mine… Cella… the rebels… she was helping Lazzor…" Tain panted. "Mr. Osei was summoned to the Cobblestone… we can't find his student… the healer's quarters… you know the ointments…" He blinked through the sweat dripping into his eyes and reached for me.

Shei bolted out of the door ahead of us. I grabbed Tain's hand and followed. Droplets of blood spattered onto the floor from the cuts littering his body. The rows of stone statues crept from the shadows of the torchlit hallways like monsters from the Ashen Desert as we rushed by.

We arrived at the entrance to the healers' wing within a minute. Cella lay atop one of the beds, wincing while Raina stitched torn parts of skin at her hip. She could barely speak. Shei dashed towards the bed and began cleaning the smaller cuts.

Lazzor paced the room frantically in the background. "It's my fault! It's all my fault!" He repeated those words over and over again. "She was helping *me*!" The healer's wing echoed with his wailing.

"Should Raina be doing the stitching?" I asked Tain.

Her hands were steady, not as steady as Mr. Osei's, but steady enough. She threaded the healer's needle through Cella's wound with an unshakeable focus and the stillness of midnight. She didn't blink once.

Tain reached for a bottle of alcohol and a clean cloth before rushing over to assist. "We all received first aid training. You will, too. Raina is as good as we've got until help arrives."

Dozens of questions ran through my head. *Is anyone else injured? Where is the commander? Shouldn't there be a healer on duty? What can I do?*

"Go fetch a wound binder and whatever else can help," Raina ordered, as if she'd read my mind. Cella was still whimpering, tiny rivulets of blood leaking from her wound from time to time. She clasped Shei's hand, squeezing it every time Raina ran a needle through her skin.

I panicked. "I'm not a healer!"

Raina's look at me was an impatient scowl. "Well, you must know something beyond our basic knowledge. Imani, hurry! I am almost done."

Alright.

My body temperature rose to a boil. Yes, I knew how to help Cella theoretically, but I'd never actually applied my knowledge before.

Think.

I pulled Mr. Osei's drawers out two at the time, searching for ointments. Luckily, all titles were penned in the head healer's perfected writing—large-lettered and easy to read.

I need a wound binder. Turmeric ointment for inflammation. Echinacea soother to prevent infection. Lavender leaf for fever. What else?

"Have you given her the healer's aid yet?" I shouted.

"No, bring some!" Tain responded.

Cella winced again. "Yes, please."

I grabbed more ointments than I probably needed and started applying them one at a time after Raina finished the stitching. My fingers shook as I worked. Cella had fallen asleep from the healer's aid, and Tain, Raina and Shei assisted me where they could. Lazzor still paced the room in the midst of what seemed to be a surge of panic.

"My childhood friend is dying because of me!" He pulled at the silver coils on his head, not hearing a word we said in an attempt to soothe him.

"She's not dying," Tain said. "You are not the one who flung the knife at her, either. Look, Imani is fixing her. She'll be fine."

Lazzor swayed, breathing at a rapid rate, almost choking on air. His chest rose and fell quicker than his heartbeat, and it looked like he might faint. "What if she dies? She's always been there for me ever since we were kids!"

Raina looked at Tain. "Go talk to him."

"Why me?"

She pinched her fingers together. "Because I am this close to knocking him out."

Raina, Shei, and I continued rubbing ointments on Cella's cuts for another hour, stretching our backs after we were done. Dizziness buoyed my head like a floating log swept by the river current, and my hands and forearms were sore.

"Cella will be fine," I judged. I checked on her forehead—the fever was fading. *Thank the moons.* I mumbled one of Mother's prayers quietly. It couldn't hurt, I figured. "Where are all the healers? Mr. Osei isn't the only one who works here."

Tain returned after comforting Lazzor, wiping crusted blood off his neck with a wet cloth. The blood dried to a scaly texture, ribbed with small, symmetrical creases, similar to a serpent's skin. "A big rebel ambush took place at the edge of the Gutter," he pointed out. "Izaak is still there. They summoned all the healers, but we were already on the way here. There was no time to turn around."

Now that we had treated Cella, I took a good look at him. Too many blade cuts to count had torn his uniform apart, exposing the raw, bloodied skin underneath. "You're hurt."

"It's nothing."

My fingers wrapped around his sleeve, locking around his muscled upper arm. "You were all hurt, and don't tell me it's nothing," I snapped, giving each patrolling legionnaire a thorough look. Lazzor calmed down at last, plunging his face into his palms.

"Shei, get more ointment jars," I demanded. "The rest of them need patching."

We cleaned all of Raina's, Lazzor's, and Tain's cuts, tending to them the best we knew how, before sinking to the floor around Cella's bed. Raina cuddled next to her on the mattress while Lazzor fell asleep with his back against the wall. Shei rested her head on my shoulder, and Tain propped himself up with Mr. Osei's chair cushion. Commander Izaak stormed inside at last, accompanied by two unfamiliar healers. He was soaked in blood that did not seem to be his own—there wasn't a single cut in his uniform.

"Thank the goddess," he uttered, his eyes falling on Raina. The healers ran to Cella first, checking her stitches and fever.

"We are fine," Raina said to her father, hopping to her feet. "I am fine."

"Everyone find a bed in here, including the two of you," Commander ordered, pointing at me and Shei. I didn't have the strength to protest, laying down on the first empty mattress I found. More healers poured in, including Mr. Osei, who took over Cella's care. We were not allowed to fall asleep until they made sure everyone was in good health.

"You did well," Mr. Osei said to Raina while inspecting her reflexes. "The stitches will hold up."

Fatigue sagged her shoulders, her body folding over as though four giants tugged at her limbs. "Thank you. Imani's knowledge of ointments helped," she said, and Mr. Osei smiled at me with fatherly pride.

Soft candlelight soothed my eyes once the torches were put out, and the calm of the quiet allowed me to breathe. Half of my face was submerged into the pillow, sinking in. Raina tossed back and forth on the next bed, while everyone else was fast asleep. Our gazes locked, and we stared at each other wordlessly for a moment.

"You helped save Cella's life tonight. You are one of us now," she said and closed her eyes.

Chapter X

The Bard

The wounded legionnaires were given time to recover after the patrol, which meant that Shei and I got all of Commander's attention for the span of an entire week. A permanent ache settled in my bones and muscles from practicing combat moves against Commander Izaak himself, but I was becoming more confident in my skills. He was strict, never holding back on criticism, but he also encouraged me whenever I showed improvement.

I got to spend more time with Miss Yamane as well, and focus on my bending. I was slowly gaining control over how much sei I released, and I was hoping it was almost time to begin drawing from outside of myself.

Shei and I staggered into our legion's salon after dinner, finding everyone but Cella at the table for the first time since the night of patrol. Cella was, understandably, still recovering in the healers' wing, but Mr. Osei worked his magic, and we were told she would be back on her feet in no time.

"Shouldn't you all be resting?" Shei asked.

Raina, Lazzor, and Tain sat around the seven-pointed table, sipping on mint tea, each focused on a different task. Lazzor's eyelids narrowed on a heavy warrior tome with a quill stuck behind his ear. Tain clutched a knife next to him, carving a pointy shape out of a patch of dark brown leather. A cluster of neatly arranged tools surrounded him, and he was so focused that he didn't even look up when we walked in. A mint branch rested between his teeth, and I glanced at Shei, who pretended not to see it.

He is Gutter-born, after all.

Raina walked back to her chamber, retrieving a gem-beaded box stacked with pins, cuffs, and jewels. She sat back down and started crafting a necklace using some of Tain's tools.

No one said a word.

Shei and I traded a puzzled *what-did-we-just-walk-into* grimace.

"Since it appears to be crafts time, I'll go grab my knives," she said.

"Meet you back here in a minute."

I strode into my bed chamber, taking my powders and oils out of the bundle underneath my bed. I had been meaning to mix the powders Mother sent via guards a few days prior, but I was always too tired to do it.

Going back to the table, I settled in an empty chair and opened two jars of indigo eye powder. One to add color and one for shimmer. I scooped three teaspoons of each, pouring them into a tiny clay container. Then, I added a drop of glue and began mixing. Shei leaned in to watch before turning to sharpen her knives.

Curiosity crept into her voice. "I never knew you also made makeup powders," she said, unsealing my containers, sniffing them out one at the time. Mother liked to add a pinch of rosemary oil to the glue, and Shei closed her eyes, inhaling the fragrance.

"I am a woman of many talents, what can I say?" I winked, and she rolled her eyes. "Do you want me to make one for you?"

The clash of her blades screeched like a wounded creature. "Pfff, why else would I be friends with you if it wasn't for free gifts?" she joked. Choosing a light blue shade as a base, she matched it with silver glitter before pointing at one of the sparkling dark gray powders. "Maybe you can make one for Cella, too? I think she'd like this one."

"Great idea!"

Raina peered at my jars from the corner of her eye, looking away every time I noticed her. *She is as stubborn as they come.* I continued to stare at her without blinking until she could no longer pretend not to see me.

"Yes?" she asked, polishing a topaz charm for the necklace she was making. The charm emitted a golden halo that reflected in her chestnut eyes.

"Would you like eye makeup to go with your necklace?" I asked. The work on my first powder was complete, so I closed the lid, putting it aside.

Raina twisted her mouth, but she selected the color she liked anyway. "Don't make it too glittery," she said, returning to polishing the topaz.

My gaze fell on the crystal. "Your birthstone?"

Zana taught me all about sun and moon signs, and about magic-bearing crystals, before I learned how to count or write. It was the only knowledge that mattered, or so she claimed. The first knowledge of our ancestors.

"Mhm." Raina bobbed her chin. "Topaz is my birthstone."

"That makes you, what, a Scorpio?" Shei asked.

Another head bob from Raina.

"Scorpios are ruthless, stubborn, and honest. Explains a lot," Shei claimed.

The boys were silent, still focused on their crafting and reading, although I could tell Tain was paying attention to our conversation, chuckling occasionally when we joked around.

"What is your sign then, Miss Gutter?" Raina's voice was sharp.

"Gemini."

"Gemini are wanderers, self-reliant and often two-faced. Explains a lot."

Shei stuck her tongue out and went back to her knives. They both selected a set of traits they associated with each other and conveniently assigned them to their sun signs.

At least they are beginning to get along in their own way.

"How are you feeling?" I asked Raina.

"Fine," she said. "I am ready to go back to training."

Both Lazzor and Tain glanced up from the table at the same time. "We were given time to rest for a reason," Lazzor said.

Raina bit into her cheek, the edges of her face sharpening faster than Shei's knives. "What do you have to rest from? You didn't do anything!"

Tain shook his head with a sigh. "Raina…"

"No!" She dropped her necklace on the table, the topaz crystal contrasting with the blue torchlight that reflected in it. "I am so tired of him refusing to do what needs to be done!"

Shei's nose wrinkled. "What are you talking about?"

"Oh, you don't know about Lazzor's rule? You see, he signed up to be a legionnaire, but he refuses to kill." Her arms shot up, palms facing the ceiling.

To kill or not to kill.

Couldn't say I blamed him.

Lazzor's jaw stiffened. "I only refuse to kill the innocent."

"The innocent?" Raina's stare widened. "That rebel almost murdered Cella, for moons' sake! An inch closer and she would've been dead!"

Lazzor slammed his book shut. Lingering grains of dust danced around the leather-bound cover. "I didn't know he had any knives left, or that he was going to aim at Cella unprovoked!"

She snorted. "You were the closest one to him! What else would a rebel cornered to a wall do? Come and shake her hand?"

"I…I mean…" Lazzor struggled to drag the words out of his throat.

Tain was silent, his stare darting between Lazzor and Raina as they spoke. The mood in the salon had changed, everyone hanging from the edge of their seat.

"How many of us have to die before you get off your high horse and do your part? Or is it all the same to you if we live or die, as long as you get to play warrior—a useless one at that!" Raina shouted, and I could tell she plunged her knife where it hurt. Lazzor's palm pounded at the table, spilling particles of powder from my jars, coating my hands in glitter.

"You don't get to speak to me like that! What happened to Cella was my fault, and I will never forgive myself for putting her in danger." Lazzor bared his teeth, closing his fists to vanish the flashes of starlight that kindled in his palms. "But to call me useless? I saved your life alone countless times before. Fine queen you will make, if nobles vote for you in the first place!"

He pushed his chair out and stormed into his chamber.

Tain followed behind him.

Shei and I continued to sit in silence, motionless, although she seemed far more entertained by their fight than me. Raina wiped a tear from the corner of her eye and headed out, slamming the doors behind her.

"I knew I would find you here," I said, crawling my way towards the edge of the rooftop.

Tain was alone, sitting under the cloudy night skies that hid all three moons from us. "Now that you've seen the ugly side of being a legionnaire, I hope you don't regret joining us."

I cackled. "Are you kidding? I wish someone would have warned me to bring the herb crisps! Jokes aside, it is natural for friends to fight sometimes. Especially in our circumstances."

Tain paused to think, brushing a silver strand away from his face. The scent of leather in his hand was rich and all-consuming. "Lazzor is like a brother to me, but I agree with Raina, though not with her delivery. We can't afford the luxury of mercy these days."

"To kill or not to kill," I said, grazing my palm over the jagged stone surface. "It won't get easier, will it?"

Tain shook his head solemnly, glaring at the distant darkness that was the Ashen Desert. Eerie and pitch black, the desert surrounded Lumenor like an inescapable void.

"Anything I can do to cheer you up?" I asked.

His fine features molded into a thinking face. "You can go back to your chamber and put on the most colorful items of clothing you own."

"Come again?" I tossed my braid over my shoulder, turning to face him. His nose floated inches away from mine. "I know you live in the palace when you are not on duty, but I am no court fool."

He chuckled, and I inhaled the scent of mint on his breath. "I don't take you for one, but now that you said it…"

I elbowed him gently, and we both laughed.

"Meet me at the salon in fifteen minutes," he said. "It is time you meet the bard."

I squinted. "Who?"

"You'll see."

It turned out the bard was him.

Tain stepped out of his bedchamber, dressed head to toe in the gaudiest set of vibrant garments I had ever seen. From the ridiculous red hat that hid his hair to the patched cloak embroidered with starry charms in every color possible, and the pair of paint-smeared boots, it seemed that he had tried hard to emulate a singing rhymester. He even brushed some of the coloring palette under his eyes, gold and green shimmering against his moon-colored cheeks.

I giggled. "What in the world are you wearing?" Despite being dressed quite hideously, he still looked handsome.

"And here I was, thinking I looked charming." He tossed a lute case over his shoulder, and signaled me to approach. "Come, you need some paint to blend in. Also, we need to find a way to hide your braid. Not many hill girls just happen to walk down the streets of Old Town."

I remained in place. "First of all, I am not letting you anywhere near me with a brush," I said. "Canvas paint is bad for your skin. I'll use my powders. Secondly, the braid stays. But I will wear a ridiculous hat if you have another one, one to match my feathered silver shirt and cyan pants."

"On it," he muttered and ran back to his chamber.

We snuck out of the base by bribing a guard who had no choice but to let the queen's son go as he wished. Tain fully embodied his bard costume, bowing to people in the streets, humming with his hoarse, out-of-tune voice. He twirled me around, serenaded to the passing ladies, introducing me to everyone as his assistant.

"What does a bard's assistant even do?" I asked.

"No clue."

We turned a corner onto the Harpist's Road—a wide street spawning off the Queen's Alley, packed with loud, wine-smelling taverns. The lanterns swung from the window frames, and visitors laughed and chattered tipsily. They were all dressed in fine silks, jewels sparkling from their faces, hair, and clothing. Sapphires and emeralds, rubies and citrines, and of course, the moonstones—all of them representing each of the five crystals that powered the world with starlight.

Tain paused in front of the tavern called *Kirrah's Cloak*. A female singer was in the midst of a dramatic chorus, singing about the goddess' last day on earth. Kirrah was believed to have hidden all five crystals around the world before departing for the star lands in the skies. She tucked the moonstone beneath the hills of Lumenor after all the others, making it the last place where her feet touched the earth. Tain was smitten with the lyrics, watching the singer over his shoulder as he bought us drinks.

"My favorite tavern in the city," he said.

"And no one ever recognizes you in here?"

Tain's hand ran down his colorful cloak, adjusting the creases. "They never even look at me twice. No one assumes the prince would dress like this, even if I look like myself a bit. You will see what I mean during the ball."

I rose my cup to my lips, swallowing a gulp of a delicious red wine. "The ball?"

He gave a nod. "You didn't hear? Mother is hosting a ball next week."

My mouth fell open. "Who throws a ball in the midst of war preparations?" I tried not to sound judgmental, but it came off that way anyway.

"My mother," Tain replied, his voice firm. "We could all use a distraction."

"And I am invited?"

"Well, of course," he said. "All elite legions attend the queen's balls."

I had never even seen the queen let alone thought of myself as elite in any way. A part of me liked the sound of it, another part felt guilty, thinking of my family. No one would ever let them attend such an occasion with me. No one would let me attend, either, if I couldn't bend potently. The silver gates of Old Town opened only to those with fat pockets or powerful palms, and that was it.

"And what are you supposed to wear to this ball?" I asked, thinking about the clothes I stored inside my dresser back at the base.

None were fit for such an occasion. "It's not like I keep a gown in my closet just in case I get invited to a lush party at the palace."

Tain lightly pinched my shoulder. "Just borrow something from Cella or Raina, they own dozens."

No surprise there.

"You're growing muscles," he went on, "they will fit you nicely. Don't think I haven't noticed."

I bit into my cheeks, feeling the heat from the wine rush to my face.

Last time I found a handsome boy, he chased me down the hills with a knife. What will it be this time around?

I was in no rush to find out, so I changed the subject. "Thank you. So, will the bard be singing for us tonight?"

Tain tilted his hat, tucking loose strands underneath. "Not a chance. That would surely break my cover."

"Probably a good thing," I joked. "I'm not sure I can handle any more of your screeching."

He brushed his shoulder against mine and pretended to be offended.

The night passed faster than a stream of starlight. We danced and poked fun at the occasional drunkards that passed. We didn't talk much of our lives or the Akani. Tain needed to forget about the things that troubled him, so I played along, jesting about his clothes and his horrendous singing voice. He was not the stoic, serious legionnaire I had come to know on the training grounds. He laughed more in one night than he had during all the time I'd spent around him. His eyes glittered at me fondly, surely softened from the wine and music.

"You need to take the bard out more often," I said on our stroll back. It felt good to breathe the clean air, untainted by sweat, liquor, or perfume oils. "He is quite fun to hang out with."

We were almost back at the base, so we took our hats off, my braid finally falling free to my shoulder.

"In that case, I will," he said, bribing the guard once again to keep quiet about our outing. I couldn't imagine that Commander would be thrilled with two of his legionnaires sneaking out in the night after what happened to Cella, despite Old Town being heavily guarded. He already thought me reckless and foolish; I didn't need to add any more mischievous deeds to his list.

We entered the empty legion's salon at last, stopping in front of my chamber door.

"Thank you for letting me borrow it," I said, handing the hat back.

"Anytime."

"Hey Tain," I started as the door to my chamber swung open. I whispered to avoid waking the others up. "Why are you so kind to me? Why did you take me with you tonight?"

Tain's face stiffened, his fingers digging into the velvet hat in his clasp. "Because I wish someone did the same for me when I first arrived. We are not outsiders, Imani. This is our city, and we belong in any part of it," he said, wished me a good night, and went back to his room.

Chapter XI
Half-Burned Letter

Cella was released from the healers' wing, but she had to wait another week before going back to training. Shei and I started spending more time in her chamber, talking and laughing late into the night. Raina frequented our gatherings as well, having yet to make up with Lazzor.

"I am not apologizing," she hissed, sorting through Cella's hair pins. It was the eve of the queen's ball, and the two of them had offered to dress Shei and me up.

Cella cleaned and bandaged her wound, her legs tangled in the spread of underdresses atop the bed. Seas of tarot cards had overflown her desk, moon reading charts hanging from the walls. Towers of obsidian crystals peaked from every flat piece of furniture Cella could have placed them on, and a cloud of opaque mist swam inside a large crystal ball in the corner of the room.

Shei brushed her wet hair next to Cella while I painted her nails.

"Stay still," I scoffed, gripping her free hand.

Cella cleared her throat, looking sideways at Raina. "You should apologize—what you said to Lazzor was unkind."

"Don't even get me started on him!" Raina puffed loudly. "He talks about being a fierce warrior all the time, then hesitates when it matters the most."

Dimples pierced Cella's cheeks, the edge of her mouth curving. "But he also regularly risks his life for us. For you."

Shei whistled to tease Raina, something she had grown very fond of as of late.

I raised my brows, looking at Raina. "Are you two…?"

"Kirrah's cloak! No," she replied briskly. "I don't have time for distractions. I have a battle to fight and a crown to win."

Of course.

I finished painting Shei's nails, instructing her to blow onto her fingers and to stop touching things until they got dry—advice she found nearly impossible to follow.

"A little distraction from time to time wouldn't kill you," Cella suggested, clipping a black choker around her neck. "No one is asking you to pick a husband."

"I will do as I please, thank you very much. I have a lifetime ahead of me to pick a man, but I can only win the crown once," Raina said with determination and dropped Cella's golden pin into her pocket, borrowing it for the night. "What qualifies the three of you to give out advice on such matters anyway?" she asked. "Alone, alone." She pointed at me and Cella. "And a hopeless case, I am sure," she concluded, poking her nose towards Shei.

"I would refrain from insults before I lose the only friends I have left," Cella scorned. "And Shei is not a hopeless case!"

Shei's cheeks blossomed like red poppies come springtime, but she remained silent.

"Kirrah help me," Raina moaned, "you three are my only friends. Who would have thought! Come on Imani, time to get ready."

I followed Raina into her room, which was as beautiful as I imagined the queen's chambers to be. Unlike her father, she was very fond of color—her sheets mirrored the night skies, sheer drapes veiling her bed like liquid gold. A set of ancient warrior blades hung above her admirable collection of jewelry—gold, silver, precious crystals, you name it. A sculpture of Uche, Lumenor's famed heroine, gazed back over her shoulder while a slayed stone head representing her opponent swung from her hand. The air in the chamber was spiced with the same rose and cinnamon scent Raina wore on her skin. A portrait of a woman with chestnut eyes was painted on the wall above the desk, a crown of silver curls contrasting her twilight skin. *That must be Raina's mother.* I wondered what happened to her, but I knew better than to ask.

I gasped. "You live like a queen!"

"I intend to be one."

"So you say."

She clicked her tongue in annoyance. "And why not? The choice will fall between Tain and me. What has he done to prove he would make a better ruler? Why should I step aside for him?"

Why indeed?

"I don't really lose sleep thinking which one of you ends up on the throne," I admitted, imagining each of their silver-haired heads embellished with the ancient, five-jeweled crown. Zana described the crown as the most intricate piece of jewelry she had ever seen, and Zana loved jewelry. "Doesn't make much difference to the Mounds-folk either way."

Raina held out a cup of lime water, three golden rose petals floating on its surface. "But what if I could *make* it matter?"

"Let's say you are crowned the next queen of Lumenor. What then?" I asked, climbing into the carriage in front of the base. I pulled up the sapphire-colored silk of the long-sleeved dress I'd borrowed from Raina to avoid stepping on it. She did the same with the voluptuous golden gown that fell down her back.

A flicker of moonlight flashed across Raina's diamond-shaped face before she followed me into the carriage. The makeup powder she wore spilled over the warm tone of her skin like a a river of gold. Her eyes were the color of deep chestnut, gleaming like two brown crystals in the night. She'd applied a subtle face shimmer to accentuate her cheekbones, her face framed by her crown of glossy curls. Raina was not the queen just yet, but she certainly looked the part that evening.

"I am not at liberty to discuss my plans until I bring them to the noble council first," she replied. "But trust me on this—I make a much wiser choice for a ruler."

My nose wrinkled. "How come?"

Raina crossed her legs into a lady-like posture. "Because despite what you think of me, there are boundaries I would never cross. Can you say the same for Tain?"

I paused to think. "I don't know him well enough to answer one way or another. He seems kind to me." I shrugged off. "What are you implying?"

She let me simmer in my curiosity for a moment. "Well, it might be worth your time to pay close attention during your little outings with him. Don't be so surprised, I am a light sleeper, and I keep one ear to the wall, always."

Of course she does.

I swirled saliva in my mouth, hoping to avoid getting into trouble with Commander Izaak. I couldn't handle any more of his punishment laps around the pit. "I would appreciate if you kept our outings a secret."

Raina snorted. "As Cella would say—get a grip! I have more important things to worry about than reporting Tain to Father. I will win the crown the proper way."

Shei and Cella abruptly opened the carriage door and climbed inside. Their faces were painted in a similar fashion, with bejeweled wings that spawned off the outer corners of their eyelids—Cella's favorite design. Voluminous locks curled down her heart-shaped face while Shei had pinned her silky hair up tightly. Even their gowns were matching—bare-shouldered and flowing down their waists with a knee-high slit, differing only in color. Cella's dress was black. Shei's was light gray.

"You are late!" Raina cried out. "Tain and Lazzor have gone already."

"Don't worry, they're not choosing the next ruler at the ball," Cella snapped back, gazing upon the melt of silver and blue makeup on my face. Raina insisted I let her apply the evening sky-toned powder to my lips, and I couldn't resist matching it with one of her sapphire necklaces.

The carriage stopped at the foot of the palace, and my mouth dropped upon seeing it from up close for the first time. A marble staircase stretched towards the entrance. Three gilded domes shone brightly, mirroring Tora, Assan and Shei in the sky. Silky, night-colored drapes veiled circular windows, gently swayed by the breath of the evening. Twisting columns held the palace's mineral-rich stone foundation, textured with imageries of old deities. Even the guards and servants were dressed in fine, bejeweled clothing.

I didn't know if Kirrah's star lands were real or a product of our desire to give our goddess a home, but if they did indeed exist, this was what I imagined her palace to look like.

"Incredible." I sighed.

"I know," Shei said with her mouth half-open.

The inside of the palace was just as heart-stopping as its exterior. Three crescent moon sculptures made of glass served as a center piece in the reception hall. Bouquets of blue roses laid around, dipped in the sand clock-shaped vases. The walls illustrated scenes from Lumenor's popular tales, offering a glance into the old worlds from our rich history. Harp players and singers cast a spell on the palace with their ethereal music, their voices dwindling into the night.

"My parents are here." Cella pointed at a couple of middle-aged Old Town nobles nearby. "Come, I want you two to meet them."

Cella's mother greeted us with a half-hearted smile. She was a woman of an oval-shaped face and red-undertoned mahogany skin. Shoulder-length locs touched the velvet of her emerald dress, pearls beading her neck and fingers. She had the elegance of a lady and the typical stare of concerned mother. Rich or poor, it didn't matter—mothers were mothers.

"Nice to meet you, Shei and Imani. Good evening, Raina." Her dark brown eyes focused on Shei and me, as if she were inspecting a broken pin, looking for the missing piece. "How are you two adjusting to the Old Town after hiding for years? I hear Imani has trouble containing her power."

"Mother!" Cella cried out, her cheeks reddening.

Cella's father affectionately placed a hand on his wife's shoulder, extending his welcomes. Pale strands fell down his moon-skinned face, and a fashionably-cut beard disguised his chin. He had a way of tilting his nose down when speaking. "What my wife meant to say is that we are grateful for your aid the night our sweet girl was injured."

"We *are* grateful," her mother agreed, "but that does not change the fact that the threat is looming over our heads, and you must be prepared."

Easy for her to say.

We moved into a vast ballroom that fit the entirety of the Old Town's elites. Ruby, sapphire, emerald, and just about every other jewel tone of their silks blended like an oil painting. Black roses accented the ballroom, and the torches emitted a deep blue hue into the air, painting everything like a dream.

Sei-san performers entertained crowds from the stage, showcasing astounding bending tricks. Some were juggling big balls of starlight, while others shaped flecks of sei into characters and stories. One woman even conjured a full-sized figurine with her power, pretending to have a conversation with Kirrah herself. I suddenly wished my sister was present to see it. Zuri had been a big admirer of bending arts ever since I could remember. She would have been smitten by their performances.

My heart sank.

Our legion was designated the table that crouched inches away from the stage since Tain and Raina were known contenders for the crown. We only settled down a minute before I decided to look for a powder room. *Surely there are hundreds of them within the palace.* Raina excused herself right before me, mumbling that she was off to greet a friend, so I followed her tracks given that she knew her way around the palace. Also, it helped that no one dared stand in her way, so I advanced through the crowds quicker.

Her silver crown of curls soon vanished behind the main exit, turning into one of the side hallways. I trailed a couple of steps behind, hoping to catch up with her and ask for directions. I could have asked one of the servers, but they all rushed past me in haste, carrying plates and wine bottles. And I would have rather wondered around than asked any of the nosy nobles who couldn't resist the opportunity to ask about my training.

"Hey, Raina! Wait!" My voice finally grabbed her attention down an empty, somber hallway lit by only one azure-flamed torch.

Her eyebrows knitted. "Were you following me the entire time?"

Gasping for breath, I trotted towards her. "Yes, sort of. I'm looking for the powder room."

Raina's big eyes fluttered about, and she pressed a finger against my lips. "Shhh, you fool. Powder rooms are located at the back of the ballroom, not here! Everyone knows that."

"This is my first time visiting the palace."

"Oh, yes. I forgot. Well since you are here now, you must come along," she whispered, turning around.

I clasped the back of her dress. "Wait. Where are you headed? I thought you were meeting a friend."

Raina waved a hand dismissively, and her golden bracelet caught a gleam of blue light. "I don't have that many friends, remember? I am going to the queen's chamber, and you are coming with me."

My palm fell on my forehead. "You are going *where*?" A tear of sweat ran down my cheek, and I shook my head. "Commander will have me sent to the Ashen Desert if you get me in trouble!"

I tugged at her sleeve, but she was already in motion, hauling me along.

"My father, you mean?" she asked, as if I needed a reminder. "Wake up, Imani. He can't afford to send you anywhere. Did you not hear what he said about the Akani Warriors? Despite being an undeniable pain, and a clumsy aimer, the sphere you conjured while dueling me was more than any of us can forge from within. That is why we took you in, despite your lack of training. You are not going anywhere."

I couldn't help but grin.

"Also," she continued, "it is me you need to worry about if you keep wasting the little time we have. You cannot go back on your own—you'll get lost, or worse, caught wondering about where you are not supposed to. Hurry up, now. It will be worth it, trust me."

Worth it? She might not get me expelled, but she'll surely have us both jailed!

But I had no choice but to stay by her side. "You are so sure of yourself," I muttered, trailing behind her.

"I have the goods to back it."

Raina was as big of a pain as she claimed the others to be, but she was not wrong.

"How are we going to get past all the guards unseen?" I asked.

It turned out you could bribe just about anyone in Old Town, as long as you had enough coin, which Raina surely did.

The fluff of her gown hid deep pockets, and she must have taken enough silver and gold out of them to buy ten moonhouses in the Mounds. Silence in exchange for coin. Guard after guard embraced the payment with a nod and continued as if we were never there in the first place. Even the two legionnaires in front of the queen's doors took the bribe, only casting a suspicious look at me.

Everything here seems to have a price, even loyalty.

"You can trust her." Raina soothed them, shutting the doors behind us. "Watch and learn, Imani," she whispered, tiptoeing towards the end of the dim hallway. "Servants who have no love for their queen are quick to betray her."

We lit a single candle wick after emerging into the queen's office from half-darkness. Raina already knew the way. Candlelight illuminated the giant marble sculpture of Kirrah behind the queen's engraved ebony desk. A cyan-colored chair, wide enough for three people to sit in, squatted behind it.

"What now?" I asked.

Raina darted towards the table, motioning for me to approach. "Now we dig for information on the Akani. I am certain the queen is not telling us everything she knows. Take the right side of the drawers and turn out every piece of parchment you can find."

What if she's right?

"Alright." It was reasonable to bend the rules if it was for a good cause, or so I told myself.

In spite of knowing that I was putting myself in danger, I had a great time doing it. My little adventure with Raina reminded me of the days when Summer and I would sneak out as kids and run to the walls. Watching the endless Ashen Desert from the abandoned watchtowers of stone, we talked for hours about who we wanted to become one day. Summer had known ever since she was young that she wanted to be a merchant in charge of her own coin. I, on the other hand, had pretended to consider many false destinies since I couldn't tell her the truth. Sorting through the queen's drawers during one of her fancy palace balls, however, was not one of those destinies.

I squinted, my eyes hurting from reading under the faint halo of a single candle. Letter after letter, the queen mostly dwelled on everyday matters—ruling on grain supplies, tax collections, and rebels' prison sentences. Raina didn't seem to have any more luck, scoffing every time she turned out another demand or receipt.

My fingers drifted across the rugged edge of a parchment placed underneath a rolling stack of quills, and I tapped Raina's shoulder before sliding the parchment out carefully. The bottom half of it was burned. She impatiently snatched the letter from me and began reading.

"It is addressed to the queen of Lumenor," Raina said, her chestnut stare dashing down the papyrus, her features stiffening with every new line of words.

"What does it say?" I asked. "Read it to me!"

"Uhm, it's from the Akani," Raina replied, her voice trembling.

A shudder pulsed down my back. If Raina was shivering…

"Read it."

She cleared her throat, and began in a half-whisper. *"I write to you from the ruins of Vatrion, with the ruby crystal in my hand. I am Kalon, and I want you to remember my name because I will be the one to take your life, unless you hand us the moonstone. Give the crystal up, and we will not burst through your gates or hurt a single person in our way. Sei does nothing but tickle our skin. Hold the moonstone back, and you deserve every bit of wrath that will fall upon you. We discovered your ancestors' secret, and we will tell the whole world about it. We know that…"*

She stopped reading.

"They know what?" I cried out, my words ringing in the silence. My insides were thickening and twisting, mouth growing dry like the Ashen Desert.

Raina bowed her chin, reading through it one more time. "The letter stops there. That hag of a queen burned the bottom half!"

Curious.

"What is Kalon talking about?" I demanded. "Commander said nothing about a secret!"

She shook her head. "I don't know, I swear it on my father's life. I doubt that he knows, either. He would never hide something like this from me. But I mean to find out. Becoming a queen will have to wait."

"Count me in," I said.

Clamor echoed from the hallway—a woman's laughter growing louder with each step. *The queen*. Raina threw the letter inside the drawer while I blew the candle out, and we hid behind the giant sculpture of Kirrah right before Queen Astra walked inside. Raina freed her palms by her side, barely daring to breathe. My mind was stuck on Kalon's words, repeating them time and time again in my head.

And I thought Commander was a person not to be messed with!

The queen was accompanied by Cella's mother, whose voice I recognized in an instant. They came by to refill their drinks, both quite loose-lipped from all the liquor they had already consumed.

"Your daughter appears rather close to the two newcomers—the girls from the Gutter and Mounds," the only other voice in the room spoke—the queen. A drop of bitterness flavored her tone like a lemon peel inside a cup of cool water.

The sound of a bottle opening was followed by the pouring of a drink. "Oh Astra, you know what the youth is this like these days. They claim to care about what happens beyond the silver gates while still living lavishly off our coin. It will pass," she said, taking a big gulp of her drink. Heat struck my forehead, and I clenched my fists. "Besides," she continued, "your boy is quite fond of the Mounds' girl himself from what I am told."

Queen Astra smacked her lips. "From what you are told, hmm, I wonder who is telling you such things. He is a boy of eighteen, of course he is fond of some pretty girl he just met. As you said, it will pass. My son knows that a hill girl could never make a suitable choice for his queen."

Raina squeezed my wrist, shaking her head in silence upon seeing the anger burst out on my face. The silk of the gown I borrowed from her stuck to my skin, choking me.

Kirrah curse her! Curse all of them!

I always knew the way the nobles thought of me and my kin, but this was the first time I'd heard my insecurities spoken back into my ears.

They departed at last, Queen Astra rushing to make her speech. Raina and I slid to the floor once we were alone, catching our breath.

Think.

Focus on what matters.

"You need to find someone in Old Town who is familiar with old histories, and who knows more about our ancestors and this secret," I gauged, "while I work on getting Tain to talk. He must know more than he claims."

"That is a good idea," Raina said with a touch of surprise. She helped me to my feet, and we inspected each other's gowns for dirt and stains. "And you are certain you can work behind his back? You, too, seem a tad fond of him."

I swallowed bitterly. "You heard the queen—it will pass."

"Where in the world have you two been?" Cella asked after Queen Astra finished her enlightening speech about the unity within the city.

The queen's voice was tuned perfectly like a lute string, striking all the important notes. Guarding the moonstone. Barring the city gates. Growing the sei-san numbers. Building weapons. Giving permission to kill Akani Warriors, as if anyone needed that. Utilizing the underground safes to store gold and jewels. Lengthy statements about her duty to protect and give back to the city. Raina kept coughing and rolling her eyes the entire time, so much so that Commander Izaak shot her a pointed look from his seat once or twice.

Although the queen's power was fading, the same could not be said about her beauty. Her face was the color of the moons, just like Tain's, blue eyes glazed with firelight, reminding me of Shei. The silver strands of her hair were sprinkled with snow-white threads, her skin creased around the eyes, highlighting her graceful aging.

The crown on her head was just as beautiful as Zana had claimed. A twisted thread of white gold peaked in five places, a different crystal in each base. The blue of a sapphire contrasted with a blood-red ruby, the green of an emerald glistening in the golden reflection of the citrine next to it, and the moonstone crystal in the middle shone like a full moon, swimming in starlight.

"Imani wanted to see more of the palace, so I showed her around." Raina made an excuse, her glance stirring towards Lazzor.

The entire legion but for Tain was at the table, drinking wine and eating one of the seven dinner courses. A servant placed a plate filled with a single slice of fine yellow cheese and three grapes in front of me. Yes, three whole grapes! I tapped his shoulder before he left, asking when the next course was coming – if three grapes and a slice of cheese could be considered a course in the first place. He laughed my question away, thinking I was joking. My belly growled even though I ate off both mine and Raina's plates. Despite loving the wine, she didn't like the textureless nature of grapes or their bitter seeds. Coming from the Mounds, I didn't have the luxury of being picky. All food on Mother's plates had to be polished away.

My mind kept returning to the Akani, and to Kalon's half-burned letter.

Our ancestors' secret? What is Queen Astra hiding?

Raina looked equally entangled in her thoughts, her eyes unfocused and distant, while Shei and Cella giggled to themselves, at least until Cella's mother came to drag her daughter away to greet other prominent nobles. Lazzor engaged in a playful banter with passing legionnaires, palace lads, and ladies. He appeared to be somewhat of a favorite amongst our group, the one person everyone wanted to talk to.

Tain wandered from table to table alongside his mother with a blank face. All his movements were stiff: the way he walked, the way he shook people's hands. He was as far as one could be from the boy who roamed the streets of Old Town by my side, dressed in a patched, colorful cloak.

"How has your night been so far?" I asked Shei, attempting to distract myself.

She pressed a hand against her chest, fluttering her eyelashes. "Better than I care to admit. Cella and I had a good time while you were browsing the palace. We poked fun at the knife throwers—did you know that knife-throwing is a competition here? And I thought I was fancy, aiming to save my life!"

"I've heard of it, yes. Thinking of entering?" I smirked.

Shei winked. "You know I would gladly take their coin if it wasn't for Commander. He would send me straight to the Ashen Desert if he found out." She indecisively glanced back at Cella from afar. "Should I… ask her for a dance? Her mother doesn't seem very fond of me."

"Her mother…" I stopped myself before blurting out everything Raina and I had witnessed earlier. "Go dance the night away. We may all die in the battle, anyway. Who cares what these people think of us?"

Shei fixed her dress, gave me a hug, and skipped away eagerly. Raina and I exchanged a hardened look, knowing it was not safe to talk here. Her arms were crossed, jaw stiff, and she pointedly glared over at Lazzor every ten seconds.

"Kirrah's cloak, your stubbornness will be the end of you!" I yelled out. "Hey Lazzor," I called, and he stopped mid-sentence with a smiling legionaire. Raina kicked my knee under the table.

"Yes?" Lazzor asked, quickly glancing at Raina's face.

"Raina here is pouting, but she is hoping for a dance," I said, and she kicked me under the table again. "She has something she wants to say to you."

Lazzor was not persuaded, having known Raina for too long. "Is that true?"

She swirled a drink in her mouth, biting into her lip. "It is. I am sorry for being harsh on you. I do think that you hesitate for too long at times, but I should have chosen my words better. You are no coward, and you did save my life plenty of times."

"That was not so hard, was it?" Lazzor scoffed, but the corner of his mouth curved up.

Raina grinned, shaking her head. "Alright now, don't push it."

He gave her a gentle, caring hug that Commander might have deemed too close if he was around to see it and led her towards the dance floor. Tain only approached once I was left alone at the table.

His mother's claims echoed in my ears. *My son knows that a hill girl could never make a suitable choice for his queen.* I had no ambitions of becoming one, but her words still stung.

"Are you enjoying yourself?" Tain asked, clueless about my stroll through his mother's possessions and about what I overheard her say. The mint in his breath swam towards me after he settled in Shei's chair, dragging it closer to mine. I wanted to remain composed just as I told Raina I would be, but his proximity, the way he looked at me, gnawed at the wall I was trying to build between us.

"Not as much as I did drinking at a tavern with a certain bard," I jested. Raina wanted me to ask him about the letter, suggestively staring at us over Lazzor's shoulder, but the ball was not the time or the place for it.

Tain's broad smile vanished. "Don't talk about that here," he demanded in a stiff, Commander-like voice.

I twisted my neck around, surveying the room. "No one can hear me?"

"Still. It is one thing that is my own, and I want it to stay that way."

I took a closer look at him. Tain's hair was styled in an orderly manner, with every strand in place. The cloth of his dark gray jacket was as straight as Commander Izaak's uniforms, outlining his shoulders. His eyes jumped around at every sound—listening, watching, soaking everything in. It appeared as though the boy I'd met at the rooftop was wearing a mask. His desire for the crown turned him into someone else—a well-behaved prince that he thought people wanted him to be.

He wants to be the king so badly he's forgetting to be himself.

"I came here to ask you for a dance," he said at last. "You look beautiful tonight."

I took a sip from Raina's half-emptied cup. "Thank you. Are you certain the queen won't mind you dancing with a girl from the hills?"

Tain grimaced, curiously furrowing his brows. "Well, the hill girl in question is one of the most potent sei-sans in Lumenor. I think she'll forgive me."

I wished he'd said he didn't care about what his mother thought of me instead. I swallowed my pride begrudgingly and took his hand. I had a secret to uncover after all, or so I told myself.

A young noble began singing a ballad, the harpist behind him forging a heart-breaking melody. The lyrics told the tale of a heroine of old whose lover fell in battle. She burned his body under the stars of Kirrah's Cloak, sending him off to the star lands.

I rested my chin against Tain's shoulder, breathing in his scent. Our fingers intertwined, his free hand gliding across my upper back. I could feel his heartbeat, his measured breathing against me. A dream-painted ballroom spun around us, and yet the only thing I could think about was the ancestors' secret.

He must know about the letter.
But how do I get him to tell me about it?

"I know you don't like talking about it here," I whispered gently into his ear, "but meet me in the salon tomorrow at midnight. It is time I show you the best view in the city."

Chapter XII
Kirrah's Temple

"The Mounds will have to wait until tomorrow," I told Tain the next day. We dragged our feet back to the base after the knife-throwing lesson we had in the evening. The skies above us were dimming to a cloud-glazed shadow, the traces of Tora, Assan, and Shei forming against the sinking sun. "Miss Yamane insisted I meet her in the courtyard for a lesson tonight."

Tain looked disappointed but nodded. "Fine, as long as you take me tomorrow. I can't wait!"

Shei caught up with us and swung her arm around my shoulder, pulling me away without acknowledging he was there. "You're getting the hang of throwing blades, tree burner—you struck the farthest target twice in a row today!"

Wrapping my arm around her waist, I laughed. "Did you forget that I'm only in your company so that you can teach me how to aim daggers?"

"Are you certain it is not my irresistible charm that makes it impossible to stay away?" She winked.

"As certain as one can be," I replied sagely.

A group of older legionnaires departed from a nearby armory, tucking their knives into their belts as they walked towards us at a slow pace. Amounting to a dozen or so, they clung to each other's sleeves just as babes clutch onto their mothers' skirts. *The legion's bond is made for life,* Raina had once told me.

Yet I didn't know them.

The sei-sans' bases all squatted next to one another, their inhabitants divided by age. In spite of living in the same base as several other legions, we scarcely interacted due to our schedules. When we were at the pit, they were throwing knives. When we were eating or resting, they were bending sei. The schedules were designed in such a fashion in order to take full advantage of the resources at our disposal, isolating us from our peers. And the older folk certainly had no interest in interacting with us beyond the usual pleasantries.

Shei and I kept to the edge of the road to let the mature legionnaires pass. As they neared us, a woman wearing her hair in an indigo-dipped braid emerged ahead. She had a pair of striking, wandering blue eyes I recognized immediately.

"Good evening." She paused as our paths crossed. Her peers continued on their way without much thought, except for one of them who bowed his chin with a kind smile. "Always glad to see a familiar face."

Shei cocked her head at me, mouthing questions I was not able to discern.

"We've met before, while I was still in the Mounds," I elaborated before turning back to the legionnaire. "Forgive me, I never learned your name," I uttered, extending my hand with awkwardness.

She embraced my hand with a warm touch. "It's Tarah."

"My name is Imani and this is my friend Shei."

Shei greeted Tarah timidly, as though she'd been asked to shake a tree branch. The rest of our legion crept past us, twisting their necks nosily. Only Raina stayed behind without introducing herself. She always assumed people knew who she was, and she was annoyingly almost never wrong.

"Your parents are fine people," Tarah said, running her fingers over the blade pommels in her belt. "They were very polite and welcoming. Your father brews an excellent nettle tea."

My nose wrinkled, heart beating fast. "You were at my home? How do you know my parents?"

She grinned, flashing a set of wine-stained teeth. The sun had sunk an inch further, tinting the skies to a deepening blue shade. "Do not fret, I only picked up the items your mother wanted you to have once or twice before. A true Mounds' woman, Kamari is."

Mother.

My chest felt inexplicably tight thinking of Mother's warm hugs, and I could almost feel her arms tightening around me.

"How is she doing? How are all of them doing?" I asked in one breath.

Shei put her hand on my shoulder and pressed it firmly. Her fingers dug deep into my flesh, the same way I plunged my hands into the earth when planting in our garden.

Tarah turned her head towards Raina before answering. "They are doing well, but…I'm afraid I am at no liberty to say a thing more. Izaak's orders."

I would have cursed the commander's name if Raina was not right there, staring at Tarah with her chin pointed up.

"Well, I'm glad to have run into you," I muttered, judging from Tarah's tight-lipped demeanor that she was not willing to disobey Commander Izaak's demands, especially not in the presence of his daughter. But then a thought crossed my mind. "One more thing. How did you know that day at the market? I didn't think I gave a sign of being able to bend. And why did you choose not to report me?"

Tarah paused mid-breath. "Oh, dear. I figured it would have come up by now."

"What would have come up by now?" Raina demanded, her voice firm like her father's.

Tarah swallowed and then murmured. "This is no time or place for such talk, and I beg your discretion—I can get in a lot of trouble for not reporting a young sei-san." She looked to see if anyone was approaching from behind and lowered her voice further. "I knew you were one of us the moment you mentioned your sister's sickness. I didn't report you because it sounded like your family needed you, and I've been in those shoes myself as a young girl."

Raina's gaze widened before trailing to the ground. "The sibling's curse…" she mumbled to herself.

"What?" Shei snapped. "What's with the gloomy atmosphere? Raina?" Shei stared at her while I felt a chill prick my skin.

The sun had completed its dance around earth, drifting into the dream land of stars. Shade fell across Tarah's pale face. My pulse quickened before anyone answered.

A part of me knew already. I chose to look away for years and selfishly keep my sanity. There had to be a reason why Mother never sought out the help of ordinary healers for Zuri's condition—why she always went to fortune-reversers, magic brewers and such. She knew.

My hands, jaw, and knees began shaking uncontrollably, and a lump clogged my throat.

"The sibling's curse," Raina repeated, clearing her voice. "I would have said something, I never knew you had a sister…"

"You never asked!" I felt the sting of anger spear my belly. My joints felt seared into place and my blood ran warmer and warmer until it felt like boiling.

"What in the world is a sibling's curse?" Shei frowned. "Breathe, Imani."

Tarah and Raina looked at each other solemnly, their expressions a mirror of the same morose emotion. "Sei-sans are not meant to have siblings," Raina replied finally. "And if they do, the second child always grows ill. They don't live very long, either. Most don't live to be more than fifteen, sixteen…at *best*."

My throat felt tight, like it was closing up. I gasped and reached for my neck, squeezing my eyes shut.

My knees gave up. I began sobbing on the ground, gnawing at the collar of my uniform, tearing at my hair with my heating palms.

Zuri is twelve. Moons help me, Zuri is twelve!

Raina and Shei fell to the ground beside to me, mouthing words in an attempt to console me. I couldn't hear them. I couldn't breathe. I couldn't think. I couldn't stop crying. I couldn't stand to live another moment while my sister was dying.

And I'd been having *fun*—training, learning to bend sei, going to fancy balls. Thinking about Tain. I'd been playing with pretty lights and all sorts of people while my sister *wasted away*.

A stream of starlight beamed from my palms. Raina screeched and linked with it, redirecting it away from the surrounding buildings before they were burned to soot. The beam burned a crater in the pavement nearby, alerting the guards on duty that were posted at the next corner. Two of them rushed to our aid, but Raina waved them away.

"Imani..." Shei wiped my tears away. She had tears of her own running down her face. "Imani, breathe...I am so sorry..."

"Zuri..." I uttered between the sobs. "Zuri is twelve..."

Tarah stood above us, gazing down at me with pity. Raina and Shei latched onto my arms and carried me back to the base. My feet dragged across the dirt, my skin itching—burning. I wanted to rip my uniform apart entirely, take one of the knives fastened at my belt and plunge it into my belly.

Shei instinctively reached for my belt with her free hand, as if she could hear my thoughts. Unbuckling it, she snatched the blades away, tossing them aside. Their edges kissed the ground with a clang that rang in my ears.

"Zuri is twelve...only twelve..." I muttered over and over as the girls dragged me up the stairs into our legion's quarters. The boys and Cella stormed out of their chambers upon hearing us, panicked from the commotion we caused. Tain embraced me from Raina's and Shei's arms and carried me into my room. The rest of them whispered behind us as they followed. I collapsed onto my bed, crying.

Zuri is twelve.
Zuri can't die!
Only twelve...

Shei reached for one of my shoulders and flipped me onto my back gently. Every bone in my body was hurting. I could not stand the way they were looking at me, all of them. I didn't want their compassion nor their pity. I didn't want any of it.

Shei fetched me a cup of water while Raina propped the tasseled, constellation-embroidered pillows behind my back. The boys settled at the foot of my bed, Tain watching me warily in silence.

"There is no cure, is there?" I asked, searching their faces. A sudden thought occurred to me. "I need to see Mr. Osei."

Cella pulled me back reluctantly, her hands shaking. "I am afraid there is no cure. There is nothing Mr. Osei can do."

"So that's it? My sister is dying a slow death while I am here playing at war?" I tilted my head, pushing away another cup of water Shei tried to get me to drink. "I think not. I will do whatever it takes."

Lazzor and Tain traded a dour look. Every glance at my friends' faces chipped away at the strings of my heart.

There's a cure out there. There has to be one out there.

"There is nothing you can do to change your sister's fate. I really am sorry," Raina told me, and I knew she meant it. She tapped her toes against the soft carpet, avoiding my stare.

"Even if I died?" I asked.

She shook her head. "Not even then. Some sei-sans have ended their lives in the past, and their siblings still didn't survive."

"Moons help me!" I plunged my face into my palms which throbbed with the warmth of sei.

"It is a well-known thing in Old Town, at least. None of us have a sibling for that reason," Raina went on.

"I had a twin," Cella cut in, her voice catching. Judging from Lazzor's tightened mouth, he was the only one who already knew. "My brother was born with a hole in his chest where I had pierced him while we were still inside the womb. My mother survived childbirth by a thread." She paused, picking at her chipped nail without looking up. "We named him Eli, after my grandfather, and we celebrate my birth night for the both of us. I still feel like there is a piece of me missing sometimes."

Raina lifted a translucent calcite crystal from my desk, gazing at its smooth surface. Her eyes seemed rimmed with tears. "At least your mother survived. Mine died giving birth to me, as some of you already know," she said, her teeth tearing into her bottom lip.

Kirrah help us all.

"I am really sorry about that. I didn't know," I muttered. "For what is worth, I blamed my mother for the majority of my life, both my parents really. I blamed them for not allowing me to join the legions. For needing me to help out at the market, for not being able to take care of Zuri, and provide for us on their own. When it was me the whole time, who was the reason behind all our troubles."

There it was, out in the open. The ugly truth of who I really was—a selfish, sheltered girl who blamed her parents for the troubles she caused. A plague to my family, the knife at my sister's throat, digging into her skin a bit more with each new sunrise. The reason why she was sick, and why she would eventually die, leaving this world forever.

All because of me.

"Don't say that." Shei hugged me, the mint in her hair cooling my wet cheek. "You did nothing to cause what's happening to Zuri."

Except being born.

The entire legion remained in my chamber for the rest of the evening. Once I cried all the tears I had left in me, I blankly stared into the Pisces constellation on the ceiling, asking Kirrah why. Why was she so unfair, dooming Zuri to the nights of fever and bone ache. Why cast a shadow over the beam of light that was my little sister. Why grant me the power of starlight in exchange for her life.

Shei leaned against me, breathing softly into my shoulder. Raina and Lazzor whispered to each other in the corner, while Cella twirled one of Shei's mint branches between her lips, lost in thought. Tain stayed seated at the foot of my bed, still as stone, glaring absentmindedly into distance.

A knock pounded against the door one hour before midnight, and Commander Izaak and Miss Yamane stepped inside.

Raina ran into the commander's arms, disarming his rock-solid composure. It was the first time I saw him for the father he was instead of the fierce commander of armies. He embraced her in a way fathers embrace their daughters, making me crave my own father's arms. That was if I could summon the courage to appear in front of Father in the first place. He worked tirelessly for years to support our family, damaging his body and soul in the process. And there was I, ungrateful for the sacrifices he'd made for me.

"We heard what happened," Miss Yamane spoke quietly. "Imani, I need you to come with me."

I tossed the covers off of my lap, uncertain if I could rise to my feet without my knees giving up. My palms were as hot as iron plates. They kept singing the things I touched. I tried to meet Miss Yamane's eyes but found that I couldn't. "If you ask me to bend tonight, I might bring down the entire base."

I wasn't lying.

A part of me wished the Akani would show up that moment so that I could take my wrath out on someone who deserved it.

"I would do no such thing." Miss Yamane beckoned me with one sway of her arm. "We are going to Kirrah's Temple."

Kirrah's Temple?

"That is the last place on earth I want to be right now!" I snapped. The starlight goddess played a cruel game, filling one cup by emptying another. "I'd rather go into the Ashen Desert."

My sei instructor frowned but approached me with a hand held out. "I understand, but I must ask you to come anyway."

"Can we go see Mr. Osei first?" I asked. "I'd like to have a word with him."

Miss Yamane's features softened to mirror the pity on my friends' faces. "He can do nothing for you, dear. Sei-san after sei-san has tried healing their siblings with potions or magic, but nothing has ever worked. It is time we head towards the temple."

I had no choice but to get up from my bed.

"Why are you taking me there?" I asked, searching for my boots in the pile of shoes on the floor.

"I am afraid you will have to come and see," she replied, heading for the door. "Feel free to change into comfortable garments, I will be waiting in the salon."

The night air was chillier than I had expected. I followed behind Miss Yamane slowly, drowning in my feelings. I didn't pay attention to my surroundings, letting time pass me by until we reached the silver gates of Old Town.

Three night priestesses waited for us on the other side, their deep blue cloaks swaying in the rhythm of the wind. The white-gilded dome of Kirrah's Temple eclipsed the sky ahead, the marble steps leading up towards it spilling from the entrance like milk. The sculpture of Kirrah stood behind it, cloaked in shadows. I was tempted to crumble it with starlight, to get back at the goddess for all the misfortune and sorrow she brought upon my family, but I kept walking.

The temple walls glinted with silver lettering kissed by moonlight, spelling out endless prayers in an ancient language I didn't know. A tall entrance archway offered a gaze into the temple's calming, candlelit interior. I would have been thrilled to visit it on any other occasion, having stayed away for years. Mother always feared I would be found out if I ever came along with the rest of my family and Zana on holidays.

The air inside was saturated with myrrh, incense burning from the altars dedicated to various gods. Kirrah was the main deity worshiped in Lumenor, but we recognized others as well—the gods and goddesses of sun, midnight, sea, earth, firelight, harvest, and countless others. Their gilded sculptures kept to the rounded walls of the temple, overseeing cloaked priestesses who labored quietly. The choir chanted a midnight prayer from an inner balcony, their soft melody reminding me of my pain.

A woman who could be none other than the high priestess of the temple approached, gliding elegantly across the floor. She was younger than I'd expected—only a few years my senior from what I could tell. Silver twists fell down her back, and eyes dark as night narrowed on me. She donned a black velvet cloak, glittering with moonstone charms that clanked like wind chimes every time she took a stride.

The only cloak of its kind.

Kirrah's cloak.

"Welcome in, Imani. Please follow me, the prayer chamber is this way."

I trailed behind the priestess and Miss Yamane wordlessly, exhausted from the black tar of emotions in my belly. The prayer chamber was a small, circular room at the back of the temple, illuminated by a ring of bright, blue candlelight. Miss Yamane crouched in the back of the room while the priestess asked me to accompany her to the cushions in the center of the candle ring.

Setting a bundle of sage on fire, she blew the smoke into my face, chanting in an ancient tongue. Dipping her hands into rose oil next, she pressed her fingers against my temples and ears. I followed her instructions mindlessly, not seeing the point in resisting. I did not see the point in whatever she was doing either, but I had no fight left in me to question her.

"Take a deep breath." The high priestess' eerie voice echoed through the prayer chamber. "And another."

I struggled to breathe evenly. Herby smoke burned my nose, reminding me of the hills come festival time. My shoulders sagged, the tensed muscles relaxing at the mere memory of oak trees and the fresh herbs I grew up around.

"Good," she mumbled, reaching for a golden goblet at her side. The goblet was inscribed with an ancient symbol, one of the few I could recognize—the one for eternal night. "Close your eyes now."

The priestess dabbed droplets of rosemary oil over my shut eyelids and continued chanting in a low, ethereal hum. Note after note, my mind sank farther into a dream state, void of thought and light. I was so tired, I was afraid I might fall asleep.

Before long, the priestess wiped the oil from my face carefully, using a soaked cloth. "Open your eyes," she said, handing me a cup. I could not identify the potion by smell or color. Strange. There weren't many concoctions I couldn't name. The liquid was a dark blue brew with the thickness of the milk. It had a sour, earthy smell.

"Drink it."

I glanced at Miss Yamane over my back. She shut her eyes and bobbed her chin, signaling it was safe.

As long as I get to go back to my chamber after this.

I drank the potion slowly, its mineralized texture chafing against my throat.

My mind stopped dead in its tracks.

An invisible force began to pull me down. I fell back onto the cushions. The star constellations on the ceiling shifted in front of my eyes, as though the earth's spin around the sun suddenly changed its course.

"What is this? What did you give me?"

Even if the priestess responded, I could not hear her. My ears felt as though they were stuffed with straw. Panic somewhere far away squeezed my heart. Suddenly, my muscles felt like writhing snakes. They twisted and cramped around my bones.

What is happening to me?

Just when I felt as though my throat would close up and my bones would splinter, the pain vanished. I felt…empty. Hollowed out. There was no pain, nor was the flood of guilt and worry swirling around in my head and stomach.

I felt…good? I couldn't feel any of the emotions that plagued me earlier, despite knowing they were still there inside me. It was like looking at myself through a window, the me on the other side still wrecked. But everything felt far away and harmless.

"What happened?" I asked once the pain completely subdued and I was left with nothing. "What did you do to me?"

The high priestess sealed the lid of the potion bottle shut, securing it with care. "I gave you a different strain of the healer's aid, spiced with a bit of magic."

I opened my mouth, but I didn't know what to say or how to react. The use of ancient magic was forbidden, yet the high priestess of Lumenor had just administered it to me without my consent.

I should have been livid. I would have been livid if I could feel anything.

"How…how dare you?" I stumbled through my words, turning back to Miss Yamane.

The soft lines of my sei teacher's face remained still. "I apologize for this indiscretion, but we had no other choice. We have a battle to fight and cannot afford for you to sink into a permanent state of despair."

I so wish I could get angry right now.

"So you decided for me?" I tried to demand. The words lacked any sort of ire I'd hoped to infuse it with.

"*We* did," Miss Yamane replied, tilting her neck with her brows raised. "And if you knew what was coming, you would be thanking us."

Thanking? Us?

I grimaced in disbelief. "How am I even going to be useful to anyone in this state? All this talk about feeling my emotions while bending. I can't feel anything."

Miss Yamane stood up, gathering her skirts before gesturing for me to follow her back outside. The priestess stayed behind. "You will feel things again as early as tomorrow," my sei teacher explained as we strolled back towards the arch that now offered the view of the sparkling night skies and the Cobblestone. "The pain will return slowly, in waves, so that you can learn how to manage it."

I swayed my head away from her, failing to recognize the beauty of the temple I had previously admired. "You betrayed my trust," I said, passing through the arch. "You lied to me."

Miss Yamane clasped my forearm, leading me back towards the silver gates. Her grip was not the touch of the soft-spoken lady who had trained me how to bend. Her features molded into a cold, harsh expression I had never seen them make before.

"Not a word more, Imani," she uttered in a brisk tone once we stirred away from the temple. "You will go back to your room and leave it tomorrow with a big smile on your face, if you know what is good for you and your family. I will explain everything during our next sei lesson." She looked back ahead and murmured quietly. "You are in danger."

Chapter XIII
Magic Potion

I felt nothing.
No fear, no pain, no guilt.
Yet, I knew those feelings were tearing at my insides… only, I could not sense them. I wondered what kind of danger Miss Yamane spoke of, counting time until our next session the following day. I should have been sick with worry, but instead I could not bring myself to a point of discomfort let alone fear.

"Mr. Osei." I walked into the healers' quarters at the crack of dawn, right before combat. Feelings or no feelings, I was not going to sit around waiting for my sister to die.

My voice startled the head healer, his neck twitching above the blue collar of his attire before he realized it was me.

"I heard," the healer whispered.

"About my sister or about what Miss Yamane did?"

"Both," he replied, taking a discrete peek at the door. "But I will only discuss the former with you for now. It is not safe to talk here."

His reaction made me pause. What could not be spoken in the privacy of an empty chamber?

"Is there a cure for the sibling's curse?" I asked, wasting no time.

Mr. Osei patted my shoulder. "Unfortunately not. I am sorry, Imani."

Not good enough. It was difficult. Even the feeling of determination felt distant, but I thought of Zuri and persisted.

"What have you tried thus far?"

"Everything," he responded, staring at his hands. "Everything I could think of. I've never told you the reason I became a healer, did I?"

I shook my head.

"I, as you are well aware, am Mounds-born like you. Being one of our kind, I faced the same challenges in my youth. And yes, I could once bend, too, though not very well. Either way, the matters of seisans' were never discussed in the hills in my day. Many more of us were in hiding back then. My poor parents did not know what they were getting themselves into."

"You had a sibling?" I asked, although I had already anticipated the answer.

He took a deep, drawn out breath. "A brother, only a year younger than me. His name was Silon."

Oh, no.

"How soon did he…?"

"He died at fourteen." Mr. Osei's voice trembled.

Only fourteen? My eyes widened.

"I'm sorry," I murmured, knowing it was the right thing to do. Yet I could feel no compassion, no share of his pain, despite that pain cutting close to being my own.

"Thank you, child. My heart still aches thinking of him. I vowed to find the cure and have traveled the world for three long decades in search of it. I didn't want anyone else to experience the pain of losing a sibling or a child. I tried everything—potions, ointments, spells. Nothing has worked."

There has to be a way.

"Zuri is only twelve," I said, my tone lowering to a whisper. "Raina claims the siblings never live past sixteen. Mr. Osei, I can't sit here and watch her die."

"Maybe you won't have to," he proclaimed. I flinched. "Now, I beg you, don't get your hopes up. I mean it. Hope is a bitter medicine." Judging from the sour twist of his mouth, it was a medicine he had once tasted, too. "But I have something in mind, and before you ask, no, I cannot tell you until I know for sure. Not until the time is right."

Until the time is right?

We only have weeks before Akani Warriors arrive.

"What can I do?" I asked.

"You can continue to train. And listen to Miss Yamane, she is on your side no matter the appearances. Now go, before you are late for combat. Trust me on this."

Trust him?

Miss Yamane said the same thing before letting the high priestess poison me.

The door of the healers' wing burst open. Shei came in looking for me. "Tree burner! We have to go, the sun is almost up, and you know the punishment for being late."

"Coming," I said, rising to my feet.

"Imani," Mr. Osei called before I stepped through the doorway. "Not a word about this to anyone."

After the night I'd had, I was not likely to trust anyone with my secrets, let alone the one that could save my sister's life.

"I promise."

"Today we begin dueling with sei," Commander announced at the beginning of combat.

No one was allowed to aim starlight at Shei or me since we couldn't deflect their streams. The rest of the legion was tasked with bending at titanium shields that the commander had flung into air without warning, tasking them with deflecting our attacks at the same time. Shei and I were given permission to try anything we wished with the goal of helping the others train against an unpredictable threat. If I were my ordinary self, I would have been thrilled, but I felt indifferent towards the whole ordeal.

Shei's turn came first.

"We shall see how much you've learned," Commander said. "Cella, would you like to start us off and fight Shei?"

Cella walked towards the center of the platform as though she was taking an aimless stroll through nature. "I am not sure she is ready for me," she joked, her full lips blossoming into a smile.

"Don't flatter yourself," Shei retorted. "You might want to take your necklace off before you choke on starlight coming from my palms."

Her warning made Cella laugh. "Let's see if you can live up to your vivid imagination."

Commander whistled and both of them shifted into a fighting stance. Shei wasted no time before going on offense. Her streams were short and pointed as always. Cella deflected them with ease while simultaneously bending swirls of magic that intertwined like threads of silk, weaving them into shields. Even with all of Shei's skill and precision, she could do nothing to distract Cella before she tired out.

"My necklace is still intact," Cella teased her after they were done.

Lazzor faced Shei next after a quick break, releasing only as much as he needed to, teardrops of sei trickling away from him like particles of rain. He could strike even the smallest of the targets, never missing despite Shei's efforts. Tain's streams, unlike Lazzor's, were as long as spears, spinning about their axis before crashing into the shields. Shei gave all she had dueling him, almost causing him to miss one of the target shields.

Almost.

"Remember everyone, deflect first and attack second," Commander advised. "You are of no use to anyone if you are dead. Raina and Imani, ready for a rematch?"

"I am willing if she is," I said, my voice even-toned.

Raina cracked her knuckles. "Try not to end up in the healers' wing again."

And so we began.

I aimed at her once, twice, thrice, releasing controlled amounts of sei without breaking a sweat. My chest did not burn, my vision did not blur. I could think clearly and focus on my bending. My streams, however, were only about as potent as everyone else's, which was disappointing.

"Is that all you can summon?" Raina scoffed after a long series of deflections that folded her spine.

I asked the legion to behave as if nothing had happened the previous day, wanting no part in anyone's pity. Cella and Shei, even the boys, struggled to follow my instruction, but one could always count on Raina to deliver on her promises. She was raised by the most disciplined soldier in Lumenor, after all.

"You speak as if you could handle my full power," I said to stir her pot and hopefully get her to slip. "As you once said to Shei, retract your claws before you get bitten."

I was in no position to make such threats, but I did it anyway.

And it worked.

Raina's stare narrowed on me with the look of a hunter who had just spotted her prey, lingering in quiet while gathering her strength.

"If I see you draining yourself, you will be building weapons in the Ashen Desert for the rest of the week!" Commander threatened.

I didn't care.

I was no longer afraid of the desert or its beasts. In spite of my lack of fear, the voice inside my head kept whispering to me. *Don't do it.* The voice also whispered many other things. *A poison to my family. My sister's killer. Ungrateful, spoiled child.*

"I will behave, Commander," I promised.

With potency being my main strength before my poisoning, I was trained to show off the magnitude of my power while bending. Miss Yamane had taught me how to leverage the marble-sized balls of sei I took years to master for Zuri, repurposing them a bit. The trick was to concentrate as much starlight as I could within them, tricking my opponents into thinking they were but a speck of magic. Then, I bent them into blasts once they were close enough to my target to inflict damage.

However, I was not sure if I could make them powerful enough now that I was weakened by ancient magic, or whatever it was that I had drank.

Raina clicked her tongue after yet another failed attack. "I am getting bored."

I will make it thrilling for you, then.

She smirked at the sight of tiny balls that left my fingers, focusing instead on aiming at the titanium shields. My mind was so clear without my emotions to overwhelm me, and I bent the balls to my will without difficulty, making them do anything I desired.

So naturally, I decided to bounce them around Raina and disorient her.

I split both clusters of starlight into five, juggling them in circles around Raina's head. She had trouble linking since there were too many to focus on at once.

Good to know.

The balls of sei hopped about, bouncing off the currents of air to everyone's amusement. I burst the first one, and Raina had a split second to deflect the blast.

She did it successfully.

Then another.

"Keep your focus," Commander urged his daughter with a breath caught in his throat, "the shields are coming your way!"

Raina struggled to remain patient, a trait my usual self shared with her. She had trouble splitting her attention in so many different directions. She persisted, aiming back and forth between my attacks and the flying shields. She worked hard and was left exhausted after we were done, folding over her knees. While she managed to deflect all of the attacks, she'd missed two titanium targets.

I passed her by on my way towards the rest of legion and the commander. She was still hunched over, panting.

"Who is the dead girl now?" I asked, and walked away.

"Your sei instructor made you drink a magic potion that numbed your feelings? Without informing you beforehand?" Shei was livid after I told her and the girls about what took place at the temple.

The four of us gathered in Cella's room after the knife-throwing drill in the evening. Lazzor and Tain had to attend their bending lessons, so we decided to skip on card games that night.

"Everyone claims the ancient magic is forbidden, yet the high priestess of Kirrah's Temple administered it to you!" Cella moaned, shaking her head.

Shei rolled her eyes. "Are you really that surprised? The laws in Lumenor don't apply to the ruling class. They never did."

That remark earned her a sideways look from Cella, who remained tight-lipped. I sometimes forgot we came from different worlds despite growing up in the same city.

"You aren't wrong," Raina agreed, playing with the twisted golden chain of her necklace. "That will all change once I become the queen."

Shei twirled a mint branch between her fingers, passing a leaf to Cella. "Right. Only you will be able to break the rules, then."

"Oh, shut it," Raina snapped. "But nobles or not, that was a despicable thing to do. I will ask Father about it the first thing in the morning."

Cella tilted a black teapot against the four bronze cups on her desk, filling one at a time. The red rooibos tea, imported from the southern lands, poured out of the pot like a stream of blood. Her eyes darted to me as she turned. "Can you feel *anything*?"

"No, not for the most part." I shrugged. "Miss Yamane said the emotions would start coming back in waves as early as today, but I'm still waiting."

Shei took tea from Cella, tracing the carving of Kirrah's face on the cup with her thumb. "I know Mr. Osei said you could trust her, but I'm suspicious."

Cella held a cup out to me next, but Raina slapped my hand and took it herself. "The tea is spiked with rum. And you, young lady, are not drinking anything tonight! You have an important task at hand."

Shei and Cella traded a puzzled glare.

"A task?" Cella asked, taking a comfortable seat atop her bed. "What task?"

Raina took a deep breath. "There is something we've been meaning to tell you. We snuck into the queen's chambers the night of the ball."

Cella spit a mouthful of her drink onto the velvet sheets. Luckily, they were dyed in the color of obsidian, impossible to taint. "Kirrah's cloak, Raina!"

Shei, on the other hand, looked offended, her palm falling to her heart. "And you didn't invite me? What, that's the kind of ball I would like to attend," she exclaimed upon taking a note of reprimand on Cella's face.

Cella's cheeks dimpled with a smile. "So you didn't have a good time with me?"

Shei look back at her, almost timidly. "Of course I did."

Raina waved her hand dismissively. "Anyway, we found a curious letter. The bottom half of it was burned."

Cella leaned onto the carved ebony headrest, propping her back with feather-stuffed pillows. "Who was it from? What did it say?"

Raina spun the end of a loose curl around her finger. "It was from Kalon," she replied, and Cella covered her mouth. "He threatened to murder the queen if she does not give the moonstone up. That, and he also threatened to tell everyone about the ancestors' secret, whatever that might be. Like I said, the bottom half of the letter was burned."

Cella rolled off her bed, inching towards the crystal ball in the corner. The translucent mist still swam inside it, emitting a faint halo. She lifted the ball out of its base, and brought it back to the bed. Beginning to hum, she closed her eyes, lowering her fingers to the glass surface.

Raina frowned at her, clicking her fingernail against the topaz charm around her neck. Unlike her, I had never witnessed someone attempt to merge their mind with any magic other than sei, and I watched, thrilled, afraid to blink and miss something.

Unfortunately, Cella gave up on her efforts a few moments later. "It's not working."

"It never does," Raina mouthed into her chest. Needless to say, she didn't believe in telling, not from cards nor from magic balls.

Shei let the upper half of her hair out, the starlit strands spilling out, framing her narrow face. "What could it be? This secret?"

"We don't know, but we mean to find out," I said. "That's why Raina doesn't want me drinking. I am seeing Tain tonight. I'll try to get him to tell me."

Shei slapped her thigh. "I knew *he* had something to do with it! But why would he tell you of all people?"

"Because he likes her, dummy!" Cella giggled.

Shei's sharp gaze snapped to my face. "Ugh, Imani. *Him* of all people?"

"Get a grip," Raina cut her off. "It is rather useful to our efforts. They've been sneaking out of the base at night, presenting a perfect opportunity for Imani to ask questions now."

I pointed my finger up, wrestling with Shei's judgmental stare. "It happened only once, alright? Raina is exaggerating."

"What is all the fuss about anyway? Tain is not a bad person," Cella mumbled, avoiding Shei's poignant glare that darted her way. "It's not his fault that he was adopted by Astra."

"Don't go on defending him now," Shei hissed.

"A bad person or not, he must know something, being the queen's son and all," Raina added. "And Imani will try to get it out of him."

Chapter XIV

Hills of Lumenor

"I must admit, I *am* a bit scared of you, after what you pulled off earlier today. You were showing some real improvement," Tain said on our way southward. Three waning moons followed us down the folk-packed streets of Old Town, enkindling the road ahead.

If Tain knew about the potion I'd been given against my will, which I was certain he did, he spoke no word of it. I played along, preferring to avoid discussion on the matter, attempting to act as my ordinary self.

I cocked my head, casting a daring glance at him. "You're right to be scared." I winked. He smiled, looking to his feet.

The girls and I had come up with a plan before departure. I was to take Tain to the Mounds, since he'd already told me he knew of a hidden passageway out of the Old Town. I was determined to memorize the path in case I needed to use it in the future. Under no circumstances was I to visit my family, not that I could bear seeing their faces anyway, not yet. Despite not being able to feel much, my thoughts still haunted me everywhere I went.

A poison. A plague. A murderer.

I covered my ears with my hood, hoping to silence the relentless voice in my head. Tain led the way towards the southern edge of Old Town. We'd wrapped ourselves in black linen cloaks, ones that had reminded me of the one the temple priestess wore the previous night. Ours, unlike hers, lacked the fine embroidery.

"How are we going to get past the silver gates?" I asked.

Tain slipped his hood over his head, too, hiding his face in the depths of shadow. "We aren't. They are heavily guarded and impenetrable for a reason. The gates might be silver but they aren't *actually* silver. They're titanium." He shrugged. "But you're forgetting that a portion of the hills belongs to the Old Town territory."

No Mounds-born ever forgot about that, yet we chose not to speak of it. The Old Town squatted in the western part of Lumenor, and all the hills that surrounded it were inhabited by what we referred to as the old blood families. The elites amongst elites. Not even the rebels dared try their luck and sneak into the Old Town through their lands.

The Mounds' mothers used to scare their young ones with made up tales of children who crossed the old stone walls and ventured there. Some were eaten, some skinned alive, never to return, depending on the story, or the child. I was an audacious, mischievous child, so Mother's versions of the tale often involved blood-thirsty beasts and monsters. The truth was, not many animals or creatures roamed Lumenor, unless they were bred to be eaten, provide blood for potions, or produce milk. And the ones that couldn't be tamed were hunted in the Ashen Desert and killed mercilessly.

"I finally get to meet the fanged beasts my mother told me about," I half-joked.

Tain's brows furrowed. "Meet what?"

I gave a dismissive wave, remembering he was Gutter-born. "Just something that mothers from the Mounds like to scare their children with. The shapeshifters, chimeras, banshees, that kind of thing. They were said to roam this place, looking for lost children."

Tain scratched the back of his head through the hood. "Umm, they're usually caged," he said without a note of jest in his voice. "Although I have seen one or two break loose before."

I paused in mid-stride, taken aback. "Wait, what do you mean? The old blood here *actually* keeps monsters in their backyards?"

Instead of answering, he began climbing the southernmost hill that hugged the tall, old fence of jagged stone, towards the glooming darkness that were the hills of Old Town. *Don't follow him,* the voice inside my head said. I ignored it, ascending behind Tain, adjusting my wind-tussled cloak.

"They keep the creatures for the entertainment purposes only," he replied at last, as if that made it any better.

What kind of entertainment involves a murderous banshee?

I figured I was better off not knowing.

A shred of a feeling passed through me, and I bit my tongue, the disapproval in my voice rising. "And I thought the tarot readings my mother dragged me to every moon cycle were a strange form of keeping the mind busy."

Climbing up the hill didn't disturb my breathing or muscles, and I could have climbed five more if need be.

I'm getting into shape.

Luckily, we didn't run into anything out of the ordinary while plodding through the hills. I couldn't see any of the manors, either, thanks to their high-walled fences. Regardless, the hills were still hills, roaming with water streams and the scent of blooming flowers. Copper-eyed owls spied on us from the swinging branches of oak and evergreen trees, an occasional silver ant crawling up my boots.

Tain found a portion of the wall that was so weathered, it was easy to grip. We mounted it effortlessly, and a flavor of familiarity etched into me the first real emotion I'd felt since the previous evening.

I'm home.

My boots touched the ground. The stretch of farms sprawled into the distance, the round moonhouses looked ready to roll down the Mounds like pebbles, and the cool moonbeams in the vast stretch of greenery greeted me. Farm animals were already asleep, but the hills otherwise vibrated with life. They vibrated with the things I grew up around—clanking wind chimes, fragrant piles of hay, swaying colorful clothes on the racks, and the whiff of nettle tea.

"Take the lead," Tain said, and his face lit up. "I am dying to see the view you spoke so highly of."

I wrapped my arm around his, pointing southeast. "The view will have to wait a bit. There is something I need to do first."

"That was not a part of our deal," he protested, coming to a halt.

I tugged at his elbow, pulling him along. "What deal? I said I'd show you the view, and I will. Don't worry, I am not taking us to see my family."

"I'm not worried about that."

"Then what?" I uttered. "You always ask me to trust you. Now it's your turn to trust me."

Tain was reluctant at first, but he tentatively walked behind me. I decided it was best to follow the clamor of the nearby river fork, knowing it would take us exactly where I wanted to go. Choosing to cross the hills through the woods, I hoped we wouldn't be seen. Although a small part of me wanted to run into Aubren and give him a good shake for betraying me.

Rebels do as rebels wish, and they always get their way.
Not anymore.

In spite of returning to my part of the city, to the same old, familiar hills, I was no longer the same. I left the Mounds a naïve, wide-eyed girl of eighteen without an idea of what the rest of my world was like. I returned to them in the uniform underneath my cloak, with the prince beside me, yet what little part of me could feel wished that I had never left the comfort of my home or family.

"We're here," I whispered. A mid-sized moonhouse, veiled in moonlight, rested inside a neatly kept yard, sprinkled with blue marigolds.

Summer's favorite flowers.

Tain's eyes narrowed to the slits of gray mist. "Who lives here? What are you doing?"

I tossed a small rock at Summer's window, where the attic was. Then another. A candle lit up behind the blood-colored curtains, and not a minute passed before a burgundy crown of curls stepped out from the round doorway. Summer advanced towards us in her night robe, stopping beyond the yard entrance.

I slipped my hood off. Tain did the same upon realizing she was frightened; she was staring at strangers wrapped in midnight from head to toe.

"What are *you* doing here?" she asked, crossing her arms.

My feelings continued to come back at the sound of her voice, the memories of our childhood flashing in front of me: our first day at school, the day she broke her ankle climbing a tree, and when I carried her home. The first cup of wine we shared in the woods where our parents couldn't find us.

"I came to see you and make sure you are well."

Summer pursed her lips. "Yes? How thoughtful of you! You are about two months late, Imani."

I bit on the inside of my cheek, taking a step towards her. She backed away in an instant.

"I would have come earlier if I could."

She pointed her chin at Tain. "Who is this?"

"He is a member of my legion," I said awkwardly. "His name is Tain."

Summer squinted, bringing her face closer to inspect him, before gaping. "Tain? Like Prince Tain?"

I guess I was the only one clueless about him.

Tain bowed in a prince-like fashion, and I wanted to slap him. "It is an honor to meet you."

He chooses to be a kind-hearted prince now of all times?

Summer backed away another step. "You come here at night and bring *him*? Are you out of your wits? They already suspect I am one of *your* kind!"

My kind.

"But you aren't," I said.

Summer's hands shot up. "I thought you weren't either! But the rebels didn't believe me. They questioned me and my entire family for three days after you left!"

I swallowed, looking at her bronze-kissed face. Summer's full lips quivered with rage, but her gaze was cold and unfamiliar. Something inside me cracked open, crumbling the wall that kept away my feelings.

"I didn't leave, I was chased by no one but Aubren!" I told her, my tone sharpening. "You said he was Senar's friend, not a damn rebel! If I didn't run, he would have killed me."

She brushed a burgundy curl from her face. "I didn't know he was a rebel, just like I didn't know you were…"

"A starlight bender?" I interrupted.

She blinked away a tear, twisting one side of her mouth. "You know what hurts, Imani? You put me in danger all those years without telling me. We grew up together, for moons' sake! And what's even worse—I wouldn't have cared, and I would've let them torture me, if need be, before giving you up. Yet, you still chose to lie to me. You were my closest friend, and I didn't know the first thing about you. And that hurts."

I shifted my weight to my heels, my eyes falling to the ground. "Mother didn't allow me to…"

Summer smacked her lips, cutting me off. "Your mother didn't allow you to tell me? Is this the same mother who didn't let you run to the walls or drink wine when you were sixteen? The same mother who would've grounded you for a year if she saw us blowing up potions in the woods? Oh yes, *prince*, your little girlfriend here did all those things with me!" Anger warped her features, and I thought she may hit me, if Summer had a violent bone in her body in the first place. But she never did. "You *chose* not to tell me. And now you get to live with that choice. Goodnight, Imani. Don't come back here."

I tried calling for her, but she wouldn't hear it. My childhood friend stormed back inside her moonhouse, taking the years of our friendship away with her.

The emotions kept rushing up my throat, searching for a way out. I drew an exhausted breath, twisting my neck up to the skies, gazing at the moons.

At least Tora and Shei will always have each other.

Tain's fingers caressed my back. "Imani…"

I pushed his hand away. "Don't say a word. I've had enough of everyone's pity for a lifetime. Let's go, we have one more stop to make."

He did not protest that time around, following me quietly into the yard of a different moonhouse. Purple curtains veiled its windows, the squirrels nibbling on the walnuts Zana had left on the doorstep for them.

I knocked once, and she answered within seconds. The teller often dwelled deep into the night, studying moon charts or reading myths with a cup of rum by her side.

"Is it really you?" Zana cupped my face, her emerald eyes sparkling, pressing her moon-tattooed forehead against mine before noticing Tain. "I am so glad to see you. Who is your friend here?" She flashed her eyebrows inquisitively.

"This is Prince Tain," I said to avoid another awkward introduction. "And he is here for a reading."

Zana gaped, then masked her reaction with a grin, welcoming us in. Tain leaned in, speedily blinking an *are-you-out-of-your-mind* grimace at me. I failed to acknowledge him on purpose, stepping through the circular doorway.

Mimi, Zana's firebird, was asleep in her cage, but everything else looked as it always did. Cushions of comfort, air flavored with myrrh, colorful embroidery on the second-hand furniture, and clothing housing years of my memories.

Another drop of my feelings seeped in.

Zana shuffled the cards after pouring us each a cup of nettle tea. Fortunately for both Tain and me, the tea was spiked heavy-handedly. I was back in my habitat, but he was completely taken out of his, squeamishly throwing his cloak over the chair. Still, I liked seeing him there, in the hills I called home. A legionnaire or not, I remained a Mounds girl at heart, and I wanted him to know that part of me.

We sat around the tea table, and Zana complimented the way the legionnaire uniform fit me. "Have you gone to see your mother?" she asked, scattering cards around the tabletop.

I shook my head, hoping she wouldn't ask why. I was not prepared to tell her that I had learned the cause of Zuri's sickness, which she surely knew already. Mother and Zana had no secrets, which was the foundation of their decades long friendship.

I can't lie to my friends ever again, not even for their own good.

"I am glad you didn't go home, I'd advise against it," Zana judged. "The rebels are watching your house day and night, hoping you'll return. Don't fret, they haven't harmed your parents or Zuri, but they will surely harm you."

"They can try," Tain muttered through his teeth, putting his cup down with force, making both Zana and me twitch. "Imani here is not to be messed with."

My lips cracked into the first resemblance of a smile ever since I was told about the sibling's curse.

Stay focused. You have a task at hand.

"Is that so?" Zana chuckled. "Well, I am glad to hear that. Her mother will be most pleased. Now, dear, pick a card. Let your intuition guide your finger, not the other way around," she repeated the familiar instructions. "You get to draw three times."

Tain repositioned himself uncomfortably, too well-mannered to refuse her.

I counted on that.

"This one," he said after hovering his hand over the starlight-colored deck Zana chose for the occasion.

She flipped the card, revealing Kirrah's face.

"Strange," she said, tapping her chin. "Only the powerful starlight benders ever draw this card, though it is usually the last one they pick. Few have drawn the goddess first over the years, your mother being one of them."

His mother?

Tain straightened up, adjusting the sleeves of the light gray shirt that stuck to his arms without much room to breathe. "My mother? My mother doesn't believe in telling."

Zana winked. "No?"

His mouth pulled into a soft smile, and he shook his head in disbelief.

"Are you saying you read the queen's future? Does Mother know?" I asked. "What did the cards say?"

She motioned stitching her lips. "The teller never tells, you know the saying. One's future is only for the ears of those who were present to hear it. I only shared that one draw because both of you already know the queen can bend starlight. The whole world knows that."

Amusement broke across Tain's face. "I will never let her hear the end of this."

He picked another card. Cutting eyes framed by the sharp cheekbones of a young, short-haired woman stared from its front seductively, a knife clutched in her hand.

"Oooh, interesting!" Zana's emerald-green eyes alighted, the candlelight making her ashen face appear blue. She licked the rum off her lips with one swipe of her tongue. "You drew Ilma, also known as the Hidden Lover. Anything you wish to confess while we are here?"

When I thought about taking Tain to see Zana, I failed to consider her delightful albeit bold nature and probing eyes. She couldn't only tell one's future from the cards—she could also read their faces.

Tain blushed and he ignored her question. "Why is she holding a knife?"

Zana grinned. "Well, you said it yourself. She is not to be messed with."

I laughed, brushing my shoulder against Tain's. He flinched but tried to hide it by reaching for his cup.

"Alright, alright, let's get this over with." He chose the last card. I was not familiar with the draw despite sitting through hundreds of tellings over the years.

Zana stared at the tarot card with a creased brow. A portrait of a young man was painted on the front. He held a stone in one hand, a flower in the other. "This card is known as the Wanderer. You will have a tough choice ahead of you, a choice between two paths. You will do well to think hard before making it."

"And why is that?" Tain asked.

"Because one choice will lead you towards everything you have ever wanted, and the other will mean your end."

"That was thrilling, I'll give you that. Though I don't really believe in telling," Tain said after we left Zana's moonhouse, starting for the edge of the hills.

The teller only let us depart after asking every question she could think of first, serving as Mother's mouthpiece. Was I feeling well? How were they treating me? Was I drinking water? Was I eating enough green vegetables and meat? Was I sleeping well? What was the Old Town like? Had bending been draining? Had I patrolled the city yet? Had I received Mother's packages? Was I mixing my ointments? And so on. I answered them the best I could while having Tain there to listen.

Zana carefully observed the movements of my face, gazing deeply into mine. It seemed as though she could tell something was not adding up, having known me my entire life. We hugged before Tain and I departed her doorstep, and I slipped a piece of parchment into one of her many pockets.

I'd scribed the letter to Mother before leaving the base.

"Do not worry, Mother. I am well. As well as one can be while training day and night. But I am getting better, and I can protect myself now. Again, I don't want you to worry, but there is something you should know. The high priestess of Kirrah's temple made me drink a magic-bound healer's aid, numbing my feelings. They are slowly coming back. It's a long story. My starlight teacher said you could be in danger. Keep your eyes wide open, and hug Zuri and Father for me. I'll make things right from the other side of the silver gates. I love you."

I could resist going to see my family, but there was no way in the world I was coming to the Mounds without leaving a word for Mother.

"Zana is quite something, isn't she?" I asked, wondering how much Tain knew: about the ancestors' secret, the Akani, whatever danger Miss Yamane spoke of.

Get close to him.

We reached the edge of the Mounds, passing by Vasin's farm. The drift of spiced air lingered by us, and Tain's nostrils flared.

"Your first time in the Mounds?" I asked.

He wagged his chin. "No, I've been up the hills before. Just not like this."

"You say you want to be a king," I began, tossing my cloak over a wet patch of grass and lowering myself onto it. Tain did the same, settling down a hair away from me. "Maybe you should watch people from other parts of the city, not just the Old Town."

The reflection of Lumenor swam in Tain's eyes, his face enamored with the expanse of the city in front of him: the sunken, centuries-old roads and houses of the Gutter, merchant stores and markets of the Cobblestone, and the manors and palace inside the Old Town.

"You were right. This is the most beautiful sight I've ever laid my eyes on." His gaze paused at my lips. "Thank you for bringing me here. I mean it."

The flicker of a flame kindled in my stomach, only to disappear the very next second. "My pleasure."

His face grew bone-pale. "I am really sorry, you know. About your sister."

Another sliver of pain plunged its sharp edge into my chest like a blade. "I'd rather not talk about that now."

Tain's palm fell on mine, his fingers weaving their way into the gaps between my knuckles. His fingers were warm and callused from combat. I locked my hand inside his. We said nothing for a while, my mind wrestling the slowly returning feelings so much so that I began to crave another sip of the magic healer's aid.

I gathered my thoughts and proceeded with the plan.

I have him in my palm quite literally.

"You know what's really sad?" I asked softly.

"What?"

I tightened my fingers around his. "All of this, our beautiful ancient city, may become but the crumbles of ruins in four weeks. Centuries of history erased in one day."

Tain's jaws stiffened, the acute lines of his face casting shadows onto the grass. "I told you I won't let that happen. No matter the price."

Empty promises again.

"How can you be so sure? We know so little about the Akani. Why are they after the starlight crystals if they can't bend themselves? Of what use is the moonstone to them?"

"They simply don't want us to have it," he replied in a half-whisper, staring ahead. "Away from the moonstone, our power wouldn't vanish, but it would decrease."

He is not telling the whole truth.

I know there is more to it.

I paused to think on how to phrase my next question without seeming too eager. "I still don't understand why warriors from the other corner of the world care about us? We don't invade or start wars, and we trade. Lumenor has done nothing wrong to the rest of the world!"

Tain glanced at me suspiciously, growing impatient. "This is not about us. What do you expect from killers whose only common cause is to invade and steal? We don't need to know their reasons, we only need to know how to defeat them."

I clicked my tongue.

He is stubborn or simply accustomed to telling half-truths.

"How do we defeat them, while we are at it? Kelpies, the ancient blade, immunity to starlight—"

"Sei," he said. "Not starlight."

That was the first time he'd corrected me.

I bit into my tongue. "You didn't answer my question," I pressed on. "How do we defeat them? What does your mother have to say about all of this?"

Tain's fingers unraveled from my hand. "You know everything I know, you tell me. It is getting late, anyway. We should head back to the base."

"Fine," I said, and snatched my cloak from underneath him.

Chapter XV
Tora's Chamber

"That bastard!" Shei cried out, stabbing her fork into a roasted piece of cayenne-spiced chicken breast. We were alone with Cella and Raina in the dining hall. All other legions were busy training, and the boys were gone, attending their sei lessons. "I knew Tain was going to remain tight-lipped! Tell me once more about his reading."

I sighed, rubbing my temples. "We already went over it thrice. He drew Kirrah first, then the Hidden Lover, and lastly the Wanderer. That combination can mean many different things. Besides, even Zana says that the cards can be misinterpreted easily."

I didn't want to admit it to Shei, but I'd wondered about Tain's last draw myself.

What kind of choice will he have to make?

"I would really like to meet this teller lady," Cella mumbled, cutting roasted broccoli seasoned with imported lemon zest. "I want to deepen my tarot reading abilities."

Zana would love that.

"I'd be glad to take you to her after the battle," I said, swallowing a spoonful of herby mushroom stew. Chunks of beef and carrots swam to the surface, colliding with the sprinkles of parsley.

"Focus," Raina shouted. "We have more important things to discuss than some fortune telling!"

"You need to wait before you question Tain again," Shei said with her mouth full. "But what do we do in the meantime? Try sneaking into the queen's chambers once again?"

I pushed the empty stew bowl away, taking one last bite of the freshly baked rye bread. "Even I am not that eager to get killed. Raina, did you talk to your father yet? He must know someone inside the Old Town who is familiar with ancient history."

Raina rolled her eyes. "I have. He scolded me for an hour about sneaking into Queen Astra's chambers before telling me to drop the matter altogether," she complained. "He said he will look into it on his own. He wants me safe."

Sounds familiar.

"He also told me to watch out for Lazzor and to keep my mind on the battle, like I am some stupid child," she continued, crossing her arms.

"Lazzor!" I jumped out of my chair. "We can really be thick sometimes. Who reads more historical tomes than him? He must know who scribes them!"

Cella slapped her forehead. "Why didn't I think of him?"

"It might be your turn now to use your charms." I winked at Raina.

She scoffed, grimacing sourly. "I'd rather choke to death. I can just ask him. Unlike your prince, Lazzor doesn't have divided loyalties."

"To be fair, we don't know that Tain has divided loyalties either," I retorted. "We are only assuming."

Shei scowled at me but said nothing.

"I will go find Lazzor and report back in the morning," Raina spoke before leaving the hall.

"I must go, too," I muttered and began making my own exit. "I'll be late for my sei lesson."

"Good luck!" Cella's voice trailed behind me.

―――

Miss Yamane was already in the courtyard when I arrived. The titanium shields stood posted all around, reflecting the faint radiance of the late evening. We trained at night at times to hone my precision in low visibility. Stars twinkled above our heads, the constellation of Aries coming into Lumenor's view on the clear eve.

I cleared my throat. "You claim I am in danger."

My sei instructor licked her peach-painted lips that contrasted with the sapphire shirt she was wearing. "Good evening, Imani. Our session tonight will take place elsewhere. Follow me."

"No." My boots rested firmly on the patch of dirt-packed ground. "What danger am I in? What about my family? You said they could be in trouble, too. I am not going anywhere before you tell me."

It was not proper to give attitude to an elder, let alone to the one who trained me—a person of authority. Mother would have upbraided me in an instant. However, Miss Yamane had me poisoned with magic two nights prior, after all, and that would earn her much harsher punishment from Mother than a few cold remarks.

"Both you and your family will be in danger if you don't learn to contain your sei," Miss Yamane whispered at last, inching a step closer.

My mouth twisted in confusion. "My sei? What does my power have to do with that magic poison you made me drink?"

Miss Yamane's features stiffened, folding into a sour frown. "Don't blame me for your recklessness." She took an intentional pause, waiting for her words to sink in. "And yes, I would have shoved the magic-bound healer's aid down your throat if you'd refused. Astra's orders."

My blood ran cold. "The queen is behind it?"

"Who else?" Miss Yamane snapped. "You nearly crushed an entire building when you'd heard about the sibling's curse. If Raina had not been there to deflect your sei…!" She trailed off. "Your actions have consequences, child. Learn before it is too late."

The sibling's curse.

I dug my fingernails into the soft flesh of my palms at the thought of it.

"You can't blame me for being shocked. My sister is dying for Kirrah's sake!"

Miss Yamane's eyebrows leapt up the same way Mother's did whenever I talked back. "I cannot blame you for feeling sad, that is natural, but I can blame you for not being able to control yourself. I have taught you better. You could have hurt someone, the potential future queen of Lumenor included. Whether she likes it or not, Astra must protect Izaak's girl from harm as much as she protects her boy. It is the law."

"But I didn't hurt anyone!" My palms shot up to the skies. "And it was Raina who redirected my starlight, just as you said. I couldn't hurt her of all people, even if I tried!"

Miss Yamane's head shook in disappointment—I did not relish seeing my instructor's face with such an expression. "And if she'd not been there? How many people could you have injured or killed?" she asked. The pin in her sapphire-hued hair caught the moonlight, glowing like a pearl from the depths of the sea. "The queen's reaction is inappropriate, I agree, but her concerns are not. Your power is out of your control at times, which brings me back to our lesson. Follow me and stop whining. Time to grow up, girl."

I was not sure which Miss Yamane I preferred—the gentle, encouraging one, or the one who told things as they were, without a trace of embellishment.

She does have a point. I could have hurt someone.

"Where are we going? I asked.

"To Tora's Chamber, of course," she replied, walking towards the courtyard exit.

I stalked her eagerly.

Visiting Tora's Chamber was one invitation I would have been mad to refuse, even if Kalon himself was there waiting for me. How could I say no to seeing one of the crystals that powered the world with starlight? Goosebumps prickled my skin just thinking about it.

Miss Yamane's silhouette cast a shadow on the walls as she led me through the heavy doors in the basement corridor which were usually locked and guarded. The guards were still there, but they let us through without a word.

I walked behind my sei teacher in silence, the blue silks of her skirts dragging across the floor like waves on a shore. With every step we made, the air became warmer, more humid, until we were entirely immersed in a cloud of translucent mist, similar to the one dwelling inside Cella's crystal ball. Miss Yamane took my hand, guiding me blindly through its jasmine-scented glint.

A marble archway thirty feet in height towered over our heads once we passed through, opening to a slippery, pale bridge without rails. Tora's Chamber was surrounded by five arches, and from each one spawned a bridge barely wide enough for three people to cross at once. Colorful gemstones patterned the arches on the inside, representing each of the starlight crystals—moonstone, emerald, citrine, sapphire, and ruby.

The chamber was built entirely from marble and reached the heights of the base's rooftop. A constellation of the starlight goddess stretched across the ceiling, marking the location where Kirrah's palace was believed to reside amongst the star lands. The bridges met in the center, merging into a round platform. From a whirlpool of haze emitted a pale corona of light around a glimmering object in the center.

The moonstone.

I peered over the bridge in front of us before crossing. The pool of endless darkness from the abyss chilled my neck, and I instinctively stepped away from it.

"There is nothing to fear," Miss Yamane said, proceeding to cross the bridge as though she were taking a leisurely stroll across the Old Town. "Falling into it will not kill you. You would simply be trapped in a dream-like state until you were rescued. Only, there would be no dreams, just an emptiness of the mind."

I leaned over again—it was just as bone-chilling as the first time. "How can anyone survive such a fall?"

The answer was obvious in retrospect. "Ancient magic," she replied.

I stayed as far from both edges as the narrow passing allowed, focusing instead on putting my feet in front of one another without straying.

I really despise heights.

The platform on the other side of the bridge grew larger with each step.

The moonstone's proximity had an effect on me—my hands were hot like burning timbers, my chest vibrating with excess energy. A flood of emotions contorted my muscles, condensing everything I should have been feeling during the past two days into one minute. Pain, anger, and fear tore at me.

My Zuri.

I would do anything to reverse our roles and be the one who is dying instead.

"Breathe," Miss Yamane said, "the remaining traces of the potion in your body are denying you the link. Hopefully we can break them."

I fought an urge to bite my tongue, to pull my hair out of my skull. My feelings had returned, entangled inside the knot in my chest. "The link?"

"Yes, the link," she responded. "We came here to work on your linking, amongst other things. Before you can link to other sei-sans' power, you must learn to connect to the moonstone's first. Most of our kind have no trouble merging their sei with the one of the crystal, though the deed poses danger to them."

There is always a catch, isn't there?

"What kind of danger?" I asked.

Miss Yamane gestured that I follow her, disappearing into the whirlpool. I clenched my fists and tramped behind her reluctantly.

A lukewarm, yet harsh, blow fought my muscles as if trying to knock me off my feet and toss me out of reach—to prevent me from coming in. The stiffness of it beaded my skin, the flax of my uniform sticking to my limbs. My braid jerked in the wind, slapping at my cheek, and my palms beamed with starlight ready to burst out of me.

"There you are," Miss Yamane said once I came out on the other side, panting as if I had just finished running twenty laps around the pit.

My eyes were immediately drawn to the glowing crystal carved in the shape of a full moon. It rested atop a tall marble base. It was quite small to my surprise, small enough to fit into my palm. Smooth and silver and shimmering—it looked like Tora on a cloudless night. The moonstone emitted an intricate silver glow, like a single lantern in the night or the sun itself illuminating the entire planet with its rays. I grew stronger with each blink, standing speechless in front of it.

"You know now. You can feel it," Miss Yamane said in a voice that was two notes deeper than her usual tone. "I remember the first time I glanced upon the sapphire crystal in my father's palace, an experience that even a girl of six does not forget and keeps chasing for the rest of her life."

I fidgeted. "Umm, wait. Your father's palace?"

She sighed, waving me away. "I forget you are not from the Old Town sometimes. Yes, my father is the ruler of Moreo—the empire built on the shores of the Sapphire Sea."

I figured she had to be some sort of nobility from her manners, clothing, and speech. But a daughter of the western emperor?

"How long have you been in Lumenor?" I asked, my gaze diving into the depths of the moonstone, drowning in its beauty.

Miss Yamane's fingers touched the marble railing around the crystal, sliding across its smooth, wet surface. "Years."

"Since before the last expansion of the Ashen Desert?" I asked. "Is that why you are still here?"

Her features tightened, and she scoffed under her breath. "No pile of ash stops me from going anywhere. I am here because I choose to be."

Why would anyone choose to spend years away from their home?

"But why stay in Lumenor of all places? Won't you be an empress one day?" I asked, imagining Miss Yamane in the emperor's seat.

She swung to face me, the sapphire skirts stirring around her legs. "My sister is first in line for succession, not me. I have no interest in ruling. The truth is, I could care less about who presides over Lumenor, too. But I do care about what happens to the moonstone. I cannot leave until the battle has been won."

The battle.

I swallowed. We had about four weeks left until the Akani's estimated arrival, and I was yet to learn to link or deflect.

"I'm sorry about doubting you before," I said, the guilt flickering across my face. "But I know how the nobles see me—even the queen thinks of me as a simple hill girl not befitting her son's company. I should have known better than to loop you in with her."

The warm tips of Miss Yamane's fingers grazed my cheek. "Do you know what the nobles here think of me? Of my sisters?"

I shrugged.

"They deem us gentle like water lilies, soft-spoken, and harmless," she said, swallowing a bitter breath. "So I play my part, let them see what they want to see, and strike when they least expect. The fools never see it coming."

I chuckled, but caught myself nodding along. Miss Yamane was full of surprises. "I see."

"The way the others fail to see your shine is not your weakness, Imani. It is theirs. Use it against them."

Glancing back at the moonstone, the urge to touch it called upon me. "I will, I promise. Can I try to link to the moonstone now?"

A satisfied grin spread across Miss Yamane's fine features. "I will repeat before we begin—linking to the moonstone is incredibly dangerous. We have not spoken of it before, but do you have trouble letting go once you begin bending?"

How does she come to know everything?

I bobbed my head.

"Well, think of that feeling, then multiply it by a hundredfold. That is what it feels like to be one with any of the five sources of starlight but especially the moonstone. It is the crystal of strength, the most powerful of them all. At the moment, when the link feels unbreakable, when you think you can drink all of its magic, you must let go."

"Or, let me guess, I'll die?" I asked.

Her hand latched onto my wrist once more, pulling my hand towards the crystal. "That, or you will remove the crystal out of its base entirely."

I jerked my hand back with my mouth gaped. "The moonstone can be taken out of its base? What in the world is it still doing here?! We could just take it and hide it! Make a run with it, even!"

Miss Yamane laughed, and not in the way that implied she found my suggestion entertaining. "You are more than welcome to risk your life and give it a try. I would be careful in your place, though. Even Izaak's girl and Astra's boy refrain from it, and those two are as pompous as they come. And they don't attempt such a deed for a good reason. Death is one state no amount of magic can bring you back from. It is not worth the risk. Besides, Astra would have you killed before you made it out of the legion's base. You are powerful, but you are not powerful enough to duel an entire city of sei-sans alone. No one is."

Bringing my fingers a hair closer to the moonstone, I tugged them back once again. "Is that how Kalon stole Vatrion's ruby crystal? By linking to it?"

"Kalon is not a sei-san, none of the Akani are. He deploys a different tactic."

Miss Yamane must know about the ancestors' secret!

I couldn't blurt my question out fast enough. "What tactic? Do you know anything about the secret he threatened to tell the world?" I asked before sucking my breath in.

"Better question is how do you know about such affairs?" Mis Yamane arched a brow.

"You didn't answer my question."

"Of course I know," she snapped, looking down at me as though I asked if the stars were bright or flames hot.

I gasped. "Well? What is it?"

My sei teacher pointed her nose towards the moonstone suggestively. "Your job here is to learn, not meddle with matters that are not yours to meddle with. Astra will not kill you over your untamed power, but she will certainly murder you over the secret." I peeled my lips back, ready to retort, but Miss Yamane shushed me before I could say anything. "We need you alive for the battle so eyes back on the moonstone. Enough chattering. Hover your palm over the crystal, a little closer, that is good."

Ugh.

Holding my hand above the moonstone burned as if I held it over a raging flame, yet it didn't harm my skin. The magic of life coiled with heat, the crystal beaming with starlight, almost reaching back for me.

"Now, close your eyes," Miss Yamane instructed. "Don't look at the moonstone, touch it. And not with your hand. Linking is the matter of spirit, not of mind or body. Feel it. Bend its force to your will."

I knew what she meant, what I needed to do to accomplish it. Starlight was not just inside the moonstone—it was everywhere around me. Inside Miss Yamane, inside the air, inside every crumb of matter that ever came to life. And as a sei-san, I had the power to summon it.

Calming my breathing, I called upon the crystal wordlessly. Releasing but a trickle of my own magic, I twirled my fingers, interlocking my own threads with starlight that surrounded me. I didn't need anything but my sixth sense to guide me through the process—I instinctively knew what to do. I kept drawing, but for the first time ever, I was not drawing only from within.

With a look of bliss on my face, my mind bent a growing sphere of magic around us. It felt so effortless, so easy.

Why would anyone ever draw from within if they can do this?

I was finally bending starlight that originated outside of my own body, and I liked the feeling of it. Loved it. I felt as though I could breathe life into the rest of the world. As though I could turn into Kirrah herself, if only I remained linked to the moonstone long enough.

Miss Yamane rocked my shoulder. "That is enough, let go."

Just one more minute.

"Imani! Right now!"

But it's so magnificent.

"Don't make me say it one more time!"

Ugh.

I begrudgingly let go of the crystal and of all the starlight my mind was bending, shivering as though I'd ripped the clothes off my back or the food out of my belly. Only the emptiness remained behind, an emotional and physical ache, my body and mind going through withdrawal already.

The sphere vanished back into the moonstone as if it was never there in the first place, feeding the crystal with my magic. I wiggled my fingers, realizing I had not drained myself one bit. In fact, I could have started bending again immediately if need be.

"You will need to exercise more control, but I am otherwise satisfied with your skill given that it was your first time," Miss Yamane said. "How do you feel?"

I cast a confident glance at her. "I may never become good at aiming, but linking… linking I can master."

Chapter XVI
The Scriber

Knife-throwing in the midst of hot summer day was no easy feat.

"Lazzor gave me the name," Raina whispered before rushing towards her designated aiming station, fanning her face to escape the heat.

A swoosh of a flying knife passed by my ear. I turned around to find Shei giggling.

"You know I hate when you do that," I snapped. Lazzor began laughing behind her, half-bent over and holding his stomach. "Don't laugh—you're only encouraging her," I hissed before turning back to Shei. "What if you miss?"

Shei shrugged. "I don't miss."

Commander Izaak called upon the legion, motioning us to get into place. The day was so warm and sunny—it forced him to strip to short-sleeved linens. "The first one of you to hit the center of their target seven times in a row gets a morning off. Shei does not count."

She immediately tossed her arms up in the air. "That's unfair!"

"Deal with it," Commander grunted. "You've had plenty of free mornings while your peers trained for years."

That was his favorite comeback whenever Shei or I lodged complaints. Unfortunately for us, he was right.

Tain positioned himself next to me, facing a wooden plank in the distance. The targets were marked with concentric circles drawn with white paint, and indented from throwing. "That's one!" He started a count, showcasing his precision with one aim.

Gutter-born after all.

Raina aimed on the other side, working hard to best him. "Two over here!" When I started paying attention, no longer burdened by constant aches, the two of them never failed to find a way to compete. No matter how menial of a task, each had to win favor over the other.

Tain hit the center of the target once again after running to fetch what he claimed to be his lucky knife. "I'm right behind you."

Not interested in adding any logs to their fire, I pulled one of the throwing blades out of my belt and tried to concentrate. The knife was entirely made from palace-forged steel, without a pommel to hold onto. Light as air, it was dull-edged but sharp at the peak. Designed for aiming.

Any blade could be thrown with or without the spin. Only Shei, Tain, and Raina could aim without one. I had to focus on the amount of spin I was releasing based on the distance of the target, which was immensely challenging. Shei recommended I grip the blade by its dull edges instead of the smooth steel handle, which helped a bit.

Being left-handed, I put my right foot in front like she taught me.

Aim, pull back, release.

The knife left my hand, spinning around its axis once before it buried itself in the mark at the very center of the plank. A cheer left my throat. I grabbed another blade out of my belt, leaning into position once again. I released too late on the following try, and the dull side of the blade bounced against the wood with a thump.

"You're flicking your wrist too much," Shei noted, throwing three knives in a row at rampant speed without missing.

"Thanks," I said, focusing on my next aim. "Yes! I did it! Did you see that?"

She released another blade with the focus of a hunting blood-eagle. "I did. Good job! See, you'll be a fine thrower before the battle begins, just like the many Lumenorans before us."

Knife-throwing had been leveraged ever since more of us began bending starlight, replacing the longsword from ancient battles. Only a fool would be mad enough to approach a starlight bender within arm's reach. And since sei-sans couldn't bend without draining themselves eventually, they needed to learn to aim knives, too. The tactic proved itself rather useful for the upcoming battle against Akani Warriors, who were unbothered by starlight, carrying longswords and shields we didn't know how to wield. Commander kept reminding us to resist bending at their gear unless they were close enough to harm us in order to prevent ourselves from draining.

"Seven in a row! I have seven!" Raina cried out.

"Eight over here." Tain smirked at her with his nose in the clouds.

"Liar! I didn't see you hit it eight times!"

Tain exhaled irritably. "It just so happens that your perception does not shape reality. I've hit my target eight times in a row, regardless if you have seen it or not."

"Whatever." Raina walked over to me with a pout on her face. "My room tonight after dinner. We will tell the boys we are sneaking out to the taverns, so splash some powder across your face. Wear all black, but dress for running just in case. Let Shei know, she can tell Cella."

"Who did Lazzor name?" I asked. "Where are we really going?"

Raina looked about to see if anyone was eavesdropping. "The hills of Old Town, where else? That's where all the old-blood historians live."

Clad in shadows and powders, I stepped out of my bedchamber to meet the girls.

"Enjoy yourselves, ladies," Lazzor said after the four of us crept past him, leaving our legion's quarters. Tain, on the other hand, was nowhere to be found. He hadn't said a word to me ever since we'd returned from the Mounds.

Don't think about him now.

Cella adjusted the obsidian choker that tightly hugged her neck, shutting the salon doors behind us. "I don't like lying to Lazzor."

"You don't like lying to anyone," Shei said.

The rich black silk of Raina's pants curved with her lean muscles as she led the way down the mineral-sparkling hallways. A distant hum of the harp vibrated alongside the tone of her voice. "We had to lie. Lazzor is all about the legion sticking together. He trusts Tain."

I gave a nod to a passing legionnaire, remaining silent until he vanished behind the corner. "Then what did you tell Lazzor when you asked about the scriber?"

"I didn't tell him anything. I simply asked him," Raina replied. "I told you already—Lazzor trusts me."

Shei clicked her tongue, trotting behind us alongside Cella. "He'll learn his lesson sooner or later."

Raina brushed her remark off, having grown accustomed to Shei's teasing. We snuck out of the base at last. The Old Town was quiet, lacking the usual clamor and music. Something felt out of place, but I told myself it was all in my head. Now that I was no longer under the influence of the potion, I wished it hadn't worn off when it did.

I can't believe I let Tain lead me through the Old Town hills so nonchalantly!

The scarce groups of nobles bowed their necks to us in passing, especially after recognizing Raina. The closer we got to the battle, the more fearful everyone became. I didn't feel particularly bad for them, knowing that the elites would be the last to suffer if things went sour. The people of the Gutter and the Mounds would have to deal with the Akani's wrath first, and I didn't see the Old Towners losing sleep over it.

The gloomy veil of night covered the hills, giving them an ominous look. The scriber that Lazzor named resided in the far west, which Raina was not too happy about.

"That's where all the old mad-heads live," she had claimed. She'd also asked me to braid my hair differently, recommending a halo braid popular amongst the Old Town's ladies. We couldn't afford to be found out by the old blood families or their monsters. Cella forced Shei to dress in her never-ending supply of black garments, which Shei complained about the entire time. Apparently, the silk was too soft and too slippery down her arms and legs.

"If anyone asks, you are from here. Remember my address, the back story?" Raina inquired for the tenth time. "These knuckleheads don't want those they consider strangers roaming the hills, legionnaires or not."

"They sound lovely," Shei sighed. "Let's mount the hills."

Cella and I climbed the inner most mound behind Raina and Shei. The plan was for Shei and I to stick with one of them if we were forced to separate, as both Raina and Cella came from prominent families and could vouch for us. Despite being legionnaires fighting to preserve their lush, comfortable lives, we were still not welcome.

I should have stayed in the Mounds and let them fend for themselves!

A wail echoed from the depths of the hills, pulling me away from my thoughts. The gut-wrenching sound made my teeth clatter. It was twisted, loud—unnatural.

Shei shuddered. "What in Kirrah's sky was that?"

"Probably one of their beasts," Raina replied in an even tone.

"Beasts? What do you mean, beasts?" Shei glanced wide-eyed at me over her shoulder.

I rolled my eyes, puffing. "The nobles keep creatures they've caught from the Ashen Desert for entertainment."

"I feel bad for the creatures," Shei squealed.

Cella shushed her, pressing a finger against her black-painted lips. "Lower your voice and look ahead. This is no time for questioning. We don't have a choice. We must go on."

The hills of Old Town were unsettling. Manors hid behind their high, pointed fences, and everything we could see looked as though it were still stuck in the last century. The small, uphill alley we plodded through was deathly silent and tucked between two long rows of merchant shops. Cobblestones rolled beneath our feet and a tall, ebony tree forked two narrow carriage lanes. Something shrieked again, startling Shei.

"Moons curse this ghostly place," she muttered, twisting her neck to face the wind. "I want to go back."

A doll swung from the merchant store sign ahead. She was very life-like, both in size and appearance. Her silver hair was braided into a halo, just like mine at that very moment, and her skin was painted a warm shade of deep brown. She'd been built with long limbs and had been given black eyes that peered from a narrow face. Her bowed lips pouted not unlike my own.

I was not the only one to notice the resemblance.

"That's odd," Cella said, pointing upward. "That doll kind of looks like Imani."

Shei squinted, gazing up while the shadows danced on her daylight-colored face. "How splendid, you can earn coin by posing for them once the battle is over!"

I chuckled, slightly uneasy with the apparent similarity. "No, thank you. Besides, I doubt they would want that. What if the children turned out like me?"

"Good point," Shei said. Then, she swirled sei in her hand and pierced the doll's face with the flick of her wrist. "There it goes—now she won't have to suffer the will of some spoiled brat."

Raina grabbed the silk on Shei's back, yanking her aside. "You bloody fool! Must we alert everyone that we are here?"

A candle wick flickered from the top floor of one of the shops, and my skin prickled.

"Come on, hurry! And get a grip, will you?" Cella urged. "We don't want to be seen, but we must not run. Shei, slow down!"

"I told you we should have left her behind," Raina mumbled.

"Too bad you couldn't," Shei said, cupping her shoulder playfully. "You're stuck with me."

Raina smacked her lips, but she didn't shove her away.

Hill after hill, distant cries echoed into the night. Clusters of trees reached for the skies, rooted in rolling blades of grass. Low evergreen bushes rustled, causing me to flinch every other minute. Squirrels ran past us, always in the opposite direction. Even the air was foul with the stench of rotting flesh. The further we advanced into the belly of the beast, the quieter and more gut-wrenching our surroundings became.

As if the Old Town wasn't blood-curdling enough already.

"Where does this man live, in the desert?" Shei asked, gritting her teeth.

"Shhh, we are almost there," Raina's voice dropped to a whisper. "The last manor to the right."

We came upon a flat hilltop where three manors hung to each side of the cobblestone path. Their fences were lower than the others, and we could see the upper floor of each house. Most had no candles or lanterns burning inside, looking deserted—left behind in the past like a grim, fading memory.

Raina knocked on the fence door of what Lazzor claimed to be the scriber's manor, only to find it unlocked. "This is not a good sign."

"Fine, let's head back," Shei said, turning around, but Raina pushed inside to her disappointment. "I guess not."

The front yard of the manor had overgrown with weeds and wildflowers. The manor itself was in no formidable shape, with silky webs of dust sticking to the corners of the entrance. Then, light illuminated the room behind heavy emerald curtains on the floor above.

Cella blinked. "Someone is upstairs."

"Well, thank Kirrah we didn't come all this way for nothing," Raina said and walked through the front door.

The scriber's manor was so neglected, it looked like a disposal of old items for burning. The walls were practically peeling off, shedding layers of skin. The glass tears of a chandelier dangled in what was once the reception hall, some pieces broken and lying across a carpet caked with grime. We had to watch our steps to avoid getting broken glass stuck in the soles of our boots. Once blue furniture had turned brown and gray, and everything appeared as though it had come from one of my nightmares or Mother's scary stories.

Maybe the Mounds' tales were true after all.

"Who comes my way?" The voice of an old man rasped from the upper floor.

Cella pulled at her choker, speaking in a high-pitched, innocent tone. "Just four friendly Old Towners, sir. No reason to worry!"

We ascended the carpeted staircase, trying not to touch anything in our way. The upper floor reeked of burned papyrus and the saccharine scent of perfume oils. Cella led the charge, being the most polite of the four of us. If anyone had a chance of getting on the scriber's good side, it was her. Needless to say, we made Shei and Raina go at the tail, since they were not so successful at masking their scowls.

Cella pushed the door timidly, and the four of us entered the chamber in file.

Azure flames lit up the only room in the entire manor that looked like it belonged in our century. Flawless, fine velvet cloaked the windows. Rosemary-scented sheets stretched across a mattress in the corner, books piled high around it. The entire room was spacious and neat, holding more tomes and scrolls than the Mounds' library.

An old man of eighty or so had his spindly legs stretched out before himself, sitting on a round, knitted cushion. His face was ashen, his skin loose and paper-thin from the passage of time. The man's eyes were, however, warm and sharp, and they were the golden-brown color of the fall leaves. A heavy, leather-bound book lay split open on his knees.

"You come here, uninvited, and you bring a Mounds and a Gutter-born with you," he said, surveying each of us carefully. His gaze paused on our faces, observing our stances and clothing. "You must be in need."

I arched a brow. "How do you know where we are from?"

The man rose his palm slowly. "Please don't take it the wrong way, dear. I don't mind. I am only observing. And such things are easy for the trained eye to spot. It is the way you carry yourselves, if you insist."

The way we carry ourselves?

I didn't know if I should feel flattered or insulted.

"Why is your house in such poor shape?" Shei asked. Raina tugged at her sleeve with a glower. "What, I'm just asking!"

The scriber swallowed, his stare glued to the carpet. "Because I made enemies at the palace, and the retirement coin stopped coming. My safes are empty, gold given to my children who were stranded in the west. I have no one left to care for me, or the house, and I cannot manage to do it myself. My wife perished fifteen years ago, almost to the day."

He is all alone and lonely.

I scratched the side of my neck, rolling up the sleeves of my shirt to avoid looking at the scriber. Old Towner or not—we all deserve dignity. Even Shei's face dropped upon hearing his story.

"I will make sure you are taken care of once I become a queen," Raina uttered, blinking at a rapid pace.

The man's smile was a warm ray of sunlight. "That is *if* you become a queen. I appreciate the sentiment either way, dear. Raina, is it?"

Her chest perked up. "How do you know my name?"

"It is my job to know things and to ink them down," he replied with a curve in his upper lip. "Coin or no coin, my quill still works the same."

A grin spread across my face.

We found our scriber.

"So tell me," he said with growing curiosity in his voice, "why are you young ladies here?"

Shei puffed, getting comfortable in the cushions, stretching her legs out across the floor. "Because the queen is a hag."

The scriber burst into a throaty laughter at her words. "Gutter-born to her core."

Cella took a deep breath. "Get a grip, for Kirrah's sake, and leave the speaking part to me, alright?" She settled in one of the cushions beside Shei, and Raina and I followed her eagerly, our feet tired from all the climbing. "We came because we found a letter from the Akani Warriors inside the queen's chambers."

The man's sunken face froze before his smile widened into a beaming grin. "Oh, thrilling," he said, rubbing his hands against one another before taking hold of some fresh parchment and a quill. "What did the letter say?"

"It was from Kalon, their leader," I replied, and he jotted my answer down. "He threatened to take the moonstone and tell the whole world about our ancestors' secret unless the queen hands the crystal to him. Do you know what secret he was referring to?"

The scriber cupped his chin with a thinking face. "I can only guess."

"Well?" Raina tapped her thigh, impatient as always. "What is it?"

"Our ancestors' secret? Only thing that comes to mind was not much of a secret many years ago when it took place, but our scribes seem to forget to mention it nowadays," he replied.

Shei leaned forward. "Forget what exactly?"

"Only the biggest slaughter we committed in history, of course."

I paused mid-breath. *"We?"*

"Sei-sans, starlight benders, whichever you prefer. Yes, we. Don't let my old age fool you, I was once as potent as you kids. And it was our ancestors who put an entire nation to death in the name of life."

Kirrah have mercy on us.

Cella licked her lips, adjusting her choker once again. It was somewhat of a tick, her way of finding comfort. "And what nation was that?"

"The nation of mei-sans, of course," he replied, "or the midnight benders, if you will."

The midnight benders?

A moan brewed in my throat. "Umm, come again?"

Raina pressed both palms against her temples, rocking her torso back and forth. "Midnight benders are real?"

"You heard the man—it's mei-sans, not midnight benders!" I corrected.

I couldn't resist.

She pretended she didn't hear me. "Father used to scare me with their stories as a child whenever I misbehaved! I thought they were a children's tale."

The scriber gave her a dire stare. "Oh, they were real. As real as all of us sitting here."

Cella opened her mouth, then closed it. Then opened it again. "So the Akani are... midnight benders?"

"It would explain why they are immune to sei," I judged.

The old man shook his head. "That is where you are wrong, child. Even the strongest of mei-sans were not immune to sei. The Midnight Rider, the last of their kin, died from a pierce of sei through his chest. Our most potent sei-sans are not immune to mei, either."

Midnight Rider. A shudder ran down my spine. That was one of the cards I drew during my last reading with Zana.

He destroyed all life on earth once before—may his like never be seen in our lands again. He brings bad luck.

I swirled drying saliva in my mouth, almost choking on my own breath. How could he have destroyed the world if he was killed? And why did I draw his card the night before hearing about the Akani's invasion? There had to be some significance to it, no matter what the scriber said.

Raina sighed deeply. "Are you certain?"

The old man grimaced, looking offended by the question, and continued as though she never posed it. "Besides, if a potent mei-san destroyed Vatrion, we would know. No such secret could be kept. If they bent midnight to conquer our sister kingdom, only black tar would be left of the city. We would feel them coming, too. I am afraid something else is at play."

I didn't know if I felt better or worse for it. If the Akani Warriors were indeed midnight benders, at least we would know what we were up against, no matter how scary the thought was.

"Wait, what do you mean by we would *feel* them coming?" Raina asked.

The scriber set his parchment aside and closed the book on his lap. He seized another, heavier tome, flipping the pages with such care that only a true book lover would have the patience for. "A powerful sei-san will always feel a potent mei-san. It works both ways. If a horde of them was approaching, all our bones would fill with chill. And this summer has been rather hot and humid, wouldn't you agree?"

Something is still not adding up.

"But what about the ancient magic?" I asked, rubbing my flustered cheek. "Apparently, Kalon's mother is some kind of sorceress, and she forged him a magic-bound blade. Maybe they found a way to bring the midnight back? It would explain their motive, why they want the moonstone."

The scriber shook his head again with unshakeable conviction. "The presence of the moonstone would only weaken them in such a case. Just as the obsidian, onyx, hematite, jet stone, and black goldstone once weakened us. The five midnight crystals."

Cella ripped her obsidian choker off in dismay, the night-colored crystals digging into her skin. "*Once* weakened us?"

The scriber flipped another page filled with tiny, curving letters etched in black ink. "Yes. All five midnight crystals are gone today, of course."

This is only getting worse. The Akani are somehow tied to the midnight benders, no one can persuade me otherwise.

"But the ancient magic—" Cella began.

"Impossible, dear," he cut in without letting her finish. "People have tried for centuries. Just like starlight, midnight cannot be conjured in unnatural ways. There is no brew powerful enough to turn one into the death bringer."

Yet death is coming to our gates all the same.

"So we are back at the beginning," Shei said.

"I don't think so, not entirely at least," the scriber concluded. "Something tells me things are connected, only I cannot see in what way."

I sighed, my head swimming with more questions than ever before.

Kirrah help us.

Chapter XVII

Patrol

"Are you ready?" Shei asked, clipping the arrow brooches to my titanium-plated combat uniform on the eve of our first patrol. We only had three weeks left until the battle based off of the recent reports of Akani sightings from the edge of the northern forest of Aquarius. Therefore, Commander deemed it was time for Shei and I to experience real combat.

"I'm panicking a bit," I admitted, wetting my lips. "What about you? You haven't been back to the Gutter ever since we were first captured. What if we encounter someone you know?"

Shei secured the last arrow across my shoulder and jerked the chain to test its strength. The titanium links clanked, but they held on. "I will deal with it as it occurs," she said with determination, yet her hollow cheeks told a different story. "Let's go downstairs now. I don't want to be late."

Cella walked in circles around the healers' wing, talking quietly to herself while the rest of the legion lined up for a taste of muscle aid potion. Commander Izaak covered his mouth, cautiously whispering into Mr. Osei's ear, both their gazes filled with concern. Shei and I sheepishly posted up behind the others, and Mr. Osei administered us an extra drop each since it was our inaugural patrol of the city.

Commander Izaak cleared his throat once everyone drank their fill, signaling the legion to quiet down. "A few things before you leave. Don't separate. Raina, I am looking at you. No chasing after the rebels. Use your best judgment while bending. And keep an eye out for Imani and Shei. It is their first patrol."

As if anyone needed a reminder.

The night had cooled down a notch, and I was already shivering from fear on our way out. Training to be a legionnaire was quite different from actually fulfilling the duties of one.

"Everything is fine. You'll be fine." Lazzor smiled upon taking note of my angst. "It's natural to be nervous your first time. I, too, still get jitters sometimes."

My teeth clattered, and I locked my jaw into a close-mouthed grin. "Thanks, Lazzor," I gritted out.

Tain led the charge, doing everything in his power to shake off my pointed glances. Raina looked around for danger by his side while Cella calmed her breathing, perking her neck up. "I always found the Cobblestone to be the most charming part of town," she said, picking up her pace.

"It can be quite charming," I agreed, observing the twisted columns that held up townhome terraces, their painted mosaic windows illuminated from inside. Each piece was stained to fit in like a puzzle, mirroring a broken, colorful image on the ground beneath.

Shei checked if anyone was at our tail every other minute, clutching the knives in her belt as she strode alongside me. "The night is quieter than usual. I don't like it."

Tain finally acknowledged that the rest of us were there. "The battle is near. Can't blame folk for being scared. Eyes ahead, we are almost there."

I looked forward, letting my feet carry me towards a corner of Lumenor I had never visited in my eighteen years. Mother forbade me from going to the Gutter in fear that I would be discovered by rebels, so this patrol was my first time seeing the eastern part of the city up close.

The Queen's Alley flowed into the Gutter with a noticeable change in our surroundings. The paved road began to crack and was mottled with dirt and debris. Small, displaced pebbles stuck to the soles of my boots. The air was grainy with dust and thick with the smell of wet decay. Vines gripped at the buildings, thick and wild from decades of lacking proper care. Many didn't seem to have homes to go to; worn and tired-looking folk clung to mounds of possessions in the mouths of alleyways and at the corners of streets. I'd spent so much time around rich velvet, glass, and ebony as of late, and the sight of the Gutter made my stomach uneasy.

No wonder most of the rebels are from here. Violence is wrong, but no one deserves to live like this, forgotten by their full-bellied, deep-pocketed neighbors.

I looked to Shei, who walked by my side in silence—without her signature jesting. She was biting her nails, staring ahead with the blank expression of someone who had seen a monster or a ghost. In a way, she was seeing one.

This must be hard for her.

"Commander wanted us to patrol the north-east," Tain announced, turning a corner. "We'll begin with the market."

"That is exciting," I said, clapping my hands. "I've never been to the Gutter market!"

"Nothing about this is exciting," Tain muttered in a bitter tone and sped up.

This will be a long night.

Luckily for us, the first hour passed without much commotion. We circled the market with no success in identifying any rebels. We ran into the occasional traveler, often children, threading through the alleyways that smelled of the mines. Many of the miners were Gutter-born if they were not from the hills.

Lazzor paused and bent over to tie his boots when the first slice of a knife cut through the silence. It missed his shoulder by an inch. We found ourselves at the poorly lit crossing of two lanes, far from the Queen's Alley—in the bleeding heart of the Gutter.

Everyone's palms ignited with sei.

Our necks made sudden twists, surveying each of the four ends of the street. But the blade didn't come from the street—it had come from one of abandoned buildings towering above us. I glanced up, but my sight couldn't penetrate the darkness behind their broken windows.

The rebels counted on that when picking their vantage point.

Another knife was flung in our direction, revealing our attackers' station. Tain shattered the dagger with starlight, motioning we follow him into the rebels' hideout.

"Stay calm," Cella said before bolting behind others. "Keep your ears open and palms free."

My belly churned. We were playing no game, there was no opportunity to build myself back up should I take a misstep. The cool evening breeze slipped in through my uniform, making me shudder. My palms flickered with rising emotion, like candle wicks in the wind.

I could really use some of that numbing potion right now.

Lazzor breathed heavily as we mounted the stairwell, almost like he was wheezing. I turned back, about to ask if he was well, but Cella insisted I keep my eyes forward.

"You will get yourself killed if you don't stop talking," she reprimanded. "Lazzor knows how to take care of himself."

Tracing her steps in almost complete blackness of the abandoned building, I thought I might faint. No amount of sei or combat lessons could prepare me for what I was experiencing. Fighting skills made up for only a half of the ingredients needed to brew a good legionnaire, while the other half required having the stomach for it. And my belly was spoiling with concern, accustomed to the quiet life of the hills.

We couldn't stop making noise no matter how hard we tried. A clutter of loose items crowded the floor, crunching beneath our feet. Vanishing sei to avoid being seen, we relied on nothing but our hearing and Tain's instincts to guide us forward.

"This is a trap." I pulled at Cella's uniform. Ahead was a squared entryway to the attic. A trickle of light mingled in through broken windows, enough to tell things apart but not enough to see the rebels.

"Shhh. Of course it's a trap. They like to lure us into tightly packed spaces with lots of room to hide. Stop talking."

"Over there, to the left!" Raina cried out, and Tain's spear-like stream of sei spun around with a swoosh, crashing into the back wall. Everyone opened their palms, lighting up the attic cramped with broken furniture.

Tain signaled we freeze in place, grabbing a grubby cup by his foot. He threw the cup across the room, shattering a mirror, and one of the rebels jumped out of a wardrobe, his back turned to us. A small spear of starlight plunged into his spine, and his body fell down with a thud. I gasped, alerting the remaining rebels in hiding of our location. Shei yanked me aside a second before a flying knife struck my throat, escaping it by a hair. My body fell on top of hers, rolling away in haste.

"Up, Imani, up, now," she shouted.

I rose to my feet, keeping my palms steady and in position. Broken wardrobes splintered and crashed, brought down by Cella's sparkling waves of sei. Her streams intertwined and knotted, causing destruction to everything in their way.

Tain and Raina aided her efforts, bending at the remaining rebels. Lazzor began coughing, tears of sei shooting out of his palms, bursting the closets before he almost collapsed, his body folding over at the waist.

"Lazzor, are you well? Lazzor, what can I do?" I asked after shattering all the blades that were flung our way, helping Shei cover for the others while they counter-attacked. The rebels dispersed, rushing towards the exit in the back.

Lazzor's forehead was drenched in sweat, and his shoulders slouched, hands resting on his knees. Cella, Raina, and Tain drove the last of the rebels out. Shei clung to the wall in the background, short of breath, before running over to help.

Raina caught my shoulder, and moved me aside to get to Lazzor. "Deep breath, take a deep breath. Now another."

"I can't… I can't breathe…" he panted amidst labored inhales.

I looked to Tain. His face was pale, skin gray, eyes dashing across the attic as his nose wrinkled. "There is something foul in the air. A poison, maybe. We can't stay here. We'll be ambushed."

"I can't… leave me… go…" Lazzor uttered breathlessly.

Raina patted his back, helping him loosen the collar of his uniform. "We are not leaving you behind. Come on, we must go if we don't want to witness more bloodshed."

It was too late.

Voices trickled in from the street, dozens of boots storming in our direction. My throat tightened. *What now?* I blew scorching air out of my lungs, stirring the floating grains of closet debris.

"The rest of you find a place to hide. Don't leave until it is safe," Tain instructed. "I will lead them astray."

Raina glanced back at Lazzor with a worrisome look. "Father said we shouldn't separate—"

"Izaak isn't here," Tain cut in. "Lazzor can't go on. Get him to safety. I'll be fine."

My hand tightened around the cloth of Tain's sleeve. "You are not going alone," I said, straightening my back to exude the confidence that was not there. "I am coming along."

Raina and Tain protested at once. "Absolutely not! You are new, this is your first patrol!"

"I *am* new. They know nothing of my power," I said, my mouth forming a smirk. "And what better bait than a potent, young legionnaire and the prince they despise?"

"Remind me to never propose something like this again!" I complained, running alongside Tain and away from a dozen rebels. He suggested I bend the bursting, marble-sized balls into an abandoned shack nearby to create an obstacle and slow them down. With jitters in my stomach, I couldn't make the balls condensed enough, and I wound up with a fistful of sei in each hand instead.

"Now, Imani! Release!"

I exhaled. I began bending starlight with intent, bursting it into my target.

The shack didn't just collapse—its foundation turned to dust with a loud blast that was still ringing in my ears minutes later. The collar of my uniform choked me, dirt and debris filling my mouth. It hurt to breathe with the grains scratching the back of my throat. All I could do was keep running in alternating patterns to avoid knives, while occasionally swinging my arm and blowing up the ground behind us, preventing the rebels from closing in.

Tain bent four spears of sei at our pursuers and turned into a narrow back alley packed with piles of stinking trash. We only had seconds before the rebels caught up. He swung one of the backdoors to what was presumably someone's home wide open, and we stormed inside.

"Where are we?" I asked, my back sliding against the door. Acute pressure punched at my temples, at my entire body. My uniform was a soak of sweat and dust, my mind scattered.

Tain's dirt-stained finger pushed against my lips. "Shhh, you are safe. We are safe."

That much was true. The rebels inspected the alley briefly before another burst of sei turned their attention west.

I hope that's not the rest of our legion bending to get away.

I looked about with my back leaning against the door. We were indeed inside someone's home. Heavy thuds pounded against the ceiling, coming from the floor above. A woman's voice laughed eagerly—a mother playing with her children. We found ourselves in the kitchen area, where cleaned, albeit chipped, pots were drying face-down on the table. There were no crystals, moon charts, or sun calendars—only the bare-boned necessities required to survive.

"Father! The princeling is here!" A child's voice startled me, and I almost bent at the girl of eight or so that giggled across from us in the hallway. Her tawny skin was freckled at the cheeks, relaxed curls braided and beaded. The girl's height barely reached the edge of Tain's jacket as she ran into his embrace.

Where in the skies are we?

A man, who could only be the girl's father, rushed down the stairwell breathlessly. His pale hands were darkened with tar, dark green eyes sagged from the lack of sleep. He had the look of a man who had not rested properly in a century. A look I knew well, having witnessed it on Father all throughout my childhood.

He is a miner.

The man and Tain exchanged a knowing look in silence. Tain had been there before, his arrival was no surprise to their family. Even the little girl knew he was the prince. But why? Why would a family of hard-working miners help the infamous Gutter-born prince? Why risk the wrath of rebels for him?

Tain dropped a bundle of coins into the man's palm before following him down the hallway. The bundle, judging from its size, carried more coin than a miner earned in months.

With low wages and steep prices—what other choice does he have?

A glimpse of the unsettling reality of our neighbors made me feel guilty for enjoying all the Old Town luxuries for the past three months, under the excuse that I was finally getting what I deserved.

I was wearing gowns and jewels while half of the city was starving.

The little girl took my hand unexpectedly, blinking up at me with child's curiosity. "Are you a princess?"

I chuckled at her innocence. "No, I am afraid I am not a princess."

"A queen, then?" she asked, fluttering her eyelashes. "You look like a queen."

I looked more like a beggar, covered in bruises and debris, than a queen, but her sweet naiveness disarmed me anyway. "Thank you, dear. But I am no queen either. I am a legionnaire," I said, deciding the title suited me for the first time.

A real legionnaire after all.

The girl's father strolled down the hallway and pushed an empty dresser aside. It revealed a hidden door on the floor, leading into the basement. The door howled as the miner tugged it open, and Tain walked down the steps without saying a word. I went behind him, and right before I descended below, the girl touched my cheek.

"Can you do a magic trick for me, please?" She made an adorable kitten-like face. "The princeling always performs tricks for me."

Her father retrieved her hand, holding her at bay. "Don't bother the lady."

I freed my hands from the pockets of my jacket. "I am no lady, sir. My father worked in the mines, too, until I joined the legions," I explained. "I don't mind showing your daughter a trick."

The girl clapped her hands, enchanted by the ball of starlight I split into five before vanishing it. Her thrill made my heart heavy, reminding me of my sweet Zuri. I made an attempt at the bow I saw from the palace performers, thanked the man for saving us, and shut the shrieking door above my head.

The basement was a compact, plain space with one large, pillowless mattress. A pot of lukewarm water squatted in the corner, and Tain and I propped our backs against the wall as far from each other as the mattress allowed. We were both exhausted, and the quiet nurtured our ringing earlobes.

"I am glad you came along," he said finally, leaning further into the mattress. "There were too many of them. I wouldn't have made it without you."

The darkness concealed my smile. "Thank you for saying that," I responded, undoing my shoelaces. I wiggled my toes once I took my boots off to bring circulation back to my feet. "What now?"

Tain proceeded to take his boots off, too, sighing in relief after setting his feet free. "Now we wait and leave at dusk. Feel free to rest, I'll keep an ear out for trouble."

I slid down the mattress, relaxing my tensed muscles with a moan. But I couldn't drift into sleep right away, not without knowing if the others made it back to the base safely. Lazzor's face was growing purple the last I saw him. He'd been in no condition to run.

"Do you think the rest of the legion made it back?" I asked.

Tain stretched out his spine, clinging to the opposite edge. "I have no doubt. I will deny it if you tell her, but I place my bets on Raina ten out of ten times. She will get Lazzor to safety."

I exhaled in relief.

"Is this your safe house?" I asked, gaping about. "You were no stranger to the miner and his little girl."

He nodded absent-mindedly. "I am no stranger here. I grew up in this house," he replied after a long pause, and my eyes widened in the dark. "And no, the people who live here are not my family. But they took care of my grandfather before he passed away, and I let them live here since I have no use of it myself, other than for situations like this."

I remained silent for a while, not knowing what to say. "What… what happened to your birth parents? Are they still alive?"

Tain's jaw quivered, and I was pretty sure he let out a quiet sob. "My mother died protecting me against the rebels, if you must know. I showed signs of bending at eight years of age, and it didn't take long before I was discovered. And my father…" His stern, hoarse voice began drowning. "He is still alive, punching holes inside tavern walls with a pint of ale in his free hand. He was the one who sold me to the queen after my mother's passing. My own father sold me in exchange for coin," Tain muttered and broke down.

I rolled down the mattress towards him, biting on the flesh inside my mouth to keep the outpouring cries in my throat. I pressed my cheek against his shoulder, allowing Tain to feel his pain without judgement. His chest rose and fell back down at a snail's pace, and he wrapped his arms around my back, hugging me tightly. The time we spent in comforting silence marked the first moment of intimacy I shared with a boy, and that meant something to me.

What do I have to lose?
We might both die soon anyway.

My hand glided up Tain's neck, cupping his warm, tear-glazed cheek. My sight adjusted to the darkness, and I was beginning to make out the lines of his face. I leaned against my elbow and brought my lips an inch away from his. The scent of mint and leather swam into my nostrils as he exhaled gently, tucking his hand underneath the roots of my braid at the back of my neck. His touch seared my skin, and I pressed my lips against his, tasting him for the first time. A proud prince or a heart-broken orphan, it didn't matter. I wanted him either way.

We both smiled afterwards. "I'm sorry," I began, looking away. "I didn't mean to... I only..."

Tain traced my bottom lip with his thumb. "Please don't apologize. You beat me to the punch, anyway."

"Alright," I said, tussling his hair. "But Tain, I need you to be honest and tell me what you know about the Akani. I have a family to protect, and the queen's omission of important details isn't helping our cause."

He twisted his mouth, sulking like a mouse that had been caught in a trap. His stare scattered across the wall before he glared deep into my eyes. "Under one condition."

"Yes?"

"You can't tell anyone. Shei especially. I don't trust her."

Not this foolery again!

"You two need to stop your endless bickering, it is rather tiresome!" I snapped, backing away. "We all have the same goal in mind, she wants to save the city just as much as anyone else."

Tain puffed out loud. "Does she, now?"

"Of course she does. Shei only dislikes you because she thinks you forgot about the people of the Gutter."

His eyebrows shot up, color returning to his face. "Forgot about them? I care more than she knows. The queen, despite what you think of her, tries to help, but she has nobles to answer to. Ruling is like a game of moon phases, in order to take, you need to give. And she gives. Not enough, I agree, but her power is fading. That is where I come in. I will make Lumenor the powerful, flourishing city it once was when I take the crown. And she is only trying to help me achieve that goal."

"Trying to help you by poisoning me?" I snarled.

Tain's handsome features contorted in confusion. "Come again?"

I pursed my lips, not persuaded by his puzzlement. "You are going to tell me you don't know?"

"Know what?"

Take a deep breath, Imani.

"Know that your mother ordered Miss Yamane to take me to the temple, where the high priestess administered the ancient magic-bound healer's aid to me without my knowledge, or agreement," I blurted out in one breath, my cheeks running hot. "I couldn't feel anything for a few days."

Tain gaped. "I...I didn't know...she would never..."

My stare was ice-cold. "Well, she did the night I found out about the sibling's curse. She was afraid my *volatile* emotions would put you in danger," I snapped. A long moment of silence followed.

"She never told me..." Tain's low voice trailed off in deep thought. "I am truly sorry. I would've never agreed with that decision, I hope you know that. She had no right to take away your pain. If anything, your emotions make you more powerful, which is rather an advantage to my wellbeing. You saved my life tonight."

I decided there was no point in scolding him for his mother's actions for the time being. I needed to know the truth in order to defend the city he was so keen on ruling.

Cut to the chase.

"Are the Akani Warriors midnight benders?" I asked without hesitation, like ripping gauze away from a wound in one move.

Tain flinched, his neck stiffening. "How do *you* know about mei-sans?"

"I am the one asking questions," I replied, keeping my voice firm. "Well?"

He grunted, realizing there was no room to wiggle out of the trap I caught him in. "They are not midnight benders, though we suspected the same. Our eyes in Vatrion reported they took both the city and the ruby crystal by force, leveraging the surprise of their immunity to sei. No mentioned of mei was made."

I pondered a question for a moment.

How much do I reveal to him?

Deciding there was more to gain than to lose, I chose to take the bargain. "What about the ancestors' secret? What was their leader speaking of in his letter to the queen?"

He gasped, shaking his head with furrowed brows. "How in the world do you know about his letter?"

"It doesn't matter." I motioned the stitching of my mouth. "And don't try to stall. I have the right to know if I am to fight in the battle."

Tain clicked his tongue, examining me carefully. I didn't come empty handed like he first thought. "You don't have *the right* to know anything. You are a soldier, not a commander."

"The last time I checked, so were you."

He sucked a breath in before speaking. "I am also the prince, remember?"

My mouth tightened to his words. "Not in this room, you are not," I said sternly. "In this room, you are my friend. More than a friend," I corrected myself after he frowned. "And you owe me to tell the truth." I blinked at him softly, cracking the wall he was hiding behind.

"Imani…" Tain whispered. "I can't betray my mother, you must understand…"

"Well I don't understand! This is a matter of life and death, not loyalty. We are fighting on the same side." I raised my voice. "What is the queen's deal anyway? Why burn the bottom half of the letter? What is she hiding?"

He brushed a silver strand away from his face, stalling for a moment. "Alright. The secret our ancestors hid was that the moonstone is by far the most powerful starlight crystal."

"We already know that," I cut in.

Tain took a deep, exhausted breath. "But you didn't know that only a few sei-sans are born in Lumenor when compared to any other ancient city," he went on. "Nor did you know that our bending reaches far beyond anything their sei-sans can forge. We have kept the extent of our power a secret ever since the other ancient cities allied with us centuries ago. We are fewer in numbers, true, but we don't need much to overpower our allies if we wanted to. And telling that to the rest of the world would put a target on our back, and that Akani bastard knows that," he spat. "He is spewing lies and using the fear of sei as means of gathering forces to help him win the battle. Not on my watch."

Something wasn't adding up.

I could see why Queen Astra would not want our allies afraid of us, that would not be wise. But Kalon's motivation behind stealing the starlight crystals had remained a mystery.

Think Imani, think.

"But why steal the ruby crystal and then come for the moonstone? Let's say Kalon managed to accomplish his goal. What would he do with it?"

Tain's stare drifted up to the very corners of his eyelids, which happened whenever he was thinking hard. "Sell it to the highest bidder? The truth is, our world is changing. The Ashen Desert spread threefold in the last century alone. The lakes are drying up all over the world, wildfires plowing through the grasslands. I doubt the winter lands of Akan are immune to it. Kalon simply wants the coin. Everyone does. And what can bring more gold than starlight crystals?"

I knew that the Ashen Desert was spreading, but I didn't know about the rest of world. And war always erupted during difficult times, or so my history lecturer had claimed. People turned to stealing and invading when they had nothing left of their own to feed and clothe their children.

Too tired to think further, I laid my head on Tain's shoulder after unclipping his arrows and helping him get out of his uniform jacket. We didn't exchange another word, his lips raining kisses on my neck before calling it a night. I fell asleep in his arms, more frightened than I had ever been before.

Chapter XVIII
Gutter Gems

My mind sank into another nightmare. The Mounds ruptured, sinking the moonhouses back into earth. The moonstone rolled down the palace's marble stairwell, shattering to pieces. All three moons abandoned the skies. I stood atop the rooftop of the base, all alone, when a hand reached for my shoulder from behind.

I woke up screaming.

Tain leapt up, thinking we were being attacked. He must have dozed off despite wanting to stay awake and keep watch. After the night we had, I couldn't blame him for falling asleep.

"Everything is fine, sorry for waking you," I said, "I had a nightmare."

His chest fell down. "Are you alright?"

"Yes. Don't worry about me. I'll be fine, I'm a bit shaken is all," I replied, avoiding his concerned grimace.

"I am here if you want to talk," he said when the first rays of sunlight crept through the crack in the ceiling. "It's probably a good time to head out anyway."

The miner's wife opened the basement door after we knocked, golden accents twinkling in her locs like stars. The silver moon tattoo was faded against her golden-brown skin. She handed us two linen, gray cloaks and some freshly-baked bread before departure. I ate like

I had been starving for weeks, stuffing my face without uttering a single word until the last crumb of bread ended up in my belly.

"Thank you very much," I mumbled before washing the bread down with a mouthful of tea. "For everything."

The woman's tired beam was warm in a motherly way, her eyes tracing the ends of my braid. "You are welcome. It is nice to house a Mounds-born for a change. He usually brings one of the polished Old Town girls along."

My eyes flickered at Tain. "Does he, now?"

He blushed, raising a palm swiftly. "To clarify, she speaks of Raina and Cella."

I chuckled. "No need for clarification. You aren't exactly known as a ladies' man, *prince*."

Tain gave me the smaller cloak of the two, raising his chin. "I have no interest in being one. I have better things to focus on."

"Like winning the crown?" I asked.

He nodded with confidence. "Exactly."

I pulled the hood over my head, tucking my braid in. There was no doubt that every rebel in the Gutter knew that their infamous prince was accompanied by a Mounds-born legionnaire. And we had to slip by their traps unnoticed.

The Gutter was as lively as ever that morning. The miners that worked the night shift headed back to their homes while the day shift strolled towards the base of the hills, aiming for the southern mine tunnels. Merchants and traders posted in front of their shops, luring customers inside. Mature legionnaires and city guards patrolled the packed streets, earning themselves a side-eye from the passing folk, and barefoot children roamed about, playing with marbles. They reminded me of my early, carefree days in the Mounds. Zuri would roll the marbles down the hill as a toddler, and my task was to wait and catch them at the bottom. She giggled every time I missed one, watching me chase the marble down the river bank before it was forever lost in the relentless currents. Her laugh echoed in my ears.

I will find the cure if it is the last thing I do.

"Look to your left," Tain interrupted the bitter-sweet flow of my memories. "That bakery over there sells the best cinnamon bread in the city."

The open door of the bakery let out a strong whiff of cinnamon and warm pastries, making my mouth water. Two school-aged girls exited alongside their mother, clutching to her skirts, begging for another piece of gingerbread cake. The sight made Tain smile with sadness, as though he was reliving a long-forgotten moment of his life.

I tightened my grip around his muscled forearm. "Tell me more. You must have so many memories."

Tain bobbed his head meekly, pointing at the nearby leather shop. "My grandfather worked there for fifty-two years, practically his entire adult life, until he fell ill. I used to run to the shop as a child and cut and sew disposed patches together for hours. Working with leather put my mind at ease. Needless to say, I was not exactly a popular kid growing up."

"I find that hard to believe somehow," I said, running my eyes over leather bags inside the store display. They were crafted by skilled hands and worth far more than the price they were being sold for. The same level of artistry would earn a merchant at least twice as much coin in the Cobblestone, and only Kirrah knew how much beyond the silver gates of Old Town.

Tain crept ahead, towards a century-old gemstone shop that cast jewel-toned shades on the road beneath. A beaded thread of bells swung from the doorknob, green like the blades of untouched grass in the hills.

"I know you like crystals, so this might pique your interest." His face bloomed into a wide grin. "They sell a variety of smuggled gems, too. Under the table, of course. Some are brought in from lands as far out as the eastern jungle villages."

I gaped, my mouth wide open.

I must tell Mother and Zana!

"You were right—my interest is piqued," I exclaimed. "Can we go see them?"

"The imported ones?" he asked with the reflection of a displayed red jasper in his eye. "Not without the keyword, and I doubt that two legionnaires are likely to be given one. They would recognize us the instant we slipped our hoods off."

"Naturally." I said, pouting my mouth in disappointment.

A woman with white-streaked hair stood in front of the shop, waving an obsidian necklace that was certainly to Cella's liking in front of passers' faces. "Protect your home and loved ones from the starlight benders! Three silver pieces only, practically free!"

"Practically free, right," a passer scoffed to her husband. "Codswallop."

She made me laugh, but Tain pulled me to the store entrance, nevertheless, and began speaking to the shop worker.

"How does a necklace protect one from starlight benders exactly?" he asked with a forged wonder. "My wife here and I are most concerned about our safety."

His wife?

I decided to play the role for entertainment. "Yes, we most certainly are. Don't let his height fool you, my Aubren here couldn't aim a knife to save his life." I didn't know why, but that was the first name I thought of.

It is rather fashionable name in the Gutter, unless Aubren lied about that, too.

Tain frowned, but the woman's eyes lit up, thinking we bit on her bait. Having sold ointments for years, I knew every trick at her disposal. "Yes, yes, I understand," she said with compassion. "My Therion is the same, he'd be a corpse long ago if it wasn't for my aim. Come in, we have much to offer to a handsome young couple such as yourselves."

We took a step away from the entrance in unison.

"I am afraid we must come back a different time, my mother is sick with worry," Tain said, which was not technically a lie. Although the mother he was referring to was the infamous queen of Lumenor, not some elderly Gutter lady like the shop worker likely assumed. "We'll be back, we promise."

The woman's expression shifted to disdain as though someone had thrown a pint of cold water in her face. "Aye, aye, let me know when your promises can help fill my pockets."

The Queen's Alley came into view, and right before we reached it, a blade shop on the other side of the street caught my attention. A pale-skinned merchant in his fifties labored inside, making me wonder if he was Shei's uncle. I knew the chances were slim considering dozens of knife shops were sprouting all over Gutter—they were practically never out of business.

Still, I was curious.

"Would you mind stopping by that knife store across the street before we move on?" I asked, making the kitten face the little girl used to gain my favor the prior night. "I think that might be Shei's uncle."

Tain cast a grim glance across the road. "What more reason not to go in?"

"Shut it," I scoffed, dragging him along. "It will be fine."

Three tiny bells swinging from knotted rope collided and rang as I pushed the door open. The shop was much more spacious than I could tell from the street, but still cozy, filled with celestial-inspired blue carpets and cushioned chairs. A fair-faced merchant stood behind the counter, but there were three other men in the background—lads of Tain's and my age. All their chins shot up when they spotted us.

I slipped my hood off upon noticing Shei's fire-blue eyes watch me across the counter, only this time they belonged to the middle-aged merchant instead of my eighteen-year-old friend. "Good day, sir."

The merchant was sharpening a knife, leaning against a glass display filled with intricately carved blades. Pommels of emerald and sapphire gleamed against the daylight that snuck in through the window. Dents in the handles were etched to shape various deities, celestial bodies, or ancient symbols, each uniquely designed and polished. And they were being sold for a rather hefty sum.

"What business brings a hill…" The merchant stopped mid-sentence, his fire-lit eyes stuck on Tain's face.

I rested my palms against my hips, just in case. "We are Shei's friends, sir."

"I know who you are," her uncle muttered, and the three lads behind him stood up abruptly, holding sharp throwing knives in their hands.

Tain grabbed my shoulder from behind. "Let's go. We are not welcome here."

"Damn right you're not!" one of the lads shouted.

My stare narrowed on Shei's uncle. "We are not here to cause trouble, I promise. We were in the neighborhood after patrol, and I figured we would stop by in case you have a message for Shei. I know she'd love to hear from you, and Commander won't let her send any more letters."

Shei's uncle's ice-cold expression softened at the mention of his niece, but he maintained a threatening composure. His palm leapt up, and the young men behind him disappeared into the room in the back. "I will speak to you, but *he* shall wait outside."

"No way," Tain groaned. "Imani, let's go."

Shei's uncle made a puzzled expression when he heard my name. Maybe I imagined it, but I had a feeling he was familiar with it already.

Shei must have mentioned me in her letter.

I swayed my hips to face Tain. "Wait in front. Shei's uncle has no reason to harm me."

He leaned in, whispering into my ear with the stubbornness of a bull. "We should stick together considering what took place last night."

"Trust me. I can take care of myself. This is important to me."

Tain grunted, turning the rusted knob. "Five minutes, and then I am bursting inside." He posted outside the entrance like he was guarding the place, blocking onlookers from coming in.

"Shei is doing well, and she…" I began, but her uncle cut me off.

"I didn't ask," he said to my surprise. "I raised my niece to know how to care for herself. Now tell me, what is a bright, young girl such as yourself doing with that scum of a boy?"

I shrugged, not exactly prepared for the lecture I was receiving. "Tain is a member of our legion, sir."

His asymmetrical frown reminded me of Mother whenever she caught in me a lie. "Is that so? Do you hold hands with every member of your legion, then?"

Am I really being lectured about boys by Shei's uncle?

My gaze fell to the floor. "No, I don't."

Shei's uncle shook his head like a disappointed parent. "Your father stopped by the shop a month or so ago, you know, inquiring about you all around the Gutter. He was worried after the recent ambush, when one of the Old Town kids got wounded. He was happy to hear you were not patrolling the city that night."

The night Cella got hurt.

I clenched my jaw, wishing I could hug Father at that very moment. He was not the kind of person who always expressed love with words, opting for playful jesting instead, but he never failed to show it with his actions.

"How did you know I wasn't there?" I asked.

Silver sunlight touched his eyes that gleamed like the aquamarine charm around my neck. "I knew my niece wasn't, and by that logic, neither were you. I have my men keeping an eye out for her in case she gets into trouble."

Where were these men last night when we needed them?

I swallowed those words before I spoke them out loud and got myself kicked out.

"Thank you for putting my father's mind at ease," I said, bowing my head. "It means a lot."

"Mhm."

"And I know you don't think much of Tain," I continued, "but he didn't forget about where he comes from. He is not bad at all, just misunderstood."

Shei's uncle clasped a second knife and ran the blades' edges against each other. The screech made my skin prickle. "Thank Kirrah he's got you to understand him, then," he said with undeniable sarcasm in his voice. "Spare me, child, but be careful. I can't guarantee your safety outside this shop. Go back to the hills, burn that uniform, and live whatever we have left of this life before the Akani come. No matter what you think right now, *he* is not worth it. No lad is."

I am not in this fight for Tain.

I inhaled deeply. "You know I can't go back. Who would help save the city if we all run to our homes?"

Tain banged on the window, signaling incoming trouble. *Time to go.* The last thing I wanted was to put Shei's family in danger. She would never forgive me if I did and rightfully so.

Before I could twist the doorknob, her uncle reached for one of the sapphire-pommeled knives in the display worth four gold coins.

Four gold coins! He held it out for me. "Take it, I will not take no for an answer," he said after I refused, pushing the blade away. "Knife-throwing has been a Lumenoran custom for ages, and you are as Lumenoran as they come. You helped save my niece's life without hesitation the day you two met, and for that I am forever in your debt. Take it."

I embraced the blade, admiring its artistic design and acute tip. The moon-carved sapphire pommel complimented the deep umber in my skin as my fingers wrapped around it. Shei's uncle's gift was the prettiest and the most expensive thing I would ever owned. "Thank you, sir, I will keep it close and sharp."

He winked in the same fashion as his niece. "I expect no less. And Imani, one more thing before you go. Keep your eyes open and your morals intact. Don't allow the Old Town to corrupt you."

I wanted to ask him what he meant by that, but Tain ran inside and dragged me out before I could say goodbye. Too many rebels began to roam the streets and eye him sideways. We had to go quickly.

Tain and I were both sent straight to the healer's wing as soon as we arrived at the base's doorstep. In spite of mingling rebels, our journey back to the Old Town was rather uneventful. Patrolling legionnaires recognized us the moment we stepped onto the Queen's Alley and sent for a carriage.

"The queen had the entire city looking for you two," the guard at the base entrance informed us after the carriage wheels stopped rolling and we climbed out.

We came upon the healers' wing for inspection in no time. Mr. Osei arrived while his assistant was helping me out of my uniform behind the curtain. Tain was changing in the next section.

"Where are they? Where is Imani?" the head healer demanded.

I stuck my head out through the curtain. "I am here, Mr. Osei, still in one piece!"

Mr. Osei slouched his shoulders and went on to inquire about Tain's condition. "Is his majesty in good health?"

His majesty?

I'd never heard the healers call Tain anything other than his first name. But then I learned that one of the queen's guards was posted inside, waiting to alert *her majesty* about her son's return.

"I was not injured," Tain yelled out behind the curtain. "Tell mother not to worry, I will go visit her as soon as I am free to go."

The queen's messenger scuttled out of the healers' wing, and I split the curtains open, dressed in my leisure garments. Mr. Osei made me lay atop one of the firm healers' beds and examined my reflexes, temperature, bruises, and lungs.

"I was not harmed," I said, my eyes tracing the head healer's moving finger per his request. "Is Lazzor well?"

"He was fine as soon as he left the ambush," he replied, then went on to rub a turmeric ointment over the bruise on my elbow. "He will suffer from cough for a day or two, but he is healthy otherwise."

Thank the moons.

Mr. Osei opened his mouth once again but refrained from speaking as Tain came out, settling on the healers' bed next to mine. I wondered if the healer had any news about the cure for the sibling's curse. I intended to ask him about it the first chance I got.

The doors to the healer's wing flew open, and the remainder of our legion rushed inside. The girls gathered around my bed while Lazzor went to Tain.

"Are you hurt?" Shei asked.

"Where were you?" Cella followed.

"We were worried sick!" Raina hissed.

My mouth cracked into a smile.

It feels good knowing people care about you.

It took me a moment to soak in their faces. It was nice to be back amongst friends. "We had to fight at first, but we mostly hid in Tain's safe house for the night." There was so much I wanted to tell them, but I had to wait until we were back in my chamber.

Cella smirked at Raina. "See, I told you so."

Shei put her hand in mine with a concerned look on her face. "As long as you made it out alive, tree burner."

I smiled. "I met your uncle this morning."

Her mouth opened widely. "My uncle?"

"Don't worry, I caused no trouble—we stumbled upon his shop is all. In fact, he gave me a little gift. I'll show it to you later."

"You better show it to all of us immediately," Raina demanded in the commander's tone.

I untucked the sapphire-pommeled knife out of my folded uniform, and even Raina sighed at the sight of it.

Lazzor glimpsed over her shoulder. "That is some wicked blade! The design dates all the way back to the Ancestors' Era—I've seen similar drawings in historical tomes before. No offense, but who gave *you* that weapon? You aren't exactly a master of knife-throwing."

"Get a grip!" Cella smacked the back of his head. "You can't say anything you want just because you claimed no offense!"

Shei grinned proudly. "It is my uncle's work. He gave it to Imani."

Raina frowned. "I thought you were… well, not wealthy?"

"Do I need to hit you, too?" Cella asked, hurrying to Shei's defense. "You two need to learn some manners!"

"It's alright," Shei said softly. "My uncle gives most of what he makes to the nearby orphanage. Besides, not many people in the Gutter can afford his weapons nowadays. The sales are slow."

Commander Izaak stalked inside the healers' quarters, interrupting our conversation. "How are they?"

"As good as new," Mr. Osei replied, done examining Tain.

Commander nodded along. "Good. Everyone come to my office. You have five minutes."

Commander's lifeless office shimmered with color coming from the vibrantly-painted scrolls that laid scattered across the long, rectangular table. They were maps. Blue lines for rivers, green circles for grass fields and hills. Gray squares for buildings, brown lines for roads, all wrapped in the city walls. A star stood in place of Kirrah's Temple and the five-jeweled crown symbol was in the location of the queen's palace.

"You will learn every line, every curve in the road," Commander demanded after we settled into the wooden chairs around the table.

"Don't come out until you can see every inch of Lumenor's map with your eyes closed," he said and slammed the door shut behind him.

"With our eyes closed, moons help me!" I sank my forehead into my palms. I could orient myself in the Mounds by using the stars, but the same could not be said for the streets of Lumenor.

"Take it easy, will you?" Raina sneered. "How many streets could there be to memorize? We should know half of them already."

Cella flipped one of the maps over, examining the carefully-penned curving lettering on the backside. "Only three hundred and four, if the legend at the back of this map is correct."

Three hundred and four?

"That number only accounts for major alleys and broad streets. But if it makes it any easier, half of them lead to dead ends, at least inside Cobblestone and the Gutter," Shei added, running her fingertip across the map.

"Dead ends are the most important ones to memorize," Tain added, earning a frown from her. "We need to learn to recognize them in case we have to get away during the battle. The last thing we want is to come upon a dead end while running away from a threat."

"Running away?" Raina scowled, extending her arm to flip the map back to its front. "I have no intention of running away from anyone like a coward. I will face the Akani head on, no matter how many warriors I am up against."

"You are welcome to get yourself killed." Cella gave her a side eye. "I will learn the name and the path of every single street in the city, thank you very much."

We split in two groups to study. Shei, being the most well-versed in the dirt-paved roads of Lumenor's stone landscape, taught Raina and Cella. Tain and I grabbed the chairs next to Lazzor, the most well-read person in our legion, if not the entirety of Old Town.

Lazzor grounded his finger at the root of the Queen's Alley, clutching a clean cloth in his free hand to cover a loud cough. "We will start at the gates and follow the widest alleys first. Those will be the ones to avoid."

I squinted at the map. "Why is that?"

Tain leaned over the table, breathing softly and narrowing his stare at the scroll. "Wide alleys will be packed with horseback riders and fearful folk, should the Akani penetrate the gates." He paused and swallowed bitterly. "Or in this case, kelpie riders."

I knew as much about kelpies as I did about the ancient magic. I only vaguely recalled one of the ancestral myths I read a long time ago. A hero whose name I could not remember rode a kelpie all the way from the northern snow mountains to the southern tip of the hot desert lands. The kelpie was said to be as cunning as a fox and faster than wind, but I always attributed those traits to embellished storytelling and nothing more.

I figured I best ask, even if I had to reveal my ignorance.

Better to be thought of as dim-witted than dead.

"These kelpies," I said, clearing my throat. "I know they can swim, but are they like regular horses otherwise?"

In spite of my embarrassment, neither of the boys laughed.

"Is a hummingbird the same as the blood-eyed eagle?" Lazzor asked.

I shrugged. "Umm, obviously not?"

"Well, the same rule applies here. Kelpies are like horses only if you amped the horse up with ten drops of muscle aid and made it read a book."

Tain nodded along, cupping his jaw. "They are also one of the most intelligent old species. One kelpie was worth the price of twenty-five horses in the olden days."

Lazzor pointed a finger up. "It was forty-five horses, actually, but that's beside the point. All I am trying to say is, you don't want one chasing you. They run at the speed of a banshee and have the nose of a predator despite being grass-eaters."

"Don't tell me they are immune to sei, too," I uttered, the despair in my voice rising.

We barely escaped the rebels last night, and they were on foot!

Lazzor shook his head. "Far from immune. Only Akani Warriors seem to possess that power."

And they will be here in no time.

I plunged my face into my palms again. "We are all going to die, aren't we?"

Tain took a hold of my hand across the table, and I could feel Shei's poignant stare from the opposite corner. "Look at me," he said, and I lifted my chin. "That is fear in you speaking. You crumbled buildings with your power and set the hills ablaze. Don't allow your fears to consume you. Remember, you are one to fear, too."

That was the first time I ever saw Shei smile at anything Tain had said. I smiled, too, and went on to study Lumenor's streets for the next five hours. We quizzed each other until our tongues and brains gave up and cheered every time someone got the answer right. Lazzor was quite a good teacher, providing little scraps of history to help us memorize.

"Which street was paved right after the Queen's Alley?" he asked, curving his upper lip. "And where is it on the map?"

I closed my eyes to dig out what little information my mind had preserved, imagining a tangle of streets, looking for the right one. "Hmm, the Merchant's Road? No, no, I take that back! It was the Fool's Alley!" My finger touched the root of a narrow street that flowed down the Cobblestone like a meandering river stream.

Lazzor's face lit up. "Correct! And which street springs into the highest number of dead alleys?"

I tapped the map again, remembering his tale about the traveling musicians who once rose their tents inside dead alleys of Lumenor come summer solstice festival. "The Harpist's Road! The Harpist's Road!"

Lazzor grinned proudly. "You can join the ranks of city tour guides after the war, Imani Stone," he said and the heat rose to my cheeks. I did well with numbers, but I was never good at memorizing names before.

"Thank you Lazzor," I said, blushing. "You should really consider teaching once you are done being a soldier. You have a knack for it."

He shrugged. "I am a scriber at heart but never say never."

We finally gathered the scrolls and arranged them neatly in the corner before our departure, our bellies crying for food. It was dinnertime, the silver sun vanishing beneath the dimming horizon in the window.

Commander Izaak awaited in front, seated in an uncomfortable chair with a map in his lap and quill between his fingers. We ran headfirst into him on our way out.

Was he listening in the entire time?

No wonder Raina sleeps with one ear to the wall.

"All done?" Commander asked without raising his chin.

"All done!" Cella bobbed her head.

"Good. You are free to go, and don't think I won't quiz you tomorrow," he said, getting up from the chair. "One more thing before you leave. Put the shawled uniforms on when you wake up, we are visiting the Ashen Desert at dawn."

Chapter XIX

Ashen Desert

Seven gray horses awaited in front of the base at the crack of dawn.

The canvas of rock-colored skies mirrored the horses' satiny hair, and the sun rising in the east smeared rays across the thickets of clouds. The horses nipped at the courtyard's neatly kept grass, fresh with morning dew, and were ready to be mounted.

Shei eagerly rubbed her sleep-stricken eyes. "We are doing something fun for once!"

"My apologies if training you to survive has not been *fun* for you." Commander's scold turned into a yawn. He had not been sleeping well as of late, showing up to the training sessions in the mornings with dark circles around his eyes. "Keep your shawls down until we reach the desert. Let's go."

I raised a hand. "Commander Izaak, will you show me how to ride first?"

"You never rode a horse before?" Raina asked with surprise.

I shook my head.

Many families in the Mounds owned a mount, although folk mostly got around the hills on foot. My parents never had a need for one, having worked in the market and the mines. Not that we could afford one, anyway.

"Come, I will show you," Raina said. "I have been riding horses since I was a child."

Naturally.

Commander paired each horse with a rider. The two largest stallions went to Tain and Lazzor since it required more muscle to support their weight. My match was a calm, black-eyed mare, the middle of the herd in terms of size. Still, I was reluctant to approach her, stalling while others got in their saddles.

"A couple of things to remember…" Raina began the demonstration with the help from her white-streaked stallion. "Greet your mare. Mount her with confidence, and keep your posture up. And be gentle with the reins," she said and began to walk away.

"Wait, that's it? That is all there is to horse-riding?" I asked.

She rolled her eyes, watching me over her shoulder. "For a smart girl, you ask stupid questions. That is all we have time for. You are more than welcome to ask the Akani all about the ways of horse-riding when they arrive. Get on now, before Father leaves us behind!"

"For a smart girl, you get your facts wrong at times. Akani Warriors are kelpie-riders." I smirked.

Raina tugged the reins, joining the procession led by the commander, everyone falling in line behind each other one rider at the time. "Same difference."

"Same difference?" Lazzor moaned after a theatrical gasp. "Kelpies and horses couldn't be further apart! If you take a look at their anatomy…"

Raina twisted her neck, her gleaming chestnut eyes blinking at the gray skies. "…I would die of boredom, that much is sure. Come on, Imani!"

Alright. I can do this.

I half-stepped into the mare's view, my leg muscles tense, ready to jump aside if she decided to attack. The two onyx crystals that were her eyes watched me approach with caution. I patted the right side of her face with soft touch, taking a deep breath to calm my angst. The mare appeared indifferent towards me, but that was a good start from what I could tell.

"Imani! Hurry—we are only waiting for you!" Commander's voice echoed from the front of the line. That was only half true with Shei's slender mare spinning about in circles while she giggled, calling herself the conqueror of the wild. Needless to say, she'd never ridden a horse before, either.

I shifted to my mare's side, running my hand across her sleek yet firm body before I thrusted my boot into the strap.

Mount her with confidence.

Relying on my strap-supported foot, I threw the other leg over the mare's back with one swing of my thigh. Holding onto the saddle to prevent a fall earned me a side eye from Raina before I gripped the reins with my free hand.

"There you go!" Her smile held the sense of accomplishment. "Keep balance with your legs and torso, and loosen your grip on the reins before they permanently imprint on your palms."

"But what if I fall?" I had trouble maintaining my posture as soon as the mare began moving, holding onto the reins as if I was swinging from a cliff by a rope.

"You *will fall* if you don't follow my advice," Raina yelled out, piercing me with an acute stare. "Loosen the grip on reins already!"

I managed to stay alive by sheer luck alone. I didn't complain, saving myself from hearing Commander's favorite *"you would have learned how to do it if you joined us ten years ago like you were supposed to"* response. Keeping my eyes on the road ahead, I fixated on Raina's silhouette in an attempt to follow her without straying.

The city woke up to a cloudy day, humid summer heat rising from the pavement. The Cobblestone greeted us with a grim face upon passing through the silver gates—many of the merchants barricading their front doors, hoping to preserve their tools and materials. Those who didn't have enough saved kept their shops open, and the folk poured in, stocking up on supplies and weapons. It felt as though the entirety of Lumenor turned tide overnight, heading into battle preparations, and with the sudden shift in their mindset came a great appreciation for the legionnaires.

"Thank you, thank you." Shei waved at cheering crowds. "What, it's nice to be celebrated every once in a while!"

Cella rode ahead, shaking her head. "I understand, but you must be vigilant in the saddle. Watch out for the apple cart ahead!"

It took Shei three brushes with fate before she calmed down in the saddle and started paying attention.

The outer gates of Lumenor soared above the roofs from the tail of the Queen's Alley. Built all the way back during the Ancestor's Era, with thousands of iron arrowheads patterning a giant crescent moon across their surface, the gates were intimidating in their own right. Impenetrable, hopefully. One big block of titanium was all that stood between us and the Ashen Desert and between the Akani Warriors and the moonstone.

Commander instructed the guards to open the gates, and all I could think about were the old tales of desert beasts: chimeras, ghouls, banshees, veelas—you name it. The creatures were believed to reside deep inside hidden underground caves, stalking wanderers and feeding on their flesh. The immediate expanse surrounding the city was regularly patrolled, making it almost impossible for the creatures to roam around without being spotted from the watchtowers atop the walls.

Almost impossible.

The gates opened, and my mare's mane matched the grayness of the view ahead. The somewhat lively city landscape composed of stone, glass, and dirt was replaced by the endless realm of ashen hills and flatlands. The sea of cinder stretched into horizon below the rising sun, making the particles sparkle like minerals. The ground beneath our horses' hooves was black basalt, sprinkled with an inch-thick layer of pale dirt.

No one knew exactly when the desert first formed, the earliest records dating from the Ancestors' Era. All we knew with certainty was that our ancestors, the original founders of our city, came upon grass-covered fields that bloomed into the distance with overgrown fruit trees and herbs. The scribers' notes diverged vastly from there, ranging from the ancient magic myths to the studies of earth, each coming up with its own explanation as to how the desert first formed.

Not that it mattered—it was there, nevertheless, glaring back at me blankly.

Lazzor's loud cough disturbed an eerie silence, and I looked to my side for the first time since mounting my mare. "Remember to put your shawls over your nose and mouth, everyone!"

Dusky linens layered the legion's desert uniforms, designed to blend into the palette of our grayish-white surroundings. We were equipped with shawls, wrapping them around our heads to prevent sunburn. Not that our once golden, now turned silver, sun emitted enough light to cause severe burns. Still, it was nice to have protection from the relentless grains that seemed dedicated to clog my nostrils.

The horses dispersed, no longer limited by the constraints of paved roads. Tain came to ride by my side, but I was in no mood for a chat. My bleeding came that morning, the fatigue burdening my lower back. My mind got lost in the haze of dizziness, my thighs burning, aching from the discomfort of the saddle.

"First time in the desert?" Tain asked. His back was straight, formidable leg muscles clutching onto the stallion as he rode.

I nodded. "It's not as scary as I imagined it to be."

"It gets scarier once you lose track of the gates and find yourself in the middle of the ashen sea."

I peeled my lips. "Well, when you put it like that…"

"Is he trying to terrify you with some milkmaid's tales?" Lazzor teased. He and Cella rode side by side while Shei struggled with keeping course, now cursing at her mare and at the particles in her mouth, as well as anything else that happened to cross her mind. Raina took Commander's side at the head, leading the procession.

Tain chuckled, running a quick glance across my lips. "I was just getting to it."

"Don't joke about such matters." Cella's tone displayed a vestige of concern. "The desert is frightening enough as is."

He shrugged. "At least no one is aiming knives at us for a change."

"Yeah, I guess that is nice."

A rider appeared from the far east, heading in our direction. He was undoubtedly a legionnaire judging from the uniform that resembled ours, save for the coat of ash glued to the cloth of his shawl. The grains rose behind him like a splash of murky water, making his appearance rather dramatic, like taken out of theatre play.

"Who is that?" I asked.

"One of the desert unit commanders," Tain replied. "We are going to visit the weapon forges."

"Why are some of the forges located in the desert? I've always wondered."

Commander's and Raina's horses picked up the pace, rushing forward with a gallop. I almost flipped over my back once my mare sped up without warning, catching up with Tain's stallion.

"They are here so that the blow up potion can be brewed safely, why else?" he said once I steadied myself atop my mare.

My eyebrows shot up, and my mouth froze in a half-gape.

A blow up potion?

They mean to blow the Akani up to shreds before they can break through the gates?

The blow up potion was the most delicate brew in existence, highly volatile and dangerous if mixed improperly. Mother had warned me against trying to brew it, threatening to pull my limbs out herself if she ever saw me with the ingredients alone. She made sure I knew that she would end me quickly and efficiently rather than have to collect my remains from the blast, if any were left in the first place.

The desert commander met us at last, his green eyes glowing like the malachite crystals Zana favored in her jewelry. "Your majesty," he said, nodding at Tain, before he greeted the rest of us. "Izaak, my dear friend, and our fellow sei-sans, welcome to the Ashen Desert."

Raina scoffed at the *your majesty* part, but she held her tongue back out of respect for his rank.

"Thank you, Marken, my friend," Commander said, pressing a fist against his wide chest. "Lead the way."

We rode deeper into the desert. The thickening, powdery layer of ash softened the terrain, the desert mouth swallowing us whole. Rolling dunes shape-shifted, roused by the hoofs of our mounts or the breeze.

"There—the weapon forges!" Cella called out, pointing further east to where fifty or so legionnaires labored inside the valley. We dismounted the horses, leaving them tied to a post to cool down and drink from pots of muddied water. I patted my mare before departing, and she nickered, leaning into my touch.

Three small huts provided the only shelter from the weather and creatures. The overhanging roofs made from oakwood planks looked as though they were ready to collapse at any second. The only guarded hut housed the potion supplies, where three sei-sans dwelled at the door, protecting the ingredients.

My feet sank into the pillows of pale particles on our descent down the hill, and Tain took a hold of my hand, pulling me out whenever my boots got stuck. His skin was warm to the touch, as always, and I wished I could place his hands on my lower back that had continued to throb.

Marken, the desert commander, gave us a tour upon our arrival. "We press the nightshade berries at the first station over there to extract the juice." He gestured at the group of legionnaires sitting in the circle with berry-filled granite mortars and pestles, big enough to fit a small child. They were in good spirits, singing ancient hymns and enjoying playful banter.

"Now that I am here to see it, I wish I was sent to the Ashen Desert instead," Shei whispered into my ear. "I'd much rather sing songs and press fruit than patrol."

Tain snickered behind her. "Until one of your peers' attention slips for a moment and they blow you up to pieces."

Shei pouted. "Do you have to try to ruin anything, or is it a natural gift of yours?"

"I am not sure," he replied, molding a thinking face. "Imani might have an answer for you, though. She knows me rather well."

My lips cracked into a smile. That was before Shei scolded me with an angered frown, and I straightened up.

"Here we crush the white snakeroot flower and soak it alongside chopped blue oleander petals," Marken continued the tour. Every ingredient of the blow up potion was highly poisonous, enough to end one's life on its own. "Over there… stay behind the line young man," he upbraided Lazzor who stumbled upon what he didn't know were the stores of the deadliest poison known to humankind, "over there, we boil the chimera's venom."

Lazzor stopped in his tracks. "The chimera's venom? How did you get your hands on it?"

The desert commander curved his lip with pride. "We hunted them, of course."

"You hunted chimeras?" Cella asked, looking half-frightened, half-amazed.

Marken nodded. "There is no other way to get the venom. We only needed to catch four or five to meet our demands."

Only four or five?

"I take that back," Shei squealed, "I am very glad to be patrolling the city."

The desert commander walked us through the rest of the station, listing the ingredients as well as the way they were being prepped for the final brew. I listened carefully, curious if their recipe matched the one I found in Mother's famous potion book she kept hidden in the basement. As per usual, Zuri and I overturned our moonhouse once to find it while she was away visiting Zana a few summers ago.

The legion came upon the last station, and Marken explained that was where they brewed the mineral-rich, magic-fused sand and water before mixing all the components together. However, one ingredient from Mother's recipe was missing.

"What about the gargoyle blood?" I posed the question. "My mother is an experienced potion brewer, and her recipe claims it to be a crucial ingredient of the blow up potion."

Raina tilted her head. "I thought you only mixed healing potions and makeup?"

"I do."

"You said nothing about knowing how to blow things up, tree burner," Shei added with a mischievous grin. "Wicked, I'll admit."

Cella slapped her forehead. "Please never teach Shei how to brew one, or we will all end up in the star lands before our time is due."

"I certainly didn't intend to," I responded, laughing. "And you can all calm your nerves. I only know the list of ingredients, I've never actually brewed one before."

Commander shot me a stern look. "It better stay that way or I will personally throw you into the dungeons beneath the palace."

I had no doubts that he was serious.

Marken, however, looked at me with a fond eye. "You are very knowledgeable, Miss Stone. We could have used your talents here," he said, eyeing Commander with a pinch of spite. "And we tried using the gargoyle blood," he went on, "however, every drop carries a different amount of explosive. That trait alone makes it hard to predict the size of the impact. We lost two legionnaires over it."

Our discussion piqued Tain's curiosity, and he craned his neck over my shoulder. "What is the gargoyle blood needed for?"

"It thickens the brew," I said, "increasing the blast by at least tenfold."

Tain's jaw split open so widely, he could have swallowed an entire apple in one bite. He turned to the commander. "And we are not using it? Was this mother's... uhm, the queen's decision?"

The two commanders exchanged a loaded stare in silence.

"Yes," Marken replied. "Queen Astra forbade the use of gargoyle blood after being warned about the dangers."

Tain puffed out loudly. "That is unwise—what other option do we have if we are to defeat the Akani?"

Commander Izaak could have sliced Tain's face with the blade-sharp stare he shot at him. "We are not using it and you will speak no more of it." Tain gulped, ready to argue, but Commander continued. "And if you do, you can go gather your belongings and run back to your mother. See if the princeling crown fits you better than the uniform."

I covered my mouth to try to stop the gasp that had already left my throat.

Tain face reddened a shade. "But—"

"No complaints. It has been decided, and the last time I checked, you were no king. Not yet. You are under my command, and you will do as I say. Understood?"

"Understood," Tain replied, bitterly biting into his underlip.

Commander says—you do.

It really was as simple as that.

Prince or no prince, his daughter or a stranger, Commander's rules never changed, and I admired him for it. No principle stood its ground if it was conditionally applied, he taught me that.

Raina and Shei made no effort to conceal their smirks, each feeling as if they'd won a personal battle against Tain.

"Good," Commander concluded. "I believe our tour comes to an end. Anything else you wish to show us?"

The desert commander's glare darted southbound. "My soldiers found a banshee sneaking about last night. It took nine of us to tame her. You might want to take a look."

"Thing are taking an unexpected turn," Shei said, climbing the ashen hill on our journey south. "I'd like to go back to the city now, please."

Cella threw an arm over her shoulder. "Am I hearing this right? Is our invincible knife-throwing master saying she is afraid of some corpse?"

Shei twisted her mouth. "If the corpse belongs to a blood-thirsty monster, then yes, I am very much afraid. You should be, too."

Lazzor overheard her and went on to give her a good scare. He snuck up on Shei and grabbed her shoulders from behind, screeching in a shrill, unsettling voice. She jumped at his touch before beginning to chase him about. "This will be the end of you, you fool! I've had enough!"

He held his stomach in a groaning laughter while making a run for it. "You will have to catch me first!"

Cella watched them scurry around with a kind smile. "Those two were bound to meet. I am not sure which one of them is madder than the other."

"I am not sure if Lazzor is the one Shei was bound to meet," I said, flashing my eyebrows.

Shei tripped over her own feet, falling face-down a short distance from us, splashing the grains. Lazzor scuttled towards her, burying her legs underneath a thick blanket of ash, before Commander lost his patience and demanded they begin to act like grownups.

Cella's head spun back towards me. "Sorry—I forgot. I know the two of you are very good friends. You became legionnaires together. Meant to be for sure."

I was not certain if I believed that anything was *meant* to happen. I preferred to think that only I could decide what was stored in my cards. However, if one good thing came out of me joining the legion, it was getting to know Shei.

"Maybe," I said, "but I wasn't talking about myself, either." I winked and sped past her.

The smell of rotting flesh became so strong that I started breathing in through my mouth. The fallen corpse came into view, resting lifelessly atop the low hill ahead.

The banshee.

Banshees were believed to be the original inhabitants of the Mounds, uprooted from their homeland by the ancestors. Once free-roaming inhabitants of the hills of Lumenor, beings of magic as old as earth itself, their souls were bound to the moonstone. Yet they never had the power of bending starlight. They didn't need it. Their voices, once known for pouring rivers across valleys and rising mounds from dust, made magic of their own, bringing harmony to life.

Until they were banished.

A female figure laid on her back, her silver waist-long hair tussled in a tangle of dead desert flowers. Her skin was ghostly white, her fingertips stained with crimson streaks of blood. A pale dress on her back faded into an ashen hilltop, the desert feeding on her remains. A gaping hole was all that was left of her chest, seared flesh from starlight marked the wound that ended her life.

The hairs at the back of my neck rose. "How long ago was she murdered?" The banshee's face muscles were cramped into a permanent frown, her fangs shining in the cloud-filtered gray sunlight.

"Eight, nine hours ago, if I had to guess," Marken replied.

Cella crouched, leaning over the corpse and blinking away the dust. "She was quite beautiful. What a tragic destiny, to die all alone, left to decay, forgotten by time."

Tain squatted by her side, squinting at the corpse's delicate features. "Banshees are never alone," he mumbled. "Best to get on with it and blast the corpse with a blow potent enough to turn her into stardust before nightfall."

"Or what?" Raina asked, shifting into an unsteady stance, jerking her head side to side in an alerted state.

"Or her friends will come," he said.

"Her *friends*?" Shei and I exclaimed at once.

Tain rubbed his temples and stood. "Her friends, yes. Mother's, I mean the queen's reports suggest the Ashen Desert is swarming with banshees, their numbers multiplying year over year."

Raina shook her head in disbelief. "And you are just telling us this *now*?!"

Commander Izaak's palm touched his daughter's back. "All commanders are aware of the strange happenings in the desert. But we must face our opponents one at the time. We shall head back to the city, we have seen enough."

Thank Kirrah.

I had enough of the desert for one day, and I was not eager to encounter an undead banshee now that I had seen a dead one. But unfortunately for me, the banshees were seemingly eager to meet us.

A synchronized wail rang through the vast expanse, scattering ash about. I covered my ears, feeling heat flow to my palms. Sei was ready to defend me before I was ready to defend myself.

"Turn your backs to each other and pair up!" Commander ordered.

Tain pressed his back against mine, squeezing my hand before he let go, shifting into a fighting stance. Raina and Lazzor did the same to my left, Shei and Cella to my right. Everyone's palms flashed with starlight while the two commanders in our midst took their knives out. They watched for the incoming threat with a calmness that could only be gained with experience.

A whirlwind of air lashed at our cheeks, the screaming growing louder, coming from the south-east.

"Whatever you do, don't run," Tain shouted.

Lazzor coughed the dirt out of his mouth. "How many?"

"Three or four, judging from the sound!"

Tain's estimate was correct for better or for worse. Four very-much-alive banshees came into view, gliding across the hills to our right.

I swallowed.

The banshees' long, clawed fingers weaved through their never-ending strands of hair, combing them. Their eyes were red rubies, droplets of dried blood. They stood at average height, their bodies slender without muscle. Yet no one could deny their ethereal beauty, making their petrifying appearance somehow poetic.

The banshees watched us patiently from atop the hill, their throats vocalizing the ear-shattering cries. Then they dispersed, hurrying at us faster than winter winds. Coming to collect a meal and avenge their fallen sister. Despite their frail appearances, they had physical abilities that easily surpassed those of humans. The tales did them no justice.

My mouth was dry, my pulse quickening. I had a hard time containing the sei within me, holding back until the opportunity presented itself.

"They're so fast!" I shouted to overpower their cries. "I don't know if I can aim precisely enough!"

In truth, I knew I couldn't.

Not with my shaking hands or the shivers up my spine.

"We can work together," Tain said, stepping around me, his hands falling to my side. "Can you draw from outside of yourself?"

I bit into my cheek. "Yes, I think so. I did it once, I can do it again."

I conveniently left out that I only drew from the moonstone before, and that I was not sure how that ability was going to translate when bending starlight from our dead surroundings.

The banshees were almost on top of us. Shei's knife-like streams swooshed past Cella's intertwining weaves of sei before they both merged with Lazzor's raindrops of starlight. Raina preserved her power, keeping an eye on the commander. The banshees danced for their life, avoiding sei with speed. Their wails grew so loud they pained my eardrums.

"You be our shield, and I will be the spear," Tain said, forming two lengthy streams around his fists.

I didn't know how to be a shield, but I had to figure it out and do it quickly. Despite all the clamor, I closed my eyes. Took a deep breath. Calmed my raging mind. Felt the starlight within me, within Tain and my friends, even within the banshees. I swirled my fingers, immersing my mind into the currents of air fueled with life force. I opened my palms, binding the sei around me to the sei that came from within, creating the link like Miss Yamane showed me.

There you are.

I opened my eyes to find everyone in a tussle of limbs and starlight. Tain was relentlessly aiming sei-spears at the banshee that was circling around us. One swing of her claws would have been enough to tear our flesh, one bite of her fangs enough to rip our throats out. My job was to keep her at a distance while Tain attacked, and I bent a sphere only a quarter as large as the one I forged while dueling Raina during the trials. However, I didn't feel close to draining this time around.

The only problem was, I was yet to master bending the starlight I drew from outside of myself. My mind was struggling to keep the links from breaking, and the sphere shrunk a substantial amount after one of the banshees almost ripped Raina's heart out, distracting me. Luckily, Lazzor was quick on his feet, saving her life. I couldn't see Commander Izaak or his companion, and I didn't exactly have time for a careful examination. I glimpsed Cella and Shei, who were closing in on their banshee, when I realized my links broke off, splitting the sphere in half, creating an opening.

Damn you, Kirrah! Can you make it easy for me just this once?

The ruby-eyed banshee was a well versed fighter with the hollow expression of a ghost, yet she shared the same determination to kill us that Tain and Raina had for winning the crown. Tain was, however, equally if not more determined to end her life, and he took advantage of the gap, aiming spears through it.

But the banshee was smart.

She changed direction rapidly before I could redirect the sphere. Nothing stood between Tain, myself and her any longer, save for a patch of ground. She played into our surprise, and thrusted herself atop Tain before he had time to bend. Wailing, screaming, clawing. I vanished the sphere, launching myself into her torso, swiping her away. We rolled down the hill together, her claws tearing at the flesh on my forearm.

"Imani!" Tain cried out, clambering behind us. "Hold on, I am coming!"

He refrained from bending, probably afraid he would harm me in the process, which was highly likely given that even I couldn't tell where my body began or ended, my limbs braided together with those of a monster hungry for flesh.

The knives at my belt were out of reach, all my strength used to hold back the banshee's fangs away from my face. I landed atop her at the base of the hill, which saved my life. Even with the weight of my entire body I struggled to contain her.

A blood-curdling realization flashed through my mind. I couldn't only feel the starlight within the banshee—my mind could reach for it. Maybe link with it, even.

No.

Find another way.

The solution was simple the moment I started thinking about it. Without any time to waste, I gathered the heat in my chest and let it rush down to my palms. Sei burned through the banshee's struggling arms, turning them to dust. Piercing her heart was even easier once she had no arms to claw with. I blasted a small ball of sei inside her chest, making sure I only bent from within to avoid killing myself. Only inner starlight could not harm the sei-san. Not the same was true for the starlight we linked with.

I was still sitting atop whatever was left of the banshee when Tain reached us and lifted me up. His face stopped within an inch of mine, his arms inspecting my bleeding forearm. I wanted to scream the second the rush left my body. The pain was excruciating.

"Here, here, I got it," Tain panted. The shouts from the top of the hill grew silent at once.

"Where is the rest of the legion? Tain, where are they?" I panicked.

He secured my arm, tearing at his shawl with his teeth before wrapping my wound to prevent me from losing too much blood. "They must be fine," he said, "or it wouldn't be silent. I am sorry. I failed you."

Failed me?

My chest perked up. "Failed me how?"

He wiped the sweat from his ashen forehead. "I lost focus, and I put you in danger."

"I put myself in danger by losing grip on my bending," I corrected him. "I put the both of us in danger. I am the one who should be apologizing, but I won't do that. I will, however, promise to do better next time."

He nodded, blowing a puff of air out. I cupped his pale cheeks, planting a kiss on his lips still soft despite the ashen coating. He embraced my kiss eagerly, letting a throaty moan out, lighting a fire in my belly. I knew it was inappropriate, imagining Commander Izaak's frown if he saw us, but we almost died.

"We might need to run into danger more often," he whispered, "if this will be the outcome each time."

"The Akani Warriors will grant your wish in no time," I said.

Tain's face hardened in an instant. "Let's go check on the others. You need your wound properly stitched."

That much was true, judging from the tear in my forearm.

We found the legion encircling a pile of dead bodies in the middle of the hill. *Shei, Cella, Raina, Lazzor, Commander Izaak—all alive, thank the moons.* My shoulders slouched, relieved of tension. But then I saw a dead body on top of banshee corpses. It belonged to the desert commander.

Tain and I looked at each other, both our expressions blank. Marken didn't survive the attack. Raina thrusted herself into her father's arms, who, despite his fading bending power, had no visible scratches after fighting banshees.

I don't wish to know how powerful the commander was in his prime.

"Oh, Imani," Shei hurled into my hug. I winced, my forearm wound biting at my flesh. "What happened? Are you well?"

"Yes, I just—"

Tain cut me off. "She is not well, she needs stitching. The banshee's claws got her pretty good, but the wound is mostly superficial."

Shei puffed. "Right, thank you for that assessment, *Mister Head Healer*. Remind me to never leave you alone with her again."

I rocked her shoulder with my healthy arm. "What happened to me was my own fault," I proclaimed. "Don't look at me like that, and stop blaming Tain for everything under the sun. He did nothing wrong."

She rolled her eyes. "This time, *maybe*."

"Enough," Commander said. "We will send my lifelong friend to the star lands the proper way. Lazzor, Tain, separate him from the beasts."

Everyone but for my injured self proceeded to build a bed of ash for the fallen commander. Lazzor and Tain carried his corpse over, laying it down on his back atop the pile. Commander swirled his fingers, and Raina's eyes widened.

"Father, you must be careful," she urged, "you drain quickly these days."

One stern look from Commander Izaak was enough to silence her. "I will send my friend off the way he deserves."

"One of us could do it, there is no need…"

"No." Commander had made up his mind. He closed his eyes, mouthing a silent prayer. I couldn't bare to look at Marken's dead body, plunging my face into Tain's chest. He brought me closer, breathing in the jasmine scent in my hair. Shei took Cella's hand, tears filling her eyes.

"Until we meet again in the star lands," Commander whispered and set the corpse ablaze, turning it to stardust. The breeze scattered his remains across the hill, uniting the desert commander's body with the earth once again, allowing his soul to depart. Raina sobbed quietly, all of us bowing our necks in respect.

"Life is precious," Commander said, wrapping an arm around his daughter. "Protect yourself and those you love at any cost."

Zuri's laughter echoed in my ears, lumping the knot in my throat.

At any cost.

Cella cleared her throat. "Uhm, Commander," she said after we stood in silence for a while. "I would like to apologize in advance."

Commander's brow creaked. "Apologize for what?"

"This." She turned to Shei and kissed her.

Lazzor and I both gasped at once. "Awww!"

Commander sighed and walked away, but I could swear I heard a soft chuckle as he turned. Even Tain cracked a smile. Despite all his differences with Shei, he was fond of Cella, and we could all use a little bit of love on such a death-ridden, gloomy day.

Well, maybe not all of us.

"Don't even think about it," Raina hissed after Lazzor glanced at her with a keen eye.

Some things never change, I thought, treading back to the desert base with heavy feet. Tain helped me along the way, his arm hung around my non-injured shoulder. Shei and Cella strode past us hand in hand, both of them blushing. My eyes met Shei's for a brief moment, and she winked, mouthing a happy scream she was surely going to let out in the privacy of her chamber. She was happy, and I was happy for her.

Maybe Cella was right—maybe the two of us were meant to meet after all and become friends.

Chapter XX
Mounds-born

I spent two nights in the healers' wing following our desert outing, which Mr. Osei used to his advantage, teaching Shei and me how to apply first aid. "You will go into the battle without knowing the fundamentals of healing over my dead body," he proclaimed, handing us each practice dummies for stitching.

Shei butchered the cloth practice arm in a poor attempt to stitch it together, squinting as she threaded the hair-thin string of silk. I was already done with mine, in spite of limited mobility of my right arm.

"Ugh," she moaned. "I have no patience for this! If I get torn apart in the battle, feel free to leave me behind."

"And if Imani gets torn apart?" The head healer gave a measured head tilt. "Keep practicing, you will get a hang of it soon."

Shei batted her lashes. "You see? The things I do for you."

"Why are you so impatient anyway?" I asked, putting my needle back into the practice tool case. "Do you have somewhere to be?"

She elbowed my healthy arm. "Shut it, Imani."

Mr. Osei quizzed me on potion ingredients and their applications, giving up after I answered every question before he finished reciting it. "You are thrilled to be visiting home, I suspect?"

Commander had announced the day prior that we would be allowed to visit our families during one of the city's four major holidays, the Assan's Night. Lumenorans annually celebrated the night when the youngest of the three moons ignited our skies for the first time, joining Tora's and Shei's eternal dance around the earth. I was beside myself, barely containing my excitement, counting hours until the following morning.

"Beyond thrilled," I replied. "This is the longest I've ever spent apart from my family."

Shei crossed her arms in her lap, bowing her chin. "I think I will stay behind."

"What? Why?" I asked. "You always talk about how much you miss your uncle!"

She was done butchering the practice arm, completing her first semi-satisfactory stitching assignment. "I do miss him, but I don't want to put him in danger. The rebels would swarm the shop and our living quarters on the floor above if they knew I was there. And what little protection Commander offered to send along could do very little in the heart of the Gutter. You saw it yourself during the patrol."

Mr. Osei tongued the corner of his mouth, putting the practice dolls back into the ebony closet that shouldered his desk. "I am very sorry to hear that, Shei."

"Wait—I have an idea!" The words rolled off my tongue with zest. "Why don't you come to my house? I know it's not the same, but my family would love to have you!"

Shei shrugged, her chin shrinking further into her chest. "No, no, you need time alone with your family, not a stranger in your house."

I softly touched her wrist. "You are no stranger. I will not take no for an answer."

"But—"

"You are coming! Off you go, pack! We leave with the first light."

She pressed her lips together. "Alright, alright. Thank you, tree burner." She left the healers' quarters with a skip in her step.

Zuri will be thrilled to meet her!

"You are smart to keep a friend like her around, she is a good child. Little hard to tame, but still good, nevertheless." Mr. Osei chuckled after Shei shut the doors behind her. "Anyway, I have a couple of things to discuss with you before you head home." The healer's face grew serious.

My ears perked up. "About the cure?"

Please be about the cure. I could use good news, now more than ever.

"Amongst other things," he replied. "First things first. I visited your family some days ago."

My palm fell to my heart. "You went to the Mounds?"

I didn't know why, but it was strange imagining Mr. Osei inside my family's moonhouse. He had grown up in the hills, but the years he spent living in Old Town made him adopt a certain noble-like presence—one, I had suspected, he'd adopted in his attempt to adapt to his surroundings. To survive. Knowing how the queen and her noble friends were with the hill folk, I couldn't say I blamed him. It didn't make him any less Mounds-born, nevertheless.

We all get by whatever way we can.

The fatherly kindness melted over the healer's onyx face. "I go to the hills all the time, although I have my way of slipping past the gates unnoticed. You've learned of those ways, I hear, taking Tain along with you. That was not wise."

My wrapped forearm shot up, and I winced, remembering it needed another day or two to heal. "Why is everyone against Tain? He is not a bad person!"

Tain had come to visit me at the healers' quarters every chance he got, bringing me red grapes and his favorite book to pass the time, which was sweet. The book was, however, quite a dry read, going on for pages about the nature of good and evil and how to recognize each within one's self.

"No one claims him to be bad," Mr. Osei said, "but he is the queen's son. And she, might I add in confidence, is not exactly what you call a good person. Cunning, efficient, powerful, surely. But not good at heart."

No kidding.

"Anyhow, I came to an agreement with your parents," the healer continued. "Your lovely sister will take refuge at my house during the battle. The Old Town will be much safer than the Mounds. I would've taken your parents in, too, but I am afraid I am not able to sneak them past the guards. They are being posted at every corner of Old Town as we speak, and only your sister is small enough to fit into the supply chest. And if things go as planned, she may be a step closer to healing the next time you see her. Not cured entirely, but granted a much, much longer life."

A river of tears ran down my cheeks. I threw myself into Mr. Osei's arms, sobbing. "I can't thank you enough! I am so worried—I've been having nightmares for months. Thank you for helping my sister. What is the cure, if I may ask?"

The healer's kindness was the kindness of my people—the people of rolling hills and whispering rivers that never ceased to amaze me. We always came together during difficult times. It was the reminder I needed.

My reason to fight.

Mr. Osei pulled a handkerchief out of the front pocket of his robe and handed it to me. "You will learn when the time comes, but you must be patient. Besides, you are the one I should be thanking," he said as I mopped my tears away, "you are doing all the hard work. Risking your life to protect your sister, to protect all of us."

I wiped my tears away. "Don't thank me just yet, Mr. Osei. I could barely keep a grip on sei I linked with in the desert. My aim improved, but it is still not precise when my target is moving. I... I don't think I will be of much help."

A bitter flavor settled in my mouth at the realization.

It was all for nothing—three months of hard work, and all I have to show for it is a marginal improvement. I will be dead from the second Akani Warriors attack. I am useless. Moons help me—I am useless! I will only stand in the others' way. What if I end up between Kalon and the moonstone all alone? He will take it in no time.

I was short of breath, and my stomach began tingling. Then the tingle spread to my arms and legs, followed by a sharp chest pain that struck me like thunder out of clear skies. One moment I was fine, another I thought I was dying a painful death.

The head healer gestured inhaling a deep breath, patting my back. "It is alright, you will be alright. Imani, look at me. Breathe. Breathe deeply. Slower. That is better. Don't try to speak, just breathe."

I tossed my healthy arm above my head, opening my ache-ridden chest. *Useless.* The first breath of air slipped into my lungs. *Useless.* Then another. *Think and calm down.* I exhaled loudly, then repeated the process.

Mr. Osei handed me a cup of cool mint water after I established the breathing rhythm. I drank it in one pour, relishing the chill as it passed down my throat.

"May I be candid?" he asked.

I bobbed my head.

"No one expected you to become a master of bending in three short months. It is impossible. I am astonished by what you have been able to accomplish, we all are. But unlike Shei, your bending skill was not the reason why you were accepted into the most powerful legion in all of Lumenor."

I squinted. "Then why?"

He glanced at the door. "You already know why. Think about it. Where does your strength lie?"

"Uhm, in the amount of starlight I can summon from within?" That much was obvious from day one.

"Precisely," he agreed, "and it is that ability that distinguishes you from others. Your raw talent."

I wrangled my fingers behind my back. "'Not worth much without skill."

The healer tilted his head with a confident, pointed stare. "That is where we disagree. Think again. Why would Izaak accept a low-skilled sei-san into his elite legion in the first place?"

I took another sip of mint water to cool down my blood that was once again running hot. "He intends to use me as fuel, right? In case the others are drained, they will link to my power and direct it."

I was afraid Commander thought me better leveraged building weapons than being one. I didn't know it at the time, but I was a weapon all along.

One drawn out nod came from the healer. "Yes. But you are not going to let them drain you. Preserve your power until the end. Remember your first priority in the battle."

I leaned back in my seat. "Which is?"

"The moonstone. Not your friends, nor the walls, not some young lad. Keep your eyes on the crystal."

I reached for my braid, finding comfort in running my fingers down its silky, curly texture. "I will. You have my word."

I wasn't sure if I meant it, but I decided I would stay true to what I said. Saving the moonstone meant saving the city, there was no other way around it. And with my sister safe in the Old Town, I knew that was where I needed to be, too.

"One more thing." Mr. Osei tossed another glance at the door. "Shei is the only one here you can trust. Remember that."

His words stung like the banshee claw in my arm. "But Raina, Cella?" I thought of Tain too, but knew what Mr. Osei would say.

Tain is the queen's son.

The healer shook his head. "Only Shei."

The carriage almost rolled backwards while wheeling uphill, shaking Shei and me inside like two pebbles in a jar. One of Shei's throwing knives slid out of her linen sleeve, almost slicing my finger in half. She bent over, picking it up with a sigh.

"We could've come on foot!" Shei held onto her stomach, unaccustomed to the carriage rides. "Kirrah damn Commander and his rules!"

I licked my bottom lip. "You want to get out and make a run for it? We are only a quarter mile away from my moonhouse anyway. At this point, Commander Izaak can't do anything but let us fight in battle."

"Now that's what I call a good idea!" She peered out of the tiny, circular window through the drapes, then wiggled her eyebrows. "Follow my lead, tree burner. And careful with the pines now that we are back in the Mounds. I know you must be tempted."

"Ha-ha. Just go."

She kicked the carriage door open while still in motion. In all fairness, we were moving at a toddler's speed. Jumping out didn't pose much danger to either of us.

The coachman in the front didn't notice us leaving, but two guards trodding atop their stallions behind surely did.

"Get back here!" they called, but I instructed Shei to cut eastbound, through the thick scatter of trees leading up to my family's moonhouse. The guards' mounts refrained from following into the steep hillside and they lost our tracks.

Shei gaped once we reached the depths of the forest, inhaling the soothing aroma of surrounding pines. Copper-eyed owls blinked in the heights, their heavy-set eyes twinkling like fireflies. It was crisp outside for the tail end of summer, as if even the clouds could smell the bloodshed riding its way toward us.

Any day now.

Shei's face lit up. "Where is the hill you infamously set ablaze? I want to see the remains of this slaughter I keep hearing about!"

I rolled my eyes. "You are the one who keeps bringing it up. I am afraid it is further down, and we don't have time. But do you see that pine over there?"

She looked in the direction of my pointed finger. "Another one you tried to take down?"

"Sort of." I gazed upon the slender evergreen tree with the sense of pride. "That hole in the bark marks the first time I hit anything with one of my starlight balls."

Shei wrestled one of the blades out of her belt, trotting towards the pine. Proceeding to carve something in the tree crust right beneath the hole, she made me turn away until she was done. "You can look now."

Two crescent moon carvings indented the tree bark when I opened my eyes. One of them was bigger than the other, their position in relation to one another mimicking the feminine moons in the sky. "Tora and Shei?" I asked.

She tossed her hands in the air. "I was named after the bloody moon, wasn't I? You can't blame me for a bit of symbolism."

"We are missing our Assan," I noted, tapping the bark where his position would have aligned with the skies.

Shei frowned with the hint of shrewdness in her twisted mouth. "We don't need some knucklehead coming in between us." Judging from the distaste in her voice, she was referring to Tain.

"I would never betray you for him, or anyone else for that matter, you know?" I asked, my voice deepening. "It's important to me that you know that."

"I know," she replied, averting her stare. "Imani, I…" Shei paused mid-inhale. Then her expression shifted from discomfort to calmness in a split second. "I know."

"Good," I said. Spinning around my heel, I beckoned her to follow my footprints.

The receding tree line soon hollowed out an opening for my house, and I sped up. Dull, gloomy skies served as a backdrop, nothing more than an empty canvas. In the center of the view crouched a round, rough-textured moonhouse dressed in the robust coat of leaves and flower buds. Summer vegetables and herbs bloomed out of garden beds with warm, rich soil. The decades old, thrice-repainted wind chime rang in the breeze, Mother's potion flasks shining on the outdoor table, left there to dry.

The familiar smell of nettle tea called me home.

Shei nudged my back. "You've been blabbing about the hills ever since we talked inside the prison cell for the first time. Go on, now!"

I swirled saliva in my mouth, the soles of my boots glued to the dewed grass blades.

"You can do it," Shei went on upon noticing my hesitation. "It's your family—the only group of people in Lumenor that isn't trying to poison you, use you, or kill you. What is there to be afraid of?"

The truth of the matter was, my family knew the girl who left home—their stubborn, albeit well-meaning child. That was the Imani they loved. But they didn't know the girl who bent starlight, threw knives, and patrolled the city with a legionnaire uniform on her back.

Will they still love me after they see who I've become?

I will never find out unless I go inside.

"Race you to the door," I blurted out and bolted.

I didn't really care about racing Shei—she was a faster runner than me by far. However, I figured it would be easier to rip the bandage off and storm into my home before I could turn away.

One thing I forgot about after spending three months away from the Mounds—the hill folk had their own way of dealing with intruding rebels. And Shei practically looked like one, dressed in a layered, gray outfit, covered from head to toe, knives sticking out from every fold and chasing after me.

Mother jumped between us, from seemingly out of nowhere, with the blacksmith's hacksaw swinging from her arm. "You will not harm my daughter!" She launched herself at Shei, who was too stunned to say anything or move aside.

My reaction was involuntary, an instinct at that point. I swirled my fingers, and a short stream of starlight shattered her weapon. "That's my friend! She is not a rebel! For Kirrah's sake, Mother, what are you doing with the hacksaw?"

Mother's chest fell down and so did her emptied hand. "What are *you* doing, running away from your friend like that? You scared me to death, child."

Her lips quivered before she finished speaking, a tear glazing her umber cheek. I threw myself into her arms. "I missed you so much."

Mother's firm hug was all the comfort I needed, and we held on for a while. "Is that a mint scent in your hair?" She sniffed at the roots of my braid twice.

I could feel Shei's sneer from behind. "It's a long story," I replied, hoping to change the subject. "And since we are talking about mint, Mother, please meet Shei. She and I joined the legion together, you saw her during the pit trials."

Mother's midnight eyes glistened like the starlit night sky. "Of course—Shei! Your uncle is a fine man. My apologies dear, I didn't recognize you in all the haste." She gave Shei a hug, welcoming her inside. "That commander of yours sent no letter ahead of your arrival! I would've swept the dust if I had the notice that you were coming and bringing a guest, at that."

Shei twisted her neck, taking everything in. She told me she had never been inside a moonhouse before. "What dust?" she asked, winking. "Thank you for having me, Mrs. Stone. I was afraid to go back to the Gutter."

Mother invited us to wait in the living room, while she fetched Zana from her house and Zuri from the neighbor's yard. "Say no more, dear. You are welcome here anytime."

The azure-hued embers burned inside the fireplace despite the temperature outside. The fire was always kept alive for Zuri, even in summertime. Moonhouses were never too warm, thanks to the ancestors' thoughtful design. I shed my jacket, bringing a dried branch of rosemary from the incense tray to my nostrils.

I am home.

A black-and-silver moon calendar sprawled across the wall, my family's birthdays and all the major holidays circled in red. A rainbow of Mother's favorite crystals—citrine, amethyst, rose quartz, aquamarine, ruby, and topaz—cast colorful shadows on the floor, arranged in the familiar order on the window base. My and Zuri's childhood drawings hung beside chipped moon phase garland that was nailed to the inward curving wall. Playing cards, planet charts, mythology books, and carved incense trays—every item in our moonhouse held a piece of my memory.

Shei reclined her back into the cyan cushions on the floor, hovering her palm over the burning candle wick, its twirling flame licking at her skin. "I like it here. It's cozy."

It was strange to see my sharp-edged and sharp-witted friend inside my living quarters. She felt out of place, but then so did I. "Thanks. It isn't exactly made of glass, ebony, and velvet, but it's home. It will always remain home."

A giggle came from beyond the window slit. "Imani is here! Imani is here!"

I dashed through the round front door of our moonhouse, and Zuri ran into my arms. Her silver braid clattered with moon charms, heart-shaped lips stretching into a wide smile. "You are here!"

I couldn't believe my eyes. *It's really her.* A crescent moon tattoo sparkled on my sister's forehead, silver ink contrasting with the deep shade of umber in her skin.

"When did you get your tattoo?" I traced the moon with my thumb. "You are a big girl now!"

Mother must have been out of her mind to let Zuri get her tattoo before she turned fifteen, or maybe she was worried that she would never live long enough to get one. The sibling's curse and then the war atop of it. At least we had the cure for one of them.

I prayed that whatever Mr. Osei created work as promised. I couldn't bring myself to think of the alternative.

"Come inside, girls," Mother called. "Your father is at the market buying supplies for the Assan's Night. Zana is fetching her cards before she comes."

I cackled. "Naturally."

Zuri had about a thousand questions for me and Shei, whom she met once we came inside. She immediately took a liking to her. "You bend starlight like knives, and you throw real knives? Wicked! You must show me!"

Mother stuck her neck out from the kitchen. "No bending inside the house! Or outside for that matter—you never know which oak those damn rebels are hiding behind these days."

"Don't worry, we won't bend," I said, realizing I felt no need to talk back or contradict Mother in any way for the first time in my life.

Father's wisdom came to mind. *An unchained dog does not bite.*

"You should see Imani bending these little balls of starlight," Shei told my sister, gesturing the move. "She splits them into five balls each, then blasts them into targets," she narrated in a theatrical tone.

Zuri's long-lashed eyes widened. "The balls!" She clapped her small hands.

"You see—I juggle, and I use them to attack," I said and smirked.

Shei grimaced with a thinking face. "I don't remember seeing you juggle. Is that a new skill you acquired?"

"Oh, shut up!" I slapped her thigh, both of us laughing.

"Watch your mouth, young girl," Mother yelled from the kitchens. "You are still under my roof!"

Zuri mouthed Mother's reprimand alongside her, giggling. *A tiny beam of light.* My throat tightened watching her have fun with my friend, her child-like innocence coming through every word. *She is still a child. A sweet, innocent child.* I almost began crying before Father stumbled inside, dropping the bundles of market supplies at the doorstep after he spotted me.

"My sweet Mani," he cried out, wrapping his big arms around me. His hands were no longer calloused, those ebony eyes well rested, without dark circles around. He was no longer bound to the eternal darkness of the mines, no longer a ghost of a man, laboring his life away for us.

For me.

The aches, the close brushes with death, every bruise and punch— it was all worth it just for this moment alone.

I could never pay Father back for the sacrifices he made my entire life, but it felt good to know I could at least help him live the rest of his life out in peace. Kirrah knew he deserved it.

Zana crashed headfirst into us in the doorway, thrilled to see me. I teared up a bit in her and Father's arms, then introduced them to Shei while Mother brought the nettle tea out.

She looked at Zuri with a familiar *I-told-you-not-to-do-that* face, before my sister's fingers could wrap around the handle of the clay cup. "This batch is for adults only."

I pressed my lips in temptation. "Does that include Shei and me?" I couldn't resist. "We are grown legionnaires, you know. Not young girls anymore."

Mother scoffed, narrowing her eyes to slits. "Like that ever stopped you before. No more than two cups!"

"Where you find two, three come," I jested.

There was no arguing with Mother after she put her foot down. "Two cups, and not a slurp more."

"Fine." I gave up testing my luck.

Shei gulped the spiked tea faster than the quickest hill streams poured into the Mounds river. "Now this is some proper brew. Better than that stale, overpriced Old Town wine we drink every night."

I grimaced a scowl. "Seriously?"

"What?" Her mouth gaped, filling the second cup.

Mother waved a hand. "Don't scold your friend like I don't know what you do when I am not around. I was young once, too."

"Why is that so hard to believe at times?" I asked, intertwining my fingers between hers.

Zana lowered herself into the cushions next to Shei, watching her in deadly silence with the keen eye of a desert hawk. Attempting to read the acute lines of her face. "You are from the Gutter, I gather?"

"Mhm," Shei mumbled, squirming in her seat as though she could tell she was being studied. Meeting Zana for the first time had that effect on people.

"Would you like a reading?" the teller asked. "I am quite skilled in the ways of the ancestral arts."

Shei leaned deeper into the cushions, guarding her chest with crossed arms. "No, thank you," she replied, her voice rising a note. "It's not that I don't believe in it," she stammered sheepishly, "I just…"

The ray of sunlight collided with the emeralds that were Zana's eyes. "You'd rather not know, I presume?" She smiled politely. "No worries, dear, I figured I'd at least offer. One's destiny is in their own hands anyway. All I can do is provide guidance down the path."

Shei bowed her head, but she still refused. "You would love my girlfriend. She swears by the ancestral customs, for better or for worse."

Spending time around my family was the medicine I needed—their mere presence powering my spirit with the relentless desire to protect those I loved, no matter the cost. No matter the fear. Commander knew that. That must have been his reason to grant us the freedom to visit home—he wanted us to remember why we needed to fight.

Night fell in the blink of an eye, or it felt that way to me, and the time had come to burn herbs in Assan's name. The moons watched us in the waning phase from the night skies as we exited our moonhouse, clusters of silver-and-gold stars surrounding us. The beauty of Kirrah's cloak never failed to stop my breath, even during dark times.

Zana arranged garden pebbles in the shape of a crescent moon and placed the bundle of sage, mint, rosemary, nettle, coriander, and thyme in the center. My family and Shei gathered around it, holding hands while she recited a prayer in the ancient tongue. She used a garden torch to light the bundle on fire, its deep blue flames feasting on herbs in no time, immersing everyone in the firelight. I breathed the scent in—smelling the earth colliding with fire in its ultimate demise.

Smoke wafted out into the sky, and I closed my eyes. The presence of starlight around me was staggering. Sei was everywhere—in the night, in the herbs, grass, and trees. In the members of my family. The life force could be felt much more potently in nature when compared to the city lines. It was consuming, overwhelming, the last gulp of air to a choking lung. I could smell it in my nostrils, taste it in my mouth. I felt called to touch it with my mind, to link to its magic.

No.

Starlight doesn't control you, it's the other way around.

I drew a deep breath, watching the reflection of flames in my family's eyes. "Mother, Father—I need a word with you alone."

Their enchanted faces turned to stone, exchanging a look of fright. Mother bit into her cheek, her nod but a twitch of her chin. "Sure. I have herbs to sort out in the basement, why don't you two join me?"

My knees wobbled, stumbling down the now repaired stairwell. Having Father around all the time must have made Mother's life easier, and her aura blossomed despite the incoming threat. We found the basement packed with more supplies than we otherwise gathered in a year, and my mouth went agape at the sight.

"What…what is all this for?" I asked.

The question was foolish in hindsight.

"We had to prepare," Father laid out, squatting onto the pile of drying wood, before Mother hushed him away. She pulled a chair out of the scatter of garden furniture that had been stored away since the winter. He sank into it, careful not to lean onto his left foot. It had never healed properly from the accident he'd had in the mines.

"With the war coming and all, we did what we had to do. Thanks to your legionnaire coin, we were able to gather enough supplies. I am so proud of you, dear," Father said chokingly. "But enough about that. Tell us everything. How is it, being a famed legionnaire of Old Town? You are making the hills proud, too, not just us."

His deep voice soothed my unease, reminding me of the bedtime tales he used to read to me before heading to work. Father was a master of storytelling—he gave every character a unique flare, bending his voice at greater lengths than I bent starlight. He once told me that he'd wanted to be a performer as a young lad, but life had other plans.

It always does.

I looked up at the ceiling, wishing I could delay the inevitable. "There is no easy way to say this, but I must." My vocal cords trembled like violin strings. "I know… I know I am the reason behind Zuri's sickness."

It broke my heart to say it out loud, to admit what they already knew. I was the reason behind all our troubles, the blade in my sister's heart. But what shattered me wasn't the lingering silence that met me from the other side—it was the looks of guilt that painted their faces gray.

Father broke down at last. "My Mani... don't you think even for a second..." He choked on his words, and I bit into the flesh inside my mouth so hard, I was surprised I didn't rip it out, bloodying my teeth.

"It's true," Mother said, her sharp words slicing through his sobs. "Your sister is sick because of your power. Now, let me finish before you open your mouth, dear. Despite that being a matter of fact, it is no fault of yours. No, Imani, I don't want to hear it, the fault is not yours. It's mine."

Huh?

I gasped, covering my mouth, afraid we would be heard on the base floor above. "How could it be your fault? You didn't know I could bend before she was born! I am only six years Zuri's senior, and I didn't show signs of bending until I was ten."

Mother's stare was distant, her mind traveling far from the looks of it. "I knew. I knew of your power before you made your way out of my womb, child. I knew."

My legs collapsed and I fell back into a chair, feeling the heat of bursting starlight.

Not now.

"How could you have possibly known?"

Mother's face remained a blank papyrus, her throat vibrating in a low, self-soothing hum. She closed her eyes, and began quietly. "I was only four months with child, my belly only beginning to swell. I was cutting herbs in this very basement when I felt the kick. You were a feisty infant, always turning and twisting in my womb." She took a measured pause to prevent her voice from cracking like a walnut shell crushed by a rock. "And then it happened. I cuddled my belly, and this beautiful, translucent light ignited my palm and my stomach. A bond forming between mother and her bending child, as Mr. Osei revealed to me a few days ago. But even without that knowledge, I knew. I *knew*," she admitted and began to cry.

Father limped across the room with a stiff ankle and put his arm around her. "It was *our* fault," he emphasized. "It was *our* choice to have a second child. We wanted another daughter. Five years had passed, and we thought maybe we were wrong. Maybe you weren't able to bend. Maybe Kamari imagined the light. Maybe…"

He didn't complete the rest of the sentence, and we dwelled in the quiet for some time.

"It's not fair," I moaned, "it's not fair that I am gifted with the power of life while she is doomed to her death."

Mother willed her tears away, wiping her face with her sleeve. She walked over and cupped my hands in a tight clasp. "None of this is fair, such are the ways of life. But don't you dare think of it as your fault."

"But—"

She tilted her head with a raised brow. "No buts. Besides, the healer found a cure, or so he claims. I believe you heard Zuri will be staying at his manor during the battle. What do you think of that choice?"

My lips froze in half-gape. This was the first time Mother had asked for my thoughts on any of her decisions, and I'd lived in her house for eighteen long years. "You can trust Mr. Osei," I said with confidence. "He's done nothing but helped me the entire time I've spent in Old Town. Don't let the sigil on his healer's robe fool you— he is a true Mounds-born at heart."

"Good," she said. "Now, tell me everything. How does that hag of a queen intend to defend Lumenor from this warrior clan? I gather they are pretty skilled, you should hear some of the hill folk's tales about them. They talk of their leader as though he is some winter god."

A winter god?

I chuckled, thinking of the roaming superstition that swarmed the hills whenever a rumor was out. And this was a juice-filled peach of a rumor, stuck on everyone's mind.

I hope it is truly a superstition without a grain of truth to it.
For the sake of all of us.

"The queen is as crooked as the nettle snake's tail," I admitted, "but I like her son."

Father covered his ears playfully, reminding me of his natural silliness that Zuri inherited, too. "Oh, we heard. And I would appreciate hearing no more of it."

I giggled, but Mother was not in mood for jokes. "Be careful, will you? The fruit tends to fall near the tree, or whatnot. You know the saying."

"I know." I puffed out. "I am careful, besides, it's not like I am in love. He's just…"

Mother fluttered her eyelashes. "He is just so handsome and smart," she mocked in a poorly-executed imitation of my voice, "and he is a prince. I get it. I told you, I was a young woman too, once."

"I still find that hard to believe." I straightened my spine against the backrest. "But this Kalon worries me. You remember my reading the last time we were at Zana's?"

Mother opened her chest, the same thing seemingly lingering on her mind. "How could I forget? You don't think he can really bend midnight? Yes, that rumor is also out."

I gave a deep sigh. "I don't know. Tain says he cannot, but I am not persuaded. We located a distinguished Old Town scriber, and while he doesn't think it's possible, he admitted it must play a part. You tell me."

Talking things over with my parents provided the clarity I needed. We stayed in the basement for an hour, discussing everything I knew. I told them every detail, everything that happened to me ever since I joined the legion—from being poisoned with magic to linking with the moonstone and killing a banshee in the Ashen Desert. Their mature reasoning helped ease some of my worries, empowering me with confidence.

So what if you are not precise? You won't need to bend far if someone is within arm's reach with a sword. They may not even make it through the gates if they are blown apart in the desert. Leave them to the beasts, you stay in the Old Town. Remain near your sister in case of trouble. We will be fine, barricaded in the basement with the neighbors and Zana. You might not even need to fight the Akani in the end. I caught myself nodding along, my mind quiet for the first time in months.

I can do it. I will survive.

Mother caught my arm as Father limped on his way up the staircase. "Remember to *think*—think no matter what takes place in battle. I believe in you," she said with conviction, putting a smile on my face, "and I hate to admit it, but I should've let you join the damn legion a long time ago. You had to learn to protect yourself. I was afraid you would be hurt, or worse. I am sorry."

I shook my head, grazing her watery cheek. "Don't be sorry. I may not have known it then, but I know now. You protected me, and Kirrah knows my headstrong self needed protection. And in doing so, you gave me the most precious gift of all—my childhood."

We shared a firm, tear-ridden hug and went upstairs.

Shei was fast asleep, snoring softly, sprung across my bed, but Zuri was still up. Her wide awake eyes sparkled in the soft dimness of our bedroom in the attic.

I snuggled into her covers, smelling the rosemary extract Mother used to wash the sheets. "So, how do you like Shei?" I whispered.

"She is awesome! She showed me how to throw knives in the yard!"

Mother is not going to love that.

I laughed. "Of course she did."

"Hey Imani," Zuri said timidly, "I am really sorry for holding you back all these years. I know Mother wanted you to stay behind and help her take care of me."

I contained my tears with a lump in my throat. "Oh, sweetie," I sighed. "No, I am the one who should apologize. You would've never gotten sick in the first place if it wasn't for me."

Her night-kissed fingers tightened between mines. "You are not to blame for that. You didn't choose this anymore than I did. Besides, Zana says we always have Kirrah to blame, if we need to blame someone." She gave a kind grin that softened the pounding in my chest.

"I will do anything to keep you safe," I said, my voice shaking. "Mr. Osei is a good man, the kind you can trust. He'll take good care of you. Oh, I almost forgot, I brought you something."

Her face alighted with thrill. Zuri loved presents as much as she loved Mother's cherry pies. I reached for my pocket and handed her one of the arrow brooches I tore out of my uniform jacket. "Here," I said, "a little piece of me. Wherever you go, remember—I will find you and protect you. I can do that now. One perk of bending starlight."

My little sister closed her fingers over the brooch, storing it within her palm. "You promise?"

"I promise."

Chapter XXI
The Night of New Moons

Cloud-gray eyes watched me from the other corner of a feathered pillow the evening upon my return from the Mounds. "I was afraid you wouldn't come back," Tain said, glaring at me longingly.

I let out a puff. "And leave the care of the moonstone to you lot? Think twice."

He pressed his lips against mine, and a soft moan left his throat. "Did you tell your parents about me?"

I blinked up as if searching for an answer in the ceiling. "I can't remember, did I?" I winked at him. "Don't fret. They already knew."

Tain was half taken aback, half pleasantly surprised. "How?"

I shrugged. "I don't know. Shei's uncle, Mr. Osei, Zana—your guess is as good as mine."

Shei stormed into my chamber without knocking, grimacing upon seeing Tain on top of my covers. "And we were all wondering about the prince's whereabouts," she said. She no longer tormented Tain per my plea and opted to tease him in the name of kindness instead, which he took on more eagerly than I'd expected.

He only wants to be accepted like the rest of us.

"Is there a reason why you are here, apart from to check on my wellbeing?" he asked, arching a brow while I giggled into the pillow. "Not that I don't appreciate the concern."

"Don't press it, now," she snorted. "Commander wants us in the pit, to go over linking formation at nighttime."

We had already practiced linking at noon as soon as we'd returned and then again before dinner. The task was rather simple in my case—all I did was bend a sphere, drawing mostly from my surroundings. The rest of the legion proceeded to merge with my sei and disperse it into a hundred different directions. In spite of holding a bit of a grudge against Commander for concealing his attentions for so long, I was content when he managed to justify his choice. He wanted me to take training seriously, worried about me slacking if I thought my precision didn't matter. He was wrong about that, wrong about me. I wanted to learn, but I also felt powerful fueling others, letting the legionnaires link with my magic.

The sun was long gone when our boots touched the familiar dusty platform. The night was so silent, I could hear every grain of dirt rolling down the pit floor. The entirety of Lumenor was holding its breath for the battle that was about to start any day, any hour now.

Raina twirled a soft silver curl around her finger. "At this point, I am ready to roll the dice. Will they come already? The anticipation is killing me!"

Lazzor placed a hand on her shoulder. "You're telling me! I can't fall asleep at night."

Cella wrestled loose strands of Shei's hair, trying to contain them with a tie. "Stop moving for Kirrah's sake! Look—Commander is coming."

Commander Izaak strode across the yard with slow steps and tired eyes. His uniform wrinkled in few places, which was a first. "Thank you for coming. We will keep this short, I know you are all tired. Step into formation one last time."

The legion got into the practiced position, shaping a triangle—Raina, Shei, and Tain at the head, Cella and Lazzor right behind. I was at the tail, helping form a reverse pyramid from my angle.

One deep breath was all it took to establish the link. *Miss Yamane will be so proud,* I thought of my sei instructor with whom I practiced day and night. I saw her so often in the weeks leading to the battle that I'd imagined her face next to Commander Izaak's, who watched us from the side.

Only I wasn't imagining—Miss Yamane was really there, whispering into Commander's ear.

When did she get here?

"Halt!" Commander cried out, and everyone twisted their necks in confusion.

"What now?" Cella's asked.

Commander and Miss Yamane scurried towards us, their chins pointed up. Three new moons slept in earth's shadow in the skies, making Kirrah's Cloak nothing more than a deep blue velvet blanket above our heads. A gust howled from above, rising the dust. I shielded my eyes to prevent the grains from blinding me.

"Are the Akani here?" Lazzor shouted. The howling grew so loud that we could barely hear each other.

Commander shook his head, and Miss Yamane trudged to my side in a protective stance. My braid lashed at my cheek, tussled by the raging currents of air. A shrill sound rang from above, like a cry for help from the stars.

What is happening?

Miss Yamane tugged at the sleeve of my uniform. "Illuminate the skies."

My neck twitched to her command. "What? *How?*"

"I'll guide you," she said impatiently, "close your eyes and reach as highly as you can. Instead of allowing the outside sei to fuel you, reverse the order this time. Release the sphere in the air and blast it into heights, merging into every speck your mind can find."

That was more than I dared to bargain for, even on a calm night.

But it didn't hurt to try.

Listening to Miss Yamane's instructions, I ignored the erupting chaos that swallowed us. *Close your eyes. Open your palms. Swirl your fingers, form the sphere. Good. Now, fuel it as it rises. Draw from air, from the moons if need be. Little higher. Now explode and become one with the heights.*

A web of translucent sei set the skies ablaze like a rainbow of stormlight, pulsing with life energy. Brush strokes of deep blue and bright silver twirled and melded, creating a dazzling spiral of light. My peers watched in awe, mesmerized by the starlit canvas of the night.

Cella sighed. "It's beautiful."

Miss Yamane raised her chin high, outlining her jawline. Her eyes darted up in search of something in the stars.

Raina raised her hand as if reaching for sei, her chestnut eyes sparkling with silver glitter. But the enchantment disappeared from her face faster than performers removing their masks after a play. "Look to the north!"

Shei squinted. "Is that a giant bird?"

"It looks like a stag to me!" Tain noted.

One way or the other, a giant creature wrestled the violent blows fifty feet above our heads with a rider on its back. With fur and feathers in the color of old sun, the palette of crimson and orange, the creature's coat contrasted the night. Its shriek was high-pitched, unnatural, its wings struggling to keep its course—aiming to land in the pit.

"Both of you are wrong, well, sort of," Lazzor proclaimed with a look of wonder, thrill even. "The creature isn't a bird or a stag. It's a peryton."

"A peryton?" Raina asked.

What in the skies is that?

But this was no time for discussion. Miss Yamane stepped aside, and Commander's shout was a groan of thunder. "In formation! Now!"

"I hope he doesn't mean us to fight that thing," Shei squealed as the creature struck a clumsy landing in the midst of the platform, all tired out.

I learned the answer to Raina's question after taking a closer look at the peryton. The front half of its body was indeed a stag, antlers and all. But its back legs ended in the talons of a large bird, with feathery wings to match. According to my estimate, the creature was at least ten feet tall in full height. But in spite of its intimidating appearance, the peryton didn't pose much of a threat, huffing and licking its wings on the ground.

Lazzor looked to Commander Izaak. "What do we do now?"

But before Commander could answer, the peryton's rider, previously concealed by its doorframe-sized wing, fell facedown to the platform with a thud. The rider was a red-haired woman dressed in a flaxen, ruby uniform.

A sei-san from Vatrion?

Tain and Raina leapt the rider's way, ignoring Commander's warnings, and the rest of us rushed behind. We slowed down as we neared the peryton, who raised its stag head upon spotting us before returning to licking its wings. Raina proceeded with caution, and Tain helped her flip the woman to her back gently.

A flame-shaped, red-glowing tattoo glistened on the woman's pale forehead confirming she was indeed from Vatrion. She was unconscious, yet appeared unharmed. Raina leaned over, listening to her heartbeat, while Tain checked her pulse.

"Alive," he concluded.

"She is from Vatrion, isn't she?" I asked.

Lazzor's lips peeled back, baring his teeth. "She is. I don't like this."

Commander Izaak and Miss Yamane caught up with us, approaching the peryton warily one step at the time. My sei instructor held out one of the legion's waterskins, spurting a drop into the woman's mouth. Her lips budged, amber eyes opening, startling Raina.

"Betrayed..." she uttered chokingly, "...we were betrayed...the blade...the crystal is gone...gone for..."

The silence that followed was void like an empty flask waiting to be filled. But no one knew what to say, all of us equally stunned, watching our potential future unfold in front of us.

But one could always count on Raina to speak up. "Who betrayed you?" she pressed on, but the sei-san couldn't get another word out.

The empty silence was finally filled with dozens of marching feet—Lumenor's sei-sans and guards stomping over the pit dust. In their midst was a fair-skinned woman, a five-jeweled crown glistening on her head.

My blood ran hot.

The queen.

Shei clenched her fist at sight of Queen Astra while Miss Yamane rushed to meet her, leaving the pit after whispering something into the queen's ear. Tain stayed in place, his features stiffening in his mother's presence.

"Step away, everyone," the queen demanded, her voice growing deep like Commander's. Ordering others around was a second nature to her.

Cella and Lazzor retreated at once, pulling Shei away with them.

Raina cocked her head. "Why? We were the ones who found her! She spoke to us, though briefly. Who better to take care of an injured sei-san than Mr. Osei?"

Queen Astra glanced at her with so much dismay, one would think Raina herself was Kalon, charging with thousands of Akani Warriors at her back. "You can move, or I can do it for you."

No one threatened Commander's only child, not even the queen of Lumenor. "You will do no such thing."

Cella covered her mouth in the background, but Shei smirked, mouthing *"what a hag"* silently.

Raina was as bold as she was powerful. "What, I'd like her to try!"

She knew that with the battle at our doorstep, the queen had no choice but to keep her in the fight. She would suffer no consequences from her words. After all, she was one of the most powerful starlight benders in the city, if not the most powerful one. And the mature queen, whose bending was fading, was no match for her. Her son, on the other hand... I didn't want to think of the outcome of Tain and Raina dueling.

I hope it never comes to that.

Commander Izaak's stern stare sharpened a notch, shooting an upbraiding look at his daughter. "Not a word more. Move away from the creature."

Raina was ready to argue, but Tain caught her arm, dragging her aside stiffly. The only leverage he held over her was his physical strength, and he knew she was not going to bend at him right then and there.

She, too, wanted to win the war first.

I realized I had not moved a muscle the entire time, and I sensed the queen's hesitation in threatening me the same way she had challenged Raina.

She doesn't want to test my strength with the half of Lumenor's guard watching.

Word spread across the Old Town faster than emerging starlight, and Mounds-born or not, I was almost as powerful as her son after only three months of training. And the queen wanted to eliminate Tain's competitors for the crown, not increase their number.

How's that for a hill girl?

I wanted no part in their race for power, but tickling Queen Astra's tense nerves was fun. If she could do nothing to Raina, she would surely not risk the moonstone or her son's life by harming me. *She needs me.* So I continued to stand in place, out of her way but close enough.

She sauntered past me as if I was not there.

The guards followed, encircling the rider. They each swung a heavy chain, aiming at the peryton. The iron links bit at its legs and wings with hunger. The peryton shrilled again, numbing my ears.

"The creature is benevolent!" Cella cried out. "It didn't hurt anyone!"

"Perytons are kind by nature, they pose no threat to us!" Lazzor added.

But the queen couldn't care less.

The chains ended up defeating the tired peryton, and I looked away as they dragged it across the pit, disappearing into one of the tunnels. Taking it to the dungeons Shei and I once shared a cell in.

I glanced at Tain, who stood by Raina with his head down. Judging from his sullen expression, he thought the queen's action unnecessary, too. Yet he said nothing.

"Do something!" Shei yelled out. "Coward!"

Half of me agreed with her, the other half feeling bad for him. He couldn't openly disobey his mother in front of her subjects. I didn't like the person Tain turned into in the queen's presence, as though all willpower was sucked out of him. But I understood, or at least I tried.

"Silence!" Commander's voice was as loud as thunder again. The guards picked up the Vatrion sei-san, carrying her away to the palace.

The queen threaded back towards the exit, arrogance swelling in her flame-blue eyes. "Contain your daughter next time or I will," she demanded coldly as she walked by Commander, leaving the pit.

Chapter XXII
Mint and Leather

"That wretched, crooked excuse of a queen!" Raina paced my bedchamber the following morning. Our training days were over, Commander wanting us to rest since the Akani could arrive at any second. We were required to wear combat uniforms at all times, even when sleeping.

Required to be ready to go whenever the time came to fight.

Shei echoed Raina's disapproval, sitting in Cella's lap in front of my jeweled mirror, playing with arrow brooches anchored in her chest. "I say we storm the palace and retrieve the sei-san from Vatrion. I'd like to ask her a few questions!"

Cella slapped her forehead, preparing herself for another uphill battle. "Oh, Shei."

"What? No one will stop us!"

I laid the muscle aid potion ingredients on the floor, crushing nettle leaves inside my fist. Mother supplied me with herbs and flasks before I left home, and I'd decided to give my fellow legionnaires a vial each.

They will need one if the battle drags out.

"We are *not* storming the palace with Akani Warriors a hair away from the gates," I said. "If anything, we should be thinking about who is going to betray us."

Cella's nose wrinkled. "Betray us? Betray us how?"

"Well, you heard the sei-san last night," I replied. "Vatrion was betrayed, but by whom?"

"Why don't you go ask your beloved prince?" Shei snorted. "He might have a clue."

Raina shockingly came to his defense. "Tain is not to blame for this turmoil. You don't understand him since you didn't grow up in the Old Town. And I am not saying that to offend you. The truth of the matter is, he has as much power over the queen as you or I. Less, even."

My shoulders slouched thinking of Tain's predicament, shrinking into my chest. *A son of the Gutter lingering in the Old Town, fighting for the crown.* Shei would have scolded me if she'd heard my thoughts, but I felt sad for him, nevertheless.

"Think," I said, "who has the biggest cause to get rid of the moonstone?"

Raina twisted her mouth. "Who?"

"Well, the rebels of course," I replied, feeling discomfort in saying that in front of Shei. Not all rebels came from the Gutter, but most of them did.

Cella shared my hesitation, her voice timid, tiptoeing around the subject. "You think they will join the Akani?"

I tightly wrapped my fingers around another handful of nettle to crush. Its herby puff clogged my nostrils. "I would do the same if I were one of them. Without the moonstone, the sei-sans will weaken, or at least Tain claims so."

"Well, if Tain claims so..." Shei mumbled under her breath.

"Not just Tain. And it's true," Raina affirmed, "but I wouldn't worry too much. The measures have been put in place. The rebels can't help the Akani break inside. You heard my father—the Gutter will be strategically guarded, being close to the gates and all."

I pouted. "And if they manage to break in? Then what?"

Raina wagged her head. "We run to Tora's Chamber. Our fellow legionnaires will slow them down and will be posted over the city in waves, hiding on the roofs. Remember, our task is to guard the moonstone."

After making us memorize every street in Lumenor, Commander Izaak decided it was too risky to let us fight at the front lines should the Akani break in. The order apparently came from the queen, who cared more about the crystal than she did about her people.

Commander knocked at the door of my chamber as if someone cued him, asking us to come to the salon and go over the battle plan once again. He lit the torches, unrolling the map of Tora's chamber across the seven-pointed table.

"You will bend at the Akani from the vantage point of the walls. Should they breach the gates, you run back to the base and head into Tora's Chamber. No exceptions, no excuses. The remaining legions and guards will do everything to slow them down and buy you time. Don't waste their lives on your feelings."

I swallowed, knowing that the future of Lumenor rested on our shoulders, should Akani Warriors break inside.

"There are five bridges leading to the crystal inside the chamber," Commander continued, running a thumb across the map. "Raina will take the sapphire one, Tain the emerald. Cella will be posted at the citrine, Shei at the ruby. Lazzor will guard the moonstone bridge in the back, and Imani will watch from the center of the platform." He swayed his head to face me. "Kirrah forbid, but if Kalon gets through all our defenses and comes inside, you will fuel whichever legionnaire guards the bridge he means to cross while the others rush to rush to their aid."

In spite of all the fear I felt ever since learning of the Akani's arrival, I was calm now that the time had come. Mr. Osei notified me that Zuri was safely tucked in the basement of his manor, and that my parents had barricaded themselves inside our moonhouse. With everyone being as safe as they could be given the circumstances, I only had my task in mind.

Protect the crystal.

We talked through the plan and all potential complications rather quickly. Say what you will about Commander Izaak, but he was as efficient as they come. Then he posed a question none of us expected coming from him. "How are you all feeling?"

Everyone was too stunned to reply.

Feel?

I thought Commander didn't know that word.

"I feel good, for a change," I spoke first. "We put every protective measure in place that we could think of. Unlike Vatrion, we are prepared."

Commander nodded, cracking the first big smile he allowed himself since I'd met him. "Good." He took a deep inhale. "I don't say it often, but I am proud of you, all of you. The task at hand is one I wish I could take on myself, but I am no longer powerful enough."

"Father..." Raina sighed shakily.

"The facts don't change just because we don't want to believe in them, dear," Commander uttered, patting her arm. "You will, unfortunately, experience the same with time. And I intend to see you all through the years, so don't you dare give up on yourselves. Stick together, and not even Kalon stands a chance. I know it, I trained your lot for years, after all."

"Or months, when it comes to some of us," I teased.

Commander snorted, showcasing a rather fatherly disposition just this once. "I don't need a reminder of your transgressions."

I chuckled.

Tain cleared his throat, his expression firm. "We are grateful, Commander. Me especially." All of our gazes but Shei's stirred towards him. She was the only one looking down to her feet with her arms crossed. "I was but a timid boy when I first met you," Tain added, "scared of my own power. You showed me how to be a solider, a man."

Shei rolled her eyes, but Raina and I teared up a bit. Commander Izaak only had one child, but he was a father to many.

"Alright, alright." Lazzor broke the silence. "You all are starting to sound like you are saying your goodbyes, and I am not ready to part ways or die. So how about we each say what we are fighting for instead? Little boost of morale couldn't hurt. Lumenoran warriors of old used to do it all the time before their battles."

"Finally—a great idea from your warrior tomes for once!" Cella said, straightening her spine. "I'll go first. I fight for our beautiful city that bathes in moonlight every night. For my home and every soul within our walls."

Lazzor pounded a fist against his chest. "I fight for me, for the six of us. I'd like to die an old man with a heavy book in my lap. Moons help me, I mean to write one myself when all this is over. Share my account of the battle, perhaps."

His words made Raina laugh. "I am sure the book will sing praise to your deeds. I better be included!" Her face grew serious. "I am in this fight because I want to make my mother proud," she choked up, and Commander Izaak shed a tear involuntarily.

"She is most proud, watching you from the stars," he whispered. "I know it."

They exchanged a long stare, filled with father-daughter love.

Tain went next. "For the city I want to rule one day," he proclaimed, and both Raina and Shei snorted out loud.

"My turn," I cut in before another argument started over the crown. "I fight for the smell of nettle tea that wiggles its way into the attic of our moonhouse every morning. For my sister's adorable smiles and my parents' lousy attempts at jokes. For many more moons of telling futures and playing cards while gazing at the stars."

"Beautifully said, Imani." Cella's cheeks dimpled. "Shei?"

Shei chewed on the mint leaf, refusing to look up. She filed her nails with a knife, blinking rapidly. "For my uncle and our cushy knife shop. For the three knuckleheads that work there who I call friends. For the simple life in the Gutter. It's all I've ever wanted."

"We'll make sure you get one," Commander Izaak said, rising from his chair. His work there was done. "Remember, remain in your uniforms at all times and be ready when I call. We *will* survive this storm."

"Hey, Commander," Cella called right before he swung the doors open. "Any word from the Vatrion sei-san? Was she able to reveal anything more about our opponents?"

Commander shook his head. "No. Unfortunately, the brave legionnaire from our sister kingdom didn't survive the night."

We all screamed questions at him at once.

"What?"

"How?"

"She was fine last night!"

"What happened?"

"Mother claimed she was ill," Tain replied, silencing the crowd, and Shei finally lifted her nose out of her lap, frowning. "And before you say it, I don't believe that either. But I asked her five times, and she wouldn't budge."

Commander nodded along. "We will get to the bottom of it, but not now. Focus on defeating the Akani first. We will uncover the truth after we secure the moonstone."

Sleep didn't come easy that night.

The arrow brooches poked at my shoulders, forcing me to turn on my back. And I could never fall asleep on my back. I yawned at the Pisces-painted ceiling, my ears perked up. The sound of commotion in the city would alert us of the Akani's arrival long before Commander could.

But the night was still quiet.

My thoughts carried me into the past, the long-forgotten memories playing out in my head. I remembered the first tarot reading Mother took me to at Zana's moonhouse when I turned thirteen. A woman from the Cobblestone came for a telling, hoping for good fortune. She received a troublesome letter from her family in the south—three of her cousins had been lost in the Ashen Desert.

Kirrah curse the Akani to the same fate!

A soft exhale left my lips, and I rose to sit. Folding over at the waist, I reached for my toes to stretch out.

I might not live another night.
I am not staying here.

I gulped some nettle tea that rested on my nightstand and got up.

Tain opened the door to his chamber a second after I knocked. Judging from the circles around eyes, he had trouble falling asleep, too.

His lips folded into a warm smile. "I was hoping you were awake."

I inclined my head, grinning back. "Why didn't you come to check on me?"

"I didn't know if you wanted to be left alone."

The truth was, if there was one night I didn't want to spend on my own, it was this one. Not out of fear, but because I wanted my last night to be memorable in case I didn't survive.

"Grab a blanket and come," I demanded.

The rooftop was as quiet as my bed chamber once we climbed up, the streets below void of life. The taverns had closed their doors for the first time in ages. Even the squirrels mounted the hills of Old Town in search of shelter, the birds flying away in flocks. Not a single cloud hid the stars. The constellation of Sagittarius caught my eye, shining brightly against the black backdrop, igniting the deserted city.

We spread Tain's blanket across the stone floor and used mine for cover. The night was too chilly for my liking.

"Do you remember when you took me here on my first night?" I asked, running my hand through his hair.

Tain gently cupped my cheek. "How could I forget? You barely managed to limp your way back to your room."

"Oh, shut your mouth." I slapped his hand playfully. "I'll be the first to admit it, I don't miss the muscle aches. Or the runs around the pit."

"MAKE LONGER STRIDES!" both of us yelled out at once, mimicking Tain's hundred-times-repeated instructions, before bursting into laughter.

I sighed. "Well, I guess I do miss those days a tad."

"You heard Izaak," he whispered with a wink, "our best days are ahead."

I let the silence linger between us for awhile, pulling the blanket over my shoulders to warm up. "Maybe, but we will not see each other as much afterwards. Kirrah help us, you might end up on the throne, and one can't be both a legionnaire and the king of Lumenor at the same time."

Tain's face lit up to a mere mention of him as a king. "You know that we don't have to see each other only during training, right?" He planted a kiss at the tip of my brow. "I like having you around, Imani. Crown or not."

"I like having you around, too." I blushed, feeling the rouse of butterflies. "Crown or not."

Taking a deep breath, I gazed at my reflection in his eyes. Tain's moonlit face was smooth to the touch, lips soft to kiss. He ran his fingers down my back, awakening the flames in my stomach. I bit his bottom lip, his taste lingering on my tongue. My thighs locked around his waist, pulling him close. We tore the uniforms off our backs without unanchoring the arrows, starlight enkindling my palms as I felt him for the first time.

My mind swam in the haze of Tain's gray eyes that watched me intensely, filled with passion. The storm raged inside my head, my entire body, pulsing to his rhythm. The battle never crossed my mind, the rest of the world disappearing in the night. All I could see was Tain's face, all I could hear were his deep sighs whenever our hips touched. His voice was a rasp as he told me I was beautiful. I felt seen, wanted. And that felt so good on what could very well be the last night of my life.

Tain kissed me for a long time afterwards, and we both smiled ear to ear. I laid my head on his shoulder, glaring up at the sparkling skies. The chill cooled down my hot blood, sleep coming to my eyes. I shut my eyelids, dreaming the night away with the scent of mint and leather in my nostrils.

"Imani, wake up." Tain rocked my shoulder at dawn. "The Akani are here."

Chapter XXIII
Titanium Gates

*A**kani are here.*

The stone foundation of the legion base reverberated, disturbed by the distant rumble of marching feet and hoofs. Drums thrummed from Kirrah's Temple, announcing the enemy at our doorstep. Ash rose in the east, streaking the skies with swirling dark shadows. A bad omen, if Mother's beliefs held any weight. Air hung thick with the scent of an incoming storm, the watchtowers atop the walls jagged with blades like mountains. The throats of temple fountains ran dry, their once trickling waterfalls drowning in eerie emptiness.

Lumenor shed its lively coat stuffed with mingling folk and clamor, leaving behind a bare-boned city of ghosts. Every window within the walls was shut, all doors barricaded, not a single footprint littering the stone-paved streets. The bands of armed legions scuttled out of the base at last, charging towards the titanium gates of Lumenor.

The peace we once took for granted was yesterday's memory and nothing more.

We threw our combat uniforms back on in a rush, Tain's palms flashing with sei while he tied his boots.

"Are you ready?" I asked after letting him catch a breath and gather his thoughts. His face was so pale I thought he might faint.

Tain nodded, cold sweat beading his brow. "As ready as I'll ever be. We need to go."

The high constellation-ornamented ceilings inside the base failed to dazzle my eye for the first time as we raced towards our legion's quarters. Velvet carpets dyed in the most enchanting shade of sapphire served as nothing but pads for my boots. Even the swirls of glittering brush strokes from the hanging paintings made for a reminder of what we had to do—bend starlight until we ended our enemies or they ended us. All the ancestral-inspired beauty lost its allure in comparison when our very lives were in danger.

"I was getting ready to come fetch you by your ears, you two fools!" Raina shouted after Tain and I half-breathlessly burst through the salon entrance. The crescent moon tattoo glistened on her forehead, silver ink spilling over the twilight tone of her skin.

"Sorry, sorry," I said in half-whisper. "We were only at the rooftop. We are here now."

Raina's lips peeled back, and she shifted her weight from foot to foot. "*They* are here, too."

"We know."

Cella, Lazzor, and Shei nervously sank into the ebony chairs, waiting for the commander. Lazzor's shaking knee tumbled the items atop the seven-pointed table—warrior tomes, playing cards, dice, and crystal towers rolling over the edge. My hands scattered Cella's tarot cards across the tabletop, searching for the starlight goddess, while Shei watched me with a wrinkled nose.

"What in Kirrah's name are you doing?" she asked. "Commander will be here in no time!"

I spotted Kirrah's moonlight-colored curls in the sea of hand-painted pieces of papyrus. I picked the card up and tucked it into the inside pocket of my uniform. After nearly two decades of rolling my eyes at Mother's superstition, I began to subscribe to it, too.

"I figured it can't hurt." I shrugged off.

Commander's head peered through the slit in the door before vanishing once again. "The healers' wing, quickly!" His voice trailed from the hallway.

Our dash down the spiraling staircase felt like a jog now that my muscles had hardened. All the runs around the pit had finally paid off.

Sweat ran down the midline of my chest despite an eerie chill, my veins pulsing with energy.

The thought began to sink in.

Akani are here.

They have arrived to take the moonstone.

The legions of all ages crammed the healers' quarters—soldiers whose faces I had never laid my eyes on before. I waved at the Mounds-born legionnaire across the room, recognizing her pearl-colored braid that was dipped in mounds-fashioned indigo paint at the very tip. She pressed her palm against her heart, smiling at me with the fading expression of a half-corpse. And she wasn't the only one. When I looked around the room, many of the legionnaires wore her face—their cheeks sunken, eyes hollow, praying to live another day.

My blood curdled.

Mr. Osei posted up on a wooden stool in the center of healers' wing, administering potions with the help of his panic-ridden assistant who had dropped at least three vials since I had walked inside. I lined up, waiting for my turn, catching curious glances cast in my direction. Our intense training schedules prevented us from getting to know the other legions, and a part of me regretted not making the effort to find them in my free time. We were in this fight together, bound to the same fate more likely than not, yet we were strangers.

The droplets of muscle aid and mind-calming brews trickled down my throat, fueling me with energy and focus. Shei called for me from the corner, motioning me to approach. Something about her demeanor had changed, grimness painting over her good-natured knack for humor. She tied a bright green silk thread around my upper arm, biting into her lip.

"Since you are keen on collecting good luck," she said, pointing at the threads she tied around her and Cella's arms, too. "It's an old Gutter superstition."

"I will take all the luck I can get," I replied, rubbing my hands against each other. "Thank you."

Mr. Osei left his chair, stopping me before departure. "Remember," he whispered, "Shei is the only one you can trust. Don't waste your power until the end."

I nodded, refraining from asking questions he was not keen on answering anyway. Mr. Osei liked to take time with his explanations and riddles, and our time had run out. The walls awaited our arrival.

The blow up potion blasts rang from afar as we stepped out to the base courtyard—the desert sei-sans trying to stop Akani Warriors from nearing the walls. The guards led six gray horses to us, and I bowed at the mare I rode during our desert visit. She recognized me, too, letting me mount her without a flinch, although I was still a clumsy rider at best.

All is well as long as I don't fall from the saddle and break my neck.

The reins were soon imprinted on my palms, my hands slippery with sweat. The passage through the silver gates of Old Town offered a view of the city I never dreamed of seeing. The doors and windows were out of sight, covered with wooden planks or bedsheets. Kirrah's statue continued to penetrate the darkening skies, but her jewels had lost their ever-present gleam. Even the sun hid from the Akani, yet we were marching to meet them.

Our horses didn't like the sound of potion explosions, halting their gallop every few yards. Shei struggled to keep course, shouting at her squirmish mare, her voice shrill. Cella rode by her side, asking her to calm down, her words swallowed by the bursting eruptions of ash. My ears rang, muting all other sounds. Raina's and Tain's stallions galloped ahead, driven by their riders' determination, and Lazzor twisted his neck back behind them, calling for us to speed up.

The Cobblestone had flown into the Gutter in the matter of minutes, trading pebbles for patches of uneven dirt. Even the rebels were gone, not a single resident peeking from the back alleys to my surprise. Only the buildings squatted in silence, scarred by the wrath of starlight over the years. I twisted my neck towards the Mounds, thinking of my parents and Zana.

Praying they were safe.

Hoping the enemy at our door would not harm the innocent folk.

But hope was all I had.

That, and the sei in my lungs. My angst awakened the power contained within my body, ready to burst out and protect both of us.

The nature reinforced the unbreakable contract between starlight and stardust, forged in their eternal bond that created life.

The guards embraced our horses at the the foot of the gates, taking them to the stalls at the very eastern edge of the Gutter. The legionnaires swarmed the walls like silver ants crawling to their designated posts. We were told that the Akani Warriors were yet to emerge out of the puff of smoke that had ascended high in the skies, rivaling natural clouds. The ashen smog cast a gloom over the city, dimming Lumenor to an evening light.

Yet it was only morning.

Raina stepped into view while I watched my mare's silky gray hair get lost in the crowd. "Hurry, we must take our posts. Some of the bastards will survive the blasts, and I am eager to give them a once-in-a-lifetime kind of welcome," she hissed.

"Coming," I uttered, beginning to climb the stone steps.

The ancestors had built the walls, cupping Lumenor inside their palms many millennia before my time, yet the stone stood the testament of age. Hundreds of feet tall and wide enough to host innumerable legions and weapons, it posed a threat on its own. Weathered rock held up, eroded by the centuries of wind and rain that indented its surface with sloping, barbed curves. The raindrop-sized holes pierced the gray stone like dimples, showcasing marks of the battle of nature against itself.

I huffed on my way up, more from the ongoing frenzy than fear. It was a lot to take in—the screams, the eruptions, the chaos. The day I'd dreaded for months had come at last. I twirled my fingers in practice while climbing the eroded stairwell, careful not to fall. Hundreds of boots thumped against the uneven steps like a stampede of wild animals. Even the desert creatures were aroused, wailing and screeching from afar.

Come out and help us fight the Akani.
I dare you.

The Ashen Desert stretched into the distance like a never-ending sea of foam from our vantage point atop the wall. Every so often, a blow up potion groaned in the distance, erupting in flecks of fire-glazed cinder. Mist painted over the horizon, making it impossible to spot our enemies if they had managed to stay alive in the first place.

Tarah, the older legionnaire I'd met at the market, rushed past me and wished me good luck. Soldiers of ranging ages, ranks, and skills held their breath and waited in fighting stances. Tain posted to my left, Lazzor to my right, just north of the gates. Raina, Cella, and Shei guarded the city entryway from the other side, per Commander's orders, and the inability to see them made me uneasy.

The explosions in the desert quieted down, leaving behind an unsettling silence that made my teeth clatter. I tossed a nervous glance at both Lazzor and Tain, who both inched a hair closer, neither letting a puff of air out of their lungs. The entirety of Lumenor was waiting to meet its destiny, all other legionnaires' postures mimicking ours.

The moment of truth had come.

A single warrior emerged out of the fog, and a thousand palms enkindled like lanterns in the night. The warrior's armor was onyx-colored, drinking the faint daylight. His tall stature and confident demeanor reminded me of Commander Izaak, save his age that appeared closer to my own from what I could tell from afar. The russet-brown hue of his skin shone around big obsidian eyes that peered underneath his black helmet. The Akani Warrior's hand clutched a night-black longsword, its peak catching what little rays managed to penetrate the clouds.

My throat went dry.

Kalon.

"Ready?" I asked the boys and swirled my fingers instinctively after they gave a steady nod each. Merging my sei with the choking, stuffy air, I managed to forge a small sphere. My peers, the legionnaires whose names and faces I didn't know, watched me in anticipation, frozen in the moment.

But Lazzor and Tain wasted no time.

Tain's spears of sei spun Kalon's way, twisting around their axis, accompanied by Lazzor's rainfall of starlight. They both fed on my power, dispersing it into as many weapons as they could forge in so short a time, followed by the thousands of weapons thrown by our companions. All of our efforts aimed at taking the Akani's leader down.

Yet none of them worked.

The blades, just like starlight, bounced off of Kalon's armor as though they were nothing but bread crumbs. Every swing of his sword slashed sei and iron alike. All of our attempts to stop him proved unfruitful, no matter the precision—his armor remained intact.

I gaped my mouth in disbelief.

"Kirrah's cloak!" Lazzor moaned amidst the chaos. "His armor is made of painted titanium!"

Kalon's strides were confident and long, with little regard for our efforts to end his life. The longsword rested firmly in his grasp like an extension of his armor, slicing everything in its way. I reminded myself of my task, having a hard time fueling the fight without joining it as Tain and Lazzor began to tire out.

I vanished the sphere at last. "Stop bending, sei does no harm to him even if you could penetrate the armor!"

Lazzor folded over, leaning on his kneecaps, gasping for breath. "We don't know that for certain until we try everything we can think of."

I grimaced and scolded him. "You will drain yourself entirely if you keep trying! Save your strength for the rest of them—I doubt their entire army is armored in titanium."

I was right.

Thousands of warriors left the receding smog, marching behind their leader in tight formation, resembling wooden toy-soldiers from a distance. Their kelpies were nowhere to be found, to my disappointment. I'd wanted to see one ever since I'd first heard about them, but a part of me was grateful we wouldn't need to harm innocent creatures.

It is not their fault that their riders chose to go to war.

Synchronized attacks by fire, steel, and starlight soared from the walls once the enemy stepped within range, all of Lumenor fighting back in full force. While blades bounced against the Akani's armors, they couldn't deflect sei. Starlight shattered iron into pieces, but the warriors' skin beneath remained intact.

The sight alone stopped my breath.

Kirrah's cloak!

They really are immune to sei.

The rain of knives never stopped falling, aiming for the exposed flesh of Akani Warriors after sei kissed their armors. They were composed of quite the unique crowd and seemed to come from all parts of the world. Their skin tones ranged from moonlight to midnight, hair texture from coils to strands sticking out from underneath their helmets. The lands of Akan crouched at the very tip of the snow lands, at the far neck of the planet, yet some in their midst appeared to be from nearby villages and towns that squatted at the northern edge of the desert. Stranger yet, their armor seemed off, ill-fitted to them, and it suddenly occurred to me why. They were only ordinary folk who chose to join the Akani's ranks.

Kalon's silhouette closed in on the gates, the guards dropping rocks and fire to the ground. He avoided them with agile movements, striding in unpredictable patterns, making himself a difficult target to hit. The girls continued to attack from the right side of the gate, their signature streams of starlight piercing the ground near Kalon's feet, but they never harmed him.

"He is almost at the gates!" Tain cried out.

Lazzor leaned over the wall, shouting foul words at the Akani's leader before giving up. "What now?"

I took a deep breath. "I am not drained—I can try to slow him down."

In fright, my fingers summoned more starlight than I had needed. I condensed all of it into ten fist-sized balls. Kalon's head cocked upwards. He couldn't have been more than a year or two older than me now that I could see him better. His obsidian eyes stared at me with familiarity, as if we had met before.

I swallowed.

You don't scare me, I lied to myself, asking Tain and Lazzor to help me keep the grip on my power. The balls of sei mingled all the way down to Kalon's eye level, guided by my mind and aided by the boys, bouncing in circles around his head. The Akani's leader paused in his tracks, staring up at them with a satisfied, child-like smirk.

Keep laughing while you can.

Desiring to wipe the smug look off his face, I burst the first ball. *Kirrah damn him!*

A deafening cry echoed down the walls as Kalon's longsword swung against sei, shattering it with one blow. A few of the young legionnaires began deserting their posts. I lost the hold on my power, the rest of my sei disappearing into nothingness.

I blew an exhausted breath.

This should not be possible.

Kalon continued to advance forward, raising his sword arm. The army of Akani Warriors behind him roared in unison, and a storm of black arrows whistled from the mist, flying towards us. I threw myself at Lazzor, swiping him off the handrail, falling painfully to the ground. Tain hunched to take cover, but not everyone was as lucky as us.

No!

I shrieked after Tarah's forehead split open midway through, the arrowhead poking through the center of her crescent moon tattoo. Life had left her blue eyes forever. Her corpse fell to the floor of weathered stone, laying still on the ground. She was gone. The legionnaire who extended me a rare kindness once, putting herself in harm's way, had been killed. A true woman of the hills who earned her passage to the star lands.

I wiggled my way out of Tain's lock after he tried to stop me from crawling to her. Tears wetted the flax cloth of my uniform, making my cheeks hot. I couldn't stand the sight of her lifeless face and hollow eyes, void of thought. I let out a sob, shoving away scared legionnaires who slithered away to safety on their knees, a quarter of them now running away from the fight.

One swirl of my fingers turned Tarah's body to stardust.

"Until we meet again in star lands," I whispered chokingly and mustered the will to get up.

The girls came over to our side once it was safe, relieved that they found us alive. The rainfall of arrows had stopped. *It was only a distraction.* The ground at the foot of the wall was crowded with Akani Warriors, swallowing Kalon in their midst.

"Thank Kirrah." Shei ran into my arms and squeezed me tightly.

Tain's eyes filled with anger. "We need to head back," he uttered through his teeth. "Now."

Cella shook her head, gray dust smeared across her evening-colored cheeks. "But they haven't breached the gates yet!"

"It is only a matter of time, I am afraid," Lazzor said. "We must protect the moonstone."

"Thousands will die if we leave now!" Cella protested, rocking his shoulders in desperation. "Imani could crumble the walls on top of them and prevent them from coming in!"

I turned my head south, overlooking the moonhouses that silently crouched in the Mounds. Rubbing my throbbing temples, I thought of my parents and Zana.

None of this will matter if they die.

"No," Shei retorted, "Imani would kill but a fraction of their army that way, leaving a wider opening for the rest of them to enter quickly. We depend on the gates to slow them down. Besides, Kalon is the only one we need to kill, and we can't do that when he is surrounded by his warriors. Thousands or not, the Akani can't all fit inside Tora's Chamber. That's where we get him. He will come to us if we are patient."

Raina huffed, looking over the advancing army with a blank face. "You don't know that."

Shei scoffed at her in an instant. "Think about it! How will they take our crystal if not with his magic blade? Without him their effort is fruitless. But we must wait for the right moment like Commander ordered. We'll get ourselves killed otherwise."

Think Imani, think.

"Shei is right," I decided. "I am not bending at the walls. We need to head to Tora's Chamber before it's too late."

———♡———

Memorizing the streets of Lumenor proved quite useful in the end. Shei and Lazzor decided on the escape route from the top of the walls, looking for unoccupied alleys from our vantage point. With the rising panic in the streets coming from deserting legionnaires and guards, the journey back to Old Town turned into a tedious task. Our horses were taken, forcing us to pick the most suitable route for traveling on foot.

"Take out your knives," Lazzor instructed once we descended to the base of the wall, "just in case. We must not drain ourselves any further before we unite with the moonstone."

A loud, blaring sound turned our attention towards the gates just as we passed by them and headed for the Old Town. The tip of Kalon's sword sliced through them, an unnatural, black vapor coating the titanium, the vibration spreading over its smooth surface. The gates trembled like a frightened soldier facing her enemy, and the mature legionnaires in charge of protecting the entrance lit up their shaking palms. Whatever magic Kalon's blade had at its disposal served its purpose, and the gates melted like butter, the liquid titanium soaking into the ground.

Witnessing that event alone made my mind spin into circles. I wiped my eyes with my sleeve as if that was going to do me any good.

What kind of ancient magic penetrates what starlight cannot? Only one answer came to mind. *But if they could bend midnight, why not use it against us?*

Cella gasped, her eyelids paring off, exposing the whites of her brown eyes. "The Akani breached the gates! Moons help us, they breached the gates!"

"No kidding—they melted them!" Lazzor cried out.

Shei's warm hand tugged at my wrist. "Come on, we must go!"

"Yes, before they catch up with us," Tain agreed with her for once. "To the moonstone!"

Raina stomped her foot against the dirt-packed ground. "You all go, I'll catch up." She licked her lips with a starving look on her face. "I told you all, I am *not* running away from anyone. Not even him."

Shei and Cella yelled at once.

"What?"

"Are you out of your mind?"

Before Raina could respond, Kalon's black titanium armor crossed the threshold of Lumenor, and my hands went cold. He was as calm as time, as steady as stone, beheading mature legionnaires with quick blows from his sword while his soldiers stayed behind and watched. I covered my mouth, unable to speak or move, but Raina stormed ahead without looking back.

"Come back here!" Lazzor called, watching her sei shatter the now backtracking Akani's armors and swords. Kalon's blade and armor, however, remained in piece.

"She will get herself killed if we don't help her," I shouted through my dry, coarse throat.

"No," Tain said firmly. "She made her choice, she can suffer the consequences."

I had never been so close to slapping someone across their face. "You are welcome to stay behind, then!"

"Imani!" Shei roared after I snatched my hand from hers and rushed after Raina. Foolish or not, her blood would not be on my hands.

She will not die while we watch.

Akani Warriors held the patience of growing tree roots from the looks of them. Waiting for their leader to overpower us, they took a step back behind the threshold of the melted gates. Half of the remaining legions illuminated their palms, waiting for the right time to strike, while the other half drew throwing knives in a readied position.

Bend first, throw second—Commander Izaak's instructions.

Kalon spun about his heel to face us, the sharp edge of his sword tracing Raina's strides. My eyes fell on the pommel of his blade, spotting a pebble-sized obsidian crystal that flashed with magic in the center.

That bastard!

Raina threw the first knife at his head, but his sword got to it before any damage could be inflicted. Then another. Kalon wasn't only equipped with the magic blade, he also knew how to wield it.

I picked up my pace, and the surrounding legions pulled back, hoping the two of us could handle him alone. I couldn't blame them—Raina and I were the youngest legionnaires in sight. Sets of footsteps pounded against the pavement behind, the rest of our legion dashing to help us.

Raina halted her chase five yards away from Kalon. "We meet at last, *thief*."

The Akani's leader said nothing in return.

"Raina! Wait! The others are right behind!" I called out, but it was too late.

She swiveled around the axis of her body, clasping knives in both hands before throwing them at Kalon's face mid-air. He dunked to avoid their sharp edges, then lunged at her, swinging his sword.

A scream left my throat.

Red blood splashed at his black armor, coming from the gaping wound in Raina's shoulder. She hissed at the pain, baring her teeth. The rest of the legion caught up with me, but no one dared to throw a knife and hit Raina by accident. And, unfortunately, bending at Kalon would do us no good.

Cella and Shei entered the fight, encircling him, while the boys bent at the Akani Warriors beneath the gate frame, fueled by sei I forged. I unknowingly put a target on my back, catching the sight of the Akani's disdained stares in the haste. Two of their soldiers broke through our defenses, their armors half-shattered, swords broken but still sharp enough to rip my throat out.

Luckily for me, Cella noticed them in time, and her somewhat clumsily thrown blades struck the Akani's backs before they had the chance to attack me. Their bodies fell to the ground, groaning in pain. Two villagers of my age—they were only boys. And despite storming to end my life just a second prior, I couldn't end theirs. I kicked their broken swords away and continued to bend starlight, leaving them to their wounds.

Raina's scream ruptured my eardrums for the second time.

Another wound, this time to her exposed thigh, left her almost unable to walk. Shei dragged her aside while Cella held Kalon back the best she could, aided by the bands of legions who joined the fight. I called for Tain and Lazzor to help me lift Raina up.

Shei was right—we couldn't win the fight outside of Tora's Chamber.

"Carry Raina back to safety!" I demanded of Lazzor while Tain and I posted behind the forming wall of starlight that quickly began to drain my life. *A tad longer, only a tad longer,* I begged Kirrah or whatever god watched over us. The sweet taste of bending turned sour on my tongue, my body on the verge of collapse. I only needed to keep my strength until we fell back far enough to escape death.

Watching the hesitant Akani Warriors and their leader behind the translucent wall of sei, I wished I was dreaming.

But this was no dream.

Kalon's obsidian eyes narrowed on me for the second time and goosebumps prickled all over my body. His face molded into a puzzled expression, examining my power, studying it almost. He had the keen eye of an observer, so unlike the killer that he was.

Then he reached his free hand through the wall of sei. The starlight distorted to his touch, leaving him unharmed. My vision blurred a notch, and Tain threw his arm over my back.

"Let go," he urged, "we are far enough. Imani, let go of the sei!"

"I can't..." I panted, stepping back in the rhythm of my slowing heartbeat. "We are not far enough... I can't..."

Shei knocked me off my feet from behind, and the wall of light dispersed into specks. "I'll take care of her, Lazzor needs your help with Raina!" She shoved Tain away. "We will meet you in the chamber! Go!"

Tain shook his head after helping me get up. "Fine," he said in spite of himself, splitting from our course. "You better return her in one piece!"

"Or what?" Shei snarled, nudging me towards the back alley where Cella already waited for us.

We never heard his answer.

Chapter XXIV
The Last Words

The city had reached a boiling point in no time.

Startled sei-sans crumbled the buildings down, bending at the Akani from the roofs, causing unrepairable damage to the old bones of Lumenor. The debris choked the streets, tar piling in my throat. The fissures between rolling cobblestones flooded with blood like the creeks with river flow.

The rebels came out at last, climbing the roofs, throwing blades at sei-sans. Falling corpses crushed the crowds. People screamed from all directions, frantically running away from the fight, looking for a place to hide. Disgruntled folk ran into us headfirst at every corner of the Gutter. Their faces had aged a decade in the space of a single morning.

Cella and I limped behind Shei, who knew the eastern part of the town better than I knew the hills—something I once thought impossible. The Gutter was riddled with hidden passageways at every turn. Concealed doors opened to abandoned buildings, which opened to neighboring alleyways on the other side, reminding me of the maze of prison hallways beneath the pit. The daylight came and faded again as we stalked through the lonesome gateways, losing ourselves in the labyrinth of corridors.

"Shei, slow down," Cella called, her arm swept underneath my armpit for support. "Imani has to rest before we go on. She can't fight until she regains her strength. We must count on our fellow sei-sans to slow the Akani down. Let's take a breath."

Shei nodded after running her eyes up and down my body. "I see. I know a place where we can rest, but only for a minute. This way!"

Changing the course towards the dead end of a quiet back alley, Shei stopped to listen and make sure we weren't being followed. Kicking the piles of litter aside, she exposed the door to yet another abandoned building. A pitch-black tunnel sprawled into infinity, and she ignited her palm with a twirling flame of sei before leading us inside.

"Shhhhh," she cautioned. "We might not be alone in here, and we are not welcome visitors."

Faint light soothed my burning eyes, stiff silence feeling like music to my ringing ears. Shei turned a corner, then another, opening the door after door until we entered an abandoned theatre, left behind to rot a few decades prior.

The main auditorium offered a gaze into the long gone golden age of the Gutter: the constellation of Leo half-faded on the ceiling, mold caking the drapes, the almost burnt out torch flickering with firelight from the stage still decorated with prompts from its last play. The scene involved Kirrah in some fashion, judging from the star-painted backdrop. Everything around smelled old and pungent like perished fruit. A coat of dust furnished the audience chairs, but the cushions padded my tired body, nevertheless.

Shei held out a vial of the muscle aid potion I mixed for the legion before the battle. "Here, take my supply."

I gulped my reserves first, pushing her hand away. "No. You need it."

She clicked her tongue. "No I don't, I barely bent thus far. Also, I have other means of surviving. You don't."

Her harsh words, no matter how accurate, stung a bit. "I'll be fine." The truth was, I could have used another dose, but I couldn't forgive myself if Shei drained herself, and something happened to her as a result.

Cella sprung her legs across the floor, swallowing her sobs. "So much destruction, so much death," she said grimly. "Maybe we should have given up the moonstone when we had the chance, and found another way to deal with the desert. Maybe…"

My brows shot up in darkness at first, before I realized that she might have had a point. The price of keeping the crystal was to be paid in thousands of lives of our people. Having never fought a real battle before, all my assumptions about true horrors of the war were faint in comparison to what took place in real life.

Death, demise, and destruction.

Shei opened her mouth to speak when a set of faraway doors burst open. Someone had entered the theatre, and it was only a matter of seconds before they found us.

"Behind the stage," she urged. "Quickly, up here!"

We crouched behind the night skies-painted panels that smelled of decaying wax used to dye them at least a century ago. Shei put the torch out before we hid, leaving the theatre in complete darkness that sharpened my ears. Step after step, the incomers' march grew louder, until they finally stumbled inside. Cella gripped my wrist so firmly that she paused my blood flow, and my fingertips began to tingle.

I felt my strength come back, fueled by the potion, but I needed a little bit more time before I was ready to rejoin the battle. Breathing slowly, I closed my eyes, listening to my body. I relaxed my tense, knotted shoulders, and wiggled my toes crammed inside the leather boots.

The intruders, to my relief, were not Akani Warriors.

They were rebels.

"I could swear I saw the three of them walk inside," a male voice said. He was accompanied by four others who lit their torches, trashing the place in their search for us.

A glass prompt rolled over the stage, the shattering noise echoing in the empty theater designed to carry sound. Cella covered her mouth, and Shei's chest rose and fell at blinking rate. One of the rebels had climbed the stage, kicking things about.

"And you are sure one of them was the girl from the Mounds?" another rebel asked.

I dug my teeth into the flesh inside my mouth.

They are looking for me?

Cella and I exchanged the look of fright, and she squeezed my wrist even tighter. Shei remained still to my side, short of breath, with her eyes on the floor.

"I am certain," the first rebel replied. "She was dragged along by one of the uppity Old Town girls I saw patrolling around in the past."

"Hm." The questioning rebel took a measured pause. "All is well, then. Shei will guide them according to the plan."

Oh, no.

My vision went black.

Shei was a rebel in disguise all along?

She is the Back Stabber Zana foresaw in the cards!

I had risked my life to save her by the fountains, or so I thought. But was she ever really in danger?

My anger, no matter how hot and striking, was nothing in comparison to Cella's. She broke cover, knocking the panels over, lunging at Shei. "How could you?" Cella screamed, their bodies intertwining on the floor.

All five rebels clasped their knives, yet none of them were bold enough to throw one. I gritted my teeth, my rising emotions quickening the return of my power. The rebels and I exchanged angered stares in a silent standoff, equally astonished by what played out in front of us.

Cella rolled atop of Shei, pinning her to the ground, taking swing after swing. Shei defended herself, covering her face with her bony forearms, but she never punched back. One of the rebel girls grunted, her elbow pulling back to a throwing position.

"Don't you dare," I threatened, illuminating my palm, and she lowered her hand.

I blinked my tears away, watching Cella express all the fuming rage I felt inside. Every tender moment, every secret and adventure—it was all a lie. Mr. Osei was wrong all along. Shei wasn't the one I could trust. In fact, she was the only one I shouldn't have trusted.

"How could you?" Cella repeated tearfully time after time. "I trusted you, you rotten shell of a human being!"

"How could I not?" Shei shouted, wiggling her way out of Cella's lock. "My people are being beaten and starved while your bellies are full! I could never abandon the cause my parents lost their lives over!"

Cella frowned, rising to her feet. "I am not blind to the discrepancies in this town, despite what you may think. But violence is not the way! Your parents were killers, that is why they died."

Ouch.

"And you are not a killer?" Shei slapped her thigh. "Look, it was *not* my attention to grow close to you, or hurt you. But I had to learn your plans."

I squeezed my eyes shut. "Akani knew about the blow up potions in the desert, didn't they? You told them."

Fire-blue eyes darted to me. "Of course I told them. Well, my uncle did after receiving my message."

Cella twisted the obsidian crystals around her neck in rage, almost choking herself out.

"Kalon knows where the moonstone is hidden, then," I concluded.

No wonder they penetrated every defense we planted—Shei learned all our plans from Commander Izaak himself!

I turned back to her. "Why does Kalon want the moonstone?" I demanded, my voice firm like Mother's whenever I was in trouble.

Shei fixed her belt, swaying her head to a tilt. Her expression changed, not a trickle of remorse lingering on her face. She remained silent.

"We can't trust anything she says anyway," Cella snapped. "*Traitor.*"

Taking a deep breath, I looked to the mold-caked ceiling, as though fading constellation held the answer. "I trusted you, Shei. Even introduced you to my family, welcomed you into my home. And all along you were plotting to put us all in danger!"

She shook her head. "It was Queen Astra who put us all in danger, not me! The same queen who poisoned you, in case you need a reminder. The mother of your beloved prince."

I clenched my fist so harshly that my finger bones cracked. "Don't you dare bring Tain into this! You have no right to point your finger at anyone! Unlike you, he wants to save Lumenor from the threat."

Shei rolled her eyes. "You are so blind, that even writing the truth on the back of your eyelids wouldn't help. I considered telling you at first, you know." She smirked, penetrating me with her deep gaze.

Liar.

"Why didn't you, then?"

"Because you can't be trusted around *him*. Your mother was right, you know. You are *reckless*. Reckless with your trust, and with your actions."

My feet carried me forward, and I would have surely slapped her across that pouty mouth if Cella didn't hold me back. "Only reckless thing I did was trust *you*!"

Cella gave a squeeze to my shoulder. "Don't you see what she is doing? Stalling us while the Akani advance. We need to go."

I bobbed my head, wiping sweat off my forehead. "Fine," I said, casting a threatening look at Shei. "Try stopping us, and I will gladly crumble the stage on top of you and your rebel friends."

She shrugged, looking at me with a hint of sympathy that irked every nerve in my body. "I have no intention of harming you."

I breathed heavily, following Cella towards the door behind the stage, speaking over my shoulder. "Good. One way or another, you are as good as dead to us."

Cella and I shared a long hug after we shut the theater doors behind us.

"I know, I know," I whispered, feeling her chest quiver against mine.

Her eyes were red and swollen, her voice cracking. "How could she do that to us? To me? I grew to care for her, even defended her against my mother's warnings, when she was spying on us all along!"

I would never admit it to Cella in the moment of heartbreak, but I understood why Shei did what she did. Not condoning her lies, but I knew why. After seeing how the queen and the city legionnaires and guards treated the residents of Gutter, it was no surprise they turned on us in the moment of vulnerability.

No wonder they want the moonstone gone, no matter the price.

What I couldn't forgive, however, was that Shei put our lives at risk, plotting to steal the crystal that protected Lumenor from the spread of Ashen Desert. Just like the innocent people of Gutter, the hill folk played no part in the war, and she had no right to do that to them. No right to endanger my family who welcomed her into our home with open arms.

I wiped Cella's tear-smeared face with my sleeve. "Look at me. The battle is not over, and our friends need us. I know it's hard, but you can't afford to break down. I *need* you."

She twisted her neck, blinking away at the clouds. "Alright. Commander Izaak is posted by the temple. We shall go find him, then head to the chamber."

Lumenor we encountered on our way back was not the same city I saw that morning on the horse ride to the gates. Starlight cracked the walls, dried blood smearing reddish-brown streaks over the stone. Dead bodies watched us from the ground with hollow, lifeless eyes. To my relief, some of them belonged to the Akani, but unfortunately none of them were Kalon. A thought of meeting him again rose the hairs on the back of my neck. I looked to the southern Mounds, my chest collapsing upon seeing the moonhouses squat in the hills intact.

My family is safe, thank Kirrah.

The noise of ongoing battle grew louder with each step closer to Kirrah's Temple. Screams, sei blasts, steel against steel. Every muscle in my body tensed as Cella and I emerged into the fountain area of Cobblestone that surrounded the temple, to the place where I first met Shei.

Streams of sei flashed like lightning in the stormy skies, the legionnaires fighting Akani Warriors in the stew of blood and swords. My eyes frantically searched for Tain, but we were still too far from the heart of the battle.

"Don't leave my side!" I squeezed Cella's hand, and we bolted into the crowd, entering the rapid dance of limbs and swords.

Due to great amount of sheer luck, we scuttled through the battle unscathed. The Akani were too preoccupied with their opponents, and only one or two swung the longswords at us in passing without causing harm. We had to duck, and maneuver carefully to avoid their attacks. Cella's intertwining weaves of sei slashed through their weapons, aiding our side. My eyes dashed from face to face, looking for a familiar one.

Unfortunately, Kalon was the first person I spotted. He fought five young legionnaires on the marble temple steps at the same time, his armor and blade still in one piece.

Damn him!

"Look to the south!" Cella cried out. "Tain and Lazzor!"

The boys grappled with three Akani Warriors, their backs against the wall. Their faces were almost unrecognizable, grimacing in ache and despair. And their uniforms were torn in more places than I could count. Raina was on her knees behind them, bloodied and bruised, yet she continued to bend at her enemies.

We picked up the pace, sprinting to meet them, when a rebel cut off our route. His mahogany face was dressed in a trimmed silver beard, soaked in sweat. I recognized him in an instant.

Aubren.

The boy who once chased me through the Mounds gaped his mouth upon recognizing me, too. I sprawled my hand across Cella's waistline to stop her from attacking him.

"No," I said. "This one is personal. He is mine. Cover my back."

Aubren's eyelids flew open as I forged a ball of starlight, bouncing it off my palm with a smirk. He threw a knife at me with practiced precision, but I shattered it with ease. Then the second one, third one. I defended against his attacks without breaking sweat.

I stalked towards Aubren with confidence. "I recommend you take off like the last time before you run out of knives."

He scoffed a familiar scoff. "How generous of you, *starlight bender*."

"You say that like it's an insult," I snarled back, "when I am giving you one last chance to live. I am not the girl you met in the hills. *Run*."

Aubren weighed his options in silence, before making his choice. And that choice was the wrong one. History repeated itself. His hand reached for the pocket of his pants, his fingers sliding towards the peering pommel of the knife. I knew what I had to do to survive, but I couldn't bring myself to it. I could kill a banshee without remorse, but what about a human being?

A familiar dilemma came to mind.

To kill or not to kill?

I shook my head, hoping he would change his mind. *Don't do it, you fool!* But Aubren clutched the dagger, bringing it out in the open. The blade was sharp-edged, forged in one of the Gutter shops.

And he meant to use it to crack my skull.

His elbow pulled back, opening his chest to gain the momentum. I could not wait any longer if I didn't want to die. The distance between us was too short for me to count on shattering the knife.

Kill.

The survival instinct consumed my mind, my entire body. I swirled my fingers, and flickered my wrist in his direction. Sei dispatched, controlled by my mind, and the last thing I saw was Aubren's terrified expression before his body turned to stardust.

I ended his life.

The wallop rushed currents through my veins, my temperature running hot like the sun. I couldn't think straight. I had just killed someone! I had killed the boy I knew, whose deep voice and pearly teeth made me giggle once and squirm in my seat. The boy I met the night I learned about the Akani's arrival.

Yet what other choice was there?

Kill or be killed.

Cella pushed me forward, her sei threads clasping the iron of Akani's longswords. We helped relieve Lazzor and Tain of pressure, the small sphere I quickly forged fueling their attacks at last. They both neared on the point of draining, aiming at the opposing forces while carrying Raina along.

My eyes fell to the top of marble steps of Kirrah's Temple, and my mouth dropped.

Miss Yamane was there, dressed head to toe in the sapphire-blue uniform fashioned after western customs. She didn't give an impression of someone who stayed away from the fight, that was not the surprise. My astonishment laid in her chosen side. My sei instructor wasn't fighting Kalon or the Akani—she was fighting Queen Astra.

And she was winning.

Both women's magic was faint in comparison to the younger sei-sans, yet they each held their own. Miss Yamane's streams were pointed like arrowheads, swooshing at the speed of light. The queen herself was a formidable opponent, deflecting them before counter-attacking with the waves of starlight that resembled Raina's power.

Curious, I thought, knowing neither one of them would appreciate the comparison to the other.

I tapped Cella's shoulder, and her reaction mimicked mine. "Is that your bending teacher? Why is she fighting the queen?"

What in Kirrah's name is going on?

"I don't know." I shrugged. I could not care less about what happened to the queen, but I cared about her son. "Tain, your mother!"

He glanced at me over his shoulder with a sour expression. "I know. She'll be fine. We must protect the moonstone."

Kalon turned around as if he heard him. The Akani's leader had just finished killing the last legionnaire—the girl from the Mounds I saw in the healers' wing that morning, her head detached from her body, laying in the pond of blood.

He is a murderer, but so am I.

I couldn't look away from the queen and Miss Yamane as we strode towards the silver gates of Old Town. Both of them had run out of starlight, engaging in close combat. And in that regard, Miss Yamane had the advantage. She didn't appear to be nearly as drained as the queen, straightening her spine and firming up her muscles in the fighting stance. The leg sleeve of her sapphire uniform swung about, and she kicked the side of Queen Astra face, knocking her off her feet. The five-jeweled crown fell off the queen's head, rolling down the steps, its silver peaks drowning in surrounding red puddles. Everyone around them was fighting the Akani or had already died—no help was coming.

I gasped. "Tain!"

His stare widened at the sight of his mother laying flat on her back atop the marble stairs, but the distance was too far for him to run to her side. Instead, he bent a spear with his free hand, which Miss Yamane deflected with ease, crashing it into the queen's heart. I covered my mouth with my shaking hand.

Only a pile of stardust had remained behind the queen of Lumenor.

Miss Yamane had used Tain's own starlight to kill his mother!

I play my part, let them see what they want to see, and strike when they least expect. The fools never see it coming, she had told me once, and I should have believed her.

I expected Tain to fume with anger, and run to face Miss Yamane. However, a single tear ran down his paling cheek. He wiped it off, his jaws clenched so tightly I thought his teeth might break.

Then he moved on.

I reached my hand out towards him, quickening my steps, but Cella pulled me back. "Not now, Imani," she uttered tearfully. "Don't you see? He is trying to hold it together."

The thought had finally sunk in.

The queen is dead.

Miss Yamane killed her. My sei teacher of all people!

I had no time to think. We inched yards away from the silver gates of Old Town, guarded by no one but Commander Izaak himself. I glimpsed back, noticing that Kalon began gaining distance on us, calling on his soldiers to push forward, when Commander rushed to meet us.

"Oh, my sweet child," he sighed, inspecting his daughter's wounds. He said nothing of the queen's death if he saw it. Raina had lost a good amount of blood, and needed immediate attention of the healers. But neither of the boys could outrun Kalon with her weight on their backs.

"I am fine." Raina forced a smile. "I'll be fine."

"Carry her away!" I yelled out, watching Kalon slow down, and proceed with caution ahead of his army. His cold gaze met mine like a hunter eyeing its prey from distance, and I shuddered. "Lazzor, go! Carry Raina to the healers! I will stay behind, and delay him."

Cella clung to my sleeve. "I will stay with her."

"None of you will do such thing," Commander proclaimed, and we turned around, gaping at him without blinking. "Your strength is in numbers, and you can only beat *him* in Tora's Chamber, near the moonstone. That boy is no sei-san, and none of you held a longsword before. Well, I have. I will hold him back." He bent over, and seized a blade from one of the fallen Akani Warriors.

"No, no!" Raina cried out from Lazzor's arms. "Father, no! I am not leaving you!"

Commander cupped her face, his throat tightening. "But you must. Remember, trust your own judgement, and always follow your instincts. I may have commanded the armies, but being a father of such a brave young woman is my biggest accomplishment. I raised you to be a warrior, but you were born to be the queen. I love you."

I glanced behind. Kalon was getting too close for comfort, leaving no time for long goodbyes.

"Don't say that," Raina wailed, "I love you, Father. Don't do this, I beg you! He is too strong."

Commander planted a kiss on her forehead one last time, and turned to Lazzor. "Take her. Go, now! All of you!"

Kalon was almost within arm's reach, and Tain coldly dragged Cella and me through the gates, shutting them behind us. Raina sobbed and trashed from Lazzor's back a couple yards ahead, threatening to bend at him if he didn't put her down. The emptiness of Old Town amplified her screams, and my insides twisted watching a committed father waiting to sacrifice his life.

May we meet again in the star lands, Commander Izaak.
Thank you for the lessons, and your sacrifice.
Thank you.

Chapter XXV

The Wanderer

"Put me down before I kill you!" Raina pleaded with unyielding Lazzor paces ahead of us, but he pretended like he didn't hear her. "Put me down, you fool! I will end that bastard's life from my knees if need be! Oh, Father…"

The void inside the Old Town carried her cries, ripping my insides apart. Everything around us looked as it always did, not counting the absence of people. The waterfalls of blue flower vines mingled down tall fences, untouched by sei or war. Lanterns swung from the tavern entrances, rocked back and forth by the breeze. The nobles hid in their homes, waiting for the tide of death to recede. I tightened my fist to prevent myself from burying them in the ruins of their fancy manors.

Cowards.

"Where is Shei?" Tain asked, his face and voice both stern. "Did she…"

Cella frowned, marching against the paved road. "She is as good as dead to us."

"She told the rebels and the Akani all about our defense plans," I added, lowering my chin.

Tain's nose wrinkled before his mouth opened wide at the realization. "I *knew* it," he muttered through his teeth.

I nudged closer to him, and squeezed his hand. Our eyes locked, his face muscles battling a tremble before a cold expression fell upon his face. I drew breath to tell him that the queen's death was no fault of his, but he spoke before I had a chance to say anything.

"How much stamina do you have left before you begin to drain?" Tain asked.

"Enough to crumble the base if need be," I replied, "I took the muscle aid earlier."

"Good."

The legion's base of rugged stone still crowned the deserted courtyard, neatly-cut green grass ribbed with hoofprints. Kalon was nowhere to be found to my relief. Commander had bought us more time than any of us could bargain for. Raina fainted in Lazzor's arms, her head swaying in the rhythm of his strides. We stopped in the middle of the yard to forge a new plan, given the unexpected circumstances. Cella cuddled Raina's face, wetting her lips with drops of the muscle aid.

"The potion won't help her," I gauged, looking at Raina's twilight skin that lost all the vigor and shine it usually held. "You two take her to the healers' wing. Mr. Osei promised to wait there in case anyone got hurt. Tain and I will secure the entrance, and wait for you inside Tora's Chamber."

Cella and Lazzor exchanged a deep stare, strengthened by their childhood bond. They seldom needed words to communicate what was on their minds to one another.

"And if *he* comes before we do?" Lazzor asked.

"He won't," Tain replied. Our chances were slim at best, but he refused to give up. "I will make sure of it."

None of us can make that promise.

Cella nodded, and she and Lazzor departed, carrying unconscious Raina along, leaving me and Tain alone. We watched them disappear behind the entrance when a faraway grumble turned our heads east.

"They made it to the hills!" My fingertips grounded in the roots of my braid.

Shining black armors of Akani Warriors packed the Mounds, flooding them faster than a river spill. They resembled toy-soldiers once again, only this time they were climbing the hills that I called home, slowly making their way towards the outer ring of Old Town.

And it was only a matter of minutes before they reached the southern Mounds, making my worst nightmare come true.

Mother! Father! Zana!

"I need to go," I said frantically.

Tain caught my arm. "You can't."

A familiar shrill stirred the skies, flapping of the wings blowing a gale, jerking my braid. I gazed up. Beautiful feathers of orange and crimson brightened the heights, the stag antlers poking at the darkened clouds.

The peryton.

The creature's rider was no longer the ruby-haired sei-san from Vatrion. Instead, one of the queen's legionnaires held onto its antlers with a large leather pouch hanging from his shoulder.

I squinted while the peryton landed in the courtyard, spitting flecks of dirt out of my mouth. The Akani had advanced further down the southern hills, getting closer to my moonhouse.

A surge of panic made my knees weak, but I managed to stay on my feet.

The peryton's rider never dismounted after striking the landing, bowing his head down to speak to his prince. "Your majesty."

"Is it ready?" Tain demanded.

I cut the queen's servant off mid-breath. "Is what ready?"

Tain and the legionnaire traded a dour look before he took my hands, the heat in his palms pulsing through my skin. "The way I see it, the Mounds are lost no matter how you look at it. But the hills of Old Town need not be," Tain said, squeezing me tightly. "Remember, without the moonstone we lose much of our power."

Our power?

I shook my head. "Let me take the peryton and I can guarantee you the Mounds won't be lost!"

I was afraid of heights, but I was ready throw myself out of the skies for my family if need be.

Tain wiped a smear of dirt from his cheek, exchanging another sullen stare with the queen's legionnaire. "I am afraid I can't do that. I am sorry."

"Why not?" My fingers began to shake. "And what are you sorry about? What lies inside the servant's pouch?"

Tain gave a subtle nod without replying to any of my questions, and the rider tugged at peryton's antlers. The creature snarled before storming upward, flying towards the hills.

We will protect the city no matter what, Tain once told me at the rooftop, and I was a fool not to believe him. There was only one trick he could pull out of his sleeve this late into the battle.

No.

Kirrah damn him, no!

The tremble in my fingers soon overtook my entire body. "Call him back! Call the rider back!" My fists pounded against Tain's muscled chest. "Don't be mad! Don't do this!"

He watched me with a stern expression, refusing to budge. "We will weather this storm together. Look at me," he begged, catching my arm mid-swing. "You are the hero of Lumenor, I'll make sure everyone knows that. If you hadn't told me about the gargoyle blood, we would have never had the chance of winning. A half of Akani's forces will vanish in the blasts before they can reach the Old Town."

Gargoyle blood?

Moons help me, he's gone mad!

"And what about Lumenoran people in the hills?" I shouted. "What about their lives?"

I choked on my own breath, my stomach churning. My chest thrummed harder than Lazzor's fists in combat.

I need to do something. This can't be happening. I need to do something!

I turned around, summoning every speck of starlight from my surroundings. My palms glistened like the rays of silver sun, my grip on sei slipping in the rouse of my feelings. I formed as big of a starlit cloud as I could manage, releasing what little air lingered in my lungs, aiming at the peryton's crimson wings.

Tain deflected my blow, scattering it about. I aimed at the peryton for the second time, even aimed directly at Tain after he redirected my attacks once again.

I must stop the creature before it reaches the Mounds!

The gargoyle-blood-enhanced blow up potion would have flattened the hills, killing every living soul, including my parents.

"Will you stop at nothing to protect the nobles in their homes? Is becoming a king this important to you?!" I shouted out, my voice cracking.

He said nothing in return.

I bent at the peryton, bent at Tain, but my lack of skill against him led to defeat every time. I couldn't give up, couldn't allow him to destroy the Mounds. I would have rather died than watched my home and everyone I loved perish.

But my time had run out.

The peryton reached the edge of the Old Town hills, flying above the walls Tain and I once climbed together to sneak out to the Mounds. I froze as the rider dropped a small pouch of the blow up potion, watching it descend slowly, uninterrupted by the raging winds.

He must have stuffed the bottom with rocks!

The pouch hit the ground after three longest seconds of my life, flattening the perimeter of ten hills with a loud bang.

I fell to my knees, pulling at my hair.

A veil of smoke hindered the sight, encasing the city in the ring of chaos. One after another, the Mounds collapsed like sand towers, washed away by the wave of explosions. I pounded my forehead against the ground, starlight bursting from my palms, erupting the patches of courtyard dirt around.

In the matter of seconds, the peryton's rider dropped the fourth potion right above the cluster of hills where my family's moonhouse crouched quietly. The ground trembled to the beat of my labored breathing. Soil seeped between my knuckles after my fingertips dug deep into earth, begging it to hold on. But my prayers went unanswered. I wretched as the eruption erased the hill I grew up on, taking almost everyone I ever loved with it.

My eyes burned, flooding with flaming tears. "Mother! Father! Oh, no, I can't breathe! This can't be. No, it can't be."

I wretched again.

Then despite all the chaos and rising smoke, despite all the cries of the frazzled Akani and remaining hill folk that ran for their lives, my world went quiet, leaving me alone with my racing thoughts.

My family can't be dead. They are not dead. I refused to accept what had happened. *I should go there, and try to dig them out of basement! Maybe the granite held against the blast. Maybe, just maybe, they got out in time.*

Tain rocked my shoulder, pulling me back to the present. Mere touch of his fingers made my skin crawl. I shoved his hand away with the first flavor of hatred I ever tasted.

"Imani," he whispered. Just hearing my name roll off his lips made me want to kill him, pierce those soulless gray eyes out of his head. "It had to be done, you'll understand one day. We can't let them put hands on our young sei-sans, or our gold. We'll need them both to repair the city after we win this battle."

You bloody idiot.

Shei had warned me not to trust him. And while she stabbed me in the back, Tain plunged a dagger straight through my heart, leaving behind the wound that would never heal.

Saying the truth out loud plucked out the remaining strings of my heart. "You killed my parents, you murderer! I trusted you, and you killed them!"

I slapped his fair cheek as hard as I could, imprinting my palm onto his reddening skin. I punched him in the stomach, kicked his groin with my knee. He winced, but he allowed me to do it. He didn't resist. I pulled his starlight-colored hair so harshly that a few strands remained between my fingers. I kept kicking him, slapping him, and I would have continued to do so until he bled out if he hadn't stopped me.

"You killed my family!" I screamed again, and again.

"And *they* killed mine," he uttered in a low, threatening voice while broadening his stance. Then he leaned into my face angrily. "Miss Yamane, your beloved Shei, those wretched rebels and their northern friends! They took everything from me, including you now. And they will pay for it."

You fool.

Kalon's silhouette appeared in distance, stalking towards the base with hundreds of Akani Warriors at his tail. Their armors were broken and bloody, but their sheer numbers had ensured the victory. Tain saw them too, his face paling.

I didn't care.

My life meant nothing to me in that moment.

I naively trusted him despite all the warnings, thinking he cared about me. I took him to the rooftop the night prior, and let him make love to me. I fell asleep in his arms with a smile. If only I knew what he was capable of doing, I would have plunged my dagger into his heart from underneath him.

The Wanderer, with two choices in front of him. Zana's cards tried to warn me, but I was too blind to see it. And he chose wrong.

"Kalon is coming," Tain urged, attempting to haul me towards the entrance. "The crystal."

"He can have the goddamn crystal," I yelled out, shoving him away. "There is nothing left behind for me to defend! You made sure of it."

Mother's beautiful face flashed in front of me as if she was really there, her big midnight eyes and heart-shaped lips smiling upon Father. I continued to weep, ripping the arrow brooches from my chest.

My reckless trust and my big mouth cost me the people I loved the most, robbing my sister of her childhood in one day. Leaving her orphaned at the age of twelve. She would never forgive me, and rightfully so. It was all my fault—I was the one who blabbed about the gargoyle blood, giving Tain the weapon he needed to kill my family.

He may have issued the order, but I was the one with blood on my hands, too.

And now it was his turn to die.

Ten balls of starlight twinkled from my fingers. "Since you like explosions so much, it is time you taste your own medicine."

I burst the first ball inches away from Tain's ear, and he leapt sideways to avoid it, deflecting towards the Akani. Kalon shattered the remaining sei with his blade, signaling his warriors to pause in their tracks.

Tain took off towards the entrance of the base, and I crushed the doorway before he made it through. Luckily for him, the blast poked a big hole in surrounding stone, enough for him to slither in.

"Bloody coward," I shouted, racing inside behind him, bending more sei in his direction. "Stay, and face your fate!"

Kalon's shadow roamed the walls behind me through the mineral-rich hallways, stalking towards Tora's Chamber after my footsteps. I was determined to live until I could end Tain, so I sped up, never looking back. Kalon could have outrun me if he so desired, yet he kept his distance, following my trail.

I will hand him the moonstone myself, if only to spite that murderer!

The aura inside the basement had changed, prickling my skin as I descended the staircase. A whiff of smoke mingled out of my throat as I parted my lips.

Something is not right.

The translucent, sparkling mist ahead of the chamber was cold as ice, instead of warm and humid like always. Its potent scent was gone, which was probably for the best. I couldn't stand to smell jasmine, not then or ever again.

Mother loved jasmine scent.

I winced, feeling an invisible thorn strike my chest, but I kept going.

Escaping the cold mist, I came upon the familiar, intricately-inscribed marble archway. The entirety of Tora's Chamber flickered like a flame, the moonstone's glimmer blinking like a night and day in the span of a moment.

Tain stood in the center of the bridge ahead of me, two spears of sei glittering around his fists, their quick spins shaping the light into silver rings. He was prepared to fight me that time around.

"You must come to your senses, Imani," he pleaded, leaning into the fighting stance.

"Stop saying my name!" I dug my teeth into the corner of my mouth, cracking it open. The taste of blood made my mouth bitter. "I wish I came to my senses long ago!"

For only a moment, his stare softened while gazing into my eyes, as though someone peeled the mask off his face. And there was only sadness there, peeking from the crack, but I had no sympathy left for him. I shook my head slowly, narrowing my focus on the single silhouette that faced me.

My enemy, not the lover.

"Please don't make me bend at you," Tain said, straightening up. "You won't be able to deflect it."

"But I will." A high-pitched voice came from the next bridge.

Shei.

We exchanged a quick glance, and she read my mind in an instant. If I had to work with the Back Stabber to avenge my parents, so be it. I forged a growing cloud of sei, amplified by the proximity of the crystal, and bent it to her side. She linked to it, sending the knife-shaped attacks Tain's way. He was cunning, deflecting her attacks towards me, forcing me to hide behind the engraved archway to protect myself from being shattered to stardust. Without the ability to see, I wasn't able to fuel the fight any longer. I hadn't mastered my bending that far yet.

I rubbed my stinging eyes before poking my head out. Shei stormed towards the tail end of her bridge. Tain did the same, meeting her on the platform, engaging in sei-to-sei and fist-to-fist combat as soon as they crossed paths. I grimaced as his white knuckles crashed into her temple, forcing Shei off her feet. Her daylight-colored cheek kissed the marble, but she got up.

I broke cover, rising to attack Tain from the back. I had no interest in playing fair after what he did to my family. But a hand reached for the back of my collar before I stepped onto the bridge, and I flew ten feet back, landing on my side. Kalon proceeded to stride down the path, his black armor contrasting the bone-white marble. He was headed for the center where Shei and Tain dueled restlessly. He didn't even attempt to harm me.

Taken aback, I paused for a moment to compose myself.

Think, Imani, think, Mother's voice echoed in my ears, making every cell in my body scream. Everything I knew apart from bending, I had learned from her. She was behind everything I loved. And I knew deep down that she wouldn't want me to give up, but it was so painful to keep going.

I passed beneath the arch without looking down, no longer worried about falling into the abyss. Dreamless sleep in the void sounded better than the healer's aid in the moment of my defeat.

After I avenge my family, maybe.

Kalon calmly watched Shei and Tain from the middle of the bridge ahead, and I knew better than to sneak up on him. He might have been merciful once, but who was to guarantee his kindness twice in a row?

Tain bent a spear our way upon spotting the Akani's leader, and Kalon splintered it with his ancient-magic-bound blade. The obsidian crystal embedded into the pommel of his sword flashed in the opposite rhythm of the moonstone—when the obsidian shined, the starlight crystal's glimmer vanished. The same was true the other way around.

There was only one explanation for that, not that it made much difference to me.

Lazzor and Cella arrived at last, advancing towards me in haste. "Imani!" Cella flung herself into my arms.

"He killed my family," I said.

Cella's full lips quivered in anger. "That bastard," she muttered, taking a step towards Kalon before I yanked her back.

"No, not him." My voice broke mid-sentence. "Tain."

Her gasp was ear-splitting. "We thought the Akani caused the blast in the hills! I am so sorry, dear. No, Tain could never..."

Lazzor stayed silent the entire time, watching me somberly without uttering a word.

"Well, he did," I added. "And don't come any closer to Kalon. Trust me on this."

It was too late anyway. Kalon had crossed the bridge, joining Tain and Shei on the platform. The three of us followed in file with Lazzor at the head of the chase. My heart pounded loudly, drowning in sadness and anger both.

What now?

Shei was catching her breath by Kalon's side, and Lazzor and Cella posted against them, standing right next to Tain. I stayed in place, clinging to the edge.

"Imani..." Cella called for me with a desperate expression on her face.

"He killed my parents." A single tear plopped onto the floor in front of me, and Lazzor and Tain exchanged one of their knowing looks in silence.

"It was the only way," Tain's words echoed through the chamber, and I clenched my fist. "Without the moonstone, we survive as nothing more than flies in this world. I would rather die."

"But we do survive?" I asked. "I thought the city would be overrun by the desert as soon as the crystal was taken away from us?"

He didn't reply.

I closed my eyes slowly. Everything the queen had claimed was a lie—the Ashen Desert was never going to swallow Lumenor in the absence of the crystal! But that only left me with more questions than answers.

"No one had to die, then?" My voice trembled. "If we only gave the crystal up, none of this would have happened?"

Lazzor cleared his throat. "I am afraid it is not that simple. The moonstone has been the crown jewel of Lumenor ever since its inception, Imani. Why would we give it up? We are nothing without it, and the world will treat us as such."

Cella raised her arm to cover her mouth slowly.

She didn't know.

"You may be nothing without your full power," I said, rising my chin to meet Lazzor's deep brown eyes.

Tain smirked next to him. "Says the girl who solely relies on her talent to survive."

"Tain!" Cella cried out.

I scoffed. "His words can't hurt me any longer." Cella's gaze met mine briefly before she looked away. "You didn't know about their backup plan, did you?"

Shei's fingers carefully wrapped around a throwing blade in her belt, while Kalon's black eyes peered from his helmet, observing everyone quietly in a rather calm manner considering the occasion. He was more patient than I expected him to be.

Cella tangled her fingers with the beads of her obsidian choker. "Of course I did not. And I am sorry about the loss of your family, I truly am. But that doesn't mean that Lazzor is wrong. The moonstone belongs to us. We would be too vulnerable without it."

So she has chosen her side.

The way I saw it, the battle was lost. Unless Tain had any additional tricks up his sleeve, there was nothing he could do, save for attempting to kill the Akani's leader and hope the rest lose courage or cause to fight. And I wanted it all to be over. I wanted to go find and hug Zuri. I didn't want to battle the Akani, I had no reason to any longer. I didn't care if Kalon and Shei killed Tain, in fact I wished for it. But I didn't want anything bad to happen to Cella and Lazzor.

They were never my friends if they accept Tain's actions as the necessity of war.

So why do I care about what happens to them?

Lazzor and Cella were simply making choices that were most conducive to their own survival. The choices that cost them nothing. The way they acted—what was done was done. My family could never come back to life, but they could keep the moonstone in their possession.

But that was not good enough, not after everything I lost.

Tain stared directly at Kalon, breaking the somber silence. "The moonstone stays here, you will not steal what is ours by right."

"I am not here to take your crystal," Kalon replied with mockery, his voice a rasp as though sand particles piled up in his throat. "I am here to destroy it."

Chapter XXVI
The Ancestors' Secret

"Umm, come again?" My feet carried me to Kalon, and I raised my chin to look up at his eyes. Every inch of skin on my back prickled. "You are here to destroy the moonstone?"

He gave a casual nod.

"But starlight crystals can't be destroyed!" Cella pointed out.

"I already destroyed one." Kalon smirked with a degree of satisfaction in his tone. "What do you think happened to the ruby crystal in Vatrion?"

How?

And more importantly, why?

Something was not adding up. If he could bend midnight, why not kill us all at once, and be done with it? And if he couldn't…

"Why destroy the crystals?" I asked. "You could sell them for a rather hefty price."

Kalon sneered, eyeing me down as though I was a clueless child. "I have enough gold to last me a lifetime. The Ashen Desert is not going to swallow Lumenor, but it will swallow everything around it. It spreads out, not inward. The world is becoming hostile to anyone but your kind thanks to the deeds of your ancestors."

"The scriber…" I uttered, drowning in my thoughts. I had so many questions but no time to ask them. Everything I thought true, everything I had been taught was a lie. We hid behind our walls to keep our power, and escape the danger we ourselves created.

Shei leaned her palm against my shoulder, but I pushed it away. "The scriber was right about one thing," she said with conviction in her tone. "Without midnight crystals to balance the power of starlight, many will die."

Shei is the only one you can trust, Mr. Osei had claimed. *Save your power until the end.*

And Mr. Osei was not a dishonorable man, nor a stupid one.

But if Shei and Kalon are right, and our power is the reason for all the demise...

The realization rushed tears to my eyes. "The cure for my sister's sickness…"

Shei nodded along. "Zuri will live, but only if we get rid of all five crystals. The sibling's curse was the Midnight Rider's last revenge before he died. It can only be broken by destroying the moonstone and others."

I glanced at Tain over my shoulder, my jaws shaking in rage. He met my stare without any guilt or remorse, but only a stiff, unfamiliar expression of a stranger. "I did what I had to do to protect Lumenor, and win the crown," he uttered, and raised his igniting palm. "And I care for you, but I cannot allow you to stand in our way now."

One swirl of his palm shot a whirlpool of silver light at me, and Cella let a cry out.

I could not redirect Tain's attack even if I tried. His bending was too fast for me to link to at my skill level. And I was yet to master linking to another sei-san's power. Before I could even process what was happening, Kalon tugged my sleeve violently, and yanked me behind him while simultaneously swinging his sword. The ringing burst through my earlobes, accompanied by the flash of bright light. His armor saved my life, shielding me from Tain's sei.

And so it began.

Peering over Kalon's shoulder, I watched him shatter starlight with his black sword. Shei quickly gulped the potion I prepared for the legion the day before, but so did Lazzor and Cella. Then the entirety of Tora's Chamber enkindled with translucent, silver lumen.

We were all more powerful in the presence of the moonstone, posing a threat to each other for the first time.

Shei redirected the attacks the others shot at her, but she began tiring out after a while. Kalon's arm reached for my back, and pressed me closer to his armor. "Shadow my steps if you want to stay alive," he demanded hoarsely, "and help Shei, or she will die."

The Back Stabber.

Shei also knew the truth about the moonstone and the Ashen Desert the entire time, and never bothered to tell me. But she belonged to my newly-chosen side of this war, and I had to help her for Zuri's sake. I didn't know if Kalon could beat three elite sei-sans alone. However, fueling everyone with a sphere of sei was no longer an option—the entire legion but for Raina was in one place. And our former peers would surely benefit from drawing on my power more than Shei alone since the Akani's leader could not bend sei.

I have to fight.

Kalon stepped sideways to face Lazzor. I traced his heels nervously, careful not to create an opening, and get myself killed. Shei went on to duel Tain once again, but he began gaining advantage on her quickly. I could not calm down and think, and I had to act. So I did the first thing that came to mind. I opened my palm, and bent at Tain time after time. I did not cause him any harm, but being forced to deflect my attacks, he found it harder to keep up with Shei.

The Akani's leader's sword kept slicing through blades and starlight both, and he continued to advance forward little by little until he was only a few steps away from Lazzor. I caught a sight of Cella in the moment, sweat trickling down her forehead, soaking the ends of her brown curls. Her shoulders were sagged—she was losing stamina.

On the other side, Shei and Tain continued to fist-fight while I launched attacks at him, giving her a chance. But she struggled to defeat him due to his height and sheer strength. She was not much of a match for Tain in fist-to-fist combat, a foot shorter and thin as a stick in comparison to his broad shoulders.

Tain had almost pushed her to the edge, crossing the threshold behind which Kalon's armor could protect me. But no battle was ever won by playing safe. Tain jerked his hand towards Shei, attempting to push her into the abyss, and she barely managed to slide aside in time. But she did not entirely escape the reach of his arm, she was still in danger. Given that Tain had deflected my every attack, I did not know what else to do, I had no tricks up my sleeve.

He was never afraid of me.

My power without the skill to bend it is not worth much against other sei-sans.

So I did the first thing that came to mind. I broke cover, and lounged at Tain, knowing I might not survive.

Shei took advantage of the distraction I created, and backed away from the edge. Tain did not have time to bend at me, so he swung a fist instead, landing it into my stomach. All air got knocked out of my lungs, and I fell to the ground gasping, holding onto my belly that throbbed with an earth-shattering pulse. I had to jump to my feet before I could recover after two shining spears formed around Tain's arms.

"Shei!" I screamed, and she deflected his attack before it turned me to stardust.

We both grew weary, and even Tain's face was beaded with sweat and blood. Shei squinted at me, subtly tilting her chin down towards her belt, her fingers slowly reaching for the only remaining knife she had left. The chance was slim, but it was all we had.

Moons help us.

The only thing I could do to distract Tain for long enough for Shei to throw a knife was bend. I forged as much sei as I could summon, which was not formidable any longer despite the moonstone being nearby.

But it was enough to draw his attention.

Tain began redirecting my sei immediately with an unbreakable focus. And then he suddenly stopped. He severed the link to my sei abruptly, and maneuvered around it so quickly that Shei couldn't aim at him fast enough, and she was the fastest knife-thrower I've ever met. His burning hand grabbed me by the neck, digging into my skin while shifting my body between him and Shei.

He was onto us.

"Imani, hold on! Hold on for just a minute!" Shei's cries began fading in my ears. Tain's grip tightened. I tried gulping for air, but nothing got through the firm squeeze of his hand. The agony of suffocation overcame my entire body, but my mind was calm. After everything that happened that day, after watching the Mounds turn to dust with everyone I loved, my heart was broken, and my spirit crushed.

Maybe today is my last day after all.

Zuri's big, sparkling pair of night-black eyes swam in front of me, and I couldn't forgive myself if I didn't try to survive. I let go of Tain's crushing hand, there was no point in trying to wiggle out of his lock. At the very edge of my consciousness, I remembered the knives in my belt.

I was yet to throw a single one.

My fingertips pulled a blade out clumsily, and I plunged it into the back of Tain's hand as hard as I could. He let go of me, bright red blood wetting his sleeve, running down his moonlight skin in rivulets.

A swooshing sound flew by my ear, landing in his shoulder.

Shei never misses, that much is true.

Tain growled loudly, beaten and bloodied, yet he remained on his feet, eager to continue the fight. The fight Shei and I could not win at the very end of our exhaustion. I drank as much air as I could, filling my empty lungs. Battling with other trained sei-sans was exhausting—it required a lot of sei and focus. The pain in my belly was still there, the permanent ache wearing me down. I kept losing energy with every breath, every move. The familiar blur hindered my vision, and there was only one thing left to try.

"Shei! Catch!" I tossed one of my knives to her, forcing Tain to turn around and face sideways so he could see both of us. Shei steadied herself before throwing, and Tain readied himself to block the blade with one hand, while summoning sei with another.

Now is my chance.

I rushed towards him once again before he could bend at me, hunching my back and shoving all of my body weight against his hips.

And it worked.

The clash was not strong enough to injure Tain, but it was enough to push him off the platform. He fell over the edge sideways, his silhouette disappearing into the dark abyss of ancient magic. I looked down into the pool of darkness that dwelled deep beneath, wishing the fall would stop his heart.

But I knew better than to doubt the magic of our ancestors.

"We will deal with him later," I said.

Shei folded over her knees, panting loudly. Her hair fell down in thousand directions, strands sticking to her neck and ears. Then her exhausted expression turned into a grimace I had never seen on her face before.

Despair.

The next few moments played out a couple feet ahead of me, yet I could do nothing but watch.

Cella and Lazzor were on the verge of draining when I turned around, and were now fighting Kalon with nothing but throwing knives in hand. And the Akani Warrior didn't waste a blow no matter who he aimed for. His foot dug deep into Lazzor's gut, forcing him off his feet, folding in half on the ground.

Leaving Cella to face Kalon alone.

"Back down," Shei cried out, leaning against her knees. "Don't be a fool, you can't beat him while drained out!"

Cella's eyelashes fluttered at Lazzor who was struggling to get back up. She was cornered, they both were. And even if Shei or I wanted to help, there was nothing we could do. We wasted all our strength fighting Tain.

"The entire world will turn on us if he takes the moonstone," Cella muttered, her voice shaking. "And we don't know his reasons. We only know what *he* told us."

Maybe she is right.

Maybe Kalon is only using us, gathering the world behind his cause with lies.

Yet that cause is Zuri's only hope.

Kalon proceeded to take his helmet off, dropping it to the ground. Sheen ringlets of short black hair curled atop his head, and his russet skin was smooth like silk, hued in the warmest shade of reddish-brown.

A single tear of sweat trickled down his jawline.

"I already told you," he said after a drawn out yawn, "I am here to destroy your crystal, not take it, and I am tired of talking. The choice is simple. Back down, or die."

Cella gulped a breath, glanced at Lazzor who still struggled to get off the ground, and shifted into the fighting position.

I sighed deeply.

She deployed a clever tactic, bending her sei threads at Kalon's face from up close to blind him. Swinging her leg about, she kicked as hard as she could, her foot flying to his side. But the Akani's leader was faster. Kalon's arm reached through starlight, and punched her into the chest, knocking Cella off her feet at the very edge of the platform.

"No, look at the string around her arm!" Shei screamed, pointing at the green thread she tied around Cella's and my sleeves that morning.

So it wasn't just for good luck.
Still, one good deed doesn't undo a thousand bad ones.

"She makes one step forward," Kalon threatened, reaching forward with his sword, "and I will slice her in half."

A tear glittered in the corner of Cella's brown eye as she leapt to her feet. She had made her choice, and she stuck to it. But at what cost? Bracing herself, she drew her elbow back to aim at Kalon's exposed head, but he was faster once again.

The obsidian crystal glistened as the pommel of his sword spun about, its sharp edge flying towards Cella. Shei screamed, and I closed my eyes. I couldn't bear to watch another person lose their life.

A hoarse grunt of the deep, throaty voice rang in my ears, followed by a loud thump. My throat tightened, and I parted my eyelids to the sight that left me speechless.

Lazzor had managed to get off his feet at last, and he had used the last bit of his strength to get between his childhood friend and the ancient obsidian sword. A top half of the blade's long edge bit into Lazzor's torso, tearing his flesh apart. Kalon's throw was so powerful that it broke through the plates of titanium that were sewn beneath the cloth of our combat uniforms. They were designed to stop the throwing knives anyway, not longswords.

And no one could survive such a blow, not even the strongest soldier I knew.

Cella burst into tears, curling up next to Lazzor on the floor. "No, no. Don't you dare die on me. No…"

Lazzor didn't respond. He could not speak, but he embraced Cella's shaking hand with a meek smile, and a heartbreaking gleam in his eyes.

My chest vibrated with tremor, breath caught in my throat. Despite our differences, I had hoped he and Cella would come to their senses, hoped all this could end in peace. But that was not the way of war, I learned that day.

Cella's wails filled Tora's Chamber, crying for help, for Lazzor to hang on. But no help was coming. The battle was over, and Lazzor knew that even if she did not.

"Get a grip, my friend, we lost," he whispered softly. "And I am counting on you to sing my praises far into the future."

Before she could protest, he used the last beam of his life force, and pushed her into the abyss, saving her life once again. No one knew Cella better than Lazzor, and he knew she would die trying to avenge his life. And only after her cries quieted down and the magic of our ancestors had put her to sleep, he could finally rest, too.

Sei left the body of its powerful wielder one last time, the glimmering raindrops of Lazzor's departing soul floating about him before he shut his eyelids forever.

A thorn had stricken my gut.

He is gone.

Shei winced, and twirled her fingers with a quiver in her jaw. "Until we meet again in star lands," she uttered tearfully, and set his corpse ablaze with sei, returning it to the earth.

I might have gone mad after watching so many people I loved lose their lives in one day. My parents, and our lovely Zana. Summer and Senar had to be gone, too. Ayla, even the Market King, and all the farmers with whom I shared many meals and gags at the market over the years—all gone. Tarah, Commander Izaak, Lazzor. All dead.

I wished I was dead, too.

But I could not do that to my sister.

The gaping hole in my stomach continued to expand with every new name I recalled, dread sinking into my bones. And the silence inside the chamber was deafening, making my skin crawl.

I straightened my uniform, steadying myself on my feet. I wiped my warm cheek, and looked at Kalon. "What is your plan?"

The Akani's leader picked up his blade from the floor where Lazzor's body had been. His obsidian gaze traced the edge of the sword. "It is rather simple. I shall destroy the moonstone."

"With your sword?" I asked.

He said not a word more, and instead took a measured a step forward, stopping inches away from my face with a cold, now familiar look of a killer. "If you still hold any objections, it is time to speak them now."

"You know I don't. And I am not afraid of you any longer," I hissed. A whiff of cold air mingled from my lips while I raised my chin to face him. "But don't expect my admiration, or friendship. For right reasons or not, you killed people dear to me, and obliterated our city."

Kalon creaked a brow. "Your own sei-sans did most of work, but blame me all you want."

Shei spun her head away to his words. She could have warned me, we could have found another way. Or at least we could have tried to prevent all the death that her mission sowed.

Kalon didn't grow up on the streets of Lumenor, but she did. And she let so many die without batting an eye, that Back Stabber!

"It's time." Kalon lifted a finger, and dozens, if not hundreds of Akani Warriors stepped out of the shade behind the inscribed marble archways, encircling us from all sides. They must had been there the entire time. None of them moved, but they all watched.

I swallowed hard.

"Despite what you think of me, I speak the truth," he went on. "Starlight crystals are slowly draining the world. Vatrion had already met its demise long before my army came around—the red-hued sun above the northern horizon boiled the city in scorching heat, killing the crops and livestock, drying up the wells. You go figure. Besides, I have proof of my cause."

"A proof?" I asked.

Kalon turned his head to Shei who sobbed at the edge of the platform, her gaze searching for Cella's body in the abyss.

That won't do her any good.

"They have seen my letter, I suppose?" he asked.

"Mhm," she replied warily, never glancing up. "Only a half, though. The queen burned the bottom. I couldn't get the girls to search for it before the ball."

My eyes pierced my former friend. "You couldn't get *us* to search for it before the ball?"

Shei sighed. "Who do you think gave Raina the idea to sort through the queen's drawers in the first place? I wanted you to find it."

"Oh! How generous of you!" I snapped.

I inched closer to the Akani's leader. Being in Kalon's proximity made me shiver. I knew he could feel the heat of sei within me, just like I could feel his power.

The scriber was right—it is rather cold.

Still, it doesn't explain his immunity to sei, or the immunity of his soldiers who don't seem to share his magic.

"Well?" I asked, holding my hand out. Kalon slid the parchment out of the shirt underneath his titanium armor, and placed it on my palm.

I read the letter out loud. "*Those are some big threats for a little boy.*" I snorted while voicing Queen Astra's words, her moonhouse-sized pride coming through the papyrus. "*Come with your horde, and try our defenses. Our gates stood the centuries of attempted invasions, we do not fear you. I do not fear you. When it comes to trading secrets—go ahead, tell the world. Tell the world, and I will deny it to my last breath, and turn them all against you. Lumenor will not lose its only claim to power. Besides, who will believe an intruder over the queen of Lumenor? Come and die.*"

I pursed my lips, running my eyes over the letter one more time. "It surely sounds like her, though her sigil is missing," I noted.

"It *was* her," Kalon said firmly, shifting his magic sword from hand to hand. "And now I will right your kin's wrongs."

He turned around and headed towards the moonstone. The whirlpool of mist around the crystal spun about like a tornado, beating at Kalon's cheeks as he passed through. The moonstone's halo flickered like candlelight in the wind once again, sensing the enemy close. My head throbbed from a long day, the pit in my stomach growing, eating away my insides.

Mother. Father.

I am so sorry. I should have listened to you, and never joined the legions.

I crossed my arms, tapping the sole of my boot against the marble floor. "What now?"

"Now we wait," Shei replied.

Certain that the prayers to Kirrah would bear no gifts any longer, having in mind that we just agreed to destroy her gift to the world, I prayed that at least Mother could hear me from the star lands.

We only need it to work this once, Lumenor deserves to be rid of this curse.

Please work.

"So, are you leaving with them, after this is over?" I asked, watching Shei grimly with my mouth pursed.

She nodded. "I am. There are three more crystals to destroy, and the Akani will need all the help they can get if they are to succeed."

"Anything else you want to get off your chest while you are at it?" I tilted my chin, leaning towards her. My braid spilled over my shoulder slumped from muscle ache.

She swallowed a knot. "I am sorry, I really am, for lying to you. I never meant to hurt anyone, and there were times when I wanted to tell you the truth, to find another—"

I scoffed, cutting her off. "But you didn't, and so many have died thanks to your lies! You are not forgiven."

Shei looked to her feet, stretching out her sleeves. She remained quiet with a sorrowful pout on her face.

Whatever Kalon attempted was not successful. A sound resembling a thunder grumbled through Tora's Chamber before the whirlpool ejected him into air. He almost slid off the platform, trying to keep his grip on the slippery marble.

I slapped my forehead, losing the battle with my nerves. "That didn't work, I gather?"

The Akani's leader hopped to his feet, cracking his neck before submerging into the raging whirlpool for the second time. Then third. Shei landed him a hand to get up the last time he got thrusted away from the moonstone.

"What's your backup plan?" I asked.

He shrugged. "We don't have one. There is no other way to destroy the crystals except for in their base. But the moonstone is too strong, damn your magic and your goddess! We'll have to come back after we get rid of all others. We shall leave our soldiers behind to guard the crystal while we—"

"There is another way," a faraway voice interrupted, and I flinched.

Miss Yamane's silhouette passed beneath one of the archways, gliding towards the platform past all the Akani. Her paling face was sunken, exhausted from the battle. Yet she still made it over the bridge in the matter of seconds.

"There is still one thing we can try," she claimed.

We?

Kalon's eyebrows shot up. "What is it?"

Her peach-colored lips spread into a grin. "You are looking at her." Her chin pointed at me. "Imani is powerful enough to take the crystal out."

My head shot up, peering at the painting of Kirrah's constellation in the high ceiling with a deep exhale.

Of course.

Why else would a daughter of an emperor agree to train me?

"No," Shei hissed, her features warping in worry. "She could die."

I smacked my lips. "Oh now you are worried about my life! Too late, *Back Stabber*."

Kalon cupped his chin, glancing back at the whirlpool of mist. "But the crystal must be destroyed in its base."

Miss Yamane took a measured pause. "True, but taking it with you will prevent another bloodshed once you return. You must not give Lumenoran sei-sans the opportunity to recover their strength."

I clicked my tongue. "You never asked if I am willing."

My sei instructor's confident glare met mine. "I don't need to. With the moonstone far away, your sister will feel better. She won't heal entirely, sure, but you will buy her years while you work on destroying other crystals."

Despite being glad of that turn of events, I still felt betrayed. Miss Yamane was my mentor, someone I looked up to. But to her, I was only another knife in her belt that needed sharpening.

There was nothing left to dwell over.

The way I saw it, there was only one choice left.

I turned to the Back Stabber. "Tell my sister that I love her, and that I am sorry, in case I don't come out," I instructed. "And I want you to burn my body, and scatter my ashes across the Mounds, or whatever is left of them. I was born there, and I intend to reunite with the hills when my time comes, flattened or not."

Shei shifted her weight uneasily. "Don't say stuff like that."

I puffed out an exhausted breath. "Can I count on you—yes or no? You owe me that much."

She gave a hesitant nod, her face contorting in concern.

"Not so fast, *starlight bender*." Kalon scoffed with a hint of thrill on his face. He reached underneath his sleeve once more, and pulled out a vial of green potion. "Here, this will restore your energy."

I backed away a step. The green liquid inside the flask had unnatural golden glow, and I had already tasted a magic-induced potion before to be fooled once more.

"The potion is spiked with ancient magic, isn't it?" I asked.

Kalon grimaced sourly. "What you call ancient magic is the magic of earth called *fei*. The potion was brewed by no one but the most powerful fei priestess, my mother. It will not harm you."

The history repeated all over again—a stranger offered me a sip of something I did not, could not understand. And Miss Yamane was there again to assure me of its safety.

"There are plenty of easier ways to kill you. Drink the potion, girl."

Alright. Moons help me.

I cocked the top off, and gulped the potion in one pour. My vision was sparked with golden light emitted by my body that healed in a moment, strengthening the bonds of sei within me. The earth magic did not harm my power, it increased it. I was as good as new.

Curious.

I must do my part now.

"Come with me." I pointed my nose back at Kalon.

His one-sided smirk exposed a set of perfectly white teeth. "You couldn't hold me back even if you tried."

"Ugh," I moaned, "I liked it better when I feared you."

Miss Yamane stopped me before we left. "Remember what I taught you. You must pull the moonstone out when the bond is the strongest, and not a second later. Or you will die."

"I know." I nodded, leading Kalon towards the moonstone.

The angry whirlpool of mist surrounding the crystal would have thrown me off my feet if it weren't for the Akani's leader. He grabbed a hold my shoulder to keep me steady, his touch feeling cold like ice against my skin.

"Alright," I said after we reached the flickering crystal. "I am going to try to link with the moonstone. If it looks like I am draining, fainting or else, use your sword to break my link. I am not ready to die yet."

He bobbed his head. "You didn't need to ask. I'd do it anyway."

I rolled my eyes. "I *had* to ask. I watched you kill dozens earlier."

Kalon's cold hand fell on my shoulder once again. "And I will kill ten times as many, if that's what it takes to save my home. The ice caps in the north are melting away, and the sea will soon wash over the lands of Akan if I don't do something about it. If *we* don't do something. So, come on, *sei-san*, get on with it since you are so eager."

I bit my tongue to suppress what I wanted to say in return, worried about him murdering me in cold blood if he found out that I knew. Although I had a hunch he was no fool.

He knows, he must know that I figured it out. He can feel it, too.

A deep inhale chilled my burning throat.

Now or never.

I would have lied if I didn't admit I was scared out my wits. I knew the potential of my power, yet my sei did me no good in the events that led to that point. Was I truly as powerful as my instructor believed?

Only one way to find out.

I thought back to my first sei lesson. Miss Yamane asked me what I knew about starlight, and I told her it was more precise when I was calm, but more potent when my emotions were in disarray. That much was true, and my feelings were never caught in as much turmoil as that evening.

So I decided to plunge a finger into my own wound.

I closed my eyes, playing out my dearest memories in my mind. Early mornings I spent sipping on nettle tea with Mother in the kitchens, gossiping about.

All gone.

Lukewarm spring days I giggled away, eating lunch with Summer during my breaks from work—she often came to visit my stand midday, walking half a mile from her father's shop.

All gone.

Late nights after I drank too much wine at the taverns, and crashed in Zana's cushions, attempting to sober up before going home. Mimi, the firebird, nipped at the bread crumbs in Zana's palm while the teller spoke of her and Mother's mischiefs when they were young.

All gone.

Early evenings I spent playing moon phases with Father who never let me win on purpose—claiming one had to earn their place in the world, teaching me one of his many valuable lessons.

All gone.

The nights Zuri and I spent in the attic of our moonhouse while I practiced starlight tricks and read her Kirrah's tales before bed.

All gone forever.

My palms became one with the moonstone, drinking its magical power. Linking fueled my body with energy, but unlike the last time, I had to draw directly from the crystal in order to weaken its glue to the marble base. The moonstone resisted, pulling back, drawing the life force out of me in the battle of willpower. I screamed in pain, but I didn't let go.

I will snatch you out of there if it's the last thing I ever do! For my little sister, and the people of Lumenor. I will prove myself useful, or this had all been in vain.

Every muscle in my body warped, my skin prickling with fever, ears ringing with pressure. I didn't care, I held on. Drawing more starlight than ever, my entire body glistened with beautiful silver halo that dazzled the eye.

Being one with the moonstone, truly one with the moonstone, with my every vein and every nerve drunk on its magic—it was hard to let go of the feeling of power.

But I must, it's time.

I didn't want to break away from the base, didn't want to spit out the last gulp of sweet summer wine.

Let go.

I thought I might be sick if I tugged my elbows, if I separated the crystal from the source of its power—the power that was my own, too.

Be strong.

What if I could rid my sister of the sibling's curse now, what if I could rid the world of its inevitable demise? My pulse began slowing down.

I can't do anything but die.

The moonstone drank on my life force, too, killing me one breath at the time.

I owe it to myself to try.

Letting out a screech, I pulled with all the strength I could muster. And it worked.

Starlight spilled across the chamber, the gleaming particles dispersing into air as I fell on my back with the round crystal stuck between my palms.

"I did it! Kirrah help us—I did it!" I uttered from the floor, laughing and sobbing uncontrollably at the same time. All the mist had vanished, and Miss Yamane and Shei rushed our way, falling to their knees to check on my vitals.

Kalon smirked in satisfaction, watching me from above. We exchanged a look of relief, and he grinned. " I am glad I didn't kill you when I had the chance."

Chapter XXVII

Three Crescent Moons

Akani Warriors cheered on us on the way out of Tora's Chamber to my absolute shock, but nothing short of rising the Mounds back from the ground and bringing my family back to life could cheer me up.

Taking off their broken helmets, the Akani exposed their youthful features that offered a stunning view of the intricate richness of the world. I paused to admire their skin tones, ranging from onyx, umber, russet, golden, and tawny brown, all the way to ivory; their hair locking in coils, braids, locs, waves, and flat strands that came in every color found in nature. Every person's features were sculpted to fit a different mold, as though the entire world had sent a representative to Tora's Chamber. Only a handful of the Akani came from the actual Akan—their army strengthened by the support of the rest of the dying world.

They all had stakes in the war for survival. That was the real reason why they joined forces with Kalon.

I leaned on Miss Yamane and Shei, having a hard time walking on my own. Kalon offered to carry me to the healers' wing, but I refused. The moonstone remained in my possession, its once blinding gleam faint, the smooth, round surface no longer hot.

"Uhm," Shei mumbled once we reached the tail end of the bridge. "We must get Cella out of the abyss immediately! And what about

Tain? He was still alive when Imani pushed him off the platform, although he was wounded."

"We need to fetch the high priestess," Miss Yamane replied, "only her spells can dig those two out of the dreamless darkness of the mind. It will take days."

Hearing Tain's name alone made me want to punch someone. "Tain can rot for all I care. He will answer to the people of Lumenor if he manages to survive, Raina will make sure of that. I am not the only one he wronged, and the people of the Mounds deserve to see him suffer."

Shei nodded along. "It's your call. Let's go see the healers, then."

Mr. Osei's shoulders sagged as soon as he laid eyes on us entering the healers' wing. "Thank Kirrah," he muttered a prayer, the whites of his eyes red like blood. He grazed my forehead with the back of his hand, checking on my temperature. "Zuri is safe and sound, my wife is tending to her as we speak."

I blinked a tear away, settling atop one of the healers' beds. "Does she know about... the hills?"

The head healer swallowed a bitter breath, his onyx face souring. "She must know by now, the explosion was quite ear-numbing," he replied, and both of us began weeping at once.

"It's all my fault," I cried out, "I am the one who told Tain about the gargoyle blood!"

Mr. Osei shook his head. "The fault lies with him and Astra and no one else. Their fingerprints are the only ones marking the graveyard of our people. He would've found out one way or another. Besides, he made rounds before the battle." The healer leaned his elbows against his thighs, glaring into the distance. "I never thought Tain meant to blow up half the city, ascribing his curiosity to the angst we all felt in the days leading to the battle."

Shei refused to let the healer's assistant inspect her wounds and bruises, claiming she was fine. Kalon stood nearby, narrowing his sight on the moonstone in my lap, its faded glow reflecting in his obsidian eyes.

"Why didn't you tell me the truth?" I demanded of Mr. Osei, my voice cracking. "I could've taken the moonstone out earlier—no one had to die!"

The healer cupped my wet cheek. "That is exactly why I didn't tell you. You were being watched, and the chance of you succeeding was low without the fei potion to bind sei within you. Besides, if you got caught escaping with the moonstone, Astra would have it hidden out of reach, never to be found. We couldn't risk the fate of the world without young Kalon and his army at our back."

He handed me a brew of different potions, all poured into one large, bronze cup. I drank the orange, turmeric-flavored liquid slowly, my ache beginning to fade away.

"Lazzor and Commander Izaak are dead," I announced, and Shei turned around, emptying the contents of her stomach out onto the floor. One of the healers came to her aid, but she refused to take the gut-soothing potion, her face pale like snow.

"How is Raina doing?" I asked. The future queen of Lumenor slept a couple of beds down, her wounds healing in the dream state induced by a healer's aid potion.

Mr. Osei pressed his lips tightly together before speaking. "She will live, but she will not be able to lift her right arm from the elbow up."

"Oh, Raina." I gasped.

She'd lost everything in the battle, and I doubted that the five-jeweled crown would bear much solace to her now. Ripping Tain to shreds, on the other hand… all our troubles could have been resolved if the queen and her son had done the right thing, and gave the moonstone up instead of scheming and lying without any regard for human life.

"At least we have the moonstone now," Mr. Osei said, blinking at the glowing crystal in my lap. "And you made it out alive."

I shrugged. "We still need to destroy the other three, then come back here to finish the job."

Kalon peered over the healer's shoulder. "*We?*"

I tightened my grip on the crystal, feeling our bond that lingered even after I plucked it out of the marble. "Wherever the moonstone goes, I go too. I may have played a part in my parents' demise, but I will help heal my sister of this curse if it's the last thing I do."

"Wise choice." Mr. Osei gave a forced grin. "Zuri will begin to feel better as soon as you leave with the crystal. I will keep her safe, I promise. No one but for the folk in this room knows she is under my care, I hope?"

"I didn't tell anyone." My eyebrows knit. "Why would you keep that a secret?"

The head healer brought his face an inch closer, lowering his voice a note. "Because many in Lumenor, especially the Old Town, will not be happy with the outcome of the battle. I'd advise against you staying here even if you wished to do so."

"Why don't we take Imani's sister along?" Shei suggested.

Mr. Osei wagged his head. "Because it would kill her to be in such close proximity to the moonstone at all times, let alone two other crystals once you approach the south. Besides, she is not well enough to travel on kelpies and sleep in cold weather under the night skies."

I frowned, searching for a way to bring Zuri along without killing her. If Mr. Osei couldn't find one, what could I do? I couldn't expose her to danger for the purpose of keeping my sanity.

I glimpsed at Kalon, who helped himself to more than one potion from the healers' reserves. "When do we leave?" I asked.

My mood soured at the thought of working with the soldiers who had caused so much death and destruction to our city. Good intentions or not, the battle ravaged half of Lumenor. And I was about to join their ranks.

It is the only way to achieve my goal.

The leader of the Akani Warriors licked his lips upon digesting a vial of deep green, pungently earth-scented liquid. "We leave tonight."

Tonight?

"But I need to speak to my sister first!"

Mr. Osei leaned over, swiping the parchment and quill from his desk. "Write your farewell down. We can't risk revealing her location for her own safety. I will personally hand it to her, I swear it on my honor."

How much is anyone's honor worth to me now?

I was a fool to trust a single soul in the Old Town.

It was not much, but it was better than leaving without a word. "Fine, if I must. I will leave the letter on the pillow inside my bed chamber."

Kalon had excused himself. He was headed to the courtyard to issue the order to bring the kelpies into the city for our journey south, and pick which soldiers would stay behind to keep the peace. "We leave in one hour," he tossed a command over his shoulder before disappearing behind the doorframe.

Taking a deep breath, I hopped to my feet. I walked over to Raina's bed and whispered into her ear, hoping she could hear me. I promised to come back and begged her to give Tain justice he deserved.

The justice of a slow, painful death.

I made it back to my bed chamber.

Given our method of traveling on kelpies going forward, I could only take a couple of things with me. I stuffed a leather bundle with the moonstone, a water skin, a few clothing items, and my hair and skin ointments, leaving barely any room for personal belongings.

And it was so hard to leave things behind.

Everything Mother had sent my way was precious, worth more than any amount of gold. I decided to take one item that reminded me of each person I loved. Zuri's star-shaped pillow to pad my head while sleeping outside on the great plains that lay beyond the walls. A quartz crystal that Father had dug out with his bare hands while working in the mines that he made into rings for his wife and daughters. Mother's favorite collection of Kirrah's tales, the first page of the book stained with spill from when she accidentally dropped her teacup. Summer's ruby earrings I borrowed and forgot to return, and the set of night-colored tarot cards Zana gifted me as a child that was as good as new.

This way I got to take a small part of them with me anywhere I went.

I packed everything else that mattered into a large bag, knowing Mr. Osei would take it to Zuri for safe-keeping. Stopping in front of the mirror, I took a good look at myself.

My ebony eyes were swollen beyond recognition, hollow and tired, my crescent moon tattoo needing a retouch, fading against my umber skin. I wiped the blood from my silver braid and embellished it with Mother's favorite sapphire cuffs.

There was only one thing left to do.

I pulled out a dagger from my belt and began to slash at my flaxen legionnaire uniform that dry sweat had glued to my skin. It sickened me to think that I spent my entire childhood dreaming of wearing one. I slashed and slashed, a few shallow gashes splintering my skin. I wished I had never left my moonhouse, never met Tain. Never naively thought that the queen and the nobles wanted to protect the city when they were the cause of all our troubles. Wearing that uniform to serve them was the most naive, reckless thing I had ever done.

And it had cost me everything.

I finished changing into the black pants that Mother bought for herself before realizing they were a size too small. I matched it with the blue sweater that Zana had knitted for me, embroidered with silver thread, shaping hundreds of tiny crescent moons.

Someone knocked at my door.

"Good evening, Imani," Miss Yamane's soft voice echoed through my chamber after she let herself inside. She stole a look at the moonstone that gleamed through the cloth of my traveling pouch. "You made me proud tonight."

I shrugged, gritting my teeth. "I don't feel proud of anything I've done."

She motioned for me to settle down at the edge of my bed next to her. "I am sorry about your family and the Mounds. I assure you that brainless duckling of a prince will pay for what he's done."

I swirled a bitter, turmeric-potion-flavored saliva in my mouth. "I know. But that won't bring my parents back to life. What is done is done."

Miss Yamane took a long pause, smudging a splash of the queen's blood across her sapphire uniform in an attempt to wipe it away. My blood boiled at her closeness, reminding me of the games she played with me ever since we'd met.

"Your journey only begins now," she claimed. "And your bending training is not over, you have much yet to learn."

I couldn't even think about training in that moment. I only wanted to close my eyes and dream the pain away. "Will you be coming along, too?"

"No," she replied swiftly, "I must head home and persuade my stubborn father and sister to give the sapphire up when the time comes. You lot will head to the shores of the Sapphire Sea after you destroy the emerald and citrine crystals, and I don't mean to witness more bloodshed, especially not on my own doorstep. However, there is someone else who can train you."

My nose wrinkled. "Who?"

Miss Yamane flashed a grin. "Well, my best student, of course. Shei. I trained her ever since she was a child, alongside two other sei-sans from the Gutter who died the day you met her by Kirrah's Temple."

I shook my head, tired of surprises. I'd had enough of them in one day to last me a lifetime. "That explains her skill with sei," I puffed, "and she had me believe she trained herself in abandoned buildings!"

My sei instructor winked. "Half-truths make the best lies."

I bit into the raw corner of my lip, letting the pain linger. "I am tired of lies. You, her, even Mr. Osei—you all lied to me."

She waved her hand off nonchalantly, as though my point was not worth arguing over. "I am afraid you left us with no choice."

I frowned, ready to argue nevertheless, but she didn't give me a chance.

"This shall stay between us," she went on, "but I must count on you to keep an eye on that boy, and be wiser this time around."

She didn't need to tell me that. I had no intention of letting anyone get closer than an arm's length away. I learned my lesson the hard way, didn't I? Everyone I naively trusted had betrayed me, or told me lies, including Miss Yamane herself. For my own good or otherwise—lies were still lies.

"That, I can promise. Is there any meaning to this, Miss Yamane?"

She inclined her head, the indigo-black strands falling over her shoulder. "Meaning to what?"

"My power. How come I can draw more starlight than others?"

My bending instructor gave a shrug and rose from her seat, stalking out of the chamber.

"Sheer luck, I suppose," she replied, pausing at the door. "The starlight goddess plays no favorites. But it is up to you to chose what you do with what you were given. You must make up for your lack of skill and do it fast. The power you enjoy today will diminish with every crystal you destroy. Focus on your task, and make sure that overconfident boy-soldier does not ruin our chances of preserving what little is still alive. Farewell, Imani. I will see you on the shores."

"...I am so sorry. I will do everything in my power to destroy the crystals and come back to you. Love you forever. Imani."

I penned my letter to Zuri, pouring my heart and my tears out across the both sides of the parchment. Shei stumbled inside my chamber, packed and ready for departure, as I laid the letter on my pillow.

"My clothes are packed, blades tucked into my waist," she recounted, exposing the belt of her pants that was stuffed with throwing knives. "I said goodbye to my uncle, I am ready to go."

"I hear you'll be teaching me how to bend from now on," I muttered, arching a brow. "Miss Yamane called you her best student, marking another lie you told."

The mint branch poked out of the corner of Shei's mouth. "You know I had no other choice. I couldn't risk you telling Tain of our plans."

Heat rose to my cheeks. "You think I would risk my sister's wellbeing for *him*? The wellbeing of everyone in Lumenor?"

Shei straightened the layered gray linens that fell down her back, her slim fingers patting the cloth. "Can you blame me? You did risk quite a lot sneaking around the taverns with him at night."

"Of course I can blame you! You never gave me a chance to side with your cause! To find a better way." I grimaced sourly, picking at my nails. "How do you even know that we went to the taverns?"

"I followed you, giggling and jesting about like two lovebirds."

The mere memory of my time with Tain made me want to vomit, hoping to erase his existence from my mind with time.

"Oh." Her answer left me pondering for a while. "You can't use Tain as excuse for everything, though. You could have told me the truth long before I got close to him. And unlike Cella, I wasn't raised in the Old Town! I would've understood and helped out. You *chose* not to tell the truth, pretending to be my friend."

"I *am* your friend, you fool." Shei shot me a knife-sharp look. "Reprimand me all you want, but I made the right choice, even though it didn't feel good to lie. Besides, I am not responsible for the death of your parents, I am sorry, but I am not—the Akani never harmed a single soul in the Mounds. That was all his doing—doing of the boy you welcomed into your bed with open arms."

She was not wrong about Tain's role in the collapse of Lumenor, but hearing those words out loud stung like a wasp's bite.

My fault for believing in him.

All my fault.

"Fine." I smacked my lips with dry eyes, all my tears were long flushed out. "I will train with you because I have no other choice, but we are *not* friends. And think twice before lying to me in the future," I threatened, throwing my bundle over my shoulder.

I exited the chamber and the salon ahead of her. Without looking back even one time, I left the life of a legionnaire behind me once and for all.

The evening chill felt good against my warm skin once we stepped out into the courtyard. Kalon was there, waiting atop the most magnificent creature I ever laid my eyes on.

The kelpies assumed the shape of a horse, their hair a spill of black and jade-green that shone with an unnatural glow in the night. Eyes red like rubies calmly watched me from afar, flickering like tailed red comets amongst the stars. Their manes were sticky like western seaweed, flowing down their long necks, thick like moss. The creatures of northern grasslands and plains, meant to roam the forest, and swim in crisp northern lakes while bathing in midnight were now headed for war.

"This will be fun," Shei judged.

I snorted. "You couldn't keep your course on a regular horse."

She rolled her eyes. "It wasn't me—it was that bloody gray mare! Stubborn to her core."

I wonder who she reminds me of, I would have said if Shei was still my friend. But she was not, so instead I decided to ignore her jests.

One of the foreigners amidst Akani Warriors' ranks led two kelpies by the roped reins, handing them to us. I couldn't gauge where he was from with skin pale like the moons and features molded similarly to my own. Thick locs fell to his shoulders in the color of sand, complimenting his light-brown eyes. He grinned politely, eyeing Shei down his nose. "Starlight benders—it is an honor to have you in our midst." He bowed, folding over his hips, and Shei and I traded a puzzled look.

"Is everyone going to call us *starlight benders* from now on?" I mouthed.

"I kind of like it," she replied, mounting the kelpie. "We sound much more dangerous that way."

"We sound like outsiders," I snapped, turning to the soldier. "What is my kelpie's name?"

His ochre-brown eyes flew open as if he had seen a ghost. "Only you can name your kelpie, of course! It is tradition. You inherited your mount from a fallen warrior, and with the new rider comes a new name."

I turned to the kelpie, brushing my thumb against its wet muzzle. The creature licked my fingertip and nickered, before bowing its neck to nip at the grass. "I wonder what I should name it."

The soldier gasped, taking great offense at my question. "What you should name *her*. All warrior kelpies are female, of course!"

My shoulders stiffened. "Sorry, I've never even seen one before. We thought them extinct until recently."

He shook his head with a grimace that showcased distaste, as though he'd eaten mud thinking it was food. "Extinct? Hear that, my muse! You northerners are a strange lot."

Northerners? A muse?

I realized how little I knew about the rest of the wide world outside of Lumenor, unfamiliar with the religions and customs of the lands beyond. "It is settled, then. I will call my kelpie Jade, after my sister's favorite crystal. I am Imani, by the way," I said, extending my hand to greet him.

His mouth twisted in confusion. *I guess they don't shake hands south of here.* Reaching the scraped hand back to me with reluctance, seemingly unsure if that was what I intended, he kissed the back of my knuckles. "I am Iori, the third-born son of Irok. My sister Irila will be most delighted to meet you, of course. She and many others are waiting for us in the desert."

"Nice to meet you, Iori. I am sure your sister is lovely."

I settled into the firm leather-bound saddle, securing the pouch on my back. I cast the first look over the Mounds with heaviness in my heart. They were gone, crushed to flat plateaus, nothing more but the clumps of dirt and broken stone.

I willed away the tears, looking over the moving procession composed of hundreds of black-armored warriors. *May we met again in the star lands.* I mouthed a farewell to my home, thinking of the curving walls of our warm, cozy moonhouse that now laid in ruins.

"Ready?" Kalon rode by, motioning us to follow. "I want you by my side in the front."

I combed Jade's black-and-green mane with my fingers, locking my leg muscles around her. "Of course you do. Kirrah forbid you lose the sight of the moonstone."

He smirked over his shoulder. "There is not much your starlight goddess can do where we are headed."

Shei proceeded ahead, pulling at the reins gently. It turned out that kelpies didn't need much guidance, galloping alongside their herd in the tangle of silky midnight-and-jade tails. Riding atop them felt like swimming through still waters, their hoofs gliding across the land almost weightlessly.

My groins throbbed despite the soothing ride, tired out and cramped, unaccustomed to the ways of saddle. *This will be a long night.* Wind lashed at my cheeks, my braid birling on its wings as we rode down the Queen's Alley of Old Town. The nobles finally summoned the courage to look outside their manors, leering at us with resentment from their balconies. Most cast disdainful glances at my pouch, their eyes widening in terror while watching the starlight crystal leave their possession, wadded by my clothes. I was never so thrilled to see the silver gates of Old Town, but my thrill died in an instant upon entering the Cobblestone.

The temple still stood in its position, and while its dome glimmered in the night, the marble staircase around it turned permanently reddish-brown, blotched with dried blood. Kirrah's statue remained erect, surrounded by the growing mound of bodies that the folk had dragged there for a proper sendoff to the star lands.

My stomach churned.

Hundreds, if not thousands of corpses slept the night away in the never-ending dream, waiting to leave our world. They were to return to stardust—to life's original form – so that their souls could ascend to the constellation of our goddess, meeting her in the starlit palace. My only hope was that Mother and Father were already there, watching me from above.

The stone skeleton of Lumenor took a hard blow—most of the merchant stores and townhomes missing an entire floor, their twisted columns and balconies gone, mosaic-painted windows shattered. The entire city robed itself in the coat of debris and smoke, the kelpies' hoofs splashing through the pools of crimson blood. Displaced limbs laid about, lost children screaming for their mothers. Even the night priestesses ambled around, offering blessings and ointments to the wounded. The remaining sei-sans and healers provided what help they could, and the merchants opened their homes, sharing their food with surviving hill folk. To my surprise, the rebels roamed about, too, pulling out the sei-sans stuck underneath the crumbled stone. The people of Lumenor came together at the sunset of old world, offering a helping hand to both their friends and strangers.

My mouth tightened.

We should have never fought this battle.

Kirrah help me, I would do anything to reverse the time and pluck the moonstone out before it was too late. Kill Tain and Queen Astra, and never raise a palm against another.

But that was not how time worked. Once the deed was done, the reversal was nothing more than wishful thinking—an afterthought. Dead could never be brought back to life, not by starlight nor by any other form of magic known to humankind.

The state we found the Gutter in was much worse. The buildings had sunk into the soil once and for all, the scars of battle ribbing the rock. Many more had fallen to their deaths there—both Lumenorans and Akani Warriors. A river of red spill dried down the Queen's Alley, and mothers wailed, cupping their dead children in their laps.

Shei wept at the sight, the flame of her aquamarine eyes put out. I couldn't say a word, my mouth sealed shut, but I didn't dare look away. I made sure to gaze upon every face, every pointless sacrifice we brought upon. It was all our fault—the fault of sei-sans, since we were the only ones benefiting from the moonstone's presence. The war brought the most misfortune to the those who already had no fortune to begin with.

The opening around the melted titanium gates offered a window into the Ashen Desert—the sea of blackness stretching into infinity. I held my breath while crossing the threshold of the city I was born in. I once intended to spend my entire life there, in the rolling hills roaming with river streams, and hill folk. To watch my parents grow old, and have children of my own one day. But all my dreams were dreamt away, and only one goal remained.

Destroy the starlight crystals, and give the world the fighting chance it deserves.

The fighting chance my sister desperately needs.

Three crescent moons shimmered over Lumenor, the home I left behind in search of cure. Kalon pulled his kelpie closer, galloping a hair away. His eyes traced the lines of my face, the chill he always brought along making my bones tremble.

"Hey, Kalon," I called, and our gazes locked. We rode ahead of others, immersing ourselves in the rich blackness that mirrored Kirrah's Cloak. My veins pulsed in the rhythm of Jade's strides, and Kalon's upper lip curved, feeling the eternal dance of fire and ice that rushed through my blood, too. I finally summoned the courage to say it out loud. "It is time I learned the full truth of you power. And conjuring lies will be of no use. I know your secret, *midnight bender*."

$SOFIA$ $NEDIC$ is a Slavic immigrant living in Austin, Texas with her husband and pup. She is a tech and fantasy nerd, and an avid enjoyer of ancient history, spirituality, and alchemy. When she is not working or crafting stories, she is exploring nature, reading books, visualizing her daydreams through AI art, or immersing herself in tarot and astrology.

Printed in Great Britain
by Amazon